MW01137014

Also by H. Adrian Sexton

Chemistry Matters

Altared Ego

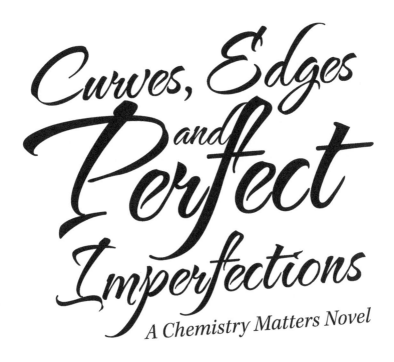

Curves, Edges and Perfect Imperfections

A Chemistry Matters Novel

H. ADRIAN SEXTON

authorHOUSE®

AuthorHouse™
1663 Liberty Drive
Bloomington, IN 47403
www.authorhouse.com
Phone: 833-262-8899

Published by AuthorHouse 12/29/2020

ISBN: 978-1-6655-1061-5 (sc)
ISBN: 978-1-6655-1062-2 (hc)
ISBN: 978-1-6655-1082-0 (e)

Library of Congress Control Number: 2020924867

Print information available on the last page.

Any people depicted in stock imagery provided by Getty Images are models, and such images are being used for illustrative purposes only. Certain stock imagery © Getty Images.

This book is printed on acid-free paper.

Because of the dynamic nature of the Internet, any web addresses or links contained in this book may have changed since publication and may no longer be valid. The views expressed in this work are solely those of the author and do not necessarily reflect the views of the publisher, and the publisher hereby disclaims any responsibility for them.

Dedicated to my GrandMa 'Tossie'
Louise 'Tossie' Robinson.
You were, and will always be, our family beacon.
Your guidance lighted our paths while you walked the earth.
And Your Spirit will forever be the Angel
that makes us smile when we look to the Heavens.

"There's this place in me where your fingerprints still rest,
your kisses still linger, and your whispers softly echo.
It's the place where a part of you will forever be a part of me."

Gretchen Kemp

01

Red Velvet

TARDINESS WAS HER PREEMINENT SHORTCOMING. At a quarter past eight, she parked her car, set the alarm, then rushed toward the busy street. Soft, bushy hair bounced above shoulders. A cream-colored scarf shielded her neck from the elements. Her belt was pulled tight around her coat at the waist, outlining her curvaceous body. A body that cursed her to a daily torrent of catcalls from undeserving men whose only interest was what lie beneath the coat; an ample bosom, a thick bottom, supple hips, and legs that stretched a mile. When a red light stopped her at the curb, she pulled out her cell phone to make a call.

"She looks happy this morning," he murmured. He was perched caddy-corner from the garage. He stood. Watched her wait. Loitered above steam vents to help loosen sixty-three-year-old joints, and cased the streets.

His morning had started two hours earlier, in the dark, humid confines of the pump house that bordered the parking garage. A cool morning, bathed in sunshine, that offered the promise of a pleasant day. After a brief, but earnest, morning prayer of *Thank You God for a new day*, he rolled up his sleeping pallet, then dressed in a black skullcap, flannel shirt, and khaki fatigue pants. He encased his feet in badly worn Army boots, gathered his knapsack and wrapped himself in a weathered Army jacket. Four blocks away at a café on Eighth Avenue owned by a short, sixty-something widow, he washed up in the men's room, then ate breakfast—a plate of scrambled eggs, smoked sausage, and potato hash, which he washed down with a watered-down glass of grape juice. After filling his stomach and reading his horoscope, he went to the counter and hugged the Filipina sexagenarian. "Tonight 'round six-thirty?" he asked in his gravelly tone.

"I closing early tonight so don't be late." Her Pinoy was thick. "My granddaughter has recital at school and I want be on time."

His breakfast was bartered. Instead of paying for his meal, he'd come back at closing and clean the restaurant. After cleaning, he'd leave with his dinner—a to-go box full of food that would otherwise be discarded.

Outside the restaurant, he dialogued with some of the elder Chinamen, promising to return to practice Tai Chi with them after lunch; they'd play Mahjong after dinner. The ancient Chinese board game helped keep his mind tight; martial arts kept his body limber.

On the trek back to the garage, to await her arrival, he spent a dollar on a dozen sticks of incense. Buying twice as many as he'd use in a week at the pump house, he decided to share half with her. *She'll like these*, he thought, inhaling the fragrant sticks as he watched her on the phone.

When the walk silhouette lighted, the Nubian queen, tall and draped in tan—three-button, knee-length, camel-hair coat and camel-colored boots that travelled up to her knees—hurried across the street with a light, graceful, yet sturdy gait. She was in a hurry again. The loose, swaying hem of her crimson dress formed a break in the monument of tan.

In pursuit, her Sentinel abandoned the warmth of his steam vent and moved quickly to keep her pace. He kept half a block behind, stopping occasionally, whenever she did, to mask his presence. They'd made this two-and-a-half block journey from her parking spot to the building that housed her dance studio every workday for the past four years, and as far as he knew, she'd never noticed him. But then again, why should she? Throughout his every day, the majority of people he passed didn't shed a glance in his direction or pay him enough attention to merely say good morning. Who gave a thought to a guy in a tattered jacket with thick, salt-and-pepper ropes of hair coiled and twisted from months without combing? She hadn't noticed his routine in over four years. Why should she now?

The rhythm of her route was well familiar to him. He knew she liked to stop at store fronts and window shop. He knew where she liked to eat. Through watching her, he learned her habits and routines with increasing interest. He had frequented the places she'd visited on several occasions and come to realize they had similar tastes and styles. Once he'd glimpsed her through a store window walking toward the renaissance book section. Later that same day the owner told him she'd inquired about the French

Revolution, so he bought her a book about Joan of Arc which she found lying on her windshield at day's end. To him, she seemed something almost divine. And whenever he thought her sensual brown eyes peered in his direction or caught a glimpse of him when she turned his way, he half believed that he was looking at an angel.

She gravitated to the unusual. Second-hand bookstores and eclectic art piqued her interest. Every now and then she'd perch outside a store window like a bird alighting on a branch and peer inside with the innocence of a toddler gawking into a candy shop. Two blocks from the garage she entered Eddie and Jack's Good Sign Bakery.

It was halftime, so her Sentinel plopped down on a bus stop bench.

Inside she greeted the baker with, "How's my favorite baker doing today?"

Eddie Bunker, a balding man in his mid-thirties, waited all week to hear those words from his favorite customer. "Mighty fine now," he replied, flashing the flirtatious smile he reserved just for her.

Strangers noticed her without truly knowing why. At first glance, most gravitated to her singular visual imperfection. An imperfection that came as penance for dealing with an awful man. But once the shock and awe of the blemish subsided, it was natural to embrace the pleasure that accompanied looking into the edginess of her hauntingly beautiful face.

Eddie licked the tips of his fingers and pulled a size-six plastic bag from underneath the counter. He opened the bag by flinging it in the air, almost as if he were swatting at a fly. Of course, he could have just slipped his finger in the bag and opened it that way, but the pop of the bag always garnered his customer's attention. Besides, quietly opening a bag killed Eddie's sense of showmanship. The lady with the beautiful, light-brown hair jumped a little as she did every time Eddie popped a bag for her.

"Here you go; hot and fresh just like you like 'em."

"I think you mean, like you like them." Laughing, she took the baker's dozen of fresh-baked scones, handed him a ten-dollar bill and thanked him.

"I put a chocolate croissant in there too," Eddie said with an unexpected urgency in his voice. "I made it special, just for you."

"Wow." She leaned close and kissed him. "That was sweet."

Although five inches shorter than her, the proprietor of the bakeshop built a six-inch platform behind the counter that allowed him to stand eye-to-eye with his taller customers. "Only thing sweeter is you," he said. Eddie's blush was even brighter than his smile. He stole an admiring glance at the length of her. The shape of her head and the turn of her neck were peculiarly noble. "Can't get no more wonderful than it is right now."

She blushed, as she did every time he complimented her. "You have a wonderful day, Sweet Eddie Bunker." Her ebony eyes shimmered on a luminescent canvas of golden wheat skin. "I'll see you next week."

"God willing," he said with an amorous candor in his voice.

"I'll be right here waiting for you to come through my door."

Eddie's smile carried her out the door and back into the last block of her morning commute to the squat, three-story, brick building where she ran her dance studio.

Her quick exodus from the bakery caught her Sentinel still sitting. He stood and a tinge of pain sparked the joints of his knees. Steps came heavier now and he labored like his feet were made of stone. A stiff, short-lived breeze came off the Sound. So stiff, it made fifty-five degrees feel like thirty-five. But protecting her was his job. And if battling a stiff, bone-chilling wind was what it took to make certain she was safe, then onward he trudged. For the two minutes it took her to traverse that final block, he followed and watched until she strolled inside the sanctuary of the squat, three-story, brick building. Just like that she was gone. And his job as her protector was complete...for now.

Out of breath from following at her elevated pace, he took deep breaths and leaned against a phone booth to start his recovery. A recovery that needed to be complete by lunch time when he'd once again return to duty as her Sentinel.

When she emerged for lunch, she had abandoned her wool coat for the lighter comfort of a cream-colored shawl. A four-inch belt matched the wide-brimmed hat that covered most of her short, light-brown hair. Cream, sling-back pumps replaced her boots, exposing sculpted calves and strong ankles.

Similar to their morning escapade, her Sentinel waited until she was moving in a decided direction before he followed. He loved the way she carried herself; simplistic, understated, but very classy. Once seen, she was forever memorable. She stood taller than the average woman and walked on long, athletic legs with a full, confident stride. Her face was remarkable, less for its imperfection of feature than for a singular and dreamy earnestness of expression. Her high cheekbones seemed to radiate sunshine when she smiled. Her lips were full and were always lightly covered with a colorful

4

gloss. She protested thick, heavy shades or dark lipsticks. Her beautifully cut mouth held a proud and somewhat mischievous expression; an air of free and easy superiority sat gracefully in every curve and movement of her fine form. To him, she seemed to glow as if a spiritual light beamed inside her. Though they'd never spoken in the time he'd watched over her, he relished her comforting, congenial demeanor.

Maybe I could strike up a conversation with her? He struggled with the urge to meet her, but knew that meeting her meant explaining, and that, he was not ready to do. *Maybe?...Well, not just yet* he struggled internally.

She stopped at a hotdog stand and ordered a bratwurst with extra brown mustard and a hibiscus-cherry iced tea. As the vendor prepared her food, she shared light conversation with a woman in a flowery hat who'd already ordered. In describing her conversation, she drew her hands in energetic animation, casted a wide, genuine smile, and tossed her head back with a laugh. Her eyes danced when she talked. Striking, hazel eyes that sparkled as she gave her waiting-companion her full attention.

How he wished she would lavish that same tenderness on him. He clamored to bask in the radiance of her warm smile; her deep giggle that preceded a hearty belly laugh and a gentle tap on the arm to acknowledge her connection. The stranger in the flowery hat didn't know how much she was taking for granted. To have one's humanity acknowledged by such a perfect woman was truly a gift.

The hotdog vendor finished preparing her meal. She accepted it, and with a wave of her hand and a pivot of her hips, she ended the conversation with her stranger friend and bounded on her way. A block south and two blocks east, on 188th Street near the Alderwoods Mall, she entered Binders and Spines—the largest bookstore in Seattle.

Her Sentinel stopped in the park across the street, found a bench that offered him the best vantage point of the store's main entrance, and waited attentively for her to exit.

May I help you, sir?" the rail-thin clerk at the information desk asked of a brown-skinned man with glasses.

"Yes ma'am," he said. "I'm looking for two books?"

"Sure. What are the titles?"

"The first is *The Negro*. The second is *The Souls of Black Folks*. Both are by W.E.B. Dubois."

The clerk took the note with her chicken scratch to the computer. As part of its Memorial Day weekend festivities, Binders and Spines was hosting book signings by three authors. He was in the Lynnwood area to have that day's author sign his pre-purchased copy of his newest novel, *Altared Ego*. The autograph was the primary purpose of his visit, but when the author's arrival was delayed, he used his time to look for those books.

Waiting patiently as the clerk performed her search, he panned the crowded bookstore watching customers wander up and down aisles fingering through covers, skimming quickly through pages and finally selecting books of all shapes, sizes and colors. His attention was averted from the stacks when the lady in line behind him barked two painful sounding coughs then struggled loudly to clear her throat.

"Are you all right?" he asked.

She nodded then smiled softly before saying, "I'm fine."

He looked her from head-to-toe. Took a mental picture of the woman standing three inches taller than him. He pulled a bottle of water from his knapsack, handed it to her, cracked a sly smile and said, "That's for sure."

She politely accepted the water but shrugged off the flattery. Her mouth formed a thin line, forming a toothless smile of her own. He lingered in her airspace, so having heard his book request, she asked, "How long have you been reading Dubois?"

"Not since my undergrad days, but I don't remember a lot from back then." He took another snapshot. Her crimson dress was the color of Sangria sprawled thinly across a tile floor. A cream-colored shawl was draped around her shoulders. Sling-back pumps and a wide belt matched the wide-brimmed hat covering most of her short-cropped afro. Her outfit brought to mind a large slice of his favorite cake as the words red velvet slipped softly from his lips. She smiled at his mention of the smooth, chocolaty dessert. If her intellect equaled her beauty, she was definitely someone he needed to know. "I'm writing a paper on twentieth century urbanization," he said, "and I need to revisit some of his works."

"If I recall correctly," she said, "Booker T. Washington also had plenty published in that era. His work may provide some insight."

This time, he cracked a toothless smile. "Well thank you, pretty lady."

She showed her pleasure in his compliment by allowing her full, thick lips to stretch into a bright smile. Her lip color was the same as her dress.

The title search for his books returned none in stock. "Excuse me, sir." The information desk clerk interrupted his attentiveness to the lady in red. "I'm sorry, but both are out stock. If you want to order them, we could have them here in four or five business days."

Before he could answer, the lady in red said, "Excuse me again." The man eagerly turned to face the lady dressed like red velvet cake. "There's an Indie bookstore in Bryn Mawr called Brothers Books." "They specialize in out of print and Afro-centric material. I'm sure they probably carry it and whatever else you might need for your paper."

He turned and told the information desk clerk, "No thank you." Then he stepped out of line and let Red Velvet have her turn with the pasty clerk in dire need of some summer sun.

After Red Velvet finished her business, she turned to see the brown-skinned man loitering nearby. The Cheshire cat grin beaming her way told that he was waiting for her. Sensing there was no way out of the bookstore without talking to him, she approached him and his eager presentation of an outstretched arm—an open hand waiting at the end.

He better not have a weak handshake. There is nothing more off-putting than a man with a wimpy handshake, she thought. *How is a man supposed to take care of and protect a woman if he has weak hands? If his handshake is wimpy, Lord knows what else is wimpy.*

His warm, inviting smile encouraged hers in return as she accepted the handshake. His hand wasn't that big, but his handshake was firm.

"I would like to thank you for helping me back there. I'm Desmond Woodson and I thought it rude to leave without saying thank you."

"No problem," she said.

"Well, Miss…?" he asked. "I'm sorry; I didn't quite catch your name."

"I didn't quite throw it," she quipped rapidly. Then, after a beat she said, "Excuse me; that was rude. You can…" she paused, uncomfortable giving her name to a complete stranger. She thought about predators and stalkers who trolled places like this looking for innocent women to prey upon. She thought about his cover story and wondered what school he was attending; what field of study required the paper he mentioned having to write. She thought about his smile and how innocent he looked standing before her patiently waiting like a red-nosed, pit-bull puppy about to get a treat. Finally, she thought about the tender reference to sweet, moist, chocolate cake that softly slipped from his lips when she was in line. Then that perfect smile returned to her face. "Let's go with…Red Velvet."

Pleasantly surprised with the jocularity of her light-hearted answer, Desmond decided to challenge her response. "Ohhh?" he chortled then asked, "And why is that?"

Without the slightest hesitation—and in a tone that would've been indignant had it not been so enticing—she boldly answered, "'Cause I got that warm, rich, extra sweet chocolate thing going on." She said it. She owned it; and she was absolutely right. Her chocolate was unlike any of the women he typically dated. Her complexion steered him more toward calling her a butterscotch or caramel, but either way her sweetness begged to be tasted.

"Well Ms. Red Velvet, could I have the pleasure of sharing your company through a cup of coffee before I get back to work?"

Her eyes followed the motion of his head to the far corner as he turned to face the almost empty line at the Starbucks. She found herself interested in, or at least flattered by, his somewhat honest attempt at chivalry. Red Velvet looked at her watch. "As much as I love a good cup of coffee, I can't right now. I'm on my lunch break too. I have to get back to work."

"What do you do?"

Red Velvet paused before answering. He was getting personal a little faster than made her comfortable. She sized him up, thinking that he seemed harmless enough, but then, she thought, *how dangerous can a guy in a bookstore be?* His build was slight, no more than five-foot nine; he couldn't weigh more than a hundred eighty pounds. If needed, she had learned more than enough in her self-defense course to protect herself from a man his size. Hesitantly she answered, "I run a dance studio."

She'd had an hour and a half before her next class started, but she had spent more time in the bookstore than planned and she wanted to finish a couple more things on her to-do list before heading back. She was, nevertheless, intrigued by the intelligent exchange of quaint banter with Mister Woodson. "Desmond," she began, "My afternoons are rather full, but I could probably do that coffee later tonight; or some other night."

Desmond's face half deflated at the thought of being rejected, but only half since she didn't come right out and say no. "Well if now is a bad time, let me suggest something different." Desmond reached into the breast pocket of his blazer and pulled out a business card. "If later is good, I would love to treat you to dinner. When you have time, give me a call so we can continue this conversation and maybe share thoughts about our favorite authors." He flipped the card through his fingers twice before handing it to her. "That is, of course, if you don't mind sharing."

She licked her lips and said, "Dinner, hunh?"

"You do like to eat, don't you? Please don't tell me that you're one of those I don't eat in front of people women."

"No Sweetheart," Red Velvet said. "I'll eat you under the table."

The innuendo in her answer surprised him. His eyebrows showed it.

"What I mean to say Mister Man…" She wanted to kick herself for the untimely use of innuendo. "Is that I don't eat like those anorexic chicks. I pack a healthy appetite. So make sure your wallet can take a hit when you're ready to feed me."

"Don't worry about that," he laughed. "I can cover the damages." The sexy way her dress cinched tightly around Red Velvet's size-six frame encouraged him to believe that nary a cookie or any slice of cake had ever landed in the wrong place on her body. "Dinner it is, then."

Red Velvet looked briefly at the card. She read, Desmond Woodson. Owner. Woody's Bar and Grill. Then she shined all thirty-two pearly whites at Desmond. "Sounds like fun." She held his card between two fingers in her left hand, tapping it with her right index finger before she slipped the card in her purse. As they walked toward the door, she said, "If I find myself in a sharing mood, I'll definitely give a call."

Outside on the sidewalk, Desmond remembered his original intention when they met and asked, "And where exactly is Brothers Books?"

"I know it's out near Renton Airport. Take the 405 exit around 118th. I don't know the exact address, but it has a huge picture of Africa on the front of a yellow sign. You shouldn't miss it."

"Thanks," Desmond beamed. "I think I'm going to head over there right now. You sure you can't join me?"

"Sorry, but no."

"Well, Bryn Mawr is a hike, so I better get going." Desmond offered his hand again.

Red Velvet gave him a firm shake goodbye then turned to leave.

"Dinner on me," Desmond raised his voice.

"I like the sound of that," Red Velvet affirmed as she sashayed away.

02

Check Please

DESMOND WOODSON WAS NERVOUS ABOUT his dinner date with the lovely lady he called Red Velvet a week prior at Binders and Spines. Dressed in a blazer, a mock turtleneck, black jeans and green suede brogans, he entered the private meeting room overlooking the restaurant floor with his hospitality manager, Denesha, riding in his wake.

"I hope everything is to your liking?" He shook hands with his guest, Stanley Bright, then introduced Denesha to the billionaire shipping mogul and NBA franchise co-owner of the Seattle Knights, assuring him that she would expertly handle all the wants and needs of his wealthy guests.

Also in the room, talking and laughing loudly near the drink table, were Stanley's brother, and Knight's co-owner, Vince; team Coach Adam Howard; team captains Jaz Stevenson and Ben Lockette; and Washington State Senator Luke Fleming. When the business conversation concluded, Vince lit a cigar and picked up one of a dozen glasses filled with champagne. He passed a palm-sized, cigar coffin to Coach Howard, who took a cigar then passed along the mini humidor. Although not part of the organization, Stanley insisted Desmond also take a cigar.

Denesha politely declined. When all of the men held lit cigars, Vince led them in raising their glasses. "A toast," Vince said, "To great food and drink, great business partners, and plenty more championships!"

Stanley tipped his glass to the others then emptied it in two swallows. The others followed suit; each clinking and then emptying their champagne glasses.

"Now, let's eat some of this great food?" Vince summoned everyone to join him as he moved towards a large mahogany table filled with charcuterie trays, fresh fruits and breads, and three more bottles of champagne. Desmond and Denesha cited the invitation as their cue to exit.

~~~

Crystal Stevenson and Sylvia Lockette, the two unfortunate player wives at the party, found themselves abandoned together at a table downstairs. Their team-captain husbands, who were only supposed to be gone for a minute, were still upstairs joking it up with their bosses. Unfortunately for the women, the men seemed content sharing their time off with management instead of with their wives. Because of their husband's status as mere players, the management wives regarded the team wives as no better than the help. Tired of waiting for their husbands to come show them a good time, Sylvia asked Crystal to dance.

"That sounds great. I'd rot like a mummy waiting for my husband to come dance with me." They stood and joined four other couples shaking and strutting across the dance floor.

"Whew. Girl, I'm beat," Sylvia spouted when the women returned to their table thirty minutes later for a much-needed break. "Outside of a Zumba class, I haven't danced that much in a decade." She lifted her half-full, mango margarita and finished the glass.

Crystal, thirsty from their thirty-minute dance-a-thon, emptied her glass of fruity beverage at a pace to match her friend. A beat later, Sylvia put her glass down and excused herself to the ladies' room.

A buzz in Crystal's purse let her know her phone was ringing. "Hello?" she said still panting heavily.

"Hey Baby, it's Dad."

"Hey, Daddy, I was just thinking about you and Mom."

"Crystal," her father noticed her haggard breathing. "Are you all right?"

"Yes Daddy. I'm fine."

"Well you don't sound fine."

"Jaz and I are out at one of his team events and I just finished dancing. That's all. Really Daddy, I'm fine." A waitress placed two glasses of white wine on the table. Crystal moved the phone away from her mouth, placed a five-dollar tip on the drink tray and asked the waitress for two glasses of water. Then she took a couple of sips of her wine. "Okay Daddy, do I sound better now?"

"If you're out with Jaz, I'll just call back later when you get home."

"Later?" Crystal challenged. "It's already past your bedtime. Why are you calling so late? What's wrong? Is Mom okay?"

"It'll hold 'til the morning, Baby. You have a good time with my son-in-law and call me in the morning. Everything will be all right."

Now Crystal was really worried. First her Daddy, who was normally in bed by eight o'clock, calls out of the blue well past his bedtime. Then he says things will be okay several times. Crystal may have been gone from the house for a dozen years, but she still knew her father's tells when he was hiding something.

"Okay Daddy, I'll call you in the morning for the details, but I'm not hanging up tonight until you tell me what's bothering you. Daddy, where's Mom?"

"Crystal, your mom is at the hospital with your grandmother. Your Papa called and said she had some pains in her chest, so your mom went over there and took them to the emergency room. Just as a precautionary measure. Remember Baby, she is 85 years old."

"Well, did mom call from the E-R yet? What did the doctor say?"

"No Baby, she hasn't called yet. I told her that I'd come to the hospital right after I talked with you. So, you rest your nerves, and I'll call you in the morning to let you know what's going on."

"But Daddy, I…"

"Crystal Marie Stevenson." Her father forcefully cut her off.

"Your Nana is at the hospital. Your mom and your Papa are there with her. She'll be fine. You enjoy your night with your husband and I will call you first thing to let you know what's going on. Shoot; as stubborn as your Nana is, she'll probably be home before you."

Crystal chuckled at her father's joke. "But Daddy…"

"Baby Girl, ain't nothing you can do tonight 'cept pray. I'll give your Nana and Papa a kiss from you when I get to the hospital, and I'll call you in the morning. Now let me get off this phone so I can go help your momma with my crazy parents."

"Okay, Daddy, but you call me first thing."

"First thing, Baby. I promise." The line went dead before Crystal could further interrogate her father.

When Crystal finished talking, she found a travel website and started a search for flights to New Orleans. She was so engrossed with her search that she didn't notice Ben, Sylvia, and Jaz approach the table.

When Jaz tapped her on the shoulder aggressively, she looked up at him as if he was a stranger. "What?" she growled.

Jaz snatched the phone from Crystal's hand. "What do you mean, what?"

"Have you lost your mind, Jared Stevenson? Give me my phone."

Ben touched Jaz's arm again, but was brushed away.

Jaz kept his hands to himself, but hovered over Crystal intimidatingly. "Who were you on the phone with?" Jaz hovered over her panting hard. His breath wreaked of liquor.

"Jared, you're drunk. Give me my phone."

"I'm not giving you nothing 'til you tell me who was on the phone."

Crystal sat back. Folded her arms intently. "Check the damn number." Jaz looked at the blank screen. "The guy on the phone was my Daddy. My Dad, Jared. Or don't you know remember him?"

Instead of checking the phone, Jaz glared at his wife.

"My Daddy called to tell me that my Nana is in the hospital. Before you so savagely ripped my phone out of my hand, I was looking at plane reservations so we could fly home."

Jaz hovered. He didn't have words, but he wasn't ready to back down.

"Go ahead Deebo, open it up. Look at the number."

Jaz squeezed the phone in his massive hand. He knew that Crystal's Nana was like a cat with nine lives. Her trips to the hospital with one fatal ailment after the next had come about twice a year for the last decade. Silently he thought, *Old Bag probably goes to the hospital to escape that simple-minded husband of hers.*

"Did you hear me Jared Stevenson? My eighty-five-year-old Nana is in the hospital and they can't tell me what's wrong with her."

"You know ain't nothing wrong with her," Jaz said indignantly.

"It's probably the only way she could figure out how to get some free time away from your crazy ass Papa. Without killing him, of course."

"Go to Hell!" Crystal attempted to stand, but Jaz blocked her. She pushed into Jaz's chest, but, even drunk, his massive frame was too much for her to move. "Move Jared!" she said emphatically.

Jaz relented.

Crystal shot out of the chair like a rocket. She grabbed her phone and moved toward the front door.

"Crys," Jaz followed calling. "Where the hell you think you're going?"

"I'm going to Louisiana!"

"What about L.A.?"

"You and L.A. can both go to hell." Crystal stormed toward the door.

Jaz had almost caught up to her when the heavy, wooden French doors swung outward. A bald-headed man just slightly smaller than Jaz started to enter. Crystal rushed by him. He turned and noticed Jaz in hot pursuit. He braced himself for impact. Jaz barreled into him like a fullback trying to cross the goal line. Both men absorbed the blow; neither yielded an inch.

"Move Fool before I move you," Jaz declared.

"I don't see that happening," the bald man said confidently.

His first instinct was to race after Crystal, but, under the influence of the alcohol, Jaz shifted towards the fight. He balled his fists and squared his shoulders towards the bald man. Before either could swing the first punch, Ben plowed into Jaz, wrapped his arms around his teammate and ushered him out onto the sidewalk near the valet. A step behind Ben, Sylvia brought up the rear, stopping briefly to apologize to the bald man.

"Calm down and I'll let you go," Ben ordered.

Jaz struggled, unable to break free. "Where are you going Crys? I'm talking to you."

"Not like that, you're not. You're being an ass. I'm taking the girls to Louisiana tomorrow with or without you."

Ben held on as Jaz struggled. Crystal's back was to him. Jaz couldn't see the tears streaming from her eyes. The air of dismissal in his voice towards the seriousness of her grandmother's illness angered her even more. She couldn't believe that her husband, a devout father and family man, chose some stupid movie audition over the welfare of a close relative.

The valet hailed her a taxi.

"I'm sorry, Baby. Come back. I'd never hurt you," Jaz yelled. "I'd kill myself before I'd hurt you."

Crystal turned and yelled at him, "Then why don't you make both of us happy and just do it?" her voice cracking through the tears. Her words were out before she realized the gravity of what she'd said. His face went blank. If she could take them back she would. The sorrow in his expression hurt her heart. She wanted to apologize. Wanted to say she was sorry, but he'd hurt her in a way he'd never done before and right now she could muster neither pity nor empathy for her superstar husband. Crystal got in and the taxi sped away. With it also sped away the fight. Jaz finally calmed down at the sight of his wife leaving. Ben released his bear hug.

Two days later, the Stevensons were both in LA. Only catch was those same initials stood for differing final destinations. Jaz was in Los Angeles. California. Hollywood. The land of sunshine, movie stars, earthquakes, and wildfires. Crystal was in Louisiana. New Orleans. The Big Easy. The land of crawfish, beignets, Mardi Gras and throw me something Mister.

03

Wing Men ... and Women

THE ATMOSPHERE INSIDE WOODY'S BAR and Grill was electric. Music played loud enough to mask the din of table talk. Most people sat enjoying their meals while the regulars checked their watches, brimming to exercise their vocals cords with their best renditions of their favorite songs. It was Karaoke night. And Karaoke night at Woody's always packed in a crowd of American Idol wannabes anxious to take home the $500 prize.

Woody's was an American–style restaurant occupying a triple-wide storefront in the middle of Short Street. The sign above the entrance was painted by an undergrad college student. The dramatically detailed mural which spanned fifteen-feet tall and twenty-feet wide was complete with a female soloist performing as the front person for a big band before a standing room only crowd that dined and danced in the foreground.

It depicted the physical layout inside Woody's, but the feeling behind the scene was more reminiscent of the clubs from the Harlem Renaissance era. The immense mural earned the young lady an 'A' as her final senior project grade, on top of the twenty-five-hundred-dollar paycheck from Woody's.

Desmond left the bar with three shot glasses and two tall lagers. He placed the glasses on the reserved table which afforded him the best view of the entire restaurant then joined his fraternity brother and wingman for the night, Solomon Alexandré.

Solomon, thankful that his friend sprang for the first round, lifted his beer, clinked glasses with Des and emptied his glass in five large gulps.

"Thirsty?" Desmond said, harboring an earnest look of surprise.

"A little heated." Solomon returned the glass to the wooden table. "It just amazes me how rude some people can be."

"What's wrong, Partna?"

Solomon sat up straight. "Check this out. I'm opening the door to come in and out rushes this fine lady all in tears and boo-hooing. A couple seconds later, some drunk plows into me trying to catch her. When I didn't clear his path fast enough, he turned and wanted to fight me for being in his way." Solomon eyed his empty glass and tipped it toward Desmond for a refill.

"You were in a fight?" Des asked. "Why didn't you call me?"

"Nobody fought, Des. Before he could think good about swinging on me, some other dude even bigger than him came out and snatched him up. I came inside when he pushed him out to the sidewalk."

"That's good," Desmond said. "I don't need no foolishness messing things up for me tonight."

"I hear you, Des. I just don't understand how some women put up with these fools."

"I feel you, Bruh."

"Hey Man," Solomon averted his eyes toward the three shot glasses. "Let me ask you a question. Why did you pick tonight of all nights to go on a blind date?"

Desmond cleared his throat, thought, and took a long, deep breath before looking back at his friend.

Solomon was referring to tonight as the same day on the calendar five years ago when Desmond's wife, Penny, died unexpectedly. Penny Roosevelt was his high school sweetheart. They married six weeks after she graduated from college. She had great teeth, a heart-warming smile and an even greater derriere. They both wanted a bunch of kids, a house with a white picket fence and a dog and a cat. They both attended the University of Washington, where she, a year younger than Desmond, graduated one year after him. She wasn't a true Daddy's girl, but she grew very close to her father during her senior year in high school when her mother caught Meningitis and passed away. Before her graduation from high school, Penny and her father came up with a bucket list of personal achievements for her to complete which included her finishing college before she married or had children. She upheld that marriage promise, but unfortunately, gestational diabetes led to complications in the fifth month of her pregnancy. She was only thirty years old when both she and their unborn baby died from complications during an emergency C-Section.

Seven years ago, the two gay partners who owned his brokerage firm shut down the business for a holiday weekend then left the company— and the country—without notice. After Desmond recovered from the funk of losing his job, he decided that the only way to prevent that from happening at another firm was to be his own boss. So he and Penny pooled their resources and bought a reasonably priced, hollowed-out storefront. After six months of some much needed restoration and the exodus of most of his savings—his sizeable savings coupled with her share of her mother's life insurance—Des opened a sports restaurant called Woody's Bar and Grill. The official opening made Desmond an independent businessman. With his original staff consisting of one certified bartender, one short order cook and three waitresses, he became what he had always aspired to be, the proud owner of an establishment bearing his name.

Penny's death hit Des hard. He relied on clear liquors to help him battle depression and mourning. His days were consumed spending more time drinking his profits and less time running his business. Ten months later as Woody's Bar and Grill approached foreclosure, Des entered rehab.

Not wanting his friend to lose his business while in rehab, Kenny Didier convinced his brother Lawrence and his friend Solomon to each chip in some money to pay Desmond's debts and bring him current with his taxes. In exchange for their contributions, Desmond gave them each fifteen percent ownership of the bar, keeping fifty-five for himself.

Although still considered a recovering alcoholic, one day every year he drinks on the anniversary of Penny's death. Desmond has always hated cemeteries, so instead of visiting their gravesite, he pours himself three double shots of his most expensive single malt scotch; one for himself, one for his wife and one for their unborn baby, then toasts their death with the phrase, *To my love for the dead.*

Solomon glanced at his watch. The woman Des was meeting was fifteen minutes late. Des' interest in this woman was the first true interest in a woman Solo had seen from him since Penny's death. "You can't even imagine how long you'll be paying me back for this," Solomon said.

"Fine ass Skylar Diggins is in town tonight and I'm missing her."

"I know."

"And, I had courtside seats." A client of Solomon's, who was out of town for the week, offered him two tickets for that night's game between the Seattle Storm and the Dallas Wings. "Des, you know I hate playing wingman for Kenny. Why do you think I'd like it any more for you?" Instead of sitting courtside watching Sue Bird square off with Skylar Diggins, Solomon, an uninspired wingman, sat in Woody's waiting impatiently for his best friend's date to show. "How did you get mixed up in a blind date anyway?"

"Come on Solo, it's not a blind date, it's a first date," Desmond responded sternly. "I told you I met her last week."

Solomon was his full first name, but Solo was the nickname his closest friends called him and the only moniker that carried any familiarity in Woody's. Solo shook his head and chortled. "The little bit of nothing you told me about her makes her a stranger, so it may as well be a blind date."

"Look; we had a great conversation when I met her." Desmond took sips of his beer as he once again recapped the ten minutes he shared in the bookstore with the lady known only as Red Velvet. "So there," he finished emphatically, "she's not a complete stranger."

"Seriously, Bruh?" Solo started, "You agreed to meet her for a date and all you know her by is Red Velvet? Why didn't you at least get her real name when she called to setup this date?"

"Dang Dad, stop trippin'!" Des took another long swig of his beer then licked his tightly pursed lips. "Look," he began, frustrated with Solo's interrogation. "She left me a voicemail saying that she was the woman I called Red Velvet at the bookstore and that she would like to take me up on my dinner offer."

"A voicemail?" Solomon thundered. "Are you kidding me? You mean to tell me that you didn't actually talk to her to arrange this madness?"

"She left me her number," Des said emphatically, as if he'd been interrupted for the ump-teenth time. "She told me that she was free tonight and asked me to text her the address to the bar; so I did." Des, now irritated with his decision to choose Solo as his wingman, picked up his glass of beer and emptied it. He belched, let out a sigh and said, "When she texted back that she got the address, I texted her again and we agreed that we'd meet here around nine."

"So, why'd you call me?"

"Because her text she said she was bringing a girlfriend. That's why I called you."

"But why didn't you call Kenny? You know this is more his thing."

Kensington 'Kenny' Didier was the third cog in their four-wheel friendship machine. The problem with having Kenny as your wingman is that he's so good looking, women normally forget all other men in the room. He's single, has money, owns a big penis and knows how to use it; and when he's with a woman, he doesn't mind spending his money on her. What more could a woman possibly want?

"And you brought her to your place? What if she's crazy? Now she knows how to find you."

"If she's crazy, I'm safer here surrounded by all of my people than in some strange restaurant where they might not know me," Des said.

"If she starts some mess here, the whole bar got my back."

Solo took a long swallow of the cool, dark lager, then looked Des dead in the eye and said, "You didn't get her real name. So as far as I'm concerned, this is a blind date."

Before Des could defend himself with an answer, two nicely dressed women came through the front door. Since Solo knew most of the regulars at Woody's, he speculated one of them was Red Velvet, as Des referred to her, and the other her wing-woman. Additionally, the lost looks on their faces showed they were strangers to Woody's. Solo tapped Des on the shoulder and nodded toward the door. The smile on his face confirmed it.

As expected of attractive women, they'd arrived late. Des stood and Solo followed. He called the hostess's name and when she looked his way, he summoned for her to bring them to the table. When they arrived, Desmond anxiously gave the taller of the two women an uncomfortable hug.

Her return hug was similarly apprehensive. She stepped back, her body language exuding that same sense of non-familiarity. "Desmond, this is my friend Sharet Thompson." Her voice was velvety smooth.

Sharet offered a perky, upbeat greeting. She was diminutive compared to her friend. Probably pretty girl as far as the eye could tell. The problem was that it was hard for the naked eye to tell because she wore enough makeup to scare a vampire.

"Nice to meet you Sharet," Des said. "This is my friend, Doctor Solomon Alexandré."

Solo thrust his hand toward Red Velvet. "Nice to meet you." Red Velvet did her justice from a metaphorical sense, but despite her pleasant face and normal appearance, Solo needed the mystery woman to have a real name; something more than a dessert-influenced moniker. "And you are?"

Desmond loudly cleared his throat to express his displeasure with his friend's forwardness.

Red Velvet held Solo's hand through the announcement of her name. "Nice to meet you Doctor Alexandré." Her grip was strong and confident. "I'm Leona Pearson."

The skirt of her gold, wrap-around dress ended halfway up her well-toned thighs. She was a statuesque, more mature-looking lady than Sharet. Her strapless, taupe, taffeta dress cinched at the waist then blossomed slightly over her hips and stopped just short of her knees. As much as Solo had doubted earlier, Desmond hit it right on the head. Red Velvet was an accurate description.

She released his hand and all four took their seats. Desmond sat in the chair facing the bar with Leona to his immediate right. Solo sat across the table from Leona, Desmond to his right. The seating arrangement afforded Leona and Desmond the opportunity to lean in and have a more personal conversation, should they choose. Solo's job was to focus on Sharet once Leona and Des made it far enough that distraction was necessary.

The conversation rotated around then crisscrossed its way about the table as the quartet slowly emptied their plates. The men finished two beers with their meals. The ladies finished a bottle of wine. The food and drink at Woody's was affordable, filling and pleasing. As the night went on, Desmond seemed to hit it off more so with Sharet than with Leona.

Citing a momentary lag in the conversation while Des called for the server to bring dessert, Sharet excused herself and led Leona to the powder room. As soon as they were out of earshot, Des told Solo he was feeling Sharet and asked him to switch seats.

Not feeling a predominant attraction to either woman, Solo agreed.

Desmond stopped briefly by the bar to have a bottle of dessert wine sent to the table before ambushing the ladies as they exited the bathroom. "Leona, may I speak to you privately?"

Sharet excused herself and left them alone in the hallway.

"Don't take it personal," Des started, "but I'm feeling your friend."

"Oh really?" Leona mused. "I could hardly tell."

Des smiled. "Let's just say that if I had met the two of you at the same time, I would have asked her out before I asked you. I mean you are a pretty woman and…"

Leona held up a hand signaling him to stop. "Hey Des, it's all good. If you like my girl that much, why don't we switch seats?"

"Are you sure you're cool with that?"

"Yeah," Leona said. "You're cool and everything, but I normally date taller guys anyway."

Accustomed to the digs on his height from his boys, Des poked out his chest and lifted his shoulders to the ceiling, trying to make himself appear taller. "Why it always gotta be about height? Everybody can't be a tree."

"Don't fret Sweetie, we're cool." Leona laughed, recognizing his attempt to look taller.

Desmond relaxed his shoulders and opened his arms to suggest a hug. Leona accepted his offering of consolation and hugged him, very briefly. Solo watched as Des and Leona walked back to the table. Her runway-model stride was sexy. Solo stood so that he and Desmond could switch chairs, but Leona came to a stop in front of Desmond's chair. Des pulled out the chair and switched seats with Leona. Leona sat to Solo's right in Desmond's previous seat. Now the men faced each other and so did the women.

Struggling to control her excitement, Sharet beamed a knowing smile at Leona before quickly dropping her eyes to her plate.

Dessert, four slices of custom-made red velvet cake from Eddie and Jack's Good Sign Bakery, was delivered to the table. Drinks were refilled while they were gone, two more beers for the guys, and a bottle of Rosè Regale for the ladies to enjoy with their dessert.

Desmond let his eyes travel Sharet's body. A devilish grin grew on his face.

"Don't look at me like I ain't got no draws on," Sharet said, in what was her first spontaneously clever remark of the evening.

Solo guffawed and Leona almost spit out her wine.

"Excuse me?" Desmond said, his eyes ogling her petite frame.

Sharet replied pretentiously, "Why don't you try having a conversation with my eyes instead of with my thighs?"

Desmond leaned in close and whispered in her ear.

Sharet laughed and scooted her chair closer to his. They quickly escaped into their own little world and spent the next half hour sharing a private conversation of which Leona and Solo could only catch snippets.

"Yuck. That puppy love crap nauseates me," Leona sniped and turned her body towards Solo, giving him her full attention. They fell into general conversation and the next hour passed like a couple of minutes. She was closed off at first, but eventually opened up. She didn't give up any solid details, but she gave enough information to no longer be considered a stranger. Enough to make them familiar if he cared to remember it all.

The conversation smoothly transitioned from one subject to another as they examined how words similar to the title Red Velvet invoked the use of food in seduction. Art and travel preceded a conversation that revealed Leona was an avid sports fan. Finally, his off-color remark about observing her athletic gait hurtled their conversation upon the subject of dance.

When Solomon asked Leona what she enjoyed about teaching dance, she leaned back in her chair, eased her fingers through her soft locks like a wide-toothed comb and joyfully explained the pleasure she received from teaching dance to children. He looked on intently, no longer grudgingly stuck in the wingman role, but enthralled in captive conversation with this attractive woman.

In between stealing peeks at the basketball game on one of the twenty televisions, Solo allowed Leona to occupy most of his attention for the remainder of the evening. The way she articulated her words led him to believe she was well-educated. The elegant way she sipped her wine exuded a sexiness that made him think of the beautiful attorney he married. In the middle of the conversation, she unexpectedly reached and touched his face. She did it without thinking. Touched his face and looked into his eyes. He gave her an uncomfortable smile. Without seeming to recognize his discomfort, she removed her hand and leaned back.

He met her gaze. His expression seemed transitive. Like watching her gave him an opium infused high. When their eye contact turned decadent, he looked away. Laughed like a shy little boy.

Leona smiled. Remained cool, calm, cold—an ice queen. Like she had to keep her walls high or the enemy might climb over. A cool breeze rushed across their faces as a group of six entered through the front door.

When he looked back at her, she was beautiful.

Solomon conceded that Leona was grown woman fine. Short, brown hair cut so perfectly you would think that her stylist was an abstract artist. Eye makeup so flawless that her eyes seemed to float on her face. Her dress showed off the finer points of her well-toned body in sexy detail while at the same time revealed nothing, despite the thigh-high slit in her hem, to make you think she was the slightest bit a loose woman. He considered her the type of fine that was far past cute and way too graceful to merely be considered sexy.

Leona steadily sipped her wine. She also did most of the talking. She wore neither a wedding band, nor rings of any kind on her left hand, but did wear with a large garnet stone set in a bronze, ankh-shaped ring on the middle finger of her right hand.

Solo wasn't there to find a woman, a date or even a friend. He was there because Des needed a wingman and he never let his partners down. Des would reciprocate, if asked, so there he sat, enjoying the company of a pretty woman—not beautiful by industry standards because of the slight imperfection on her cheek, but an attractive woman who knew how to keep a conversation rolling.

Leona bit the corner of her lip and paused as if in contemplative thought. "Would you mind if we left and went someplace else?" she hummed. "These two don't seem at all concerned with our company and I know of another get together with much more potential."

"Are you bored?" Solo said, feeling that her comment was directed toward their conversation.

"No Honey, I am far from bored with you." She rubbed her hand over his, then put her hand on his thigh and rubbed it a couple of times. Alcohol was diminishing her reserve and magnifying her desires.

"Truth moment?" She seductively ran her tongue across a thin coat of shimmery mahogany lipstick which left her easing into a smile. "I am very interested in exploring more than you can show me in this bar."

"Well, well." He eyed her for a moment. His mind wandered about this being the point where the normal player would tell her how beautiful or sexy he thinks she is in an attempt to encourage her to want to go home with him; but, he knew a woman of her obvious grace and maturity would certainly be immune to such blandishment. Finally, he said, "Yeah. Let's go explore that more interesting get together."

Leona may have talked a good game about seduction, but the wine had sped her forwardness past the seduction intersection a few miles back.

Definitely interested in finding out what her mind thought she wanted to do with the rest of her evening, Solo turned to face Desmond and Sharet. "Hey Man, are you all right?"

Desmond barely turned his eyes as he gave a thumbs up and waived his hand to dismiss them. Again, Sharet offered her excuse, but this time, she practically dragged Leona away from the table. "Hey Girl, I hope you're not upset about switching. I think I could really get to like this guy."

"Forget about it," she laughed. "You know you my girl."

"Well, Your Girl is about to work her magic on Mister Desmond.

I'll give you a call later."

"I hope you're right." Leona burst into laughter. "Because if not, I'm never going to let you live this down." At the table Leona asked her, "Are you okay getting home by yourself?"

"Don't worry about that," Desmond answered for her. "I will make sure that she has everything she needs tonight." Des hadn't dated in a while. Nice girls didn't come his way that often and she seemed like a nice girl.

Sharet giggled softly as she smiled brightly at Leona.

"Whatever," Leona walked around Desmond's chair, leaned in between them and kissed Sharet on the cheek. "Call me in the morning, Chica."

Des sat after he and Solo shook hands. He was all up in Sharet's world and his wingman was happy for him. Des asked Leona to call him in a couple of days. They had talked earlier about dance lessons for his niece. Leona agreed, pushing her handbag onto her shoulder.

As Solomon, the wingman, and Leona, the late blind date, walked out of Woody's, Leona hoped that the dinner show was but a prelude to an even more exciting after party.

04

Majac Arriving

"LET ME GUESS, HE'S RUNNING LATE?" Anton 'Majac' Charles said to the woman walking beside him reading a text message on her cell phone. She was a slender woman in her mid-forties. She'd sat next to him in first class on the flight from Chicago to Seattle. Now they, along with the majority of their fellow passengers, were on the escalator descending from the Arrivals terminal to the baggage claim area. Majac pulled his new smartphone from the right breast pocket of his sports coat. He'd owned the device for less than two weeks and if it wasn't for his sister Angel loading the pictures and ringtones for him, he'd be listening to one of those annoying elevator music chimes instead of the sultry voice of his Sade ringtone telling him once more that she was a *Soldier of Love*.

"What's up Majac?" Jaz Stevenson's voice came from Majac's phone.

"What's up Partna?" Majac answered. He turned to her, "It's my ride."

"Who you talking to?" Jaz asked.

"Hunh?" Majac exclaimed. "Oh, that's Jennifer."

"Jennifer?" Jaz said. "Damn Boy, you don't waste any time. You haven't been here two minutes and you've already caught one."

"Where are you?" Majac said, ignoring his friend.

"I got the text that you landed."

"Cool." Majac replied. "I'm on the escalator headed down to baggage claim. I don't see you."

"That's because I'm sitting in traffic near the Space Needle. Dude on the radio said they just started construction this morning. Practice ended

27

early and I would've been there on time, but the owners called a surprise meeting and it ran a little longer than I expected."

"Everything all right?"

"Yeah, everything's cool for now."

"Cool."

"I would've called Crystal and asked her to come pick you up," Jaz said, "but she's at school with the girls right now and I'm closer."

"So you're saying all that to say…"

"Yeah Bruh, I'm saying all that to say I'll be late." They both laughed at Jaz finishing his sentence. "It shouldn't be more than a half hour, once I get past Yale."

"Aiight Bruh," Majac said. "I'll grab my bags and find a place to have some lunch. Probably have time to check my email and Facebook since I ain't going nowhere fast."

"My bad Man," Jaz said. "I'll be there as soon as I can."

"No worries Bruh. It's all good."

"Hey Partna, maybe this will give you some time to get more acquainted with your new friend Jennifer?" Jaz laughed.

"Bye Jaz."

"Everything all right?" Jennifer asked as the escalator arrived at the bottom floor. The peculiarly offset of her eyes made it difficult to make eye contact. She stood tall and slender of form, with remarkably delicate hands and feet. Her fairly light-skinned complexion seemed pale beneath a close-cropped head of fine, jet-black hair. Her straight, well-formed nose, finely cut mouth, and graceful contour of her head and neck showed that she must have once been beautiful; but now her face was starting to wrinkle with lines of pain, and of proud and bitter endurance.

"Yeah," Majac said emphatically. "Everything's cool. My ride's running a little late, but no worries."

Jennifer checked her cell phone a third time for a return call from her husband. Then she called another number and held a short conversation as Majac ordered two Stromboli and two drinks from an Italian food vendor. They took their food and walked to the USO, a place he hadn't been inside since he was a young Lieutenant flying into Italy for the first time to meet his submarine. The guy at the front desk asked them to sign in then pointed across the room at a sign on the counter that read free fresh fruit, water and snacks. "Make yourselves at home," he said.

"Thank you, sir," Majac said.

"Not a sir, thank you." He raised his eyes to meet Majac's and said, "People round these parts call me Gerry, but if you feel so inclined, I prefer that you younger GI's call me Master Sergeant."

"Sorry Master Sergeant. I didn't mean to offend."

Majac eyed the ledger. His was the fifth name signed in that day and the only name that didn't have the Master Sergeant's initial behind it. Master Sergeant spun the ledger around, initialed next to Majac's name and said, "Excuse me Commander Charles, I meant no disrespect Sir. Master Sergeant, Retired, Gerald Huckabee at your service."

"Nice to meet you, Master Sergeant." Majac extended his hand and the Master Sergeant responded with a bear trap like grip that seemed accustomed to crushing men's hands. Majac smiled. The Master Sergeant released his hand, allowing it to slowly regain feeling.

"Thirty-two years United States Army," Master Sergeant Huckabee said. "Let me grab that bag for you, sir."

Before Majac could say no, the Master Sergeant scooped his bag up in one of the bear traps he called hands and placed it on the luggage shelf behind one of the chairs that sat across the lounge from a 55-inch flat-screen television. Majac sat his second bag on top of the first and escorted Jennifer to a seat at one of the four bistro table sets.

Majac pulled out his phone and sent Jaz a text that he was waiting in the USO. Jennifer dialed a number on her phone, simply said, "I'm downstairs at the USO" then hung up before the two of them peacefully enjoyed their lunch.

Twenty minutes later, a tall, captivating or moreover in a single word, stunning woman entered the USO. The room seemed to slow down as she approached the table. Her heather brown complexion reminded Majac of warm, sweet potato pie.

Jennifer caught Majac's eye, turned to see the woman approaching their table and joyfully rose to give her a hug. When they separated, Jennifer introduced her. "Anton Charles, I'd like you to meet my sister, Leona Pearson."

Anton extended his hand and embraced the butter soft grip of the stunning beauty. "Nice to meet you Leona."

"Likewise," was Leona's duo-syllabic response. The warm colors in her dress accentuated her complexion. Soft flowing lines intertwined patches of reds, oranges and yellows. A wildly artistic African broach adorned her lapel. She turned to face her sister. "And exactly where is my good for nothing brother-in-law?"

"You know Luke; I hardly ever see him."

"Okay," Leona said. "I get it; he's a busy man. But he ain't that damn busy that he can't come to the airport and pick up his wife."

Jennifer eased her face into an awkward smile, trying not to show her airline travelling partner how true her sister's words were. She offered Anton her business card and again welcomed him to Seattle. She told him to call her if there was anything she could do to help him get settled.

Leona grabbed two of Jennifer's suitcases. Jennifer grabbed the third and her purse. Then, like a brief gust of wind, the two amazon bombshells were gone.

Master Sergeant brewed a fresh pot of coffee and poured Majac a cup.

"Thank you, Master Sergeant."

"Please, call me Gerry."

"And if you would please call me Anton."

When the Master Sergeant went back to his desk, Majac looked around and found himself the only visitor remaining in the USO. He pulled out his new phone, put in his earbuds and listened to two chapters of the latest audiobook by Eric Jerome Brown.

$$\sim$$

A pained, apologetic look covered Jaz's face when he finally entered the USO a half hour later. In a deep baritone he called, "Hey Partna."

The Master Sergeant, who was now standing behind the sofa watching television, turned around to face the man calling out from the door.

"What's up?" Majac replied.

"You ready?"

"Aiight, let me grab my stuff." Majac picked up one of his bags as Gerry moved to pick up the other. "Thanks Gerry, but you don't have to."

"My pleasure, Sir." Gerry picked up the other bag in his massively powerful hand and they walked toward Jaz.

"Damn, how rude of me. Let me introduce you to my best friend…"

"Oh my God, you're Jaz Stevenson," Gerry said emphatically. "Wait a minute, let me get my camera."

Majac took several pictures of Jaz sharing a short tête-à-tête with his self-proclaimed biggest fan, the Master Sergeant.

Jaz offered to autograph a team picture posted on the wall from the year that the Seattle Knights won their second consecutive NBA championship. "Who should I make it out to?" he asked.

"Please make it out to 'My Good Friend, Ole Master Sergeant Huck'."

Jaz signed the picture, then handed it to Gerry. "Next time you want tickets to a game, call Key Arena and ask for Mister Melvin Griffiths. Tell him you are a personal friend of mine and that 'Mister Big Shot' said to hook you up with the VIP treatment." Jaz laughed. "He'll make sure you get the best seats available."

Five minutes later Majac dropped both of his bags in the trunk of Jaz's Sintered Bronze Mercedes Benz G550. They hopped in and Jaz bolted out of short term parking at SeaTac Airport past a billboard of six Seahawk cheerleaders welcoming guests to Seattle and hit the interstate.

The cheerleaders on the billboard returned Majac to thoughts of his former girlfriend Celeste. She was the cheerleader for the San Diego Cougars who declined his offer to marry him. Time revealed that she declined because she was pregnant with another man's baby. *Wonder how that turned out for her?* Majac thought. After he shook off the memory of Celeste, he remembered that Tessa Ajai, his cheerleader girlfriend from high school, had a birthday coming up soon.

As Jaz sped north like a drug mule running from the DEA, Majac pulled out his phone and sent Tessa a text. *Happy B-day Ms. Ajai. Thot I would get my b-day wishes in B4 the wknd got here and U got 2 deep in party mode.*

Two minutes later, Tessa replied, *Thanks so much 4 the b-day luv. You are a gem my friend.*

Next he sent, *After all this time, I'm just glad we're still friends.*

Tessa sent, *Ur a Sweetie. I share in that gladness. Out of town 4 my b-day. Need it. I get so busy here that I forget my name most days.*

He sent, *Well lucky for you, some of us always remember Ur name (lol), along with a LOT else about U.*

She sent, *U always know exactly what 2 say 2 me...Miss U very much, Charmer.* Before he could send his next text, she sent, *Ps. Where's my gift? LOL*

He laughed to himself and sent, *What U want?*

Tessa sent, *Hmmm (scratching my temple). Have 2 think hard & C what cumz to mind. lol*

He sent, *LOL – Really, What CUMZ to mind?*

Tessa sent, *This is the part where Ur s'posed to tell me 2 B-Have.*

He sent, *Who is Have? – lol*

Tessa sent, *Rubbin my chin now. - Ur camera still work?*

He sent, *Batteries stay charged!*

Tessa sent, *Fresh batteries would be good right about now. LMAO*

He texted, *Do U need me to bring U some?*

Tessa sent, *Are you in Tuskegee?*

He sent, *Unfortunately not. But do U need me to B?*

Tessa sent, *If you were, I could imagine some things to do with you.*

He sent, Sounds like a *Sista could use a li'l maint-nance. LOL*

Tessa sent ten tool emoji's including wrenches, hammers and nails.

Over the next ten minutes, they continued to text. When texting became sexting, she sent back, *I gotta go pack, but U really made my day.* Her change of subject offering a moratorium to his *li'l maint-nance* proposition. *Thanks for thinking of me Sweetie.*

As Jaz reached Mercer Island, Majac sent *Ur well-cum. Stay Sweet.*

She didn't send a reply.

"Thanks for picking me up, Partna." Majac was finished texting now.

"Majac you just don't know how happy I am to see you."

"Yeah, it's been a minute. A lot's happened since we last hung out."

"Man, you don't know the half of it."

Majac peered at Jaz inquisitively. Perplexed by his cryptic comments, he checked the tightness of his seatbelt and held on as Jaz almost three-wheeled the exit ramp.

"Hey Maj, you want to hear some good news?"

"Sure Partna, what's up?"

"Well, I was late because management called an unscheduled coaches' meeting. I was pissed until they announced that I was being promoted to interim head coach."

"Dang Partna, that's great!"

"Yeah, apparently Coach Bogans came in this morning and told management that he was going into the hospital to have some surgery and tomorrow was his last day."

"Wow, is everything all right?"

"I don't know exactly. Coach said they needed to do some tests and the tests left him too weak to coach. Crazy right?"

"Yeah, crazy."

"Oh, guess what else that means?" Jaz paused, but didn't wait for my response. "Since I'm now the head coach of the best team in the conference, I...am coaching the West team in the All-Star game."

"Dang Partna, that's what's up. I could hardly tell that you're happy about it with that sour puss look on your face."

"Well, that is a long story, but we got All-Star weekend to get ready for."

"What about tickets?" Majac asked.

"I got you tickets for Friday, Saturday and Sunday."

"Cool. I can hang with Crys and the girls while you coach."

"Crys has her press pass. She'll be working. So it's just me and you."

"Cool," Majac said. "All-Star weekend! This is gonna be off the chain."

Jaz regarded Majac and said, "Don't think I forgot."

"Forgot what?"

"Jennifer, Boy? Don't act like you don't know what I'm talking about, Playa-Playa," Jaz exclaimed.

"Nothing to tell really," Majac said. "We sat next to each other on the plane. She told me her cousin Michelle had just written a book titled *Becoming*, and she was in Chicago for the book release party. When the plane landed, we walked to baggage claim together. When her husband, a politician, didn't show to pick her up, she called her sister. Since we both had to wait for our rides, we sat and ate lunch together. A little while later, her sister came and got her." He paused. "Now that sister of hers...Whoo! That woman is a beast."

They laughed as Jaz switched lanes and sped past a red Audi A8.

"So Partna, how's retirement treating you?"

Jaz looked straight ahead, his eyes locked on the road, staring hard as if he was counting the white lane markers as they passed at sixty miles an hour. The twenty-three-mile drive from the airport to the Stevenson's house took right about a half hour. Jaz made good time getting home, repeatedly swerving through all four lanes, and all the while explaining the insanity that popped off between him, Crystal and Quianna at his villa in L.A.

Crystal filled the dishwasher and started to clean up the kitchen after dinner. "Jared," she started, "why don't you boys go out on the veranda for a beer?" Jaz grabbed two beers from the fridge before his best friend followed him out onto the veranda of the 16,000 square foot, seven bedroom, five-and-a-half bath, lakeside mansion overlooking Lake Washington. It'd been three days since Majac's arrival in Seattle and the body of the transplant from Washington the city was acclimating to the time zone change to Washington the state.

Fairweather Bay, in the Hunts Point section of the northern end of Mercer Island, was a private neighborhood of luxurious, custom-built homes set in spacious, deep, wooded lots located twenty minutes east of downtown Seattle just across the Evergreen Point Floating Bridge on Highway 520. Unlike other suburban communities along Lake Washington, Fairweather Bay was an oasis of tranquil, tree-lined, residential streets. Its prestigious roads, lanes and circles were exquisitely paved with either cobblestones or sparkling pea-gravel. Grand waterside mansions with private boat landings lined the beaches along the northern end of Lake Washington surrounding Mercer Island. Set in an idyllic, resolutely non-urban community where smaller houses and apartment complexes sat on the hill on the opposite side of the lake, overlooking the mansions and beach houses like onlookers peeping over a privacy fence.

Soft white puffs of air billowed from their mouths with each breath. When their eyes finally met, Jaz asked, "What?"

"You seem more stressed than usual Partna," Majac said.

"You wanna talk about it?" He had noticed during dinner how exhausted his friend looked —tired, like he'd been awake for days.

There wasn't much joy in Jaz's voice. "Yesterday, the Knights offered me a three-year contract to stay on as head coach."

"Great." They raised their bottles and touched them in salute.

"So why the sad face?"

Jaz didn't respond immediately. He leaned one leg up on the bronze-colored wrought-iron railing that separated the veranda from the swimming pool area and took a long swig of his beer.

Majac suffered through the anticipation of the long pause. He missed spending time with his best friend. He missed engaging in their intense guy talk sessions about politics, work, and of course, women, but he didn't miss Jaz's dramatics. It'd been three years since he and Jaz had been in the same room which gave them a chance to sit down and have a good, real, brotherly chat. Majac took a seat on one of the four plush patio chairs and waited for Jaz to finally talk. He took a small drink then cleared his throat to remind Jaz that he was still there.

"Last week I got a head coaching offer from the Monarchs," Jaz said, looking out across the lake. St. Louis was the team that drafted Jaz after he graduated from college. He spent seven years there before being traded to San Diego in salary cap negotiation. "Yeah," Jaz continued. "St. Louis got permission from Seattle to talk to me mid-season, which is something that never happens, and apparently they're looking to pick up a new head coach right now instead of letting the interim coach lead the team through the remainder of the season."

Majac and Jaz were so engrossed in their conversation that neither of them heard the shallow moan of the screen door when Crystal stepped out on the porch. She'd come to tell Jaz that the girls were going to bed and their baby girl wanted him to come tuck her in. But when she heard them talking, she stopped and listened quietly, hidden out of sight by the corner of the outdoor kitchen, as their guy talk continued.

"Does Crys know?"

"Of course."

"About both offers?"

"Yeah."

"So which way are you leaning?"

"Don't know yet. The Seattle thing is all of a sudden. I had no idea that Coach Bogans was gonna go out on us like that, so I wasn't even thinking about a head coaching job here in Seattle."

"Pros and cons?"

"Both teams are doing well right now. If they keep playing the way they are, they'll both make the playoffs." Jaz rubbed his right knee as he spoke.

"Wow; that really makes it tough."

"Even with my retirement, we're still having a great season." Seattle had entered this season coming off a loss in the NBA finals after winning back-to-back championships.

"How's the leg, Partna?" Majac asked, nodding his head toward the nagging right leg Jaz now habitually rubbed.

"It's getting there," Jaz said, pulling his hand away from the four-time injured right leg which had forced his retirement from the game. During a pre-season game against Portland, Jaz suffered a freakish injury when he blocked a shot from behind during a fast break attempt by Trailblazers' guard Marc Spears. When he came down, his foot and leg got caught under the hoop's stanchion and fractured both the tibia and fibula in his right leg.

Jaz said, "Doctor said I should've been out of my cast and into a walking boot in two months, depending on how the pins set." Jaz had taken a role in a movie over the summer and despite it being a sports movie, he didn't put in the work he normally would've had he been off the whole summer. He blamed his injury on neglecting his off-season routine.

"Well, that didn't happen," Jaz continued. "By the time Christmas came around and I was still having significant pain putting any weight on my leg, the doctor told me that my leg wasn't healing well and my season is probably shot. The team was doing so well without me that I didn't see any reason for me to rush back and risk further injuring my leg."

On January first, after several long talks with Crystal about their future, Jaz held a press conference in which he announced his retirement from the NBA. He reminded the press of his previous injuries, which led him to tears while he talked. During his third season in the league, Jaz ruptured his right Achilles for the second time—the first time ended his sophomore season in college. In his second year in San Diego, he tore some cartilage in his right knee and missed two months. While he was out, San Diego lost twenty of twenty-eight games and finished the season last in the conference.

Once Jaz finished talking to the press, Stanley Bright took his place at the microphone and announced that the Knights were hiring Jaz as an assistance coach, effective immediately.

A couple of minutes passed in silence. Majac listened to the beauty of the lake and marveled. Waves crashed gently against the shore.

In the darkness of dusk, toads croaked in a syncopated staccato. In the trees, birds chirped gleefully. On a distant highway, cars drove at breakneck speed making the din of tires sound like rushing water. Each man thought about their personal lives and how after all these years, how happy they were that they'd once again come to have their best friend back in their life.

"I know you've never been there," Jaz said, "but I loved St. Louis."

"What did Crystal have to say about going back to St. Louis?"

"We talked about both jobs last night."

"And..."

"And..." Jaz took another swig of his beer. "We're trying to figure it out. Crys and I agreed to wait until after the All-Star game to talk seriously about our future. Doesn't help that she's still holding this L.A. thing over my head every chance she gets."

"You my boy and everything, so I gotta ask; since it apparently is still the elephant in the room." Majac retorted. "But seriously though, Partna. Was she worth it?"

Jaz fell Silent. The weight of it appeared to crush him like an Acme piano in a Road Runner cartoon.

After a beat, Majac changed the topic. "So what did your agent say?"

"He has both offers. He's reviewing them so Crys and I can talk to him about them next week."

"Either team give you a firm deadline?"

"No. Seattle knew the St. Louis offer was on the table, so I think that's why they offered me the job so quickly after Bogans got sick instead of just making me interim and doing the customary coach search. Shoot Maj, I ain't been a head coach before and even though I am probably most familiar with the team right now, there's no good reason that they wouldn't try to bring in the best coach out there and I know that's not me."

"Sounds to me like they already found the best man for the job."

"Thanks for that Partna."

"Here's to choices." Majac raised his bottle for a toast.

Jaz reached over and they clinked bottles again. "Remember that call I took right before dinner?"

"Yeah."

"Well, according to my agent, both contracts are enough to set me for retirement. Enough money that we'll be set for the rest of our life."

"Choices, Choices." Majac joked, unaware that his sarcasm cut Jaz.

"Come on Maj, I'm being serious here."

"C'mon Man. I'm just kidding. It's nice to have those decision to make. You've earned it."

"Yeah, nice." Jaz's expression didn't seem earnest. Something in his tone said that his heart wasn't in it as much as the excitement of two NBA teams bidding what was probably millions of dollars for his services should excite the normal person. Then again, Jaz and people like Jaz weren't normal people. They were professional athletes and coaches who were used to talking about millions of dollars, and that made the gap between them and normal people about as wide as the Grand Canyon.

"Yeah, must be nice to have the stress of choosing between which two playoff contenders I want to be the head coach for and making millions of dollars a year doing it," Majac joked. "I need that horrible decision weighing on my mind."

"What's with all the sarcasm, Partna?" Jaz's irritation came to full surface.

Majac knew he was stressed, but didn't expect this reaction.

"Do you need something?" Jaz asked.

"Need something?" The implication from Jaz that Majac needed something was new. Despite Jaz having more money than Majac could ever imagine making, Majac had never asked Jaz for anything. Jaz had done a couple of things for Majac without his asking—like buying last minute first class plane tickets for Majac and his girlfriend to fly home when his Pops passed—but Majac never asked Jaz to do it and he tried to repay him the money but Jaz refused. The implication that he needed a handout agitated Majac. He knew Jaz had a lot on his mind between the coaching thing and Crys finding him with that girl in Los Angeles, so he didn't start that argument right then.

Jaz not only had himself to think about on this one, but Crystal had been on her job for a couple of years now so asking her to relocate was probably another issue pressing him. Majac took a deep breath and cleansed his mind before clarifying, "I don't need a damn thing Partna. I'm single, got no kids to pay child support for, and I got a six-figure salary—not including my bonuses. I just made Commander and in three years I'll be eligible for a full Navy retirement. Besides, your money problems ain't nothing but a headache. I don't need NBA millions to make me happy."

"Me neither," Jaz said, before finishing the remainder of his beer. Jaz, an inner-city kid from Pennsylvania who shared a three-bedroom house with his parents and three siblings as a child, sat perfectly quiet and took a moment to look out over the lake. He marveled at the beauty of his secluded suburban village. He smiled; satisfied with what years of hard work perfecting his basketball skills throughout a successful NBA career had afforded him. "But it sure is nice."

As the guys clinked beer bottles, Crystal turned around and went back inside without asking Jaz to tuck in their daughters.

"Do you mind if we watch the news?"

"You can watch whatever." Jaz tossed the remote to Majac. "I normally watch Channel Nine."

Majac changed the channel from twelve to nine then listened intently as Dustin Kiernan, the eleven o'clock news anchor, reported:

"Earlier today we broke the story that the commanding officer of the ballistic missile submarine THURGOOD MARSHALL was temporarily relieved of his command after being arrested during an undercover prostitution sting by Kitsap County Sheriff's office. Commander Melvin Gleason, a 40-year-old Naval Academy graduate from Des Moines Iowa, has been temporarily reassigned to the office of the Commander, Navy Region Northwest, in Everett, according to Steve Bassett, Public Affairs Officer for the Naval Station."

Majac didn't know Gleason but the story piqued his interest.

"According to a Kitsap County Sheriff's report, Gleason was arrested around 9:30 last night after having approached an undercover female police officer who was posing as a prostitute in the Maryland Farms area. The report stated that Gleason was driving a sport utility vehicle and had circled the area three times before he pulled into a parking lot at Pleasant View Center on Alabaster Road where he approached the undercover officer. Gleason invited to the officer to open his passenger door and the two began talking. Gleason asked the officer if she wanted a ride and she replied that she was working.

"The officer then asked Gleason if he wanted business.

"He said he did want business and asked her several times if she was a police officer. Gleason offered to pay $40 for an oral sex act and invited the officer into his vehicle. The officer told Gleason it would be better if he were to pick her up in the rear of the building, where, other officers moved in and took Gleason into custody. Gleason was charged with solicitation of prostitution.

"He was taken to a Kitsap Sheriff's Office and released after a bond hearing this morning according to the Kitsap Sheriff Public Information Officer.

"Gleason has been reassigned pending the outcome of his case. Temporary command of MARSHALL has been turned over to the executive officer, Commander Martin Danielson."

The news anchor moved on to a story about a fire at the Fish Market.
"Damn," Majac exasperated.
Jaz said, "They said that fool went to the Academy. You know him?"
"The name rings a bell. He's a couple years older than me. Probably a couple of years ahead of me too. Either way, I don't know the guy."
"So, what does that mean for him?" Jaz asked.
"What it means is that he's about to retire."

05

Gifts A Plenty

FRIDAY AFTERNOON LEONA PEARSON WAS running late for her monthly, but previously bi-weekly, anger management counseling. Two girls in her teen dance class asked could they stay and do some extra work on the routine for their upcoming performance. They were good girls who were struggling with some of the complicated steps, but they were trying hard, so she stayed and helped them.

As she rushed to therapy, she found a client waiting outside her studio. He was a widower, and a powerful man in the community who had always been one of her most respectful clients.

"You didn't call. I don't like it when people change our arrangement," Leona said. "And I definitely don't like people showing up unannounced."

"I was in the neighborhood on other business and given the nature of my visit, I thought stopping-by was less impersonal than a phone call." Sunday night he'd told her he would call to arrange for them to get together but he didn't. "I brought cash," he said.

"That's not the point," she said curtly. Normally she took payment by credit card, but because he was a faithful customer, he asked if he could pay cash just this once. Never having any trouble with him in the past, she agreed to this method of payment—this once.

A month earlier, he had approached Leona about his triplet boys turning eighteen. He spoke of how he admired how nurturing she was and asked if he could hire her to teach them the right way to have sex; explaining how, despite their age, he wanted an experienced woman for their first time vice fooling around with some teenage girl who knew less about sex than they did.

The boys were high school seniors, all with scholarships to prominent universities. Their father didn't want their futures disturbed by some girls who might—in his words—fall in love; or get pregnant; or God forbid... give them something worse.

Leona had asked, "What makes you so sure they're still virgins?"

"They're my sons," the arrogant man had said bluntly. "We've talked and I know."

Leona huffed her disgust at him, then moved toward the parking lot. He followed.

If the traffic gods smiled on her, she could still make her appointment. At the parking lot entrance, amidst a third round of apologies for his transgression, the widower grabbed her arm to interrupt her perpetual motion. Being manhandled was something she'd never tolerate again. She spun on him, pulled away angrily, shot daggers from her eyes, braced herself and balled both hands into fists. Anger bubbled up inside causing the skin of her heather brown cheeks to glow red.

When her anger boiled over she took things to the extreme. The last time it boiled over she wound up in jail. She didn't want anything like that to happen again, especially on her way to a meeting with her therapist.

The widower took a step back and raised his hands in surrender.

She relaxed her brace to receive the manila envelope handed her. It was heavier than she expected, so she opened it and scanned the money. Inside was three thousand dollars. "This isn't right." She closed the envelope and shoved it back at him. "You only owe me two thousand."

He kept his hands in the air, refusing to accept it. "You're right; $2000 per our agreement and another thousand for your inconvenience. I genuinely appreciate your professionalism in not embarrassing me in front of the boy. I hope my transgression won't affect our relationship going forward. Again, I'm sorry."

Her cellular phone rang. She answered it and turned her back to him.

"Well hello Darling, to what do I owe this surprise?" The father of three stood idly by as she held court with her cell phone.

"Sounds great, I'm looking forward to it," she said, then hung up. She turned back to her client. Her expression was less angry. Again she extended the envelope in his direction. "I don't like surprises. And I don't want your charity," she boomed. "When we make an agreement, I expect you to honor it. Understood?"

"I'm sorry," he said again. "I understand. It won't happen again."

She didn't respond.

"Please accept it," he said. His hands were still raised, refusing to take back the envelope.

Defeated, pissed at him for making her later by the minute and wanting to end the conversation, Leona dropped her outstretched arm and tucked the envelope deep into her cavernous Berkeley bag.

As she turned to walk away, he asked, "When can I see you again?"

"Considering the way you handled this last arrangement, it will be a while." Leona stopped in her tracks. She gave him a stern look and told him, "Don't call me, I'll call you."

Although she said the extra thousand wasn't necessary, he hoped it would keep him in her good graces. It appeared to work, for now.

⟿

Leona Pearson was Doctor Désirée Crittendon's last session for the day. Scolding the inconsiderate father of triplets put Leona behind schedule, but the true reason she arrived late for her session was the ten minutes it took for her car to start because of her failing alternator.

Once Leona had settled in the office, Doctor Crittendon pushed the intercom button. "Vivienne, I won't need you anymore tonight. Check with Doctor Alexandré, and if it's all right with him, you can go." When Doctor Crittendon sat down, it didn't take much for her to read into the flustered expression on her client's face. She asked, "Are you all right?"

Leona closed her eyes. She'd recognized Solomon's name on the outer office door during her first appointment two months ago, but they'd never crossed paths. She thought of asking her therapist about him, but didn't, thinking it might spark too many unwanted questions of her. She dropped her chin to her chest and scratched where an itch festered on the back of her scalp. "Yes, Doctor Crittendon," she said. Her eyes were still closed. That itch was the last bit of anger that remained from the discussion outside her studio. "I'm all right."

"You don't seem all right."

"I'm just mad that a client showed up at my studio unannounced."

"A dance client or the other?"

"He wasn't wearing dance shoes, Doc," Leona rumbled. She scratched at that itch some more. She exhaled and said, "What I'm having a problem getting past, despite him giving me an envelope with three times more money than he owed me, is him taking me for granted."

"Three times? Darn, if you're that good, maybe I need to check out your services?"

"You, can't afford me, Doc."

"Then I guess I need to raise your rates."

Leona laughed away the comment. Then she slipped her shoes off and tucked her feet beneath her. "It infuriates me when people try to take advantage of my good nature. Not that I don't deserve every dollar I earn, I just don't want people to think I'm open to anything for the sake of making a buck. Don't get me wrong, money is important, but there are limitations to what money can buy—from me."

Leona went silent. A beat passed as Doctor Crittendon shared her silence allowing some of the tension in the room to die off. When they finally started talking, Leona spent the first fifteen minutes of her session telling Doctor Crittendon about the previous weekend.

She told her about the three boys with her client when he arrived on Saturday morning. How they agreed for him to bring the other boys back later that afternoon because she needed time to freshen up between sessions. Because of their age, she wanted to spend time with them individually. He agreed and left one of the boys, agreeing to return later with the second boy. As a rule, Leona never had more than two clients in one day.

Leona explained how she—spending four hours with each boy— took two days over the course of the weekend to teach all three the basics of lovemaking. How she gave each of them her Sex 101 crash course, including pictures of the female anatomy and some non-pornographic pictures of men and women engaged in sexual intercourse; how after she quizzed them on sex, she allowed and encouraged them to ask all of the questions that they could think of, no matter how embarrassing.

Leona explained that the surprise which strained the agreement came on Sunday afternoon when he arrived at the end of the third boy's lesson with a fourth boy. A fourth boy who was not part of their agreement.

A fourth boy who was not his son. A fourth boy, the son of his best friend, who'd also just turned eighteen. Leona expressed to her client that the agreement was for three boys not four.

Doctor Crittendon asked, "So what did you do about the fourth boy?"

Leona sighed heavily. "I took care of him. He needed the lesson no less than the other three so I took care of him. I was furious with my client for overstepping his bounds, but I didn't want to deprive the boy of a valuable life lesson. Besides, that extra two-thousand will buy me a great looking pair of red-bottoms to go with the dress I just bought."

Again they laughed.

Doctor Crittendon asked, "So do you regret taking care of those boys?"

"No Sweetie. I'd much rather those boys learn the right way from me as opposed to..." Leona stopped mid-sentence when her cellular phone rang. They were only twenty minutes into the session, but Leona looked at the screen anyway. She smiled when she recognized the call was from a pitcher for the Seattle Mariners. Ten years her junior, he was an incredible lover with energy to spare. She thought briefly about how great a workout he was, but unfortunately, right now was not the time for her to have him on her mind. Leona pushed those thoughts to the back of her mind, pressed ignore and returned her attention to her therapist.

"So, what else is on your mind?" Doctor Crittendon asked.

Forty minutes into the scheduled hour-long session, Leona checked her watch again and realized that due to their late start, she needed to cut the session short. "Excuse me Doc, but I need to rush to the airport. My sister from Pennsylvania is flying in."

Doctor Crittendon replied, "For some reason, I thought your sister lived here in Seattle."

"No Doc, I have two older half-sisters," Leona said. "The older of them—by my mother—lives here in Seattle. The younger—the one flying in today—is by my father."

"Interesting,"

"Believe me when I tell you, my parents truly were rolling stones."

"Maybe we need to talk about your relationship with them sometime," Doctor Crittendon said playfully.

Leona ignored the comment. "I just learned about the younger sister a couple of months ago and now she's coming to visit."

"Then I guess you better get going," Doctor Crittendon's eyes moved above Leona's to her hair and said. "Call me if that itch worsens."

Leona smiled, grabbed her bag, and with shoes in hand, rushed out of the office. The time was 5:08. Her sister's flight had a scheduled arrival time of 6:42pm. Leona hoped for light traffic, but more important, she prayed that her car's engine was still warm enough to start.

06

The Dark Knight

ON THE 14TH FLOOR OF THE MADISON BUILDING, Doctor Solomon Alexandré stuffed two folders into an aluminum briefcase. He turned off all but one light inside his office suite then locked the door behind him when he exited. As he trudged toward the elevator, the strain of enduring another non-stop day of marital bickering showed in his enervated stagger.

In the parking garage, he softly sang lyrics by his favorite musical group as he strolled to his car. I'm a laid back kind of guy, in a laid back kind of world. When the sound of an engine failing to start interrupted his singing, he looked around trying to locate the vehicle in distress. Finding it, he checked his watch before detouring to see if he could help. What he found inside the cute blue Mazda was a frantic woman yelling and screaming. Standing in the low light of the garage lamps, he glanced at her reflection through the window. She was so caught up in being angry at her little blue roadster that she didn't notice him approach. And when he tapped on the window she damn near jumped out of her skin. He mouthed *Can I help?* while motioning for her to roll down the window.

Startled, incensed, and ready to cry because nothing had gone her way all day, she rolled down the window and let out an exhaustive sigh.

"Hello Solomon." Despite his pleasant appearance, Leona Pearson struggled to smile once she recognized that it was him. Standing a hand taller than six foot, his sturdy, thick arms and legs gave him more of a superhero visage than of a regular person. What she saw impressed her, but not enough to make her smile. "Well, aren't you a sight for sore eyes?"

Solomon and Leona were both tall clotheshorses with funny colored eyes. His were more hazel and hers more of a sharp chestnut, but when she looked into his eyes, it was like looking into a mirror. Just like staring into her own soul.

Solomon leaned over and rested his forearm on the roof above the driver's door. Strong cheek bones flanked the distinctive edges of his full lips and his longer than usual eyelashes gained him plenty of compliments. Separately appealing to any eye, his face struggled for pleasant cohesion as a whole. "Hello Ms. Pearson," his voice washed gently over her face in a smooth seductive baritone as he asked, "Car trouble?"

"I'll be all right," she said. Her tone was soft and seductive like a woman in love. She sat quietly for a moment staring. In her head she reminisced briefly about their first encounter—that night in which they shared drinks at her blind-date-gone-wrong with his friend Desmond. This was the first time she had seen him since.

She asked, "So why is it that a fine man like yourself is all by himself every time I see you? Please tell me there is a woman in your life."

"There used to be."

"And now?"

"She's gone."

"Her loss."

"Not exactly."

"Then how exactly?"

A tear escaped his eye as he whispered, "She, umm…she's dead."

Leona swallowed a gulp of embarrassment. She felt like such a heel. She sat in quiet angst, her tongue now at a loss for words as she struggled to recall that detail from their impromptu blind date.

"Sounds like your starter?" he said, referring back to the car.

"Excuse me?" she asked.

"Your car," Solomon said, pointing to the engine. "I said it sounds like your starter."

"Starter. Alternator. It's all the same to me." Leona said. "All I know is that I'm late."

"Would you like me to take a look at it?"

"Yes, but I don't know if there's anything you can do." She batted her lashes. "Do you think you can fix it?"

When he stood up and inhaled, his chest expanded. He smiled and said, "That's what I do…I fix things." A charismatic masculinity radiated from his almost six-foot-four and just over 200 pounds, smooth, chocolaty-brown frame. He had a rugged sexiness that crossed racial lines and could make any woman foolishly swoon, regardless of race. In a register too low for him to hear, Leona seductively whispered, Well, if you're really in the mood for fixing something…while she looked him up and down.

"Excuse me?" Solomon flexed the deep dimples in his cheeks. He flashed straight, white teeth and replied to her suggestive smile,

"You don't want to mess with this, Miss Pearson…I'd only break your heart. And we don't want that, now do we?"

"Sounds like a challenge," she beamed, "but I don't have time to think about that right now. I have to get to the airport to pick up my sister."

"Well, let me see what we can do about that. We can't have your sister stranded at the airport." He removed the jacket to his beautiful, grey, three-piece, pinstripe suit, revealing gym-sculpted muscles bulging inside his peach shirt. A peach and white striped tie perfectly complemented his ensemble. "Pop the hood."

When he leaned into the engine, Leona admired the curve of the firmest butt she'd seen this side of a Chippendale model.

"Try to start it," Solomon said from beneath the hood.

Leona turned the key and the engine clicked but didn't turn over. When she released the key, her radio came on.

After poking around in her engine for another minute or so, Solomon stood up and closed the hood. He walked back to the window and said, "How about I just take you to the airport." The hero in him was figuratively growing larger as he spoke. A strong sexual energy radiated between them like microwaves. "Tomorrow morning I'll have my mechanic come out here and look at your engine. If he can't fix it, then I'll have him tow it to his garage."

"There goes my red bottoms." She looked at her watch, graciously accepted and rolled up her window. She grabbed her purse off the front seat, pulled her keys from the ignition and stepped out of the car. Tension started to ease its chokehold and she began to breathe again as she smiled at the man standing before her like a bona fide hero in an action movie.

Five minutes later they'd exited the parking garage and Solomon was expertly navigating his red Audi A8 down Madison Street toward 6th Street. A left on 6th and just like that they were on I-5 ramp headed south.

Sixteen miles and twenty-five minutes later, they parked in the arrivals lot at SeaTac. Solomon waited near the top of the escalators, giving Leona some space to greet her sister as the passengers of Aer Lingus flight 238, a talkative, but exhausted, rainbow-colored mob of humanity, pushed through the doors of Gate 32. The river of people rushed through the concourse, greeting family, friends and drivers. Women in colorful dresses or in jeans stretched so tight they looked painted on. Men in suits of various fabrics; wool or linen, or in the occasional leather jacket over a mock-turtleneck with jeans.

Solomon immediately recognized her outfit from the picture Leona showed him in the car.

Leona walked a beeline towards the gate. When they were within earshot, she waved and called out, Tessa?

Tessa broke her killer stride and detoured straight to Leona. They kissed on the cheek then hugged for a long moment. Following some brief small talk, they turned and walked toward the escalators. From the direction of her stare, it became apparent that Tessa was referring to Solomon when she asked, "Who is that?" Either Leona had mentioned him or maybe Tessa saw her walk away from him to come greet her, but either way, Solomon had caught her attention.

"That, my dear, is our ride home," Leona said.

"That…is one fine ass chauffeur," said Tessa.

"Fine…Yes. Chauffeur…No."

Tessa said, "I sense a story."

"No real story," Leona replied. "He's my doctor friend who was kind enough to give me a ride to pick you up after my car died."

"Damn he's fine," Tessa repeated.

"Yes girl, fine he is."

"A doctor, huh?"

"Yeah, but he is one tough nut to crack."

"I bet," Tessa guffawed and cracked a knowing smile.

Leona continued as they approached, "And despite dominating the conversation on the ride here, he didn't once make any lewd suggestions."

"Maybe he was just being a gentleman?" said Tessa.

"Too damn gentle if you ask me," Leona replied.

Tessa eyed Leona with an *Is there more behind that?* look on her face, but didn't ask out loud. She merely said, "But he sure is handsome."

"Yeah girl, he is one prime cut of beef."

Tessa laughed. Leona laughed. Then they shared a high-five. When they walked over, Leona made introductions.

Solomon saw the similarities in the curve of their lips, in the shape of their almond eyes and the gentle slope of their foreheads. Yes, they were definitely sisters.

After retrieving her luggage, the trio made their way out to short term parking. He unlocked the car and dropped both bags in the trunk as Leona joined Tessa in the back seat.

"I thought you said he wasn't the chauffeur?" Tessa asked playfully as Solomon slid behind the steering wheel and buckled his seatbelt.

"Home James," Leona playfully ordered her handsome chauffeur.

"Why Yes'um Ms. Daisy," were the words that followed from his sarcastic Uncle Tom-esque reply. "Right aways, May'um."

They dashed out of the parking lot, Solomon trying to expedite the conclusion of this taxi ride and still pick up his suit before the dry cleaners closed. He asked, "What's your address, Leona?" She gave him the address and he entered it into his GPS. Once on the interstate, the GPS estimated their travel time at twenty-one minutes. He looked in the rearview and asked, "So Tessa, where are you from?"

"Pennsylvania, born and bred."

"First time in the Emerald City?"

"Yes, but I hope it's not my last."

"Wow, that's great. I hope you have a chance to visit all of our sights."

"Thank you Solomon."

"Is there a Mister Tessa?"

"Excuse me?"

"I just asked because if there's not, the matchmaker sitting back there next to you will have you hooked up in no time."

"Oh no, I'm not out here looking…"

"Don't let her fool you Doc," Leona chimed in. "She already has her sights set on Mister Right."

"Leona, please," Tessa said. "He doesn't need to be all up in my business like that."

"Girl Please, according to my therapist—who just happens to be his partner—this man is the black Doctor Phil," Leona said sarcastically. "Doctor Alexandré is a marriage counselor. He is the perfect person for you to talk to. And from what Doctor Crittendon says, if HE can't fix a relationship, then it don't need fixing."

"But I'm not married," Tessa balked. "Why would I need to talk to a marriage counselor?" Confused with the way the conversation was heading, Tessa leaned away from her sister. "Let's just ride, all right."

Leona, ignoring her sister's request, leaned forward in her seat, cleared her throat and said, "Listen Doc, I'm going to give you the Cliff's notes version. My dear, long-lost sister has this guy friend who she's crazy about. He's a military man. They've known each other for a long time and when he used to come home to visit, they always hit it off real...real...good!" Leona poked Solomon in the shoulder for emphasis. "If...you know what I mean."

"Leona, please stop." Tessa punched her lightly on the shoulder.

Leona continued, "Now according to her, the only reason they haven't already sealed the deal is that they're never managed to both be single at the same time, or better yet, not dating, because neither one of them has ever married. But what I've taken from the last conversation we had before her trip, it seems that the stars have aligned because after all of this time, she and he are both finally single."

A silence hung in the air for a moment while Solomon digested Leona's story. In the mirror, he observed Tessa's lips poked out and her arms crossed tightly across her chest expressing her silent displeasure at her sister telling him all of her business.

"Well Tessa, since Leona is so confident that I am up to the task, let's not disappoint her." Solomon smiled in the mirror then added, "Actually, it's more appropriate to say, let's not disappoint you."

"I like the sound of that better," Tessa said after fidgeting a bit.

"That's what I like to hear."

"Okay here goes." Tessa exhaled and said, "I don't know the best way to say this Doc, so I am just going to put it out there. I'm in love with my best friend."

"Please don't be offended Tessa but some of my questions may come off as frank. I don't like to guess about my patients' meaning, so I tend to be blunt."

"No worries Doc go ahead."

"Well, the first question that comes to mind is does he know how you feel?"

"I'm fairly certain. I mean, I've always been more analytical than creative. I mean, my tongue gets twisted in knots when it comes to talking about my feelings; especially when talking to the person that I am having those feelings about. So..."

Solomon waited, but no more words came. GPS indicated there were only five miles left in the trip so he said, "Let me ask you this Tessa, have you and this best friend…ever been more than friends?"

"Yes, we dated in high school. While I was in college and we were both home for the holidays, we spent New Year's together."

"With respect to a relationship, how far did this dating go?"

"What exactly are you asking, Doc?"

"Have the two of you ever been intimate?"

"Intimate?" she echoed. "Yes, of course."

"So, you are telling me that you and he have had sex in the past."

"Yes." Now Tessa beamed. "And it was great."

"Did he think it was great?"

"Excuse me?" The question dimmed the brightness of her glow. Her response intoned that she had taken offense to his inquiry.

"I…I don't mean to offend you," Solomon continued. "But sometimes both sex partners may not always take away the same experience from the encounter. Most times it's the man saying that the sex was great while the woman says it could have been better, but on rare occasion those opinions are reversed. So, I ask again; do you know if he feels the same way about being with you?"

"As far as I know, the sex was as good for him as it was for me." Tessa looked peeved.

"Well then, do you know if you two are looking for the same things in a relationship?"

"Well, I thought we were." For a short moment, Tessa went on one of those tangents that the female species is famous for. Dreamily she said, "I've never felt more physically and emotionally compatible with anyone in my life." While she talked, she swung her hands back and forth to show the comparisons. "He has a great athletic body. I have long, thick legs, and a great mane of strong black hair." Tessa stroked her hair and segued even further. "This is the part where some women will tell you that they have good hair because they have Indian in their blood. But as far as I know, ain't no Native American swimming through my veins. All this good hair is courtesy of my hairdresser, Nancy; that girl can work some magic."

She paused.

Solomon politely laughed at her joke.

"But, all that aside, I've always felt like I've been alone waiting for someone to comfort me. I know my heart has lots of love to give and I don't want to live life alone any longer. I've been on my own for almost twenty years and when things go wrong, there's no one there to help me get through my tears. I want my prince to find me and rescue me from loneliness."

"And you think this best friend is that prince you're waiting for?"

"If I could turn back the hands of time I would have never let him get away," Tessa said. "I would have kept our relationship. Even though he said he didn't want a long-distance relationship and he didn't want me wasting my life waiting for him when he couldn't guarantee where he would be after I finished college, I know he wanted me the same way I want him."

"So, you want him. I get it," Solomon said, "but what exactly is it that you like about this man?"

Tessa turned, twisted a thick strand of hair and stared out the window for a moment. She watched as a large bird flew by before turning again to face the front. "This man..." she said, furrowing her brow. She lifted one eyebrow, thought really hard, then delivered an ear-to-ear smile before saying, "The thought of me and him together describes all of the things love means to me. There is absolutely nothing that I don't like about this man. He is everything I have ever wanted in a man. I've dated several nice brothers throughout the years. Hell, I've even been engaged once."

"Oh really?"

"Hah," preceded, "Yeah, that didn't work out."

"Sorry to hear that."

"Thank you," Tessa said, then went back to talking about him. "Everything I want, and everything they turned out not to be...he was. Everything I wanted them to be...he was. He is that person for me. When I was with them, I would find myself thinking of him."

"Can you say that he ever loved you?" Solomon interrupted.

"YES." The look on her face told that she wanted to say a lot more than that single word, but as loud and proud as she said it, there was no further explanation necessary.

Solomon said, "Don't get me wrong, but it sounds like you've got a little obsession thing going on."

"I am way past obsessed Doctor. I love this man with all of my heart. He is my world. I have loved him since I was a child. He was and still is my first love.

"I am not crazy Doctor Alexandré, and in the generic sense of the word, I am not obsessed. This is not any of that fatal attraction mess either. This man is the love of my life."

"You said is…" Solomon replied. "Well what if instead of turning back time, you make time start anew?"

That digital voice on the GPS said, "You have reached your destination." Solomon parked in front of Leona's condo off Sunset Avenue in West Seattle and pulled Tessa's suitcases from the trunk. He offered to carry them inside but Leona politely declined.

"You Sir have somewhere to be, so you better get a move on."

Leona kissed him on the cheek. "See you later handsome." She dabbed at the lipstick on his cheek before grabbing the larger bag.

Tessa stood her ground. "What did you mean start anew?"

"Is he married?" Solomon asked.

"No."

"Have a girlfriend?"

"Not any longer from what his Momma told me."

"Well then stop being afraid of yourself and go get your man."

Tessa kissed Solomon on the other cheek, then, almost skipping along the way, pulled the smaller bag up the walk to her sister's upscale, loft-style condominium.

07

Near Misses

LEONA GAVE TESSA A QUICK TOUR of her condo, finishing with the bedroom where she would be sleeping.

"I need to use the bathroom and check my voicemail," Tessa said, dragging her luggage into a bedroom immaculately decorated in blues and yellows. Before unpacking, she called her Mama. There was no answer, so she left a brief voicemail stating that she had arrived safely, she loved her and would call the next day since it was late back home.

When she opened the top drawer of the nightstand, she encountered a pair of fuzzy handcuffs and a silver rabbit that rolled to the back of the almost empty drawer. Laughing, she placed her bag on top of the dresser and decided to find another drawer for her belongings.

Tessa and Leona hadn't ironed out any plans for the rest of the evening, so after doing no more than shoving her suitcase into the closet and slipping off her shoes, she headed back out into the living room.

The layout of the Leona's single story condominium was fantastic. The foyer and living room were elegantly decorated. The teak hardwood floor looked recently restored. The focal piece of a bare brick wall in the living room was a stone fireplace flanked by Palladian windows that offered fabulous views of the Puget Sound. Numerous paintings and statues of various sizes were sprinkled throughout.

At the back of the living room, teak flooring continued up the steps into the dining room and kitchen, which sat on an elevated platform four steps above the living room. At the back of the dining room, another Palladian window provided more breathtaking views. A quaint but well-designed kitchen, with stainless steel appliances throughout, sat in an alcove to the left of the dining room. A six-burner executive cook top with built-in grill, sat as the centerpiece of a massive island. This kitchen said Leona was serious about getting her burn on.

Tessa was in the hallway leading to the bedrooms admiring an oil painting when Leona exited her bedroom. The first thing Tessa noticed was the inch thick, platinum anklet Leona was wearing. She was barefoot, making the beautiful heart floating on the anklet hard to miss. A black, satin robe with a lace burgundy belt hung loosely about her waist. The bottom of the robe ended midway down her thigh. Leona had changed into her usual loungewear.

Eighteen months younger than Tessa, she looked good for her age. Although a dozen pounds more than her ideal weight, those extra pounds made her well-toned body look even better. Deep cleavage amplified her ample bosom. Tessa admired the comfort her sister had in her own skin.

The look of surprise on Tessa's face caught Leona's eye. After a brief moment of apparent embarrassment, she eased the top of the robe closer together. "I'm sorry Honey; I didn't mean to surprise you," Leona said.

"No problem," Tessa said, trying not to blush. "But you do have something on underneath there, right?" She drew an outline of her frame in the air with her hand. Her question was more as a reassuring statement of fact than an actual desire to know.

"Yes Girl. I do."

Tessa cringed slightly as Leona loosened the knot in her robe to reveal the remainder of the 3-piece ensemble. The matching satin camisole and boy shorts with lace trim were well hidden beneath the black-satin robe. Leona smiled then closed the sides of the robe and retied the knot in the belt. "Why don't I go change?" she said and started to go back to her bedroom.

"No Honey, this is your place. You get as comfortable as you want to," Tessa said, relieved to see those last two pieces of lingerie. "Hell, I'm the one who needs to get more comfortable."

Leona laughed. Although her smile said things were cool, she sensed uneasiness in her sister's demeanor. She went over and gave Tessa a hug. "You're fine Honey; this is just how I like to relax. I love the feel of satin against my skin."

"Are we expecting company?" Tessa asked. The we—instead of

you—was to reassure Leona that she was not intending on leaving the apartment by herself, just yet.

"Not that I know of," Leona replied. "I had the most horrendous day, and now that I am in for the night I just wanted to get comfortable."

"Can't get much more comfortable than that," Tessa commented.

"Not true Baby Sis," said Leona. "If you weren't here, there would be no cami and panties underneath, and the robe would be my favorite smoking jacket."

"Smoking jacket?"

"Yeah, smoking jacket," Leona said. "On a warm summer night, 'cause Seattle rarely gets hot, I'll put on my smoker, pop the windows open to let the breeze flow, pull out my pipe and relax the night away. A pipe and a good bottle of wine are better than any Calgon take me away commercial that you've ever seen.

They laughed in unison at the reference to the old familiar commercial.

"Tessa," Leona called. "Do you eat Chinese food?"

"Yes girl."

"Good Honey, 'cause I'm starved."

Leona called and ordered Chinese delivery from a place called Happy Garden. She said it was the best Chinese food this side of Mount Rainier. Tessa ordered Moo Goo Gai Pan. Hunan shrimp with vegetables dinner was Leona's choice. Surprisingly, Leona thanked the person on the other end of the line by name and told him to throw in a six-pack of Tsingtao beer before she hung up.

"Food will be here in a half hour." Leona moved next to Tessa who was admiring a painting of a woman standing at the edge of a cliff with one foot hanging off the edge. "Do you like it?"

"Yes. I've never seen a painting with such bold use of colors before. I love all of the detail he put into her face. The model looks so lifelike, like she just wants to jump off the painting at you."

"Let's hope she doesn't, that would be some straight-out-of-a-movie scary stuff."

They both laughed. Dinner arrived and they ate without conversation. The music playing in the background was the only sound in the room louder than the two of them chomping noisily on their delicious Chinese food. Tessa didn't realize it until the food came, but she too was starved. Leona drank two beers with her Hunan shrimp. When she offered Tessa a second beer, she declined. The first made her feel bloated so she only drank one. She later confessed that she was not normally a beer drinker, but it tasted great with the food.

"I have some wine if you'd like instead."

"That would be great."

Leona pushed her chair back from the table to go get the wine but Tessa stopped her.

"I can get it. Just tell me where it is."

"Do you prefer red or white?"

"Red."

"Reds are in the little cubbies under the cabinets next to the fridge."

"Opener?" Tessa called as she entered the kitchen.

"Top drawer right beneath the wine."

She chose an Argentinian Malbec she'd never tasted before and poured two glasses. Leona's gigantic wine glasses were big enough that filling two of them emptied the entire bottle. Perfect size for an intimate dinner for two. Tessa took the glasses and joined Leona on the sofa.

"Did you get settled in your room?" Leona asked.

"Uhhh, not exactly."

"Uhhh, why not?"

"Well, I wasn't exactly sure if my unmentionables would cohabitate well with the furry little critters already in your top drawer."

Leona half-cocked her head showing mild confusion. When she realized what critters Tessa was referring to, she burst out into a loud laugh. "I'm so sorry," she said. "I forgot that stuff was even in there. I'll get it out of there after we finish eating."

"Extra-curricular activities?"

"Umm, you may need to finish that wine first before we get into that conversation."

"Is there something you want to tell me about that room?" Tessa joked. "Trick mattress, trap doors or peeping toms who might decide to come out of the closet and surprise me in the middle of the night?"

Leona had told Tessa about being a dance instructor during the phone conversations that preceded the trip to visit the sister she never knew she had. They'd only found out about each other two months prior and after several phone calls, they decided to meet face-to-face. By the time they'd finished that bottle of wine, Tessa knew of her other job. The sisters talked openly that night, divulging some serious secrets to each other, including the origin of Leona's facial imperfection. Fortunately for Tessa, when

Leona talked about her side-hustle—escorting, she didn't share many of the more intimate details of her interactions with her clients. Disregarding the ample amount of mad money escorting provided her, Leona discouraged Tessa from seriously considering pursuing her side-hustle.

Late the next morning, Leona took Tessa to brunch at a small bistro in the fish market district. Afterwards, they went to her dance studio. Leona asked what sites she wanted to see and Tessa told her all of the normal touristy stuff. The studio was closer to the north end of town, so on the drive back to her condo Leona detoured back through downtown, allowing Tessa to visit the Space Needle and Key Arena. All-Star weekend flashed on the sign at Key Arena.

"The All-Star game is here this weekend?" Tessa exclaimed.

"I would love to go to the All-Star game."

"Funny you mention that," Leona giggled. "I couldn't get tickets to the game itself, but as a birthday present, I did get us tickets to the Slam Dunk competition later tonight."

"Are you serious?"

"Yeah Honey. We can go there tonight and afterwards we can go clubbing and celebrate your birthday the right way." Leona smiled.

"You do like dancing, don't you?"

"You know it girl."

"Good, then you are gonna love Club Demeanor."

They came to the southern end of the strip and exited downtown.

As they drove back out to West Seattle, Tessa asked, "Can you tell me about...our father? I've never met him and the only picture Mama had of him was from more than thirty years ago."

"I'll tell you as much as I can, but I haven't seen him in a long time."

"Not as long as me," she said, hoping to make her feel more comfortable.

Leona drove on. She'd understood from their conversations that Tessa had absolutely no interaction with their father. They were both excited about the idea of having a sister—a second sister for Leona—and Tessa wanted to know anything that she could about their father.

"Mama told me that he was a good man, but he didn't know what he wanted in life. He was a free-spirit who couldn't be chained down with a family," Tessa said. "Nowadays, people call that a deadbeat dad. Back when Mama was young, that type of guy was a rolling stone."

Leona said, "Well Sweetie, my daddy lived with me and mommy for about six years. My fondest memory of him was that every summer, he took us to the beach. He loved the water and the beach is where he taught me and my sister how to swim."

"This guy named Gino Barkley, who had the worst breath in the world, taught me to swim at the Southside community center," Tessa said. "I hated swimming lessons."

"Never learned?"

"No I learned. I just always thought that guy was a pervert."

"I guess we know who got the better end of swimming lessons?" Leona joked.

"When was the last time you heard from him?" Tessa asked, ignoring her sister.

"I don't know where he is nowadays, but I still get a card from him on my birthday. He mails it to the studio and never puts a return address," Leona said. She smiled and reflected on something for a moment as a brief schism of joy passed through her face in the form of a childhood memory. Tessa sat quietly allowing her to keep that personal moment personal.

"He never misses my birthday."

"Have you tried to find him?"

"I've looked him up every way possible, but he does not exist in the greater Northwest Washington area. If he is still in the area, he must be living under another name."

"So you haven't actually talked with him in..."

"...In twenty-seven years," Leona said, finishing her sentence. "I gave up trying to find him about six years ago, but I've kept every card that he ever gave me." Leona wiped away a tear that came to her eye as she drove. She said, "When we get back to the house, I'll show you pictures of him and the cards he sent me."

The thought of seeing a more recent picture of her father set loose a flock of butterflies in Tessa's stomach. She was happy for Leona, but at the same time, jealous as hell because she'd had somewhat of a life with him. A tear escaped Tessa's eye as she mourned not having one solitary memory of her father to remember. "That would be great," Tessa said flatly.

That night they went back to Key Arena to watch the Slam Dunk competition and Three Point Shootout. Leona introduced Tessa to a couple of the local celebrities she knew and they even took a picture with Julius 'Doctor J' Erving. She remembered that he was all Anton used to talk about when they were growing up. Doctor J this and Doctor J that. He used to talk about Doctor J the way today's men talk about Beyoncé or Halle Berry. If one didn't know better, you would've thought he was in love with the man.

Tessa looked for Jaz Stevenson but didn't see him. So much time had passed since Jaz and Tessa had talked, that she wasn't even sure if he was still playing basketball or not.

After Key Arena, they took in Club Demeanor, an Over-30 club for the more mature crowd. It was brightly lit, had three bars and women dancing in cages. In the VIP lounge, they met up with Leona's friend Sharet, her cousin Micah, and Troy—Micah's boyfriend.

Micah was tall and skinny. A cross between Bentley Farnsworth and RuPaul. He had a round face and three-inch twisted braids. A tightly manicured goatee outlined pouty pink lips. He strutted around in a black suit; a two-toned, cotton-candy pink, striped shirt with a yellow satin tie and gold hounds tooth pocket square. The sharply dressed brother was fierce.

In comparison to Micah, Troy was a rather somber-faced man. A dapper dresser himself, his pleated white chinos hung above multi-colored socks. One couldn't help noticing how big his feet were because there was a lot of leather in those caramel loafers.

His multi-colored blue, pink polka-dots and burgundy diagonally-striped outfit proved that he wasn't scared of color. Not quite as tall as Micah but much thicker, he covered his ensemble with a tan four-button micro-suede blazer complete with satin, chocolate-brown lapels. On the floor next to him was an umbrella that matched the blue in his shirt. From the looks of their outfits, they either; dressed each other, dressed to impress each other, or dressed to outdo each other. But who was she to say what motivated them.

Tessa had never met a gay couple before. Although she didn't care for their flashy style of dress, they were both attractive looking men. Even after a couple of drinks, a heavy rain cloud of uneasiness still hung over her. Leona did everything she could to help Tessa relax, and although she truly didn't understand their lifestyle, it was easy to see their attraction.

Around eleven, the DJ announced that a coed modeling group called Sexy After 30 was in the building and was auditioning new models.

"Ooh Leona, you should audition," Tessa said.

Sharet and Micah cosigned, urging Leona to give it a try.

"You're a natural Leona," Troy said, his lips pursed in a pucker.

Leona smiled, but didn't appear too excited about the idea.

"Honey," Micah started, snapping his fingers in a z-pattern. "You know you are fierce. Take your cat walking ass out there and show them heifers what you got." He poked his lips out and pointed. "If you don't, I sure as hell will."

They all burst out laughing at the thought of Micah flitting about on the stage. If it hadn't been obvious to Tessa which of them was the female in the couple before, it definitely was then.

Leona picked up her half-full wine glass and emptied it before putting it down. "I'll do it" she said, "but only if Tessa does it with me."

"But I don't live here," Tessa said. The thought of going out there in front of all those strangers petrified Tessa. It moved her even further from her comfort zone than hanging with Troy and Micah.

Leona leaned back in the plush chair, crossed her arms and mimicked a small child. "If you don't, then I'm not either." Her poked out lips adding the finishing touch to her pouting.

Sharet, Troy and Micah cheered the sisters on until they finally gave in.

Leona and Tessa agreed then made their way down to the Sexy After 30 table where a pretty brown-skinned lady who called herself 'M-J' signed them up. From there, they went back into a dressing room, put on some of the outfits provided, then came out and ripped the runway.

Troy and Micah yelled, screamed and cat-called each time they appeared in a different outfit.

The leader of the group, a green-eyed, light-skinned woman named Koco, came on after the last contestant finished and called everyone who modeled back to the stage. She thanked everybody for trying out and called six names—two men and four women—to come back next week for the finals. Two of those names were Leona and Tessa. Even though they both knew they wouldn't be joining the group, it was the most fun Tessa had had in a long time.

*

Sunday afternoon found the sisters on Leona's patio enjoying Dungeness crab legs and emptying separate bottles of wines. In a moment when Tessa's mouth was full, Leona decided to delve deeper into Tessa's love life. "Okay Sis, if you're so sure this guy's The One, then why aren't you out scouring the earth trying to convince him that you're the one?" Leona took a swallow of wine and shifted in the two-person patio chair to face Tessa. "I mean since Doctor Alexandré thinks you should go for it, and so do I, tell me more about this Mister Right."

Tessa paused. She looked out across the water and followed the sound of a horn from a ferry crossing the Sound. She took two longs swallows of wine then said, "A long time ago I used to think we were destined to be together, but once he joined the Navy and never came home that light of hope faded. Now, almost twenty years later, he's still in the Navy; only God knows where, doing God knows what…"

"Was there a reason that you couldn't go with him? I mean, I don't know much about the Navy, but I'm quite sure wives can move places with their husbands."

"Reason? Ummm, probably…because…he never asked me.

I told him I'd wait for him after high school, but he hasn't been in touch much since our little altercation when his dad died."

"Altercation?"

"Yeah," Tessa said solemnly.

Leona sat up straight. "Oh Honey, please, do tell."

"My, unh-un, fiancée and I were downtown shopping…"

"Wait a minute," Leona burst in. Where did a fiancée come from?"

"Yes, fiancée," Tessa said. "Do you want me to tell the story or what?"

"My bad, Sis. Please continue."

"We…," Tessa rolled her eyes at Leona then took a swig of wine. "We… were downtown shopping when we ran into Anton and some raggedy heifer he brought with him when he came home to bury his father."

"Funny you say that," Leona interrupted. "My sister Jennifer introduced me to some guy named Anton who sat next to her on the plane when she came back from visiting our cousin Michelle in Chicago last week. But please continue."

"Anyway," Tessa pressed on, not trying to make a connection. "Introductions were exchanged along with some polite conversation. We acknowledged each other. Said our hellos. I said I was sorry to hear about his Dad passing, gave him a friendly hug and told him that if there was ANYTHING I could do, to just let him know."

"Okay, sounds reasonable," Leona said.

"That's when that Trick started trippin'. For no reason at all, she wedged her way in between us and pushed me back, talking about I better back up off her man before she slapped me down. Next thing I know, we were swinging fists, pocketbooks and ponytails right there on the sidewalk. But before I could do any serious damage to her ugly face, Greg had snatched me up and was carrying me over his shoulder to the car; and Anton was carrying that trick into the store. Greg forced me into the car until I calmed down, and that was the last time Anton Charles and I were face-to-face."

"And how long ago was that?"

"I don't know; about six, maybe seven years ago."

"Did you ever get a chance to tell him that you wanted to be with him?" Leona said. "I mean, have you ever told him that you wanted to get together with him since that?"

"Not in so many words. And to this day, it still hurts my heart like it was yesterday."

Leona's expression rumpled into a Mom face. "Exactly how many words?" she asked.

Tessa didn't say it, but the mom face was working. She shrunk in her chair, feeling like she was being chastised. "Exactly?" Tessa asked, ashamed to give an answer.

"Yes, exactly." Leona repeated. She didn't move and her tone didn't rise, but the presence of her Mom face made her seem to grow larger, and more intimidating, in Tessa's mind.

"Well," Tessa said meekly. "I wrote him a letter a few years ago."

"And...?"

"And nothing," Tessa said flatly. "He never wrote back. Never called. Nothing until he texted me for my birthday four days ago."

"He sent you a birthday text just four days ago?" Again Leona sat up straight. "Out of the blue? What did he say?"

Tessa could tell that her sister had switched into matchmaking mode.

"If you haven't seen him in a couple of years and he—out of the blue—remembers to send you a birthday text..." Leona's enthusiasm brought her to the edge of her seat. "...That, Sister Girl, means you are on that man's mind."

"I don't know about all of that."

"Well you need to know, because the only time men call out of the blue is because they're either horny and lonely and looking for a quick booty call; OR, they really miss you but know they can't get to you right away."

Tessa shrugged her shoulders. Let her eyes drift to the floor.

"And since you don't know where in the world Waldo is, the booty call scenario is definitely out of the question. Look," Leona said emphatically, "if he remembered your birthday, he'd definitely be glad to see you. Especially if he thinks he can get some when he does."

"Well even if he did miss me, I ain't quite sure he'd want to see me?"

"Girl, why not?"

"Hello, the last time I saw him, he came home to bury his father and I started a fight with his girlfriend."

"Did you win?"

"Leona?" Tessa was stunned. *Did you win?* was not what she expected to hear next.

"Look, if you won, then he might be mad at you for beating her up. But..." Leona paused, her eyes darting back and forth as a thousand thoughts danced in her head. She bit her lower lip then released it as a smile spread across her face. "But if you lost, and they're not together anymore, then there's definitely room for you two to get back together."

Tessa blinked away the memory of her encounter with the exotic looking; strikingly beautiful, horrible, terrible, no-good woman Anton had the nerve to bring home with him for his father's funeral.

Leona put both hands on her sister's shoulders, looked her straight in the eye. "Girl you better call that boy and let him know how you feel."

"I can't. I'd be too embarrassed. I went out on a limb sending him that letter telling him most of how I feel and he gave me nothing in return. I can't bear that rejection again."

"So you plan on just living the rest of your life as an old maid; alone in a house full of cats?"

"Umm excuse me Miss Living Single—people in glass houses..."

"Wait a minute girlfriend. I. Am single. By choice," Leona said, grouping her words. "And for your information, I have all of the companionship I desire. I'm just not ready to settle down yet."

"I bet you do."

"Watch your mouth, Girl," Leona challenged. "Don't talk about what you don't know."

Fire danced in both of their eyes as both women went silent. It was like their tongues were in a championship welterweight fight and the bell rang signaling the end of a round, sending them to their corners. They both sat back hard in the extra-wide chair. Another long moment passed as Tessa watched a seagull circle gracefully above the water. "I'm sorry," she finally said. "That was out of bounds."

Leona took another drink.

Tessa asked. "But what about having kids?"

Anger now shifted to pain. A veil covering Leona's face. She wrapped her arms across her chest and held herself, backing down from her matchmaking. "Stop trying to change the subject," Leona huffed. She rocked rapidly on the loveseat before reaching out to refill her glass.

"I'm sorry," Tessa said. "Are you all right?"

A beat passed between them as silence filled the better part of another minute. Again Leona emptied and refilled her glass. She half smirked then said, "Yeah Sweetie, I'm okay."

Tessa sat back almost in tears. "Look Leona, I understand what you're saying and I appreciate it. I don't have the best track record as far as relationships go, and I've never been real good at openly expressing my feelings to men."

Leona sat back and studied the look on her face. She smiled and said, "If I can't help you, then I think we need to get you some professional help."

"Excuse me," Tessa said.

"Tomorrow morning I am making you an official appointment with Doctor Alexandré."

"What? Why?"

Leona walked into the living room, picked up the television remote and just like that it was decided. Tessa followed her inside. Leona turned on the TV. Tessa excused herself to the bathroom, the wine telling her that it was long since time for a potty break. When she returned, Leona was sitting on the sofa watching the fourth quarter of the NBA All-Star game. Tessa stood behind the sofa for a short minute and watched. The West team was winning by four points.

Leona turned around and said, "I'm sorry I couldn't get us tickets."

Tessa's gaze remained on the game. Watching the game brought back high school memories of watching Anton play basketball.

Even though the game was tied with only seconds left when she arrived at the park, Tessa looked first at Anton who was standing near mid-court. He was holding the ball like an egg, with his fingertips the way Coach Pfister said a good ball handler does. Anton could practically dribble on rocks. She'd seen him in the rocky sand at the corner of the basketball court down at the park.

Him and Jared; dribbling and defending, dribbling and defending.

They were so good to only be fifteen years old. They'd fall or knock each other down before they'd let the ball escape. Anton was holding the ball as tenderly as he would a newborn puppy. The look on her face said she wanted him to touch her that way. When he looked up she said, "Hey Anton." Her neck felt hot. Hotter than the heat of the day.

Anton nodded at her. Spun the ball on his finger. "What's up Tess?"

Before she could answer, a blast from the air horn signaled the end of the game. The blue team jumped for joy as their fans cheered their victory. The red team hung their heads in defeat after blowing a four-point lead with less than a minute to play. When she shifted her attention back to Anton and Jared, they were huddled up with the dozen other boys on their summer league team listening to their coach tell them what he expected from the team they were about to play.

She sighed. Pushed out her lips in disgust at missing her chance to talk to him and started to feel sorry for herself. A feeling that never had a chance to mature as she slipped on a smile when her girlfriend Gabi shouted her name and hugged her from behind.

Anton's team, led by Jaz scoring 34 of their 74 points, won that game and the next on their way to winning the Memorial Day tournament.

Tessa thought of how she used to love watching Anton play.

She smiled and made a mental note to call him once she got back home.

When the game was over, Leona turned the channel before the post-game interviews.

"What are you doing?" Tessa asked.

"What's wrong?"

"You didn't even see the highlights and interviews."

"I'm sorry Honey, but its eight o'clock and my show's coming on."

The excitement of All-Star Weekend held its promise for Majac. Most of the players arrived in Seattle Wednesday night, but of course there were some stragglers who dragged into town Thursday morn.

Thursday afternoon Majac tagged along with Jaz, who'd gotten him a team pass that allowed him floor access throughout the weekend. The park outside Key Arena was all a buzz with excited fans trying to catch a glimpse of their favorite NBA stars. Inside, the arena was packed with reporters. Practices, although open to the public, were restricted to the first one-thousand fans. As the West All-Stars held their first of three scheduled team practices, Jaz let Majac hang out on the bench.

After practice, as Majac met the West All-Stars, Jaz grabbed a ball from the ball carousel, pulled a sharpie out of his shirt pocket, signed the ball then passed it around. All of the West All-Stars signed the ball then Jaz gave the ball to Majac, doting on him as his best friend the Naval Commander. Majac was flabbergasted.

The NBA slam dunk competition and three-point shootout were always fun to watch on TV, but watching them courtside was a dream come true. Now it was eight o'clock Sunday night and the All-Star game had just concluded. Majac's fairytale NBA All-Star weekend was quickly coming to a close. Jaz was being interviewed by a reporter from ESPN as the winning team coach when Majac walked up to meet him on the court holding his baby girl. He'd had the girls because Crystal was on the opposite end of the floor interviewing the game's MVP for her station. Crystal, who majored in journalism at Temple, was a field reporter for almost three years now.

The ESPN cameraman briefly panned over Majac before focusing on the baby. He put her down and they filmed her toddle over to Jaz. While Jaz collected her, Majac's eyes wandered to the beautiful young lady waiting to interview his best friend. Their eyes met and they briefly shared a moment. She smiled and pushed her hair behind her ear with her left hand revealing a hand devoid of any kind of committal jewelry. No wedding ring. No engagement ring. Just pretty skin covering the back of a dainty hand. In return, he rubbed his chin with a barren left hand and smiled that smile that implied he was interested in interviewing her.

When Jaz stood up holding his baby girl in his arms, the lady from ESPN turned her attention back to him. The baby waved at her.

She smiled and went back to being the reporter, questioning Jaz about being named interim coach and what he thought the remainder of the season held for him and the team.

Crystal was interviewing an East team All-Star in the background, but somehow didn't miss the chance to see the look on Majac's face during his non-verbal exchange with the lady from ESPN. After her last interview, when the cameras were all done recording and the majority of the players and coaches, including Jaz, had vacated the floor, Crystal strolled back to the end of the court where Majac stood with her babies. Along the way, she corralled the pretty ESPN reporter who had interviewed her husband.

Crystal held the ESPN reporter's arm in hers. They gossiped as she escorted her to where Majac stood with her babies. Her girls squealed her name when they saw she was coming to them. She kissed each of them, and then proceeded with her introductions. "Sage, this handsome man—" she snickered when she said, 'my defacto brother-in-law' "—is my husband's best friend, Anton Charles. But we call him Majac." Crystal strained to hold back her smile through the introduction. "Majac, this is my soror, Sage…"

"Nice to meet you, Sage," Majac confidently interrupted.

Sage offered her hand. They shared a light handshake. He held onto her hand and smiled. "You're taller than you appear on television."

Sage was accustomed to talking with some of the most famous athletes on the planet, but at that moment she was intrigued that this man watched her show. She didn't seem to mind that he hadn't yet let her hand go. She eyed him methodically…on the outside, she was calm, cool and collected; but on the inside, she was the shy schoolgirl who'd just met the homecoming king. "Probably because most of the time I'm on camera, the guy I'm interviewing is half a foot taller than me."

They laughed.

Majac drew in both lips, wetting them with his tongue before smiling. He was still holding her hand. Nervously twirling the microphone in her left hand, Sage struggled to maintain her composure. And Majac was doing his best to make it as difficult as possible for her to.

When Crystal looked at her soror, she noticed a couple of teeth showing as Sage anxiously drew the corner of her full, caramel-lipstick shaded bottom lip inside her mouth. He inhaled and the outline of his shirt highlighted his chest muscles. He had the build of a pro athlete, but when it came to women, he was not the player that some of the athletes were. Although Crystal saw no magic in meeting Majac, she couldn't blame Sage for being anxious about meeting the tall, sexy stranger.

Majac said. "I was telling Jaz earlier how much I enjoyed your interview and I was hoping that…"

Before he could give Sage an introductory dose of the Majac she seemed to desire, Crystal interrupted with, "Umm…Unh-hunh. Yeah. Umm…No. Not going to happen. Save it Romeo. She ain't trying to hear all of that right now."

Just then, Jaz came up from behind and patted him on the back. "You ready to go Partna?"

"Daddy!" the girls squealed in unison. They let go of Majac's hands and jumped on their daddy.

While the girls squealed, Crystal walked over and kissed Jaz on the cheek. Then she wiped her lipstick off his face and turned back to Sage. "Honey, did I tell you how gracious the guys have been?"

"No Girl?" Sage asked. "Do tell."

"Well, since you're heading back east tomorrow, they have volunteered to watch the girls tonight so we can hang out and catch up."

"Is that right?" Sage feigned surprise.

"Have fun with Daddy, Babies." Crystal kissed her girls again. "Mommy loves you."

The girls cooed and giggled in Jaz's arms.

"Come on Girl; let's go get our swerve on!"

Majac stood and watched as Crystal and Sage walked away without any hint of turning around to pay the guys any further attention.

As quickly as Crystal brought Sage to into Majac's life, the two of them walked toward the ESPN cameramen on the sidelines, and right back out of it.

"You all right, Majac?" Jaz said.

"Yeah, I'm cool."

Jaz smiled in the direction the women had just walked. "Don't worry about them Partna, we'll celebrate later at the house."

Little did Jaz know how close he was to forecasting Majac's future.

~~~

After the girls fell asleep, Jaz opened the bottle of 21-year single-malt scotch Majac sent as a gift last summer when they won the league championship. Jaz told Majac that since he couldn't make it to the ring celebration, he'd wait until he saw his best friend again to open it.

They sipped on that delicate scotch, talked, joked and laughed until well after midnight when they were both way past tired and the bottle of scotch was half past empty. Still there was no word from Crystal.

"Hey Man," Majac said, "I got some great news from the medical board yesterday."

"Let me guess," Jaz said, "You're not criminally insane after all?"

"Very funny," Majac said. He wasn't laughing. "For real though,

I passed my last physical and as soon as the doctor in D.C. finishes the paperwork, I'll be medically reinstated for submarine service."

"That's great Partna. So what does that mean to us civilians?"

"It means I can get away from these targets and get back to submarines where I belong."

"And that's a good thing?" Jaz asked.

"Hell yeah it's a good thing."

"Come on Majac, really; who in their right mind wants to be trapped in a metal tube thousands of miles beneath the ocean?"

"Me," Majac laughed. "You have no idea how crazy sailors are on these surface ships."

"Woooo, scary," Jaz laughed.

"Hey Man, you remember about two weeks ago when I didn't come over for dinner and didn't call you back for about four days afterwards?"

"Yeah. Crys cooked oxtails for you that night and she was pissed."

"Well, let me tell you how scary these surface guys are. That previous Friday, three sailors on my ship had a little house party. One of the women they invited was a female Gunner's Mate who works on the base and lives in the barracks. Well as you suspect with any party, there was a lot of drinking and apparently some of the partiers wound up having sex. Well, the report I got from base police when all of this got sorted out the next morning is that the female Gunner's Mate drank until she passed out and was raped. A couple of days later, she illegally checked out a gun from the base armory, took that gun to another party at that same sailor's house the following Friday night and shot all three of them."

"Are you serious right now?"

"Dead serious." he said. "Pun intended." They laughed.

"Aiight Partna, I get it."

"Stuff like that don't happen on subs. That's why I want to get back."

"No really, you know I was just kidding. If you getting back on a submarine makes you happy that's great; but I still don't understand how you can go out on a ship that intentionally sinks," Jaz paused, "but if it makes you happy, then I'm happy for you."

"Thanks Partna."

The next day was Majac's last day of leave before he'd check in at the Cruiser-Destroyer Squadron in Everett, so he gave Jaz a hug and made his way to the downstairs guest room, ready for a good night's rest after a long, fun-filled week. Jaz armed the security system then went to bed.

Majac was normally a sound sleeper, but around 2:30 he heard the security system chime followed by footsteps stumbling around.

Through the space beneath his room door, he could see the foyer light come on as Crystal came in loud enough to wake the dead. A couple of light giggles permeated the quiet hallway and from the sound of things, girls' night out had been exactly the stress reliever Crys needed.

A long sshhhh followed the loud clanking of keys dropped onto the glass table in the foyer. She whispered something unintelligible, but he thought nothing of it, since most drunks talked to themselves.

The light in the hallway went dark then a second later his door cracked open. From the natural backlighting of the moon shining through the plate glass window off Lake Washington, he could make out the silhouette of a female in the slightly ajar doorway. He chuckled to himself at the thought that even when drunk, the mother in Crystal checked on him before going to bed. A second later, the door closed and all was quiet again.

He rolled over and tried getting back to sleep.

Thirty seconds later, he hoped he was dreaming when he felt the bedspread pull back. He knew there was no possible way that Crystal had come in that bedroom. She'd been a second sister to him for more than fifteen years and the thought of her slipping into his bed quickly turned this dream into a nightmare. Not my best friend's wife rang out loudly in his head. Despite his hoping, the mattress shifted under the weight of another person. Please Crystal, don't put me in this position. The bedspread moved again and the sweet sigh of a woman brought sound to the quiet room.

Majac sat up and reached for the light on the bedside table. He turned on the light and said, "Crystal?"

A shriek responded to his question as the light revealed curly brown tufts of hair in the bed next to him pulling at the bedspread. Crystal didn't have curly brown hair, but he knew he wasn't dreaming. She yelled and pulled harder at the bedspread. "Get off of me," she shouted as she pulled the covers away from him and scrambled to get out of the bed. "What the hell are you doing?"

The sound of screaming downstairs initiated footsteps scrambling upstairs.

"Whoa, whoa, whoa," Majac yelled as he scrambled out of the other side of the bed in his boxers. Before either could gather their bearings, the door slammed open, the ceiling light came on, and Jaz and Crys rushed into the room.

"Oh shoot!" Jaz covered his mouth.

They all started talking at once. As all four absorbed the pandemonium, Majac picked up a pillow and put it in front of his boxers. He'd never been shy, but Crys was nearly as much a sister to him as Angel and she didn't need to see him standing there in his underwear.

"Oh my God, Sage" Crystal screamed. "I'm so sorry!"

"Sage?" Majac asked loudly.

The lady wrapped in the bedspread took a couple of steps away from the bed and turned around. She looked to Crystal and asked, "What the hell is going on Crystal?"

"Sage, I am so sorry," Crystal said again. "I forgot all about Majac being in the guest room."

Jaz guffawed, amused at what was playing out before him.

Despite the embarrassment of the situation at hand, Majac quickly caught on and reacted to Jaz's laughter with his own giggle.

Sage turned and faced him. Her golden shoulders showed naked above where the bedspread wrapped tightly about her. Her eyes met his and a sensation shot through him that required him to consciously hold the pillow a little more securely.

Jaz laughed even louder and Crystal punched him in the arm.

"Shut up Jared," she said forcefully.

Jaz retorted, "That's what you two get for getting all liquored up." He looked around the room and still laughing, said, "All right everybody let's all calm down. We're all big boys and girls here. It's obvious somebody..." he turned and faced Crystal, "...made an honest mistake."

Crystal went into self-defense mode and started stammering her excuse, "Well, it was late so...and she had already checked out of her hotel and she was leaving early tomorrow morning so I invited her to stay at our house so we could have breakfast and I could take her to the airport. We hadn't seen each other in years and I wanted us to spend a little more time together."

Jaz continued laughing. Crystal was a cute drunk. She rarely drank more than one glass of wine a day, so it didn't take much to get her tipsy. She stopped talking when he laughed at her.

Majac regarded Crystal and said, "I'll tell you what Sis. You offered her the room, so I'll go crash upstairs."

"See, that's my Partna," Jaz chuckled, "doing the gentlemanly thing and giving up his room." Then Jaz began clapping ostentatiously like a

Denzel Washington movie character. "You go boy." Not that the situation didn't warrant, but Jaz was enjoying the incident just a little too much.

Without allowing the bedspread to slip from her arm, Sage picked up her clothes off the chair at the end of the bed. "No, you were here first. I'll go to the other room."

"Look at that, a chivalrous woman." Jaz clapped, but his guffawing had subsided.

Crystal put her arm around Sage and the two tipsy women stumbled out of the room.

"Can I at least get the blanket back?" Majac yelled. The women didn't respond.

Once the women were well clear of the room, Jaz went to Majac and said, "And here, less than three days ago you got all mushy telling me how you were gonna concentrate on work and leave the women alone."

Jaz patted his best friend on the back and laughed. "I told you I didn't see that lasting too long," He said before making his way back upstairs.

Once all was quiet again, Majac turned off the light and got back into bed. Ten minutes later he heard a light tapping on the door. "Come on in, Man," he said, "it's your house."

The door opened and the ceiling light came on. It was Sage. She'd made her way back downstairs and was now standing in the doorway. And she was still wrapped in the bedspread.

Majac propped himself up on one elbow, checking that the bed sheet was pulled up above his waist. "Hey look," he said, "I'm really sorry about earlier..."

Before he could finish, Sage interrupted. "When I got upstairs, I realized that you had asked for your bedspread back."

He was somewhat stunned, but couldn't hold back a smile. "Yeah. Crystal keeps this place like an icebox."

Sage stepped into the room and shut the door behind her. She unwrapped herself from within the bedspread, allowing a view of what she so closely kept covered before. The width of his smile showed his approval. Sage gave her smile in return.

"You might wanna cover up before you catch cold," he said.

"I was hoping that you might find a couple of ways to keep me warm." Sage turned off the light. A gentle breeze accompanied her as she glided across the room. He pulled back the bed sheet to accept her entrance.

Seconds later she eased onto the same side of the soft bed she'd so hastily vacated earlier and covered both of them in the bedspread.

Majac reached for the nightstand drawer where he had put some protection. Getting his bedspread back warmed him. Getting Sage back got him hot. Majac wet his lips and kissed her.

She eagerly returned his passion. Sage had wanted him from the first touch of his hand at the arena.

Pulling her warm body and soft moans closer, he twisted her, pulled her hair, cupped her soft breasts and moved her all around the bed. Her curly coif bounced lightly. Settled around her face like a lion's mane. He loved it.

Her wish was his command. He moved his hand to her narrow hip, squeezed her plump but firm backside then pulled her closer. She was light in his arms as her winding body jerked on top of his. He touched the mound of hair above her sex. A squeal escaped her and she trembled. She mounted him and rolled her hips back and forth in a gentle grinding motion as she ran her hands through her tousled mane. The mattress swayed like the flow of the open ocean with the flow of their bodies. Metaphorical fireworks exploded as the two strangers, become bedfellows, danced a simultaneous exchange of pleasure.

Whatever peaceful rest Sage thought she was going to get staying at her friend's house instead of in a hotel, had now become an afterthought. There would be no sleeping in that bedroom as Sage and Majac exchanged one intense orgasm after another. When the ecstasy of their night culminated, Sage finally rested on the pillow next to him. Tiny streaks of light from the dawning sun strained to break through the blinds.

When dawn finally came, he sat up and touched her like she was his possession. Sage sat up and gave him a kiss; a long, warm kiss that aroused him once more. When she felt his arousal, she stopped kissing him, opened her eyes and whispered, "Thank you for the birthday present."

Hoping to creep quietly back upstairs without waking Crystal and Jaz, she got up, pulled his shirt off the chair and loosely wrapped it around her. Faint beams of sunlight highlighted the curves of her silhouette as she buried her face in the collar of his shirt, inhaling his scent as she exited the room. And as quickly as she'd come, she was gone. And as quickly as she'd warmed his bed, it was once again a little bit colder.

By the time they got home Thursday night, Tessa was absolutely exhausted. Leona had the energy of a woman half her age, which Tessa experienced first-hand being dragged all over every part of Seattle and Tacoma. Although her preconceptions about Seattle were that it rained all the time, the weather throughout her visit was absolutely gorgeous.

The average daily temperature was in the upper 50's and there was barely any rain. Monday morning, Leona took her to see some ladies who expertly treated them to the most relaxing mani-pedi Tessa had ever experienced. They ventured downtown for lunch where they ran into Dorian Daugherty, a Seattle native and third-year pitcher for the Seattle Mariners. A marine biology major, Dorian talked and joked and kept them laughing about everything except baseball. For a jock, he was humble and a great conversationalist.

They spent the majority of their afternoon window shopping and people watching before joining Dorian at the Seattle aquarium where he explained more than they ever wanted to know about fish. Surprisingly enough, his three-hour ichthyology lesson was absolutely enthralling.

When he invited them for dinner at a place he touted as having the best fried fish and hushpuppies in Seattle, Leona accepted before the period came out of his mouth. At Willie's Taste of Soul, Dorian introduced them to the owner, a quinquagenarian named Mattie, and ordered three of the house specials without telling them what the special was. When desserts came, Mattie told Dorian his money was no good there, so Leona insisted on leaving a fifty-dollar tip. Before the evening ended, Dorian invited them to join him for drinks at Demetriou's Jazz Alley on Wednesday night.

Tuesday morning started with a twenty-lap swim. As if that wasn't bad enough—considering Tessa hadn't been to the gym in over a year— Jackie, the aerobics instructor, wore out every muscle they had left lifting weights in a Body Design class. All of that was before breakfast. On their way to the hairdresser that afternoon, Leona said she needed that workout after Willie's if she was going to get into her dress for the white tie affair later that night.

Dinner, dancing and lots of alcohol kept everyone's spirits high as the Governor's Ball pressed on until well after midnight. When their car arrived at Leona's condo, their driver, Geoffrey, had to double-park the car and help both of those staggering drunks inside. Luckily for them, Geoffrey was the perfect gentlemen. If he'd been one of those crazy sexual sadists that terrorize people weekly on those insane TV shows, they'd have been easy prey in their extremely inebriated state.

Inside the apartment, the talkative drunk in Tessa surfaced as she raved about how much she absolutely loved Leona's condo. "This place is laid. I'm gonna have to learn how to dance like Debbie Allen too."

"Being single helps," Leona said. "I only have to spend my money on me."

"I'm single too, but I can't afford a crib like this."

"The dance studio is awesome and it makes ends meet, but it's the escorting that makes sure my mad money is there when I want it."

"There can't be too much wrong with it if it's how you know all of those rich people from the penthouse the other night?"

"You could say that."

"Well maybe if I were here longer, you could put in a good word for me and get me some of that part time action. I can think of a couple of things I've been dying to buy."

"Let's...just...," Leona dragged out the two words like they were scared to leave her mouth without the rest of the sentence to protect them. When she couldn't prolong the statement any longer she finished with, "...get you through this vacation."

On Wednesday they slept until almost noon, dressed then made their way to Mt. Rainier. Their trek to the summit was by way of The Road to Paradise, making several stops including the waterfalls, the glacier and the Paradise Inn near the five-thousand-foot mark where they shopped. Tessa bought souvenirs for Mama and Drake while Leona bought an Indian headdress that she proclaimed might come in handy sometime.

After exploring as much of Paradise as they could stand, they headed back down the mountain. Leona made short stops along the way to take pictures of beautiful Reflection Lake and a 1200-foot deep channel called Box Canyon. Their final stop was at Grove of the Patriarchs, an old-growth forest with gigantic Douglas-firs, western hemlock and western red cedars, some estimated at more than 1,000 years old. Some with circumferences in excess of thirty feet. The ranger explained that people come from all over the world to experience walking through those huge trees. With all of their stops, the 83-mile journey around the mountain only took five hours, leaving them plenty of time to get back to Seattle to meet Dorian.

When a beam of sunlight slithered through the curtains and poked her in the eye Friday morning, Tessa was dead tired. Tired from the dancing and drinking late Thursday night, but moreover from being out until after midnight all week. Back home, staying up past eleven was a once a week occurrence. If the headache she felt coming on didn't pass quickly, there was no way she was gonna survive another day traipsing behind Leona at her breakneck pace. And on top of that, she had no idea how late they'd be out Saturday night after the art auction. But for now, it was early and from the sound of it Leona wasn't up either, so Tessa rolled away from the sunlight, covered her face with the pillow and tried to fall back to sleep.

Just before ten she woke to her cell phone ringtone blaring in her ear. When she answered, her nephew Drake's voice surprised her. "Aunt Tess?" he said, out of breath.

"Hey Honey, what's going on?" Tessa asked. Drake was her older brother Chris' only son. She'd help raise him for a couple of years when he and his wife had some marital problems. She got him through high school and college, graduating with a Criminal Justice degree. Unfortunately, his parents were divorced, but ironically, the three of them have a greater relationship now than when they were married.

"I am at the hospital with Nanna," Drake said.

"Nanna?" Tessa exclaimed. A deathly chill stretched down her spine. "What happened, Drake? Why is she in the hospital?"

Tessa stood from the mattress but the combination of the different time zone, the late nights and the several gallons of alcohol she'd consumed knocked her back down with the power of a Mike Tyson punch.

The line went silent for a moment.

"Tessa?" Mama asked.

"Yeah Mama, it's me. What's going on?"

"Calm down Sweetie. The doctor said I'll be all right."

"All right? What does that mean Mama? All right compared to what?"

"Calm down girl and let me talk," Mama said. She was silent for a long moment, but Tessa could hear her breathing heavily in the background. "Sorry about that Baby, but they keep making me breathe through this mask. Anyway, I was at the community center playing cards with the girls and I must have passed out. When I came to, I was here at the hospital and my baby Drake was here with me. Doctor Singletary said that I passed out because my blood sugar was low. Did I mention how cute Doctor Singletary is? And he's single too. You want me to give him your number? You two would make some pretty…"

"Mama!" Tessa interrupted her mother's cross-country matchmaking attempt. "Have you been checking it? What did you have to eat today?"

"Lower your voice Missy," Mama raised her voice as much as she could. "Last time I checked; I was the mother." She took a couple more breaths from the mask before she continued. "I have been taking my medicine and I have been checking it, but I didn't have an appetite this morning so I skipped breakfast. I ate a big dinner last night with my neighbor Kelly so I thought I would be all right until lunch."

"Is the doctor in the room, Mama? Can I talk to him please?"

"No Baby, he's gone. Drake is here looking after me and the doctor said I can go home tomorrow morning if my sugar stays right until then."

With Mama in the hospital, Tessa needed to call the airline by noon to change her flight to that night or the next morning instead of Monday. It would cost a bundle, but she couldn't stay while her mother was sick.

Leona called on the house phone around ten-thirty, but Tessa let it ring and go to voicemail while she finished with Mama.

"Humph," Tessa growled into the phone. "Mama, I love you."

"I love you too, Baby."

"You take care and do what they tell you, okay?"

"Okay."

"Let me talk to Drake please." When Drake answered, Tessa told him that she was changing her flight and that she'd be coming home early instead of waiting until Monday afternoon. I'll text you my flight itinerary, were her last words. By the time she hung up with the airline, she had a seat on the last flight leaving Seattle Friday night.

08

Reunions

SINCE HIS ARRIVAL, MAJAC NOTICED that Jaz and Crystal existed in either of two opposing states—incessant arguing or unyielding silence. Now as they prepared for a visit to Tuskegee, things were coming to an ugly head. He could hear them in the kitchen arguing again, about what he wasn't certain, but their demeanors were definitely intense. The kitchen door was closed, but that didn't stop their fierce words from disseminating throughout the downstairs. Majac considered going into his bedroom, but since the family room was farther from the kitchen and he didn't want them to think he was trying to eavesdrop; he kept his position on the sofa and turned up the volume on the television. His first thought was about the girls having to hear their parents argue, but then after a second thought he realized that the girls probably couldn't hear them. Their bedrooms were upstairs at the far end of the hallway and they'd been asleep for almost two hours now. In the short time that he'd been a houseguest, he couldn't remember either of the girls ever waking up at night. Over the loudness of the television, Majac could hear Crys telling Jaz matter-of-factly, "When we get back from this trip, we are going to counseling."

"Like hell I am?"

"Then the girls and I will be gone when you get back from P-A."

A door slammed and Majac listened as Crys' heels tapped across the marble foyer then were muffled as she climbed the stairs. Majac was shocked. The discord between them made a dramatic encounter almost inevitable. The veracity of their confrontation was proof that they were definitely on one. Jaz and Crys' marriage had always perfect—the kind that people dreamt about. The only people he knew with better, longer marriages were their parents. Of the hundred people he knew who probably should have never gotten married—let alone stayed married—he could not imagine Jaz and Crys ever not being together.

When Jaz came in to watch TV, the look on his face told that things were really bad. He stood at the left side of the sofa and watched as an abandoned car rolled directionless across a busy street, stopping only when it ran into a fire hydrant.

Majac asked, "You Aiight?"

Jaz twisted the magazine in his huge hands. His voice escalated. "She said that if we don't go to counseling, then she wants me to move out."

"Damn."

"Fuhgeddaboudit," Jaz said in a low, defeated voice. He walked to the wet bar in the far corner of the room and poured himself three fingers of Gentleman Jack. Without asking, he poured Majac one also. Jaz made his neat, Majac's was on the rocks.

Even though Majac wasn't a Jack drinker, letting his best friend drink alone was not a consideration. He knew down in his gut that he should have seen it coming sooner.

Unlike the Jaz and Crys of old, they barely said five words to each other when they got home in the evening. Everything he did upset her and the past two nights, Jaz stayed up well past when Crys went to bed.

Majac hypothesized that Jaz either slept on the couch or in the guest room on both nights. Not having his own place didn't make Majac feel like he was imposing because most nights he worked so late on the ship up in Everett that he was rarely there. But if Crys had truly asked Jaz to move out, there was no way he was staying in his best friend's house with his wife when his best friend wasn't there. Since she and Jaz married, Crystal was like a sister to him. An incredibly attractive, stepsister. Continuing to stay there was a certain recipe for disaster. Despite them both saying he could stay as long as he wanted to, and in a house that size, he surely wouldn't be in the way, Majac decided right then that as soon as they got back from P-A, he needed to expedite finding a place of his own.

Majac was hungry, and if his cell phone hadn't rung, he would have made a sandwich.

"Hello?"

"Hey Majac. How's my favorite Lieutenant doing these days?"

The voice on the phone was familiar. "You got that bum knee fixed yet?"

"Admiral Griffiths?" Majac was surprised. He hadn't heard from his former commanding officer since completing his tour of duty in Japan.

Jaz drank his drink, aimlessly channel-surfing while Majac chatted.

Not wanting to be a disturbance, Majac walked out into the foyer to continue the call.

"So, Commander Charles, how's life on that tin can?"

"It's not the same as driving a boat Sir. But I don't have to tell you."

They shared a laugh before Admiral Chip Griffiths, Commodore of Submarine Squadron Nineteen at the Submarine Base in Bangor, told Majac that his name popped up on a short list of candidates to fill an immediate commanding officer billet on one of his submarines.

"You're talking about THURGOOD MARSHALL, Sir?" Majac asked.

"The news made it over to that skimmer, huh?" Again they laughed. "When I saw your name on the list, I made a call to your DESRON Commander to get permission to bring you back home to submarines."

Majac held the phone away from his face. He was stunned. It was rare for senior officers to talk across community lines. And even more rare to have an Admiral call a subordinate at home on the weekend.

"Job is yours if you want it," Admiral Griffiths said seriously. "You ready to get to work?"

"Hell Yeah," Majac shouted into the phone. "I mean, umm, Yes Sir."

"That's my Boy. We'll talk Monday. You enjoy your weekend."

"Thanks Sir. I won't let you down."

After Majac finished his call with the Admiral, he was excited, and still hungry, so he made some sandwiches before returning to the den. They sat in silence and ate as they watched a movie starring the girl who played the pregnant hooker in *Hustle and Flow*. Twenty-four hours from then, he and the Stevensons would all be back in Tuskegee, three time zones and three thousand miles from Seattle. And sometime in his near future, he'd finally return to submarines as the commanding officer of his own ship.

Majac loved Tuskegee. Trips to his hometown never failed to excite; and this trip, like many others, wasn't going to disappoint. Saturday night they arrived at the centerpiece of downtown Tuskegee—the Grand View Hotel. Ten cars were waiting to valet park. Jaz, the famous athlete and hometown hero had returned home. Crystal, his trophy wife of nearly fifteen years, was on his arm despite all of the tension between them. Pissed at him or not, she was not allowing some tramp an opportunity to help him forget who he was. Majac on the other hand, in his mid-thirties, still single, and dateless, hopped out of the passenger seat of Jaz's rental and preceded through the door before them.

People called to Jaz from all directions trying to get him to stop for a picture or an autograph. Lettering in football, basketball and track all four of his high school years, he joined nine other alumni who would receive honors that evening as the top athletes in the history of Hammond High sports. To date, Jaz was one of only seven people in the school's history who scored more than 1,000 career points in basketball; him holding the school's all-time record for points scored by a single player with 1,986.

When the awards ceremony concluded, the crowd moved downstairs to a larger ballroom where fifty or so tables flanked a dance floor and a DJ was spinning records. At the back of the ballroom, a VIP area was guarded by an off-duty police officer moonlighting as a bouncer. When the first customary line dance drew most of the crowd to the dance floor, the after party quickly gained momentum. An avid fan of line dancing, Majac joined right in. Four songs later when The Wobble instructed all of the big girls to back it up—and there were a bunch on the dance floor that night—a thirsty Majac decided it was time for him to find a drink.

The line at the bar was as long as the Susquehanna River. Majac decided to give the bar in the VIP a shot. The bouncer at the VIP entrance slowed his entrance, requiring him to capture Jaz's attention before he was allowed to enter. At the bar, he ordered two Phenomenons—his favorite concoction of spiced rum, amaretto liqueur, club soda, bitters, and lime and cranberry juices.

Two women breezed quickly behind him. The roar of the music muted their voices, but the scent of fresh summer berries trailing in their wake intrigued him. He turned to see who smelled so good and was pleasantly surprised when he thought he recognized the familiar shape of the woman wrapped inside a burnt orange dress. He stood staring until the bartender, who had returned with his drink, impatiently cleared his throat to remind him that he hadn't paid.

Majac grabbed his drink, threw a ten-dollar bill at him and without waiting for his change, quickly journeyed to find the occupant of that stunning dress. Near the back of the VIP, a row of six or seven large leather chairs of varying sizes faced the window overlooking Grant Park.

Stretched out across a chaise lounge with their backs to him is where he found the lady in the pretty dress and her girlfriend.

"Tessa Ajai?" he called loudly over the music.

Tessa recognized her name and turned to see who called her. Majac moved to the front of the chairs. His motion caught her gaze and she shifted on the chaise. Without oral invitation, he took a seat next to her. The long slit in her dress exposed slightly bent legs resting against the chair back. Now that he confirmed she was Tessa, an ex-girlfriend who he once felt passionately for, Majac eased over and made himself comfortable in the crook of her leg. His boldness excited her although she didn't immediately recognize him in the darkness of the room. "Excuse me," she said tersely, "But I don't know you well enough for you to be this forward."

Majac sat mute as stillness crowded his body like a pool of quick hardening cement setting around him. When their familiar eyes finally met, the room fell silent. It'd been seven years since they'd last seen each other, but the memories of him flooded her mind like it was only yesterday. She smiled widely as old feelings quickly surfaced. Her light, flashy eyes sparkled and reminded him of his own.

"Hello, Beautiful," Majac uttered nervously. "Long time no see."

Air escaped her and she covered her mouth.

He grinned flirtatiously. *Same beautiful smile*, he thought, *still as bright and warm as the sun.* He noticed how her body—thick and lovely in that cream dress she wore to Pops' funeral a few years back— looked firmer and more mature now.

Her eyes told him, *Flirt with me. Act like I still interest you.*

His eyes, seeming to know what she meant, grinned in reply. He smiled and she leaned into his open arms.

They hugged.

Her girlfriend, instantly feeling the third wheel vibe, announced, "I need a drink," before bouncing to her feet. She handed Tessa her drink and an unlit cigarillo then took Tessa's empty glass and hastened away.

"You look great," he announced with all the sincerity three drinks on a Saturday night could offer.

"You don't mean that," she replied.

"Yes, I do mean it. You look like a grown ass woman."

"Oh really?" she said, placing one hand on her hip in preparation to let her inner ghetto loose on him. "What were you expecting, the teenage girl you abandoned a lifetime ago?"

"No, that's not what I meant. I mean…you just look…" sensing her hostility, he considered his words carefully. "You look more mature now… is all I meant."

"Mature hunh? Don't trip Anton. If you want to call me fat, then just say it. Fat. Fat. Fat. It's just a word, I can handle it."

"All right then Tessa; Yes, you—and that dress—are fat" he said.

"Fat spelled P-H-A-T! And I'm the personal trainer you need to hire to work that fat off of you."

Smiling widely, Tessa imagined generating lots of sweat with him during a hot workout. She fanned herself then drank and swallowed hard. "You always were a charmer," she said, rolling the unlit cigarillo between her fingers and wishing it were lit. Instinctively, Majac reached in his pocket, flicked open a sterling silver torch and applied that hot flame to her fresh butt.

Great conversation filled the next thirty minutes as she gave him the Cliffs Notes version of her life since they were last in each other's company, concluding with how her nephew Drake, who the court awarded her temporary custody of during her brother's divorce. He had graduated from Morgan State University and was a recruit training with the CIA as a foreign linguist. He and his parents were still in therapy, but had progressed to the point where he now stayed with them when he came home to visit.

As casually as he could, Majac tilted his head a little, not wanting to seem too anxious and asked, "Would you like to dance?"

"What took you so long to ask? Tessa mumbled under her breath.

"Excuse me?"

"Nothing," she said and straightened. "Yes, that would be great."

Tessa took Majac's hand and didn't let go. And he didn't mind. Her delicate hand fit comfortably in his and as tightly as she held on, it was apparent that it'd be a long time before she let go. To unsuspecting bystanders, they were a couple. That thought wasn't hard to conjure up with her clinging to his arm like a Siamese twin. The more she noticed people's smiles, the tighter her grip became. Majac escorted Tessa to the dance floor, marking his arrival at the spot where they would dance by stopping and twirling her around twice. "You like?" He pulled her into his arms.

"Yes, Mister Charles, me like a lot."

Majac landed the palm of his right hand between her shoulder blades before letting it travel down the supple skin of her naked spine, where with a quick, fluid motion, he eased her even closer. Exacerbating his motion,

Tessa pressed her breasts against the chest of his Armani suit. Her eyes widened with excitement when his pelvis bumped into hers.

Tessa was immediately comfortable. She relaxed into the familiarity of his smile, melted into the security of his arms and laid her head gently on his shoulder. Dancing so close was perfect, moving in undisturbed harmony, almost as if her mind were guiding his hands and feet. When she lifted her head, he regarded her and asked, "What are we doing?"

Tessa said, "I don't know, but it feels really good." She stared into his eyes; a hard stare like her words were trapped in the maze of her mind without any idea of how to find their way to her mouth. "Hey look, it's been a long time since we've seen each other and to be honest, I came here tonight hoping that you would be here. And if you were, I was hoping that you would notice me..."

"How could I not?" The 'V' in her dress dipped all the way down her back and ended right above no-man's land. When she moved, the slit in the hem crawled up from the floor and revealed her entire left leg.

"I wasn't finished," she gently scolded him for speaking out of turn. "What I was going to say was that I was hoping you'd notice me in a way that made you want to be more than just friends."

He said, "Come on Tess, we're not in high school anymore."

She stepped back so he could get a real good look at her dress.

"I ain't been a schoolgirl in a long time Anton."

"Yeah, you didn't have half of those curves in school."

She seemed to take his compliment in the tone it was intended because next thing he knew she leaned in and kissed him. The freshness of a York Peppermint Pattie was on her breath. Baylie Smythe, Celeste Devereaux and the half-dozen other women that he'd dated before tonight were good kissers. But none of them compared to this...right here...right now.

Tessa kissed with a passion the likes he'd never experienced before.

It felt good...and true...and right for him in every way. His brain stopped thinking and his heart took control of both his emotions and his motions. Their bodies moved in unison, no longer dancing to the beat of the music, but swaying to the motion of their kiss. Tessa and Majac kissed with the fervor of prodigal, star-crossed lovers. They kissed until they were both almost out of breath. When the kiss was finally broken, he held and caressed her, both his hands settling in the small of her back.

Other couples dancing around them noticed them kissing more than dancing and stared like they were trying to translate the motion of their tongues into words. When Tessa opened her eyes, she noticed their stares. She smiled an embarrassed smile, pulled away from him, but still holding his hand, walked to the table her friend had occupied. Majac followed, feeling a high like he'd inhaled too much oxygen.

He sat and took another drink. He took her hands in his and said, "Okay Tess, I'm all ears."

"I'm serious Anton," she said. "I'm not trying to hide the way that I feel about you anymore. When you sent me those text messages before my trip to Seattle, I lost control for a while and it took me some time to get back on track."

"Seattle? Wait. What trip to Seattle?"

"What?" Tessa was so caught up in her own thoughts that she didn't hear his question.

"What trip to…" he stumbled over his words then asked, "When were you in Seattle?"

Tessa finally pulled her hand away from his. "Would you stop changing the subject? I am trying to tell you how I feel, and you're asking me about my vacation?" She stared a look of frustrated disgust at him for not allowing her to finish what was obviously so important to her.

She exhaled deeply and said, "Maybe this was a bad idea."

He recognized the frustration in her voice. With a sincerity that she immediately recognized, he said, "I'm sorry Tess; go ahead."

Again, she stared at him. They were quiet. The thoughts bouncing around in her mind ran laps across her face until she realized that making him wait had finally captured his full attention. "You know what?" she said pensively, "I really don't expect you to understand, but I want you to know that you are special to me. Special like no man I've known before or since. I don't know what is going to happen after tonight, but I guess I'll just have to wait and see…" Tessa stopped talking. The look on her face showed she had gone back into contemplative mode.

Majac, uncertain if she was finished and afraid he might upset her again, remained silent. He shifted his chair until they were side-by-side. Her hand came to rest on his thigh. He wondered if she was conscious of her hand placement. If she was she aware that she was playing with fire.

The curve of Tessa's leg pressed against her skirt. Majac took a deep breath and looked away from his attraction. "Tess, I know you're a grown woman," he told her softly. "I'm sorry for the high school thing," For the next ten minutes, they sat wordlessly. Tessa and Majac had drank, danced and reminisced until almost two-thirty. Now that the party was finally winding down, they sat watching as others said goodbyes and headed toward the exits. Majac finished his drink and looked around the room for Jaz and Crys. "Where did they go? I know they didn't just leave me," he said. "I know, they're probably out in the lobby."

"I guess we should be calling it a night soon," she suggested as she stood up and gently brushed her hip against his shoulder. Sensations rapidly shot downward from his brain bringing about an arousal that until then had remained controlled. Deliberately she said, "And I guess I should tell you that this grown woman wants to do grown woman things tonight."

As if he could see the thoughts inside her mind's eye, his eyebrows raised with anticipation. Tessa accompanied Majac to the VIP where they found Jaz and Crystal. They said their goodnights then made their way to the hotel lobby. The lone attendant giggled as they, the two drunks standing before her, stumbled once or twice before coming to a stop at the counter. Majac pulled out his wallet and said in a mock British accent, "As you can see Madame, neither of us in a condition to drive. I need to know what room you can make available so that I night sleep off the wonderful beverages I so abundantly partook of at the party."

Tessa giggled continuously at his mockery. When they weren't laughing, they looked toward each other uneasily. They both knew what they wanted to happen next, but reservations about overstepping the boundaries built by time kept them from openly broaching the topic of sex.

Tessa played with the slit in her dress, waving the flap covering her leg open and shut. She hoped the desk attendant wouldn't hear her as she whispered, "You scared of what I'm gonna put on you?"

Majac letting out a nervous laugh. "I ain't scared." His eyes scanned the lobby and looked everywhere, except at Tessa. The front desk attendant was still checking her computer. Majac turned to Tessa, licked his lips and smiled, "Well, a little nervous maybe…But never scared!"

09

Her Man and His Momma

"I'M SORRY SIR," THE DESK ATTENDANT FINALLY SAID.

Disappointment took root in Majac's eyes like squatters.

"It looks like we are fully booked tonight."

Before Majac could curve his face into a scowl contemplating which curse word to use first, Tessa suggested that they go to her place.

Majac started to text an Uber but Tessa suggested they walk. It was a stormy night when the dinner began, but the rain and lightning had passed and the breeze that blew seventy-degree air made it a great night for being outside. For the first time in years, she had him to herself and this time she'd make it last for all it was worth. She'd missed him on his last two trips home and had no idea when he'd come home again.

Tessa walked a half-step behind Anton, her arm tucked in his as they trekked the eight blocks from the hotel to her house. They chit-chatted about nothing of real importance marveling at the brilliant architecture adorning most of the older buildings downtown. Majac smiling as they passed the Maple Donuts bakery, City Park and the spot where the Macon River Bridge crossed the river by the marina where they used to go swimming in the summer. The glassy reflection from the water below, now a black mirror beneath the night sky.

Tessa smiled and held his arm tighter as they passed the Harland

Concert Hall. "You remember this place?" she asked looking up at a poster for an upcoming performance.

"How could I forget?"

Majac had taken her to The Harland on their first official date. He had used gift money from his sixteenth birthday to buy tickets to the Young Brothers of Soul concert where Ginuwine, Case and New Edition opened for Boys II Men. They had a great time. And after that night, Tessa just knew that he would be her boyfriend for the rest of her high school days. Unfortunately, her crystal ball didn't tell her that nine months later they would break up after she saw him at his locker offering another girl his varsity jacket.

It was after three when they arrived at her house. Majac kissed her neck while she distractedly searched for the door key. Then he played in her hair as she turned and fumbled in the darkness to find the keyhole. Despite her stiletto heels, she stood four inches shorter than him. Majac, always the perfect gentlemen, stopped teasing her hair and gently wrapped his hand around hers then squeezed and glided the key smoothly into the small hole. "Right where it should be," he said. The door unlocked.

Inside, he removed his blazer and came to her, his face near enough for her to inhale the sweet scent of amaretto on his breath.

"Thank you for tonight," she said. "I had a wonderful time—." *Hiccup* The unexpected noise brought on by two Long Island Iced Teas forced her face into a playful grin.

He laughed at the hiccup. "You're very welcome."

She dropped her keys to the floor. Lazily leaned into him and turned a smooth, round cheek to him. He kissed her cheek. His lips softer than she remembered. In her eyes he saw what her mind was thinking—and what he saw was sex—mind-blowing sex that made a married man in a movie call his wife and tell her he was never coming home again. When she broke the kiss, she took his hand and led him toward the stairs. Majac resisted.

When she turned to find out why, he picked her up and carried her up the winding stairs. A schoolgirl, playfully kicking her feet, her stilettos falling on the fourth and eighth steps. In her bedroom, she turned on the lamp next to the bed. The bulb in the lamp was red. It was all the light they needed.

He slipped off his shoes, approached her and intertwined his hands in hers. He pulled her close, unraveled their hands and cupped her breasts.

His large, strong hands, smooth like satin on her breasts, gently squeezed her hardened nipples.

Her body betrayed her. Her moans, soft at first, grew louder the more he squeezed. Taut nipples pressed at the delicate silk in her bra. Heavy breaths came fast. Kiss me, like when I dreamed you, was her thought.

He leaned in and pressed his lips firmly against hers. Just lips at first; but when she responded, he hungrily kissed her mouth. Just lips quickly morphed into an all-tongue-kiss sweeter than a French pastry.

When she felt his lips part, her knees quivered and she sucked his tongue hard. Tried to consume him. Tessa saw heaven in the distance... and they were still fully dressed.

Majac moved as if he knew her most intimate, unspoken thoughts. Everything about him felt good to her. She stopped him when he started to undress himself, "No. Please...let me." Tessa begged. Despite the urgent slurring of her words, she still managed to make it sound convincingly seductive. She strained to control herself, slowly undressing him down to his boxers. Then she laid him on the bed and mounted him. The long slit in her barely there, free-flowing, burnt orange dress made her movements easy.

She rested on his thighs, her eyes travelling his body, eyeing every ripple of every muscle on his athletic frame. Her hands were drawn uncontrollably to him; he couldn't have expected it, but before he realized what was happening, she rolled him over, removed his boxers and massaged him from arms to ass; then ass to ankle.

After the massage, Tessa stood, undid the fabric belt around her waist and let the dress hang open exposing her front to him. Her taut nipples pointed at him with desire. Before she could get her dress off he came to her, picked her up and kissed her again. Every time he kissed her she sucked his tongue hard. He sucked on the hollow of her neck then feverishly kissed her chin, her lips and her face. Majac shifted his grip from her legs to the small of her back and her feet drifted to the soft carpet below. Then, without warning, he smoothly dropped to his knees before her and kissed her belly. Again she gasped, as his powerful hands came to rest in the small of her back and held her in place against his mouth.

She writhed as he kissed and sucked at her belly button like it was his favorite candy. A thousand Kama Sutra positions flashed through her mind. "Oh shit!" escaped her as her left knee buckled to his passion. It...Felt... So...Good. Her body gave in. She moaned louder.

Jolts of lightning struck everywhere he touched as fingers anxiously traced her curves in the soft darkness of the red light. One hand came to rest in the small of her back again as his other hand glided down her hip.

When his hand rested inside her thigh, she trembled, and as if he had pressed a secret button, her legs parted when he brushed the back of his hand across the front of her panties. She couldn't believe the power of his touch. He pressed his thumb under the curve of her butt. He squeezed and her wetness came quickly. She'd never felt anything so strong and so good.

Majac's finger stopped when he found the silky trim of her panties.

Her mind screamed, *rip 'em off!* but he didn't. A finger found the edge next to her sex and hooked itself inside the soft silk. Her wetness had soaked them through and when her moisture hit the back of his hand, she knew he could feel how much she wanted him. That one finger rode the hem of her panties until it reached her butt, sending shivers through her body as his hand traced the velvety, shaven contour of her love.

His touch felt fabulous, marvelous and torturous, all at the same time. All she could manage were gasps of, "Please...take...me."

Her legs went weak. She fell onto the bed. Muffled a scream into the softness of her comforter. Her dress draped over him like a cape.

Anton slid from beneath her. Rolled her over. Lifted her ankles to the ceiling as he released her from those silk panties. He touched his hands to her knees and without applying any pressure her legs dropped open; full and inviting. He stood before her touching lightly at first, staring deep into her eyes as his hands travelled the length of her thighs.

The feeling they shared was sweet. Some years had passed since they'd shared sex as young adults, but now as mature man and woman, the incredibly powerful sensations almost felt new.

Tessa ached to start this ride; only, she wanted to drive; so she sat up before him, she massaged his legs with a light touch then massaged the length of him, his excited growth surging with the warmth of her touch.

His eyes closed. His moan deepened. The sensation of her mouth on him was phenomenal. His heartbeat increased exponentially.

His chest heaved up and down. He shook at his knees and hunched over at his shoulders.

Tessa wrapped her arms around him, pulled him to the bed and rolled on top of him. She straddled his hips, her satin dress a shadow in the red light hanging over them. She took him inside her as she had yearned to do back at that moment when he lit her cigar.

"Oh shit!" escaped as a quick wave of ecstasy surged through her.

She hadn't had sex in a month of Sundays, and despite being wetter than a puddle, his size brought pain. Pain that quickly shifted into repetitiously long ebbs of pleasure as she rode that stallion.

He held her face. Brushed away hair from her dank cheeks so he could see her eyes. Stroked her hair then kissed her. Wrapped his strong hands around her back and supported her weight as he rocked her gently back and forth on top of him, his hips doing all of the work. Tessa moaned, cussed and screamed as her orgasm came quick and loud.

Anton's orgasm mounted as he rocked, sat up and kissed her hard. Like he couldn't get enough of her flavor. Realizing she couldn't catch her breath, he kissed her cheeks, then her earlobes, then her neck. She squealed when he kissed her neck. Squealed and came again as his kiss became a light bite. He broke into a full sweat. Rocked Tessa. His orgasm mounting.

Forceful thrusts took her on the ride of her life. Tessa could feel herself pulsing all around him; throbbing, pulsing, contracting and opening for him as he glided up and down.

His head tossed back, eyes closed, humping fast but steady, he repeatedly brushed kisses across her shoulders, her neck and her breasts, and again Tessa cussed, screamed and called on God to save her twenty different times.

She wrapped her arms around his shoulders and accepted his fierce injections, her own hips moving rapidly in a circular motion until finally she shook all over and exploded again. The sensation was intense.

Waves of pleasure surged through her body causing her to writhe in agony as she cursed a thousand times. Her breath grew ragged as her pleasure came in one relentless wave after another. When she finished, her chin dropped to his shoulder, her mouth hanging wide in silent ecstasy.

Majac swelled as he hit bottom. In the short forever it took her to tame her long-time dormant beast, Majac swelled inside her wetness, growing both wider and longer.

Tessa gasped loudly, open-mouthed with no shame at all as a third orgasm hit her as his orgasm came hard and fast inside her.

Silent moments passed as both Tessa and Anton struggled to regain their composure. After the uncontrolled jerking stopped and the waves of ecstasy subsided, Tessa's body went limp; her arms draped over his shoulders, her hair draped down his back. Anton buried his face into the nape of her neck, unconsciously continuing to gently roll his hips.

After another long moment passed, he released a sigh accompanied by several sharp thrusts of his hips before slowing his rhythm and relaxing inside her. Tessa smiled, unable to tell if the heart beating—no… slamming—up against her chest was hers or his.

He leaned back and she lowered her torso on top of his. Her body was in a state of euphoric shock. Her emotions were all over the map.

His closeness had her heated, but her mind had her tinkering with skepticism. She had so many questions, but didn't want to scare him off. Wanted him enamored with her. Wanted him in that moment.

Anton didn't say anything to her as his breathing slowed.

Tessa wasn't quite sure what she wanted him to say.

Nervousness took over and she rolled away; a thousand questions flooding her mind as she wondered if he was comparing her to any of the other women he'd ever been with.

He found his breath. "What you thinking so hard about over there?"

She hesitated for a moment then smiled and said, "Whether or not you'll be joining me for breakfast."

He met her gaze and stared deep into her eyes. Deep like he was trying to peer into her soul. Looking into his eyes was like looking into her own. Like looking into a mirror. Like they were kindred spirits or a part of the same soul. Her eyes were a half-shade lighter than his, but the connection was eerie. She'd never been able to explain it, but since they were young, every time she looked into his eyes, she always thought there was a deeper connection between them than showed on the surface.

"Nothing would make me happier," Majac said, stroking her hair.

She surrendered to every word he whispered the rest of the night.

After a long shower, she put on a silk nightshirt that hung below her hips and a fresh pair of panties from her drawer. After his shower, he put on his boxers.

She lotioned him. His skin and taut muscles felt good in her hands. She watched his subtle reactions as she touched different parts of his body, finding found herself taking much longer than if she were lotioning herself.

The masculine side of him tried to play it off, but she could tell it tickled. He wasn't overly ticklish, but there were a couple of spots that made him smile and shift in his seat. She wondered how much more about his body she could find out if they had more time. That thought excited her to the point where she noticed her nipples pressing hard against her shirt.

When she finished, he returned the favor, somehow removing her shirt in the process. He got close up on her neck and the heat of his breath made her moist again. Her toes curled when he oiled the back of her knees and inside her thighs. He sprayed perfume across her bare chest then got close so he could take in how the scent mixed with her natural aroma.

It must have been as exciting to her as it was erotic to him because before another stitch of clothing was donned, both of them were well-oiled, sliding and climbing all over each other on their way to climaxing all over again.

～

Sunday morning following four short hours of sleep, Majac and Tessa took a cab back to the hotel to get her car. Once there, they shared a full-service breakfast before she drove Majac to his mother's house. He invited her in to say hello, but she declined. His goodbye kiss felt less passionate than those from earlier, but afterwards, she noticed that he almost skipped up the sidewalk and into his mother's house.

At home, Tessa spent the majority of the day in bed recovering from Saturday night's combination of alcohol and incredible lovemaking. The alcohol put a hurtin' on her head and her Maintenance Man put a hurtin' on every other muscle in her body. The primary reason she spent most of her day lying in bed with her legs spread wide was because she was so sore down there that she couldn't bear to sit or even keep her legs closed for any extended period of time. *And let me tell you*, she told her girlfriend later that night, *he completely wore out the muscle in the middle.*

When she woke from her nap that afternoon, she realized that similar to a drunk who keeps drinking to fight off a hangover, she either needed more of Anton to keep her feeling good or lots of ice to numb the feeling. Knowing Anton was already on a plane headed west, she trudged downstairs to fill a bag with ice.

When she woke up Monday morning, she was still feeling it. Plenty of water and aspirin got rid of the alcohol induced headache, but the throbbing between her legs told her that sitting at her desk in that uncomfortable chair was definitely not an option. Tessa got out of bed long enough to grab more ice and call into work. Her supervisor tried to get all in Tessa's business when she said she needed to take a personal day, but Tessa, being

99

the professional that she was, cut her off explaining that her mother was on the other line and she needed to take her call.

A cold compress rested on her inner thighs throughout the majority of Monday afternoon. A long hot bath soothed the remainder of the pain out of her body on Monday night.

Tuesday morning, she awoke refreshed, rehydrated and ready to conquer the world. Work went well that morning. For lunch, she accompanied a couple of the girls from the office to a new Mediterranean sandwich shop. Inside she saw Momma Charles. She intended to stop and only say hello, but found herself confessing, "Missus Charles, I need some advice. Do you have a couple minutes to talk?"

"Anytime baby," Momma Charles replied.

"Thank you Missus Charles," she said.

"All of you have called me Momma since I've known you as children. What's with this Missus Charles stuff all of a sudden?"

Right now I would like nothing more than for you to be my Momma or Momma-in-law, she thought. Tessa played with her straw. Fidgeted in her seat. She hoped that Momma knew what to say without her having to spill all of the beans.

"Child, what's on your mind?" she asked in the sweetest, kindest voice Tessa had ever heard. "From my experience, the only reason you would be acting this way is if there is a man involved. Now I ain't one to overstep my boundaries, but since I haven't seen you in a couple of months and you're bringing this to me only a couple of days after my Anton left town, let me ask 'What' has Anton done now?"

That was the problem. Anton's communications with her were so spotty throughout the last couple of years that there was nothing negative for her to tell his Momma that he had done. She thought briefly about the past weekend but out of respect for her and modesty for herself, she wasn't about to tell her any of the details about all of the wonderful things her beloved son had done with—and to—her Saturday night into Sunday morning. Just thinking about it made her blush. "Anton hasn't done anything Missus...I mean Momma Charles."

"Might this have anything to do with him being home this past weekend?"

Tessa blushed when she smiled.

Momma Charles sat stoically. She had a great poker face. She was more on target than Tessa wanted to admit.

Tessa was pining for him to do something more than provide her with merely a pleasure-filled one-night-stand. She cared for Momma Charles and the last thing she wanted to do was be deceitful, but she didn't know how to be totally forthcoming with what was on her mind. "Okay Momma," Tessa started, "let's just say that hypothetically, you are single and that guy that you always wanted to get with—or should I say, were seriously interested in, but due to bad timing, one of the two of you were always unavailable—is now single also. You think it's your chance to get with him, but because so much time has passed, you don't know if you can handle the rejection if he doesn't feel the same way?"

Without hesitation Momma Charles said, "I'd go get him!"

Tessa raised an eyebrow at how quickly she answered. "You would?" She swallowed hard and cleared her throat.

"Yes, I would. I lost love once. I wouldn't lose it again."

"So how do you approach him?"

"Shoot straight, no holding back. Look girl, if you think he is the one that got away, let him know how you feel. Like you said, you are too old to play games."

"Hunh?"

"Life is too short, Sweetie. You never know what the next day will bring, so if the opportunity is finally there then go for it!"

Tessa had not expected her to be as forthcoming and direct, but she was excited that Momma was telling her what she had hoped to hear.

Momma added, "But never-ever forget that first and foremost, you are a lady. Present yourself as a lady at all times and if he is half the man that he needs to be to deserve someone as special as you, he will step up and treat you like the precious gem that you are."

"Do you really think it's that simple?"

Momma exhaled softly. She reached across the table and held Tessa's hand. "All I'm saying Baby, is follow your heart. That's the soundest advice I can give, and if I were you, it would be enough for me. But then again...I'm a Pisces and that's what we do."

"What?' Tessa asked, unsure of what part she was referring to.

"Follow our hearts." Momma said. "That's what Pisces do. God created a great big world out there and you would be best served if you saw as much of it as you can in your lifetime."

"Yeah Momma, but Tuskegee is home. It's all I've ever known."

"And the place you move will be the next place you get to call home. That's why they call it living."

"But Momma, my Mama ..."

"But nothing, child." Momma squeezed her hand. Her voice grew gentler. "Your mother raised a beautiful woman. She is here in Tuskegee because that is where she chooses to live her life. If she wanted to go somewhere else, she would've done that a long time ago. If you were young, she would have taken you with her. If you were an adult, she would have let you know where she was going. Bottom line is that you are a single, grown woman who needs to make decisions, for herself, with herself in mind. Shoot girl, your Mama ain't gonna love you no less just because you don't live in the same town she does."

Tessa smiled as Momma eased the grip on her hand.

"Tessa do you remember the first time you left for college? She was sad, wasn't she?"

"Yes, Ma'am."

"But, she knows the rules of parenting. She got over it, and she still loves you the same way. Everybody has to live their lives for themselves. Parents know that children grow up and leave the house. Hell, I told my kids, 'If you don't ever move out, I won't have anywhere to go visit?'"

She let loose a small chuckle at Momma's analogy.

"Now, that being said, most emotional decisions are bad decisions, so whatever you decide to do, make certain you wait until whatever emotions that may have spawned these thoughts have subsided, then weigh out all of the pros and cons. Make sure it's a decision you can live with."

"That sounds..."

"Hush child, I ain't finished," she scolded. "Women are fragile, foolish creatures when it comes to a man. Nevertheless, if you are going to be foolish for any man, that man should be your husband. And, if he's not worth making a fool of yourself over, then he is not worth being your husband. No man is worth your tears, and the one who is, won't make you cry." Momma Charles laid it on thick. "Once you find the person that you love, love that person with all your heart. And take your time because the heart only knows love baby. The heart has no concern for time. Love has no time limits. I mean no limits on time. No boundaries. The heart can only deal with love. God will do the rest.

"Don't get me wrong, I loved my husband more than anything." Despite

102

the pain behind her thoughts, Momma didn't skip a beat. "I wish Manny was still here, but I am okay being home by myself."

Tessa saw the pain in Momma Charles' face as she spoke of her late husband. She sympathized that he'd been taken from her so early in life.

Momma laughed. "So Honey, if you truly are worried about leaving your Mama, let me reassure you that she will be all right. If this job is what you really want, then you take it and you go live your life. And if that man is who you really want, then you go get your man."

"Thank you Momma. I'll let you finish your lunch. I know you have to get back to school."

"Sounds to me like you've already made your decision," Momma said. "I'll tell Anton that you asked about him too," said Momma.

"Yeah Momma, you be sure to tell him that." As she walked away, Tessa thought, *If I don't tell him first.*

10

New Beginnings

As the ship's bell struck out the noon hour that Friday, Captain Tony Thayne manned the podium to commence the Change of Command ceremony for the submarine USS THURGOOD MARSHALL.

"The Change of Command of a naval vessel is a time-honored tradition passed down from the Royal British Navy. One officer is assigned to command a ship of the fleet and given the opportunity to prove his seamanship and leadership skills in the most unforgiving of arenas, the Sea. At sea, the Commanding Officer is the one person solely responsible for every person and every thing aboard that ship. As Master and Commander of a vessel, when all is said and done, not only the responsibility, but the accountability for all decisions, big and small, lie squarely on his shoulders. Today's ceremony signifies that one officer, having been found fit for command, is ready to relieve another proven Sea Warrior." Captain Thayne ordered, "Commander Charles, Commander Hamm; front and center."

Majac rose from his seat and, along with Commander Franklin R. Hamm, THURGOOD MARSHALL's acting Commanding Officer, marched over to join Captain Thayne. Captain Thayne stepped away from the podium. The two Commanders saluted him. Commander Hamm dropped his salute. Majac said, "Sir, request permission to relieve the watch?"

Captain Thayne returned the salute and replied, "Permission granted." Majac acknowledged then read his orders into the microphone. At the conclusion of his reading, he turned, faced Commander Hamm, raised a salute and said, "Commander Hamm, I have reviewed your logs and find THURGOOD MARSHALL a ship in good standing. I relieve you Sir."

Commander Hamm replied, "I stand relieved." The boatswain lowered Commander Hamm's command flag, then raised Majac's command flag, before the two of them dropped their salutes.

Majac turned to Captain Thayne, reported his relief, then took his seat.

Commander Hamm gave a brief speech thanking the officers and crew for their tireless work, then invited everyone to the reception.

⌁

Just over an hour later at the Oceanside Officer's Club, Majac was at his reception reminiscing with Commander Lorenzo Fabre about one of their liberty adventures as lieutenants in Amsterdam.

"Hey Majac, that ice sculpture is dope," Zo spouted. "And the food on the buffet is banging."

Majac's eyes lit up when the DJ played a song by Teddy Pendergrass. He fell quiet, briefly slipping back in time.

"MAJAC, you all right?" Zo asked.

"Yeah Zo, I'm fine," he replied. "Just thinking'."

"'Bout what, Partna?"

"Nothing," he said. "Forget about it."

Zo said, "I'm going to go grab another brew. You want one?"

"Sure, as long as it's cold and wet." Majac was trying to pay attention to his friend from the Naval Academy, but the sound of high heels tapping across and stopping somewhere close behind, distracted him.

"Congratulations, Superstar!" A velvety voice purred over his shoulder.

Could it really be? he thought. Only one woman he knew had ever called him *Superstar*. He turned around and standing before him was without a doubt the most beautiful woman he had ever known. *Wow*! was his only thought as he took in the full majesty of her beauty.

"Coco Ellington?"

"Anton Charles," she replied.

"Well hello there!" he said, stunned to see the lovely vision from his distant past standing right there, in the flesh. He furrowed his brow momentarily, wondering how he missed her face at the ceremony.

She sized him up. Liked what she saw then said, "I see you've put on a couple of pounds."

106

"Is that a good or a bad thing?"

"Grown man weight looks good on you."

"Thank you."

"I didn't quite expect to see a beer belly, but I'm glad to see there's more to the skinny kid that I fell in love with."

"In love with?"

In high school, Majac had obsessed about Nicolle 'Coco' Ellington since he first laid eyes on her in ninth grade. They'd hung in the same circles, but never found each other romantically. That was before a last-ditch effort by Coco during their class graduation trip brought them together.

"Yeah, *in love with*," she smiled openly. "But that was a lifetime ago."

"So how did this lifetime bring you here?"

"My ex-husband is a personal trainer. He and I own a couple of health clubs together with his brothers. His brothers run the two clubs in San Fran and Portland. I ran into your sister Angel at the state capitol building and she told me about… your ceremony. Long story short, I used a visit to the Portland club as an excuse to come out west."

"I appreciate you thinking enough of me to make that excuse." This time he sized her up. "You look great too!"

"Thank you, sir."

"And Congratulations on the success of your business. Four clubs, hunh? I guess that answers how you keep that body so tight?"

"Thank you again. But enough about me, let's talk about you. My boy is the Commanding Officer of a submarine. You've come a long way, Superstar."

"Yeah," Majac cosigned. "Who'd have ever thought? But what do you know about submarines?"

"I know everything about submarines…" Coco laughed, "I've seen *Hunt For Red October* AND *Crimson Tide!*"

For Majac, her laugh was like hearing Angels sing. The DJ played a popular line dance song and Coco started moving to the music.

"Would you care to dance?" Majac locked eyes with her as he thought about her winding her way to him through the crowd on the dance floor at a club in Ocean City. It was their senior graduation trip and she had passed him a note to join her for a dance. That dance led to them spending their one and only night together. After the graduation trip, she left for college and he left for the Navy.

Before she could answer, Zo returned with their beers. "Damn Majac, where'd you find her? I step away for one minute and there you go, keeping the finest woman in the place for yourself."

Oblivious to his mutterings, Coco and Majac smiled at each other as if they were the only two people in the building. Her face lit up the room. Her smile was infectious. In the moment of silence that followed Zo injecting himself in their conversation, her smile told Majac everything he wanted to know.

"Hey Majac, you all right?" His gaze volleyed between Coco and Majac. Irritated that Majac ignored his previous comment, Zo continued with, "Damn man." He hesitated, focusing on the lady who paid him no attention. "I ain't never seen you this wide open!"

"Excuse me for being so rude." Majac smiled at her. "Nicolle, this is Commander Lorenzo Fabre—but those of us who admit knowing him, call him Zo." Zo play punched Majac's arm. "Zo, I am pleased to introduce you to Missus Nicolle...Oh wait, it's not Ellington anymore?"

"Ellington it is," Coco finished for him. "I changed back to my maiden name after the divorce—for business reasons."

"Nicolle hunh?" Zo interjected. "Majac, I think you forgot to mention a Nicolle. But, that whipped look on your face tells me that she must be a special lady!"

Special she was...he kept his eyes locked on Coco as Zo's inquiry about her stirred the memory of the fellas prodding him for info about their night together during the bus ride home from Ocean City. The thought of that night made him smile.

"Yo MAJAC, what happened last night with Nicolle?" This was Marvin.

"Yeah boy, spill it," Johnny followed. "And don't leave out any of the good parts."

"Yeah, 'cause she got a whole lotta good parts," Marvin spouted.

Majac could see Coco a few rows ahead of him. She was talking with her best friend Treecy Chesson, but as loud as his boys were, he knew she could hear their convo.

"We had a good time, and that's *all* you boys need to know," Majac said.

Marvin said, "Damn that fool, tell us about the body man, we want details!"

"And I'm talking..." Johnny gyrated his hips to the right. "Blow..." Johnny swung his hips wildly to the left. "By," He brought his hips to the middle and thrusted his pelvis. "Blow!"

"Yeah and don't leave nothing out," Marvin demanded.

"Hunh," Jaz shrugged his shoulders. "It's a good thing you didn't come back to the room last night. I had two girls up in there with me and there wasn't enough of them for me to share with you!"

Johnny sucked his teeth and shouted, "Shut Up, Jaz! You left the club same time we did and we didn't see you leave with no two girls. And besides, your drunk ass would'a passed out before you got to the first one!"

For the first time Majac could ever remember, Jaz Stevenson was speechless. He and the fellas fell out laughing!

Majac never did tell his high school partnas about that night, and now he saw no reason to tell Lorenzo either. "I'll tell you what Zo..." His face was almost glowing when he turned away from Coco. "Let me get this dance with Miss Nicolle right now and I'll hit you up later with a little sumthin-sumthin about everything I forgot to mention!"

"That's what's up," Zo said. He gave Majac a fist bump and walked away drinking his beer.

Majac took Coco by the hand and led her to the dance floor. On cue, the up-tempo dance track faded into a mellow tune more suitable for some close hand dancing.

⚊⚊

Solomon rose before the sun Saturday morning to make the drive from Spokane to Seattle. He didn't stay late at the social hosted by the conference chairman Friday night, but in the time he was there, he had two or three drinks more than he had originally planned. The social and those extra drinks were the reason his Friday night departure was delayed until Saturday morning. The sleep was good, especially with the faint aroma of his new friend, Jordyn, still on his sheets from the night before.

Back at his house, he drove past the open end of an empty moving van parked on the sidewalk and continued down the driveway which led to the garage at the back of the property. He waited for barely a moment to see who was moving in. When nobody came out after two minutes, he surrendered to his fatigue and decided to meet them on Sunday.

His bed was calling loudly, so after he parked, he made his way past the swimming pool and up the stairs of his back porch in search of the sleep that awaited him in the comfort of his own bed.

During his first eight months as XO, Majac worked late into the evening and spent numerous nights onboard the guided missile cruiser USS WILLIAM PENN so often that he rarely found himself needing the room at his friends Jaz and Crystal's house more than long enough to say good night and good morning. His stateroom on the ship was comfortable, but knowing he wouldn't want to live onboard when the ship wasn't out to sea, he secured himself a room in the Officer Quarters at Naval Station Everett where his ship was home ported. After several weekends of battling sleepless nights over the noise of loud parties hosted by youthful junior officers, Majac found a duplex for rent in North Seattle. After his change of command, he considered backing out of the lease and moving closer to the Subbase, but deferred because the ferry landing was close by.

When his household goods were delivered, Jaz helped him move. By eleven o'clock, all of the large furniture was in place. A plethora of miscellaneous boxes lined the front yard between the moving van and his front door. After the movers left, Majac and Jaz took a beer break on the small balcony that overlooked Puget Sound.

Majac and Jaz finished their beers and were back out on the front porch retrieving the remainder of the moving boxes when the screen door on the other side of the duplex opened. They heard a voice announce, "About time somebody moved into the *Hang Suite*." They turned and saw a man in a suit coming closer. When he was within arm's length, he offered an open hand. "Wait a minute, you're Jaz Stevenson?"

"And you are?" Jaz asked tersely. He loved his fans, but guys who fawned like girls pissed him off. This guy he wasn't quite sure about yet.

"Oh, my bad." The obvious fan continued staring. "I'm Doctor Solomon Alexandré. The rental manager mentioned someone was moving in, but I didn't realize it was you."

"Nahh, I'm over on the island." Jaz knelt and picked up a box. "My Partna is moving in. Not me."

Solomon nodded.

"Anton Charles," Majac said extending his hand. "Nice to meet you." They shook hands. "A doctor right next door. That's good to know."

"So, do you work at a hospital or have your own practice?" Jaz asked.

"Actually, I'm a psychologist. I have a private practice off the 405 down in Bryn Mawr."

Now Majac picked up a box. "Why you call my place the Hang Suite?"

Solomon laughed. "Brotha who moved out used to have a runway full of Hunnies hanging out over there every weekend. The Hang Suite was the nickname me and the fellas gave it."

Jaz stopped at the bottom of the steps and turned. "Was he running whores out of here?"

"Nahh," Solomon replied. "Nothing like that. Kenny was just a lady's man. So much so, that some women didn't mind other women hanging around at the same time. He was honest about not being into long term relationships and for some reason that was enough for them."

"Hang Suite, huh?" Jaz snorted.

Majac wrinkled his nose, turned and looked at his new house. "I can dig it."

The silence told Solomon that introductions were complete. He said, "Well if you need a hand, I can tote a box or two."

"Thanks Doc," Majac said.

"You don't have to call me Doc, my boys call me Solo."

Jaz smirked. "You plan on carrying boxes in that monkey suit?"

Solomon took all of five minutes to disappear into his house and Superman from a suit and tie into jeans and a T-shirt.

"You comfy now?" Jaz mocked when he returned.

"Yeah," Solomon replied.

"Cool. Now maybe we'll get all of this crap inside in time for kickoff."

By noon, the three of them had emptied the lawn of boxes. As Majac hooked up the 55-inch television, Solomon ordered lunch and a six-pack of beer from his favorite Thai restaurant. Channel surfing three college football games while sharing a bottle of Bacardi Oakheart rum helped the new neighbors make their acquaintance as the afternoon passed.

After encountering Majac at the Hammond Reunion, and encouraged by the pep-talk from Momma Charles, Tessa Ajai took less than a month to get all of her affairs in order; she explained her feelings and her plans to her own mother, then submitted her two-week notice at work. In just over three months since her night of intense passion with Majac, she packed her things and moved to the great northwest.

Informed by Leona of her half-sister's plans, Jennifer Fleming made phone calls to a couple ladies in her societal organization and secured Tessa a phone interview for a job as an assistant with the Seattle City Manager. The interview itself was nothing more than a formality because the City Manager's boss, the Deputy Mayor, received a phone call from Jennifer's husband, Senator Luke Fleming, who stressed his desire for the interview to go in Tessa's favor.

The title of her new job was City of Seattle Criminal Justice Coordinator. It meant that she would be working with the Gangs division. Before the phone interview, Tessa hadn't realized Seattle had a gang problem, but she didn't put too much thought into it because nowadays gangs were everywhere. The City Manager described her expectations of the position to Tessa, then welcomed her aboard.

A couple of days before relocating to Seattle, Tessa consorted with Majac's sister Angel to get his new phone number, something she failed to get while he was home. After making the move and telling Leona about him, finally giving him a name, she found out that her consortium with Angel wasn't necessary because Jennifer already had his number.

Early Saturday morning, the sisters were dressed and waiting for Jennifer to arrive so they could go get mani-pedi's before brunch.

Leona loved surprises. She was ecstatic with the thought of Tessa being with the man she described as the man of her dreams. Never one to openly complain about being single, she internally pined to have her own man of her dreams to steal her away. Later that night when she called Anton to invite him out, she was so giddy with the concept of being in love that she strained to contain her excitement.

Tessa listened on the other line. She couldn't wait to see the look on Anton's face when he saw her.

The call went something like:

"Hello?"

"Hi," Leona said. "May I speak to Mister Anton Charles?"

"This is he."

Majac locked the front door after Solomon left and retreated to the back porch overlooking the joined yards.

"Hi Anton, this is Leona Pearson. Am I interrupting?"

"No, not really."

"You might not remember, but you and I met a while back when I picked up my sister, Jennifer Fleming, from the airport. I think the two of you shared a flight. I hope you don't mind, but she gave me your number."

"Yeah, I remember Jennifer," Majac said, "but to be honest, I remember her meeting someone, but I can't call your face."

"Ouch, that's a first," Leona laughed. "And here I thought I was unforgettable."

Majac laughed, politely following her lead.

"Well, I don't normally do this," Leona said, "but something recently made me think about how handsome a man you were."

"Thank you."

"And the fashionista in me loved your suit." Again, they shared a laugh. "Well anyway, this is a little embarrassing but what I called to say is 'Would you like to go out some time?'"

The line was quiet for a moment.

"Hello?" Leona asked.

"Yeah, I'm still here," Majac replied.

"Is everything all right?"

"Yeah, everything's cool. It's just, um...let's just say it's been a while since the last time a woman asked me out." He laughed under his breath before saying, *But that was a New Year's party in college...A bunch of years ago. And a million miles away.*

Holding her hand over the phone, Tessa joined in his laughter.

He was referring to the New Year's party Tessa's sorority hosted at Hammond University.

"Sooooo," Leona said trying to coax him into answer, "Unless that memory is causing a terrible aversion to being asked out a second time, I know this quaint little restaurant that serves a wonderful Sunday brunch."

"Tomorrow?" Majac asked.

"Yes, tomorrow," Leona said coyly. "I've eaten there a thousand times.

And although I'm hopeful, or better yet fairly certain that you'll enjoy the food, I guarantee you'll enjoy the company."

Majac laughed openly at her assertive confidence. Thankfully for the sake of Tessa's mounting anxiety, he didn't waste much time before he enthusiastically said, "Hell, I don't have any better offers at the moment. Let's do it."

"Okay then..." Leona was half insulted. "The restaurant is called Sazerac. It's on Virga Street. Do you think you can find it?"

"As long as my GPS is working, I can find it."

"Well, brunch starts at eleven. How about you expect me around eleven-thirty?"

"That's cool," Majac said. "But I have another question. Now that you've jogged my memory, Mizz Leona, how will I recognize you? Like I said, I remember a woman picking up Jennifer from the airport, but I don't quite remember the face that went along with that woman."

"Good question. And although my ego is a little bruised right now, I won't hold it against you." Leona paused. "Well, it's too early in the day for me to tell you what I will be wearing, but if it's all right with you, I'll text you a pic of my outfit later on tonight. I'll assume this number can receive texts also."

"Yeah," Majac replied. "A text will be fine."

"That way," Leona continued, "since you can't remember what I look like, you'll have all night to cogitate on what I'll look like."

Tessa held her hand tightly over the phone as if her smile were loud enough to be heard. She waited for the line to go dead then hung up a beat after the two of them. Her plan was coming together—but first they had to go dress shopping.

The sassy trio piled into Jennifer's pearl white Mercedes C300 sedan. Before they could decide which mall to hit first, Leona's cellphone rang.

"Hello?" she answered. "Hello?" she asked again. "Who is this?" She was silent for a minute then she said, "How did you get this number?"

Tessa and Jennifer couldn't hear the voice on the other end.

"I don't give a shit," Leona shouted. "What part of restraining order don't you understand? Don't...Call me again!" She hung up and threw the phone to the floor. "Auugggh!!"

"Everything all right?" Tessa asked, her eyes shifting rapidly.

"What was that about?" Jennifer asked.

Leona raised her hand and inhaled deeply. "Nothing. Just...ugh! Don't worry about it." She took a deep breath to compose herself. "Now what were we talking about?"

It was obvious from the stress on her face that whoever had just called had upset her deeply.

Lunch at Passion Noir was supposed to be brunch, but when they arrived at the day spa, Leona opted for a massage to accompany her nail treatments. This delay impacted their timeline by an hour and a half, causing them to miss their original brunch reservation and forcing them to settle for the less inclusive lunch menu.

Jennifer had her heart set on the Crab Almandine on the brunch menu. When the waitress informed her it wasn't served with the lunch menu, she repeatedly reminded Leona that it was her fault she was going without.

Their waitress was a mousy woman with a shrill voice, but she was ever attentive and brought everything they desired rapidly, including their food. They chatted over top of each other for fifteen or so minutes as they drank peach Bellini's, mostly listening to Jennifer complain about how much of a pompous ass her husband, The Senator, was being during the pre-election process.

After brunch, the sassy, savvy sisters left Passion Noir and spent the early afternoon apartment hunting in West Seattle. Looking at five apartments was overkill because Tessa found the perfect place about five miles southeast from Leona on the fourth try. The remainder of the afternoon they spent shopping in a variety of stores that ranged from thrift stores as low budget as Joanne's Gently Used Boutique to downright uppity venues like the Givenchy store. After browsing through ten or so stores and trying on twenty or so dresses, they finally found the perfect dress to accentuate both Tessa and Leona's shapes.

With a job prospect and a place to live behind her, and the perfect dress in hand, Tessa's Operation Get Her Man was in full effect.

In the hours following Leona's phone call, Jaz helped Majac unpack all four boxes labeled kitchen, then went home to take a nap. Through the window over the sink, Majac saw Solo sitting on the back porch. He pulled two beers from the fridge and bounced outside to share his good news with his new neighbor. A half hour later, Solo's oven timer announced that his food was finished.

"It smells pretty good in there," Majac said. "What you got cooking?"

"A chuck roast," said Solo. "My mom will be here any minute. Why don't you join us?"

"Cool, I'll grab a bottle of wine."

"Oh yeah, I should warn you; please call her Miss Vivienne. If you slip and call her Ma'am or Missus Alexandré, she'll spend the entire night commenting about you calling her old." Solomon raised his eyebrows to confirm acknowledgment. "I'll leave the front door open." Solo said before disappearing inside to check the food.

Majac breezed through his kitchen, grabbed a bottle of red wine to pair with the roast and joined Solo in his side of the duplex. Ten minutes later, the doorbell rang. Vivienne Alexandré was standing on the other side of the door when Solo opened it. "Well it's about time," were her first words. Solo gave her a kiss on the cheek and took her bag.

She pushed by him. Adjusted her eyes. Focused on the man occupying her son's living room. Not recognizing him, she charged straight at him. She was tall, just a notch below six-foot and her skin was maple brown. She was wide at the hips and shoulders, but wasn't round. Not a lot of girth, but she was hefty.

First glance made you think that a fifty-pound heavier version of the Blaxploitation actress who played Foxy Brown back in the 70's had just walked in the room. She was a *Solid Heifer*, as Majac's father Manny used to say. Majac watched her approach with that forceful gait at an intimidating pace. He immediately thought of Tessa's mother, Mabel Ajai, another formidably sized woman who never much cared for Majac since the day she found him hiding beneath Tessa's bed.

Majac hadn't done anything with Tessa other than be in her apartment after her curfew. When Mabel came home early, there was no escape, so he hid quickly under the bed. Tessa met her mother at the door, but reluctantly she didn't push the bed skirt all the way down and Miss Mabel caught a glimpse of Majac's sock as they talked. She was a vindictive lady. Instead of coming in the room and getting him out of the bed, she went to the phone and called the police. Hearing her end of the phone call, Majac scrambled out from beneath the bed and ran past both Tessa and Miss Mabel before she had a chance to hang up the receiver. That was the last time he visited her house after curfew.

Vivienne Alexandré introduced herself as Solo put the remainder of the groceries on the counter. Fifteen minutes after her arrival, they all sat down to eat. In his haste to be on time, Majac forgot his cell phone. Before dessert, he went back to his place, grabbed the phone off the counter and went back to Solo's.

Vivienne answered the door and stood in the doorway preventing his entry. Scared to push his way past her, he hesitated to enter.

"You gon' stand out there all night, 'cause I know my son's air conditioning bill don't include the front porch."

"No Ma'am," Majac said, regretting it the moment he said the word.

"Ma'am?" she huffed. "Do I look that old to you?" Vivienne sounded as though she were speaking in tongues as she stormed back into the living room. Majac followed, knowing full well not to ask for a translation.

Solo joined them from the kitchen. Instantly he deduced from her antics that Majac had called her something other than Vivienne. Some people just don't listen, he thought.

"Hey Partna," Majac said hoping to steer clear of Vivienne's wrath, "I really appreciate you helping me out with the move earlier. And since Jaz left me to fend for myself, I appreciate the company and the meal."

"He did sound offended when I thought he was moving in," Solo said. "Did he go back to the island?"

"I hope he took an umbrella," Vivienne said. "The ache in my foot tells me it's getting ready to rain something fierce."

"I assume so," Majac said. "I'll give him a call later."

"Good," Solo said. "Now let's get with this pie."

11

Late Nights and Early Mornings

THE ONLY THING WORSE THAN how the sun rose year-round into his bedroom window was the way sound travelled as easily as the wind riding the back of the waves down the Puget Sound and crashed loudly down his narrow street. From his living room, he could hear the wind chimes from a neighbor's house frantically announcing the brisk breeze coming off the Sound. Fortunately, there were only eight residences on his dead-end block, so traffic was always light, and from his love for cars, over time he'd come to recognize the sound of most of his neighbors' cars.

"I know, I know. I won't be late," Solo said before hanging up the phone. Vivienne had called to confirm that she'd made it home safely.

His television was on mute, so the distinct male voice he heard talking on the back porch came to him loud and clear. A rash of break-ins throughout the past couple of months had plagued North Seattle. Solo hustled to get his pistol, made his way toward the back door. When he heard rumbling around his neighbor's back door, he threw the back porch light switch, flung his back door open and pointed the gun.

"Whoa Partna," the man shouted. "It's me, Majac."

"Dammit." Solomon dropped the gun to his side, recognizing his new neighbor Anton Charles. "Everything all right?"

Majac leaned up against the wall. "Rough night," he said, digging his keys out of his pocket.

Solo stole a look at his watch. His day seemed longer than most considering the previous night in Spokane yielded next to no sleep. He yawned. "Why don't you join me at church tomorrow? One of the pastors is my best friend. I think you'll enjoy the service."

It was approaching ten-thirty and he still needed to press a shirt to wear to church.

Now Majac looked at his watch.

Solomon grinned. "And there's eye candy in every flavor imaginable?"

The tension of Solo pulling a gun on him was momentarily lifted as they shared a much-needed laugh. Majac opened his mouth to return a witty comeback, but paused when Solo's cell phone rang.

Solo checked the caller ID, gestured for him to wait and answered after the third ring. "Hey, what's up? I didn't expect to hear from you tonight."

Leona Pearson, who unbeknownst to Solo was meeting Majac the next morning for a brunch date, invited him to join her and her sister Tessa at Club Me where they were taping a local show called Grown Folks Dancing. "That sounds great, but umm," he hesitated, regarded Anton then told her, "I'm hanging with my boy tonight. Can I take a rain check?"

"Bring your boy with," Leona replied. "There's room for everybody."

"Hey Majac," Solo said, "My friend and her sister are inviting us to go dancing. You want to come with?"

"Yeah Partna, I'm in."

"You said Club Me, right?" Solo spoke into the phone. "Yeah, I know exactly where it is. We'll meet you there." He hung up his cell and exchanged a fist bump with Majac before they disappeared into their respective halves of the Hang Suite to change clothes.

Coming back to get his wingman for the night, Solo rang the doorbell as Majac came down the stairs dressed to impress. Majac let him in then removed the vibrating cell phone from his hip holster. The text message was from Leona. It was a headless picture of her in a dress. Majac grabbed his keys. "I'll D-D. It's probably best if one of us stays sober tonight."

Again, they shared a laugh. A laugh that was short lived. This time it was Majac's cell that rang. *Yes*, then *Yes again*. A long period of listening preceded, "Yes, I'm on my way."

Majac took a long, disheartening look at his new neighbor, exhaled enough air to fill a hot air balloon and dropped his keys back on the table. "Looks like I'm the one taking the rain check."

"Anything I can help with," Solomon said.

"No, Solo. Three of my sailors got picked up for a DUI. Besides, they're waiting for you. You go. I'm good."

"Are you sure?"

"Yeah, I'm good."

They exchanged a half-hearted fist bump, then Solo was gone.

Solomon arrived at a packed Club ME shortly after midnight. The all-male line was short. Ladies were admitted free before eleven, so most of the crowd was already inside. The dance floor was so crowded that he thought he'd need a search party to find Leona and her sister. He ordered a drink and while he waited for the bartender to return, that search party came in the way of a strobe light that pointed out two women dancing vigorously on one of the small six-by-six stages in the middle of the dance floor. Those two energetic women were switching, swinging, gyrating and partying like it was 1999. Solo retrieved his drink, slid the barkeep a ten and watched as those two dancing divas energized the crowd.

When the deejay shifted to a selection better suited for couples, the ladies relinquished center stage and exited the dance floor—stage left. Knowing all of that exertion had made his friends thirsty, Solo bought two more drinks and waded through the crowd to a small table on a raised platform where the two ladies were acting like royalty.

He caught Tessa's eye first. Leona saw her eyes light up and followed her gaze. Solo placed the two extra drinks in front of them and the jubilant duo came to their feet simultaneously to greet him with hugs. Tessa first with a quick, familial hug; then Leona. Her hug was two-and-a-half seconds longer than what made a normal greeting as she buried her face in his neck and melted in the scent of his cologne. She pressed her satin party dress tightly against his chest and a warmth sparked deep inside her when she felt the hardness of six-pack abs tensing beneath his purple, long-sleeved shirt. "It's getting late, I was starting to think you weren't going to make it," she said, pulling her face from his so he could see her poked out lips pretending to pout.

He took her hands and ended the hug. She stepped away but he didn't let go. Solo eyed her entire length then spun her around to take in the whole package. Her dress was light green with large white polka dots. It had inch-thick shoulder straps and a hemline that hovered mid-thigh to show off the well-toned definition in her legs. The dress was loose enough to be comfortable, but snugly form-fitting. "Yeah, I thought about backing out after being out all of last night," Solo said. "And I have to get up early tomorrow morning for church."

Leona pulled away from him. She whispered in Tessa's ear and when she finished conveying her message, both women emptied their drinks and slid their arms in his. Loudly Leona proclaimed, "Let's blow this lame sex factory."

The ladies followed Solomon for three blocks and parked in front of Woody's Bar and Grill. In his car, he'd called ahead to let his friend Des know he was coming, but Donna Lynn, one of the two night managers, told him Des was off. Donna Lynn knew Solomon was one of the silent partners and since the kitchen closed soon, she took a food order for him and his guests. When they arrived, she greeted them, then sat them and a bottle of Solomon's favorite red wine at Desmond's reserved booth.

Leona pulled out her cell phone and pushed it toward Tessa, who smiled uncontrollably as she read the text reply Anton sent to Leona after viewing the picture of her outfit. She fantasized briefly about the wonderful idea of being his girlfriend again. Through all the guys she'd dated since him, including the two fiancé's that didn't pan out, not one was able to make her feel the way he had. Minutes passed quickly as they sipped their wine and batted the whiffle ball of inane club conversation back and forth. Watching Solo and Leona flirt like teenagers, Tessa asked, "So how did you two meet?"

The next hour passed unnoticed as Solo and Leona recapped their introduction during her blind date at Woody's. Tessa, being no newcomer to the curvy road of love and romance, released a forced, exaggerated yawn. She waited until Leona made eye contact then said, "I don't know about you two, but I need some sleep. We—I mean I—have our...No, I—I mean we— need our beauty rest."

With that, Solo left a one-hundred-dollar bill on the table and escorted them outside.

Leona fumbled through her purse for keys, exhaling her disgust at the thought of ending her night without Solomon. Solo gave Tessa a quick hug goodnight then turned to Leona who, without a word, leaned into him and planted a wet kiss on his cheek. She said, "Tessa and I are having dinner tomorrow with my sister Jennifer and her husband out at their house on Mercer Island. If you're free, I'd love to have you join."

"I don't want to be a bother. Are you sure your sister won't mind?"

Leona knew that her sister was the ultimate party hostess. Another person at the dinner table made for more conversation and potentially more good times, not more bother.

"Wait, what time?" he said, "I'm going to the Storm game tomorrow."

"Oh well, what a pity. Jen's dinners are legendary."

"Legendary, hunh? Since I'm flying solo, I could swing out there after if that works for you. Better yet, you come to the game with me, then you can navigate to your sister's. I'd much rather listen to you than Siri."

"Can I bring my niece?" Leona asked.

"Sure, I can swing seats for three."

"Then it's a date, Doctor." Leona pecked him on the lips once, twice and then a third time and then turned and walked seductively away.

Solomon smiled and watched with growing expectation as all of the sexiness exuding from her performance whet his appetite for the woman once referred to as Red Velvet. It had been a long time since he looked at an incredibly beautiful woman with lustful eyes. A woman other than Mareschelle.

12

Seeing Double

LEONA PEARSON SAT AT A TABLE for two fidgeting with her dress. She checked her watch. Eleven-fifteen. The waiter returned and asked if she wanted to order anything or wait for her guest to arrive. Another minute passed before she looked up. Just as she was about to answer him, she received a text from Majac. He would be arriving any minute. "No thanks," she said. "I'll wait."

Remembering the disaster in Texas that was his first and only blind date, he was nervous about being late for their lunch date. His concern was that she would leave when he didn't show on time. That was before her text reply read that she had just arrived and was seated by the windows.

At twenty-five past the hour, the door of the restaurant opened. In the slow second between hope and fulfillment, a man appeared in the opening as if he'd been beamed there from the starship Enterprise. He appeared to have been running. Seemed out of breath. He glanced at his watch. His silver Movado was running slow. He was fifteen, no, twenty-five minutes late. He pointed to the window seats, suggesting to the Maître de that his party was seated somewhere in that area.

Leona took a deep breath, stood and waved. Suddenly, the dress from the text message was right there before him. She thought he gasped. Then she thought he didn't.

A nervous, semi-confident, but noticeably concerned smile carried him quickly over to her table. His shoes and the bottoms of his charcoal slacks were damp from the rain. The top two buttons of his shirt were open. His extra-long sleeves were un-buttoned and folded back once over the sleeves of his blazer. A herringbone trilby cap crowning the king standing before her was the perfect finishing touch to his casual first date outfit. "Leona?" He asked with his arm outstretched.

His skin glistened like the Sahara. His hazel eyes were mesmerizing. *Yes*, she thought, standing tall to greet him, *he's finer than I remember.* She smiled, imagining herself being lost in his oasis. She started to undress him in her mind, then stopped, considered her half-sister's obsession and pursed her lips in unspoken approval. Finally, she accepted his hand.

He kissed hers in return. His inviting smile and gentle hand instilled in her a comfort that she was doing the right thing. "Good morning, Anton."

"The pic of your dress was beautiful; but seeing you in it, absolutely stunning." The open shoulders dress had a deep cut back, was tight around her hips and ended just above her knees. The sheath of the bodice showed hints of peach and green. A tuft of her soft brown hair escaped from beneath her paper braid floppy sun hat. Despite the rain, the taffeta ensemble was great for a warm summer day.

Her beauty had a familiarity to it that he couldn't quite place and although certain he didn't know this woman, the more he observed her, the more familiar her face became.

They sat. Her cell phone rang and as the waiter finished taking his order for a sparkling cranberry juice, Leona excused herself from the table.

Ever the gentleman, Majac rose and watched her walk away, waited until she was out of sight then sat and perused the menu. *I must be seriously slipping*, he thought. *How could I have met this woman twice and not remember her. Maybe Jaz is right. Maybe I do need to just find an escort service and let them send me somebody to take care of my needs. Especially if I missed noticing somebody this fine.*

Two minutes later he raised his head as the peach dress re-emerged. She raised a finger to signal she was still on the phone and something struck him as slightly different about her. Her head was down and her hair covered the left side of her face; the side facing him. He frowned curiously, certain that earlier her hair had covered her right. Not wanting to dwell on an uncertainty and unable to grasp what was different about her, he put his head down and went back to considering his menu options.

As she arrived at the table, she closed her cell phone and stood watching him. His complexion complemented his dreamy hazel eyes—eyes that looked like hers. His hair was cut down to a shadow and lined razor sharp all around. His profile was nothing short of majestic. *Oh yes, he was fine as a new mohair sweater.* She stumbled over her words a moment, regained composure and pushed the brim of her hat away from her face revealing the long Raven's feather curl of hair flanking the left side of her face. At the time of her reveal, Majac was entranced in the menu. "Well hello handsome," she said with a touch of sweetness and all of the sexiness she could muster. "Don't you look sharp?"

Majac looked up. "Tessa?" he said, confusion dripping all over the word. Now he understood what was different. She'd come from the back wearing the same dress as Leona but Tessa's complexion was a half shade darker. A difference seemingly erased by gold-flaked body powder. *What the hell is she doing here*? Majac thought in disarray.

Tessa smiled.

He stood to greet her. "But I..." he stammered. "You?" Then Leona rounded the corner. Threw him into a déjà vu. Confusion replaced disarray. He stepped back; toppled his chair. She put away her cell phone and joined Tessa. Them on opposite sides of the chair like a pair of peach bookends.

Perspiration sheened on his forehead.

She reached for his arm but he pulled away. Fright clouded the anticipation of their reunion. Sucked the joy from Tessa.

Anger was plastered on Majac's face, his demeanor flat and cold. Tessa could only imagine what lie behind his sudden transformation as she waited stoically, preparing to absorb his next move. His body language told her he was excited to see her here, but his mind appeared to be somewhere else.

Inside Majac's head, *Is this really happening again?* echoed as his mind flashed back to an ex-girlfriend's bedroom in San Diego.

"Anton?" Leona called. He didn't respond.

This was a bad idea! resonated loudly in Tessa's ears. Nausea set in as her blood rushed to her feet. She thought a chance encounter with a happy ending would be a great way to reunite them, but instead, she seemed to dredge up some horrific memory. Desperate to save him from whatever misery was applying a strangle hold on his mind, she reached for him.

"No!" Majac shifted into a menacing pose. Braced for a confrontation.

Tessa pulled back her hand and regarded Leona. She had no idea what to do other than wait and hope that he'd soon return from whatever terrible place his mind had taken him.

An angry, anxious, crazed look danced on his face as his eyes flashed back and forth between those two Georgia peaches. He eyed them both then slammed his hand against the table. "What the hell is going on?"

People at the three tables around them watched, whispered loudly and offered personal opinions about the way *those people* acted in public.

Blinking hard to hold back the tears, Tessa cleared her throat and called Majac's name for a second time. He looked everywhere but at her. She called his name a third time desperately hoping to release him from his traumatic trance.

Finally, Majac turned and peered deeply into her eyes. His vapid gaze pierced through, instead of at, her. The glass roof of the restaurant allowed a lightning burst to illuminate the romantically lit dining area. Then, without comment, his chest deflated. He exhaled deeply. Snapped back to reality as if the lightning was the switch his light needed to turn back on. "Excuse me." His eyes broke away from Tessa's. His voice fell before he softly released, "I'm sorry for raising my voice." He turned and facetiously asked Leona. "Would you care to join us?"

"I already have, Sweetheart. Pay attention," Leona smirked, then offered her hand as a peace offering which Majac calmly accepted. She called to the waiter, "Sweetheart, would you bring me a chair and another Cosmo. And not necessarily in that order."

"Anton please forgive me." Tessa said. "I love surprises and I...well, I just...I just thought that a surprise meeting would be so romantic. I conjured up this whole thing with Leona and hoped that you would be as happy to see me as I was excited to see you. But what happens; it backfires on me and now I feel like a heel."

A chair and a Cosmo came seconds later. Leona filled the chair and half emptied the glass—not necessarily in that order. She put the glass down and decided that it was time for her to interject her two cents. Their eyes averted to her as she said, "Anton, when Tessa was out here before, she and I talked about any and everything. I told her about the men in my life and she told me about the men in hers. When she got to you, however, her tone shifted and everything became all marshmallows and puppies. Mushy and cute, if you know what I mean. Tessa told me..." Leona stopped for a moment and pursed her lips. She realized that Majac's attention had shifted to the edges of the beautiful facial scar hidden behind her hair. She eased her expression, lilted her head until his eyes came back to hers. Said, "Well let's just say she bared her soul, and afterwards I told her that if the opportunity ever presented itself, that she should go for it!"

"Unh," Tessa cleared her throat, briefly interrupting the rant that was beginning to embarrass her.

Leona continued despite Tessa's angst, "Look, this woman came all the way across the country to be with you. Now I don't know you from Adam. Have no idea what kind of man you are, but apparently, whatever kind that is, it's the kind she wants to be with."

"Unh-hunh," Tessa cleared her throat again, more forcefully.

Leona understood her meaning and concluded with, "Long story short, we're here, she's taken her shot—and now the balls in your court."

Silence sat amid the trio like a widow at a funeral parlor. The faint piercing of sunlight accompanying the absence of raindrops on the glass ceiling shifted their collective attention toward the sky. The winds had eased and the rain looked like it was ready to grant the Emerald City an afternoon befitting the splendor of the women's dresses.

Majac smiled for a moment then broke their silence when he said, "How about we start this thing over?" He stood up—Tessa followed— then stepped around to the women's side of the table and opened his arms to greet Tessa with a hug.

The breeze whisked her up into his arms. The spicy scent of his cologne travelled on the breeze from the patio, wafted up her nose and salsa danced through her mind.

He moved his chair to her left vice across from her and sat down.

Leona ordered another round of drinks as they moved their seats.

Wintergreen freshness floated from his kissable lips as he said, "So please explain to me how you wound up in Seattle and why you didn't tell me you were coming out here when I was home."

"I tried to tell you while you were in Tuskegee, but you were too busy... umm..." Tessa regarded Leona and realized that she was about to reveal a little too much information about what—and who—he was so busy doing back home, so she just said, "umm...being busy."

Majac smiled. Leona raised a curious eyebrow. She finished her drink then without warning said, "I ain't one to judge, but if I was a real man and a beautiful woman bared her heart to me, I would step to the plate and handle my business. But what do I know, I'm just a woman."

"Thank you for that pep talk," Majac chuckled. "I got it from here."

"It's about damn time." Leona said looking at her watch. "I've got a date of my own, so I think it's time this party got a little less crowded."

She stood, shook Majac's hand, said how nice it was officially meeting him. Before she turned and sashayed away, she leaned to Tessa, gave a hug and said with a tone that didn't care if he was in the room or not, "I don't mean to sound cliché, but he can get it. And if you don't give it to him, I guarantee somebody else will."

Their overeager server returned on the wake of Leona's departure. Majac suggested they forego the buffet and ordered Rigatoni Romano. Tessa opted for the Chicken Piccata with risotto and roasted vegetables. The peach dress hugging her hips urged her to pass on dessert, but Majac told the server to bring his dessert while they waited for their entrees.

Once they were alone, an uncomfortable silence squatted between them like a sumo wrestler. Despite having known each other for what seemed like a lifetime, their words didn't come easy. The look on Majac's face told Tessa that he was nervous even before he began to sweat. An adult relationship between them was still uncharted territory and the realization of the moment was a bit overwhelming.

Finally, Majac reached across the table and placed his hands on top of hers. Lightning bolts of intense chemistry jumped across the table. He smiled a smile that let her know he was happy she was there. Their dessert came and despite her initial concerns about the fit of her dress, she ate the slice of Italian wedding cake when he pressed it against her lips.

The storm passed while they ate. The remainder of the day was beautiful. The afternoon unveiled a bright blue sky with a modicum of puffy white clouds. It was warm for the season, but a slight breeze reduced the heat of the direct sunlight. Not ready to let her man go, Tessa said, "So what do you have planned for the rest of the afternoon?"

"My calendar's clear. What are you suggesting we get into?"

"Leona and I are going to her sister Jennifer's house for dinner. Would you mind escorting us?"

"Escorting two beautiful women to dinner? My pleasure!"

His yes was music to her ears. Her eyes glistened cloudy with tears before she realized she was crying tears of joy to his 'Yes'. She wanted nothing more than to be in his air. Listen to him, breathe him and visually take in all of him for as long as she could.

On a whim, she'd moved 3,000 miles to be near a man who had no idea she was coming, and now she was there with that man and wasn't ready to let him get away. Tessa smiled and said, "Well, dinner doesn't start until six, so how do you suggest we occupy ourselves in the meantime?" She wasn't trying to be suggestive or provocative; she just wanted him to know that even though brunch was over. The possibility of him escaping was not an option.

Majac looked at his watch. "If you'd like, we can head over to Market Street and wander around the Seafood Festival. I've never been, but my neighbor says it's fun."

As they walked from Sazerac to Market Street, Tessa called Leona to let her know that their two would now be three for dinner.

The festival offered a wonder of colorful booths full of arts, crafts, and of course, food vendors offering unique seafood choices. As he finger fed her fried calamari strips, she envisioned their honeymoon and imagined all of the wonderful possibilities that their future life together held in store.

In the background, a sweet old lady jabbered on-and-on about the history of the Seafood Fest. How it got its start in 1974 as a small one-day community barbeque and had since evolved into a weekend-long event. Unfortunately, her words fell on deaf ears as Tessa stared dreamily into Majac's eyes. When the history lesson was finished, they moved toward one of the two entertainment stages.

"Can I ask you a question?" She eased her hand inside his. "What do you see when you look at me?"

"I see a beautiful woman." His words came without hesitation.

"That's it?"

"That doesn't even begin to scratch the surface." He smiled. "You have a heart like Mother Theresa. I mean it takes lots of heart to raise a sibling's child. Especially when the sibling is physically capable. I see an ambitious woman. It sure takes ambition to up and move across country to a city you barely know to start a relationship with a guy who may or may not return the sentiment. It's not like its seventeen years ago and I first joined the service and you were just waiting for me to finish boot camp before you joined me; you and I have done a lot of living since the first time I left home. And among all that living, you've managed to stay good looking in the process."

"Why thank you." His compliments brought a smile she couldn't stifle.

The scent of seafood and Old Bay seasoning permeated the air as they walked up and down the two blocks cordoned off for the festival. Vendors handed out samples as they passed tent after tent, and if they weren't full after brunch, they would surely be stuffed after tasting all of that free food.

"Let me ask you something?" Majac said. "Why now?"

Tessa pointed out a mermaid logo in the back of a tent occupied by a vineyard. She said, "I'm almost 35 years old. I've raised two children—neither of them mine. I have my degree. I have a great job. I have my own place. But what I don't have is anyone to share my life with. Life is too short to be alone. You never know what the next day will bring and I want someone special to start and end my day with. Someone to tell all my secrets. And I want to listen to his. I want to come home from work and have someone there to pamper me and for me to pamper."

"And you think I'm that someone?"

"I want you to be." Tessa paused. Majac always knew how to push her buttons. She remembered never being able to tell the difference between when he was being serious or joking around. Worst part about it was how he could be absolutely joking and still maintain a serious face for prolonged periods of time. His poker face used to make her want to scream. She said, "Just because it may be something I have wanted doesn't mean it will be. Think about it; on a whim, I packed up and moved 3,000 miles without an invitation. It was an emotional decision and most emotional decisions are not good decisions. All my life, situations have been well thought out… all possible consequences explored before I considered making a decision and even then I second guessed it. Reliability and conservatism have been my default settings. Reliable trumps romantic and keeps you from nursing a broken heart."

"Have I ever broken your heart?" Majac asked. His tone now sincere.

"Which time?"

"What?"

Tessa stopped walking and grabbed both of his hands. "Look, I have loved you since high school. You left me for the service and asked me not to wait for you. When you came home to visit we spent time together but, we never committed to anything. Anton has been my friend for more than twenty years and I love him…No, that's wrong; I am in love with him. I've had relationships with other men, but they never thrilled me the way you do. I know I want to be with you and even if you don't right now, I am willing to take the chance to try a relationship and see where it takes us. We're no longer the two teens we were when you stole my virginity. I want to explore the differences in the people we are today. I want to figure out if it's possible for us to be a couple in the future. Time changes things, I know that, but this could be a good change."

"So Ms. Ajai, you're telling me that you went through all of this to tell me that you want to be my girlfriend?"

"Girlfriend?" she laughed. "I haven't been a girl in a long time. But I do want us to give being together a try. This time, for the right reasons."

"The right reasons." He smirked with the uncertainty of a child.

Tessa hoped she was getting through to him. She said, "A while back a very wise Momma I know told me that the best foundation for a lasting relationship is friendship, and despite our separation, our friendship has been rock-solid for over twenty years." Tessa wanted to believe that he recognized that her Momma reference was to his Momma. She exhaled a deep, frustrated breath and looked around the market at all of the unfamiliar faces. Quietly she wondered if all of this was a mistake.

Before she could say another word, he pulled her close. Held her there. They stood face-to-face, chest-to-chest in the middle of a marketplace occupied by a thousand strangers. "Well then, I think it's time to take that leap of faith and see if this friendship is worth romancing." Then he kissed her.

She kissed him back. Despite the seafood samples, that wintergreen freshness still lingered on his breath. In her mind, the fireworks that followed were brilliant enough to light the sunny afternoon sky. When they finished, Majac led her further up the street, holding her tight and smiling like a kid who'd just been given his favorite candy.

Through the next three hours, merchants vigorously peddled their wares. Streets full of people biked, power-walked, or merely ambled about around them. Tagalog, French-Canadian and Japanese dialects filled the air. Tessa and her new beau, Anton Charles, walked hand-in-hand around the marketplace people-watching, talking and sampling more than they should have at the unique celebration of the maritime tradition the likes of Tessa had never experienced in the landlocked state of Pennsylvania.

When five o'clock rolled around, they migrated away from the festival back towards Sazerac where Majac was parked. The drive to Jennifer's house took just more than thirty minutes, marking their arrival seven minutes into CP time. Tessa called ahead to let them know they were on their way and when they arrived, Jen, Ayrikah and Leona were waiting for them on the front porch.

Inside the foyer, Luke was waiting with Anton's new neighbor, Doctor Solomon Alexandré. Majac and Luke were barely introduced before the women whisked Tessa into the next room, eager to hear details.

Gesturing broadly with his right arm, Luke invited his male guests into his study. "So Commander Charles; Doctor Alexandré; I presume you two patriotic, registered voters prefer your cognac to be Louis the Thirteenth?" With the anticipation of sipping expensive liquor, Luke Fleming's words were more a statement than a question.

13

With the One I Love

IT WAS JUST BEFORE MIDNIGHT Friday night when Majac arrived home. A sailor was injured on his ship, and as the commanding officer of USS THURGOOD MARSHALL, he chalked up his more than eight hours late departure as a matter of duty. A torpedo hoisting strap broke, allowing a torpedo to swing loose and knock a seaman into the water during the weapons onload earlier that afternoon. The sailor escaped his unexpected dip in the drink unscathed, suffering no more than a fractured arm.

Because of the late hour, Majac took the ferry home and picked up a calzone from Mario's. This deviated from his normal Friday evening routine of stopping to visit Tessa—she lived near the bottom of the Sound in the southern section of Seattle called Bryn Mawr. He lived up north near the University of Washington.

In the weeks and months that followed their cross-continental reunion, Majac and Tessa had settled into a pattern that, if not predictable, was somewhat comforting. They took their time getting to know each other again. Majac sent flowers to her job. In the middle of their business day, they'd occasionally call just to hear the other's voice. Most evenings, after a long day at work, they'd call and talk until midnight. They would tell each other things they had previously kept to themselves. Not always great embarrassments or secrets, but simple notions, hopes and ideas.

As time passed, their interests in each other became more serious. Their long conversations became more in-depth, exploring the differences in the people they are today. They talked about finances, retirement and bucket lists. They talked about having children. Their conversations about previous lovers—relationships gone well and relationships gone bad— no longer revealed half or two-thirds truth. When Tessa spoke to Majac in their intimate talks, her words were flowers blooming before his eyes. When Majac spoke to Tessa, his words were a symphony of beats dancing on her eardrums. For the first time in a long time, Tessa hung on a man's every word. Conversation, simple and pure, connected them to each other.

Around two o'clock that morning, he finished his tasty sausage and veggie-filled Italian sandwich, then washed it down with a Mexican cerveza and an Old-Fashioned backer. Because he was cooking dinner for Tessa at his house for the first time Saturday night, he was still too excited to sleep. Uncertain of what else to do, he decided to put that nervous energy to good use and clean his house. He scrubbed and disinfected the kitchen and bathrooms, did laundry and washed the windows. He dusted and polished all of his horizontal surfaces then vacuumed every square inch of his house. Such meticulousness really wasn't necessary because he was never really there enough to allow the place to get too dirty. And when he was there, it was normally only long enough to read his mail, pay bills, shower, sleep, then wake up and dress before heading back to the ship.

By the time he felt his house was clean enough, it was almost eight o'clock Saturday morning. After jumping in the shower, he laid down and took a three-hour nap. Now it was noon. He ventured into his closet to pick out something to wear. For some odd reason he felt anxious. He didn't want to be overdressed like someone unaccustomed to having a pretty woman in his place. And he damn sure didn't want to be too casual and risk giving her the impression that she warranted nothing better. Although it was unseasonably cool for August, he didn't want to wear anything that was too heavy just in case he got nervous and started sweating. He pulled out a pair of grey slacks and a white rayon short sleeve shirt. He added a burgundy belt and grey Bull Boxer loafers then went down to the kitchen. He decided to make curried shrimp over linguini noodles. It was one of those dishes that presented like it took painstaking effort, but in actuality was ready in just under an hour.

After working late one night at the Pentagon, he decided to eat in the Executive Dining Room before going home. His favorite chef had just returned from culinary school and asked Majac if he was open to trying a new curry dish. He enjoyed the meal so much that he begged the cook for the recipe. Both times Majac prepared it, his guests raved.

At the farmer's market, he bought a colorful array of organic vegetables to make a salad. He sliced, diced and tossed everything into a bowl and put the bowl of colorful roughage into the refrigerator. Next he checked his bar supplies. He had a five pack of Mexican beers—he drank the sixth one twelve hours prior—one bottle of dark rum, a dozen bottles of wine, and mixes to make Mules. He knew the white wine paired with the dish, but he didn't know her preference, so he put two red blends on his countertop wine rack and two whites in the refrigerator to chill. On his way to pick her up, he'd stop by Mario's for Tiramisu.

Nine months had passed since Majac assumed command of his submarine and the entire look of his life had changed. He was firmly at the helm of his boat's crew. Both officers and crew thought the world of him. By the time they had finished pre-deployment workups, he was confident every man on his ship was a competent sailor ready for war.

Every day the ship was in port, he and Tessa met for dinner. Tessa's main office was in the heart of the city, but she spent most days working from the district office near the University of Washington campus since that district reported the highest rate of gang violence— and coincidently, it was closer to Majac's house. Sometimes after work he'd meet her at the Starbucks near campus. Other times when his workday would end earlier than hers, they'd share the adventures of their workday over a three-block walk from her office to the bookstore. They'd hang out at the café, scan books they'd never before thought about reading and share comments about their favorite authors: Delores Phillips, Marlon James, Zora Neal Hurston, and Chinua Achebe.

Majac realized how little he knew of Tessa—the woman. For once, he had taken Jaz's advice and not chased her like a conquest. Instead of being the aggressor, as in previously failed relationships, Majac let Tessa create the tempo of their courtship. Let her define the pace at which their relationship progressed. Things moved at her speed, her comfort level, as she learned about the grown man version of the boy she loved as a teen.

Every weekend throughout their courtship was an adventure. There was an early morning trip to tour his submarine. At least ten Saturday morning conversations over tea and muffins at the Spot of Love Tea House. One weekend he took her to the Jimi Hendrix Exhibit at the Museum of Pop Culture. Four Jamaican dinners while listening to live music at the Sound of Irie. A hiking trip at Mt. Rainier Park, and another through the trails at Port Madison Indian Reservation to the waterfalls. A day at the aquarium and another at the Poulsbo open-air mall. A weekend trip to

Portland and two to Tacoma. Dozens of kisses in public at parks, six field trips to bookstores and antique shops. And three live plays; The Wiz at Woodinville Repertory Theatre, The Color Purple featuring Fantasia at The Phoenix and Cats at Taproot. They marked the anniversary of their first kiss—Majac hadn't remembered it, but Tessa had written the date in her dairy—by having dinner at The Summit, the most expensive seafood restaurant in the region.

~

The alarm was set to away, so as soon as he pushed the door open, it started to beep every three seconds to indicate that someone had breached the only entrance authorized for entry without alarming the police and the security company. Once inside, he quickly shut off the alarm by entering his five-digit personal identification number into the white, four-inch square keypad before the thirty seconds of entry time expired and the system computer, physically located in northeast California, dispatched a signal to release the hounds on the intruder.

Excepting the basement, which Solomon had commandeered to extend his man cave, the layout in his house was the exact left-to-right inverse of Solomon's on the first and second floors.

"So this is it?" she asked when he removed the red blindfold.

"Yes," Majac said. "Welcome to my humble abode."

"May I look around?"

"Make yourself at home."

Though she figured it was a ploy to get into her panties, she decided to give him something to look forward to if he did come correct.

As she started her walk around the living room, she put in a little more sway than usual in her stride, making the hem of her silk blouse wash across her sculpted behind. She stopped at a picture hanging on the wall that adjoined the dining room.

"I love this painting."

"It's by a lady named Yvette Davies. She's an African-American artist, but she was raised in Germany."

"So it's an original?"

"Yes, I bought it one night at Jennifer Fleming's art auction."

"At her art gallery? You were there?" she asked. "Oh my goodness, I was supposed to go to that."

"I was there with Jaz," he said. "Or at least I started the night there with Jaz. That was until Crystal came and almost set it off in there with your sister. But that's a very long story—for another night."

"Boy, stop playing. You better tell me."

"If I'm going to relive that drama, I'm going to need some liquor." They laughed.

"But like I said, I'll tell you all about it. We've got time, you just got here."

Tessa let it go at that and returned to her tour. His place was neat and clean—as it should be after he spent all night cleaning. This was a good sign to her. There was no dust on the bookshelves. Shelves on both sides of the entryway that were actually occupied with books. The shelves on the left filled primarily with what appeared to be military journals, self-improvement and professional books. On the right, a mixture of fiction and non-fiction, African American authors, and to her surprise some of the classics like Crime and Punishment, and Moby Dick. "Well read are we?" she asked teasingly.

"Somewhat; though most are for show," he admitted.

She laughed.

Passing the bar cabinet and two-seat bistro table, she ran her hand along the red, felt cloth of the pool table. Majac followed her through that room and into the kitchen. The kitchen was full of stainless-steel appliances. Cookbooks had unbent spines. Dishes and cookware looked out-of-the-box new.

Her first take was that it did not get much use. A too-clean kitchen used to put on a show, but not actually cook. Beneath each sparkling clean gas burner was an aluminum inset to catch drippings. It reminded her of a habit she had learned from her homemaker mother, but hardly ever seen these days in kitchens belonging to anyone under fifty.

Majac took a baking dish out of the refrigerator, placed it in the oven and pressed a couple of buttons. An electric hum brought the oven to life.

Tessa paused to admire the decor as she traversed the corridor back to the foyer. To slow the passage of time, and to give herself a chance to absorb all of the personality in his belongings and decorations, she began to cut her steps. She was wearing black boots, blue jeans, and a silk, silver blouse with the word sushi spelled out on the front using food for letters. The way she looked, he was glad to have obsessed so much about what he was wearing. She made anything look good. He was confident his choice of outfit made him equally good looking.

She opened the door beneath the steps, turned on the light and stepped into the powder room. He watched her go in. She gazed up the wall to the ceiling, enjoying the warm, red and orange patterns of light from the copper sconces stenciled with Dinkha symbols funneled against the walls on either side of the vanity mirror. At the end of the corridor was a mirror outlined in cream and blue Iberian mosaic tiles, and she began to watch herself approach. His eyes involuntarily went to her butt when her back was safely turned. It was as if God himself went to Africa, dipped his hands into the most fertile mud possible and sculpted the most breathtaking butt the world had ever seen. It was glorious. Spectacular. And life affirming.

"What are you thinking about?" While lost in his daydream, she had finished observing herself in the mirror and had stopped in front of the living room.

"Nothing," he said. "Would you like some wine?"

"Actually, I'd like to eat. I didn't really think I was earlier, but now that I can smell the food cooking, I'm hungry."

"Then let me make you a plate." Majac took her hand and led her back into the kitchen. "Would you grab two salad and dinner plates from that cabinet?" He pointed to the glass-doored cabinet above the left of the sink.

"I picked a Riesling and a Torrontés to go with my curry shrimp. Unless you prefer a red instead?"

"Let's save the red for dessert," she said, placing the four plates on the kitchen island.

"I've never had a Torrontés, so whichever white you think is better, is good with me."

Majac removed tongs and silverware from two drawers by the sink then pulled a large glass bowl full of color from the fridge. He placed everything on the island and removed the saran wrap from atop the salad.

"Why don't you go ahead and open the wine. I'll plate the salads," Tessa said. She came over to the island and began making plates. As Tessa completed tossing salad on their plates, and setting their water glasses and utensils on the bistro table, Majac pulled out the bottle of Riesling from the fridge and returned to the island with a cork remover decorated with Asian art. If they finished it, he'd serve the Torrontés with the entrée.

"That's a beautiful wine opener. Where'd you get it?"

Majac looked at the fancy Asian trinket trying to recall in which country he'd found it. He stared for a brief moment at the picture of the beautifully garbed lady riding on the back of a blue dragon and recalled purchasing the opener in South Korea. "No real story behind it..."

"It doesn't matter," she interrupted. "Tell me anyway. I always enjoy just listening to you talk."

And so he did. As the buzzer on the oven timer indicated that the food had sufficiently warmed, he began to recount his extensive at-sea travels during his Western Pacific deployment as Executive Officer aboard USS WILLIAM PENN. Having popped the cork and poured the wine, he escorted Tessa, with salads in tow, to the bistro table. She sat the plates down and he pulled out her chair.

"Always the gentleman," she said, her smile beaming so hard that she showed all thirty-two of her teeth.

Majac sat and, after blessing the food, explained the exploits of life aboard a guided missile cruiser deployed to the western Pacific Ocean while Tessa ate her salad. His Oriental voyage included stories about the ship's visits to Thailand, Malaysia, Hong Kong and Singapore, then ended with exploits about their adventures in the Sea of Japan.

"We had finished our exercise with a Japanese carrier and were on our way to Gwangyang, South Korea," Majac said, "when we received a distress call from a merchant who reported being boarded by pirates."

"Like Pirates of the Caribbean movies, pirates?" Tessa asked.

"No," Majac said. "Like the Captain Phillips movie, pirates."

"For real?"

"Yes Baby," he laughed. "For real."

"Wow."

"Well, we radioed into the area commander and were told to proceed and help. When we reached the merchant ship, my Captain ordered me to prepare a boarding team. We called them on the radio, but they didn't answer. We circled the merchant and found this hundred-foot Orient Junk boat tied up along the aft port side. I took a dozen of my Sailors, armed with machine guns on one of our small boats and went over to the pirate ship. There was nobody onboard it when we got there, so we untied it from the merchant ship and let it float away."

"What happened to it?"

"When it was far enough away from the merchant, my Captain had the Gunner sink it with a 50-caliber machine gun."

"Really?"

Majac smiled. "Anyway; my team boarded the merchant ship. After some exchange of gunfire, we killed a couple of the pirates and the others surrendered."

The look on Tessa's face was one of pure amazement. She'd seen a hundred movies about Navy SEALs in foreign lands killing bad guys, ships at sea fighting wars, aliens, and all other sorts of stuff, including the Captain Phillips movie, but she'd never met anyone who'd done anything like that. Now she was dating one of them. Anxious to hear the rest of the story, she almost had to remind herself to blink and breathe.

"About six hours later, we finished the search for any other pirates that may have been hiding, accounted for all members of the merchant crew, arrested the pirates and took them back to our ship. Back on the PENN, our interpreter was able to determine that two of them understood English. Turns out, they were North Korean. The ship's brig was too small to hold all of the pirates, so we put them in the visiting riders berthing since we didn't have riders onboard."

"Wow, I cannot believe my ears. I never had a clue that you actually did crazy stuff like that. I just figured that was all make-believe stuff they put in movies to entertain us."

"This is where the story really gets interesting."

Tessa's eyes grew large in anticipation. They briefly went from him to her empty wine glass, then back to him. "Hold that thought."

Tessa hopped up, ran in the kitchen and returned with the wine bottle.

"After that, we got back underway to turn the pirates over to South Korean authorities. About a hundred miles off the South Korean coast on our way to Gwangyang we hailed a radio distress call.

Captain answered the call. A South Korean ship had hit a mine. We turned west, headed towards their coordinates. When we arrived, there were about thirty South Koreans floating in three life rafts"

Tessa sat in silence. She couldn't believe that her Majac was telling her first-hand accounts of these types of stories.

"So we put our boats in the water and got all of the South Koreans out of the life rafts. Now this is where it gets interesting. Because there are so many of them, and we only have the one berthing space open that none of our sailors are sleeping in, my Captain tells us to put everybody except their two South Korean officers into the same berthing with the North Korean pirates."

Tessa guffawed, almost spitting wine. "Aww shucks."

"About an hour before we got to Gwangyang, the Master-at-Arms calls away a security violation because the South Korean sailors and the North Korean pirates are fighting in berthing. Now the funny thing about it is that the Captain of the South Korean ship told my Captain to just lock the door and not let anybody out until the fighting stopped."

"What?" Tessa asked. "Stop lying."

"Honest Injun." Majac raised his right hand to the ceiling.

"But, since we had already reported the number of North Korean pirates we had captured, my Captain sent a security team into the berthing and handcuffed everybody—South and North Korean—once we got them to stop fighting."

"So you're telling me that your security team got thirty something foreigners to stop fighting just like that?"

"Not at first. But after the Chief Master-at-Arms went in there with firehoses and sprayed hundred-pound seawater at everybody moving, they all calmed down with the quickness."

"You mean like the videos of the cops spraying black people with fire hoses back in the 60's?"

"Exactly. Everybody up in there forgot all about fighting and was doing everything possible to keep from being blasted with that hose."

Tessa and Majac laughed until their stomachs hurt.

After the Wes Pac story was finished, Majac rinsed their wine glasses and refilled them with Torrontés before expertly plating the curry shrimp.

"Bravo, Sir." Tessa's face lit up as she clapped her approval. "We just might have to enter you on one of those Food Channel cooking challenge shows."

"Thank you, Pretty Lady." Majac set the plates down and took a bow.

Conversation throughout the remainder of dinner included the highlights of his tour in Japan, Texas and the nation's capital. Dinner talk was light; it was fun; and best of all she didn't ask about any of his romantic trysts with the women he'd loved and left along the way.

Her meeting the woman he'd brought home from San Diego was the worst day of her life. She didn't want to ruin dinner hearing anything about her or any others since her. After Celeste in San Diego, Majac barely put any effort into learning much about the few women he'd been with. His encounters were normally quick and furtive, with only the slightest attempt being made at meaningful conversation. Afterward, he pushed the experiences from his mind, not wanting to dwell on these breaches of willpower.

Tour de Casa Charles moved to the second floor after dinner. When they reached the top of the stairs, the open door led to the master bedroom with en-suite. Its windows overlooked the backyard. "That's where I sleep," Majac said, "but we'll come back there later. Let me show you what's down there." He took her by the arm and led her down the hall toward the front of the house. The middle room contained a Bow Flex weight machine, a wall-mounted television, rubber padding over hardwood flooring and an elliptical machine.

"This is where you get your work in," Tessa laughed, flexing her arm muscles around his hand.

"No," he said, cracking a grin. "Here is where I work out. Back there is where I put in work."

Tessa laughed—she thought his joke was funny—nevertheless, the thought that he'd put in work with someone other than her in the room she'd just left loomed large in the back of her mind.

The front bedroom was a second en-suite. Save the colorful area rug with matching curtains, a shelf-top stereo with detached speakers, a three-foot grandfather clock sitting atop an end table and a wooden card table with an empty chess board, the room was essentially bare.

"Do you play chess?" he asked.

"I know the ins and outs of the board," she said.

"You sound like you might be hard to beat?"

"I don't know about being hard to beat, but I definitely appreciate the strategy."

"Who taught you how to play?"

"I learned in college," she said. "But I remember being intrigued since middle school when I used to watch my grandfather play in the park with his buddies."

"Should I set up the board?"

"Maybe later. We've got time."

"So what do we do now?"

"Does that radio work? Or is it just for show?"

"Like everything else around here; it works."

"Good," she said. "'Cause I'd like to dance."

Majac turned the stereo on and switched channels until he found some good Chicago two-step music. He took her in his arms and escorted her to the middle of the floor. He began to show her that he could dance and she found herself glowing inside. It was nice. She looked him over as they danced through that and three more songs composed just for lovers to be close on a Saturday night. She found little thrills in every one of his good points. Those full, curly eyelashes. The lean, muscular arms and shoulders. The way his hands held her narrow waist and moved her about the room as if they'd been dancing together for years. When the dance music slowed to a ballad, she simply slowed her step and fell into his welcoming arms, her face buried in the crook of his neck, the scent of his body's aroma and the spice in his cologne practically lifting her off her feet.

Tessa stepped out of her heels and an hour passed as they danced like lovers do, shifting to the varying rhythms of ballads and step-dance songs, all the while joking, smiling, laughing and occasionally kissing.

When the DJ came on to wish his listeners a good night and announce the end of his show, Tessa asked, "What now?"

"Now…" Majac said the word more as a statement than a question. His hazel eyes—a perfect color match to hers—locked with Tessa's. He took a deep breath, blew air and started to say, "Now we…"

But he was stopped when Tessa leaned her body into him, pressed her lips against his and kissed him. Kissed him as time stood still. Kissed him as mountains moved. Kissed him as colors as bright as the northern lights shown behind his eyes.

Majac slipped his hands inside her silk blouse as they kissed, pressing his warm hands onto the smooth skin of her back. Held her tight and inhaled her, his tongue dancing a tango with hers. Held her and kissed her like she'd disappear if he dared to stop. For what seemed like an eternity, she abandoned any and all restraint and kissed her man. The only man she had ever genuinely loved. When that kiss ended, they both struggled to catch their breath. When their eyes met, their smiles turned into out loud laughter.

"So, what did you say was next?" Tessa asked.

Majac took her hand and led her toward his bedroom at the back of the house. He opened the door to a security pad on the wall just inside his bedroom door and set the alarm to stay.

Still holding her hand, he led her into the bathroom where he lit a Midsummer's Night candle by the head of the two-person Jacuzzi tub.

He turned on the faucet and poured a generous helping of the same scent bath salts into the solid stream of rapidly heating water. Then he walked her into the walk-in closet, offered her an oriental robe and told her to leave her clothes on the small chair as he walked out.

Just prior to his return to the bathroom, music began to flow from a speaker mounted in the ceiling. Majac came through the door garbed in an oriental robe of a different design, carrying a bottle of red wine and two glasses. He set the wine and glasses on the ledge of the tub, checked the water temperature and turned off the spigot to stop filling the tub.

"What-ever did I do to deserve you?" she asked.

"Just be the most amazing addition to my life," he said, pouring them each a glass of wine. "I'm the one who should be asking that question?"

"Oh, that's an easy answer for me," she said. "You're sexy, intelligent, kind and you make me feel like a queen—and I don't just mean sexually. That's what you did? Did I mention sexy?"

"You didn't say handsome. I hope I was able to appeal to your visual senses tonight."

"Not sure what you're talking about," she said. "Your visual...drives my senses...to overload! Your visual...is what my dreams are made of. Thank you for sharing." Tessa thought back to a memory of her mother telling her to *Leave those boys alone*. They don't want nothing except your special gift. Just wait and you'll find the man who truly deserves you— and your special gift. At that moment, Tessa knew that no man ever deserved her special gift more than the man standing before her. Tessa stepped into the hot tub, slipped off her robe and slid beneath the water. The bath salts smelled great, and the water was hot; but not as hot as she was going to make it once he joined her.

Majac awoke before her the next morning. He stared at Tessa's sleeping face and noticed that her eyebrows were going which and every way, and that the corners of her mouth were white.

"So, this is what it's like to wake up to her?" For a second he thought about Celeste's face in the morning and how she had looked as though she hadn't really slept the way most people do.

Celeste would wake up with no crust in her eyes, no bags under them, and her hair almost seemed to already be in place for the day.

He remembered thinking that marrying her would be like looking at an angel every morning. He would come to find out that how a woman looks in the morning isn't the most important thing when looking for a wife. It was a good thing though, because Bailey definitely didn't have that angelic morning glow, nor did Tessa. He couldn't remember anyone before Celeste having it either, which prompted him to the conclusion that it was a rare quality that he had better be able to live…without.

~~

Sunday afternoon they joined Leona, Solomon, Jennifer, Ayrikah and Luke Fleming at Safeco Field to watch the Mariner's game. The buffet in Luke's skybox suite was catered by a West Seattle restaurant called The Swinery. Their signature sandwich was a most epic bacon cheeseburger dubbed The Swinery Burger. Grilled over mesquite in the bare-bones Swinery courtyard, the Swinery burger is a true thing of beauty: one-third pound of house-ground Painted Hills beef with soft onions, covered in a mound of house-cured Swinery bacon cooked until softly crisp, then served with your choice of cheese, lettuce, tomatoes and house-made pickles on a soft, sweet brioche bun from Macarena Bakery with a side of their dynamite seasoned steak fries. If there was a better burger on the planet, Majac had never tasted it. And to top it off, some rookie named Kyle McPherson hit a walk-off double to win the game for the Mariners.

Sunday night he sat in her bedroom waiting for her to finish dressing. She was in her closet trying on the fifth pair of shoes that she didn't like with her outfit. She stepped out of her second shoe and backed into him. "What are you doing?' she asked.

"Watching you put your heels on." If thoughts could be criminal, the smile on his face would have gotten him ten years.

An implant fell out of Tessa's shoe. She forgot it was there. Majac saw it. She saw him see it. In all their time together, he didn't recall ever seeing it before. Her eyes locked on his. She was embarrassed.

While horseback riding on her twenty-third birthday, Tessa suffered a nasty fall. A snake on the trail scared her horse and he threw her. Before he ran off, the horse stepped on Tessa's back. Tessa was rushed to the hospital and into surgery. The surgeon fused two vertebrae together to relieve the pain. When she healed, her right hip set higher than her left causing her right heel to hover a half inch off the floor although her left foot was flat on the ground. After four months of continued pain, past when the doctor said the surgery site was fully healed, he prescribed her a heel implant. After wearing it for two weeks, she had completely stopped taking her pain medication. Now twelve years later, his finally noticing her imperfection brought her emotional anxiety far beyond any physical pain she'd felt in years.

"Anyway," Majac said. He leaned in and nibbled on her ear, trying to refocus their attention away from the prosthetic. "It's been a long day. If you're not up to it, we can just stay here and not go out and…" He hugged her, licked his lips, eyed her hungrily. "Either way, it's up to you."

After fighting through a fit of laughter brought on by his silliness and tickling, Tessa pushed him off of her. "As awesome as that sounds, Mister Charles, I'm good. We can go."

She placed the shoes in the shoebox and stood on her toes to put it back on the top shelf. He came up behind her, his hand finding the slit in her skirt. "Can I give you a lift?"

A smile stretched across her face as his hands slid up her thighs.

Her shoebox went back on the shelf, Majac's hands went inside her skirt, and the two of them went right there in the closet; before moving to the bathroom and finally to the bedroom. Just after midnight, a cocoon of lust enveloped them as they wrapped themselves in each other's arms.

On love stained sheets, their bodies melded together, him resting in her womb. Their cocoon was beautiful and colorful; his lips planted on hers as they breathed one air. Their hearts beating as one as they became more than a pair. In the morning, the love cocoon exploded, and broke open, allowing their bound bodies to fly onward, upward and out into the air.

At sunrise, Majac would tell her that he'd refund her the cost of the tickets for the Gospel Comedy show that they'd sinned their way through the night before. As they lay in bed, eyes transfixed on each other's souls like the universe grabbed them with both hands and told them welcome home, Tessa thought of how Ellen Page—the woman who sat in the cubicle next to hers back in Tuskegee—used to keep a stash of her favorite potato chips in her desk. When Tessa asked the story behind her obsession with the chips, Ellen told her story, ending with the moral, "Friends tell you what you want to hear to make you feel better. But best friends tell you the truth; then share their chips!" Every day since arriving in Seattle, Tessa realized more and more that she was with the one she loved. She called him Anton, but his friends called him Majac. And her Majac was the only man she loved enough to share her chips with.

14

Swinging and Singing

AN ENORMOUS FIVE-CAR GARAGE anchored the rear of the two-acre property that was home to Solomon and Majac's Hang Suite. The side-loading bay corresponding to Solomon's side housed his everyday car, a red Audi A8. A second side-loading bay, corresponding to Majac's side, housed Majac's Range Rover. Three end-loading bays opened onto a large concrete slab bordered by a hedge of purple Loropetalum that separated the yard and swimming pool from the massive parking pad. Two of these three bays each housed one of Solomon's antique cars; a 1968 Ford Mustang Shelby GT 428 Police Interceptor and a 1938 Avion Voisin C28 Cabriolet Saliot he called Fay Francis, in honor of his grandmother. On Sunday afternoons when there was zero chance of rain, he would bring this exquisite automobile out of the garage and grace the streets of Seattle with its beauty. He had won it in a high-stakes poker game. He bet his Rolex and the cash-strapped guy who called his bet was foolish enough to put the pink slip for the classic car on the table. Solo stopped gambling after that. Now the only poker he played was no stakes poker with the boys at Woody's.

Solo entered the third bay, which housed a hugger orange 1974 Ford Gran Torino. The car had a supple white leather interior and a white vinyl convertible rooftop. White, hockey-stick shaped stripes ran from the door handles to the front bumper and across the hood, outlining the grill. Backing the Torino out of the garage, he made a call. "Hello Ms. Pearson."

"Well hello, Doctor Alexandré," Leona checked her watch. "I didn't expect to hear from you tonight."

"Well if you'd prefer I didn't call."

149

"Come on now. You know that's not what I meant."

"Great. Well, I just finished with my last…umm…session for the day and thoughts of you crossed my mind, so I figured I'd call and see what trouble you might be getting into tonight."

"Unfortunately Dear Heart, I was just about out the door. My sister and I are going dancing, and, as soon as we hang up, I'll be on my way to her."

Solomon was silent for a moment. His original plans for the evening were to apply some touchup paint over the fresh plaster in the basement bathroom. But his adrenaline was in overdrive and painting was not going to satisfy him through the rest of the night. Leona put his mind at ease. Calmed him, comforted him, put him in a good mood, and after all of the day's drama, he needed her kind of cheering up.

"Hey Doc, are you still there?" Leona asked, exiting her walk-in closet. She'd wedged the phone between her ear and shoulder while she slid on her sling back pumps. Now she was dressed and ready to go. Before he would formulate an answer, her phone beeped signaling that she had another call. "Hey Doc, Tessa's on the other line. Give me a second."

As Leona clicked over to accept the other call, Solomon started the ignition and backed his car out of the garage. When her voice returned to the line he said, "Hey look, I won't hold you any longer. You enjoy your night with your sister and I'll check you out some other time."

"Well, aren't we quick to give up," she said.

"Excuse me?"

"It appears that my sister is a little under the weather and doesn't feel up to gallivanting with me tonight; much less up for dancing."

"Oh really?"

"Yes, really. Soooo…" She held onto the word, dragging it out playfully. "If you're still in the mood for company, my calendar has miraculously just become wide open for the night."

"Great," he said, zooming down the driveway. "I'll pick you up in fifteen minutes."

"Better make it twenty," she said. "A girl's gotta freshen up."

"But I thought you said you were ready to…"

"Not to go out with you, Silly." She laughed. "When will men learn?"

A dial tone pre-empted his response.

Leona wore a silk muga shawl that beamed like Mylar in the bright lights of downtown Seattle. Her blouse was tied at the bottom, revealing her navel ring. Silver bracelets jingled every time she moved her left arm. Her cropped crown owned the hue of a brown penny. Her light skirt hung wide about her hips and ended five inches above her feet. Feet adorned in straps of brown, tan, red and green atop comfortable looking pumps with almost flat soles made for dancing. Two weeks had passed since she'd last shared his company, and in that time with all the work at the dance studio and entertaining a client each weekend, she had little time to think of him. Much less call or be with him.

As was her preference, she'd tucked her hand in the crook of his elbow as they exited the parking garage. She'd forgotten how taut his muscles were. How gently weathered his skin. He adjusted his hat and again she inhaled his intoxicating scent. Pepper, musk and citrus wafted about his collar and mixed nicely with the faint breeze off the Sound. It was a good, clean, strong smell that evaporated off him like the dew off a morning glory. She leaned her head on his shoulder and smiled.

"Thank you again for fitting me in last minute," Solomon said, the fluffy ball of Leona's hair brushing against his neck. "I really needed a break tonight."

"You're welcome," she said as they reached the front door of Club Me. "Mmmm?"

"What?" he asked.

"Just enjoying your cologne," she said.

"Ummm," he started hesitantly. "I'm not wearing any. I got caught up looking for my watch and forgot to put some on. I did shower though, so I hope I don't smell too bad."

"If you aren't wearing any, then I need to bottle you."

They laughed.

"On second thought, that may be a scent I want to keep for myself. Don't need a bunch of hags hanging all over you."

Inside the club they sat at the bar through the first round of drinks before venturing out to find a table. Leona sipped on vodka infused cognac. Solomon's preference was bourbon—on the rocks. Before the night would end, his bourbon would make an Old Fashioned. Surprisingly enough, the music was soft enough that they could talk without having to yell at one another across the table.

"Are you all right?" she asked.

"Yeah, I'm fine. Why?"

"You look a little pre-occupied. As if you're expecting someone."

"Nope," Solomon said with a glint of naughtiness in his eye, "Not looking forward to seeing anybody but you."

They sat for a while watching a handful of couples, and that many more singles, rhythmically dance their way through a half dozen of the more popular line dance songs.

"I have a question for you, Leona."

"Fire away."

"If you could travel anywhere on this big ball of dirt and water, where would you go?" He asked in that easy, confidant way about him that made her melt inside.

"Well, Doctor Alexandré..." Leona exhaled loudly, stopped talking and considered if the good doctor's question was meant to psychoanalyze her. She took a long swallow of her drink to calm her angst. Calmed a bit, she then tried to conjure up an honest response to what was, for now, an innocuous question in a meaningless conversation. "If I could choose a place, it would have to be far away from work. I'd like to go somewhere outside the states. Someplace with no cell service and no computers.

"Somewhere where one day is just like the next and tomorrow is just like yesterday. Somewhere where I could lose all sense of time and absolutely relax. Someplace where my only concerns are what I want to eat today and is the thunderstorm going to stop me from getting in the water. Oh, and I'm talking about a really reclusive spot, no concrete, no shoes, just sand and palm trees. A place where nobody can invade my privacy. Somewhere I can go with somebody who would hold me the right way. Hold me close while we watched the day fade into night. Where we'd talk and he'd listen earnestly as time passed by unnoticed and that same night faded back into day." She smiled and blushed at how carefully he watched her when she spoke.

"So, if such an opportunity came about, do you think the studio could do without you for a week?"

"They better."

The music shifted from line dances to a couple popular songs while the house band set up onstage. The lead singer introduced the members of the band while they warmed up with some unrecognizable scattering of notes and sounds. Their introductions concluded; the lead singer invited anyone that felt the groove to join them on the dance floor. The first series of tunes was an easily recognizable cover compilation of a popular nineties' girl group. The drink and the popular tunes put Leona in her zone.

"Come on Doc. I'm ready to dance." She grabbed his wrists and pulled Solomon off his stool. The radiance of her smile almost blinded him. She repeated beg my pardon and excuse me as she politely, but firmly, pushed her way to the middle of the dance floor. There, she took his hand, wrapped his arm around her waist and guided him through a series of intricate steps. She turned him this way and then the other. She spun him out on the length of his arm, a fly at the end of a fisherman's pole, then rapidly reeled him back in. The band played one upbeat tune after another and Solomon worked to follow the steps.

In the back of his mind, Leona tossing him around on the dance floor was the most fun he'd had in a while.

The combination of steps wasn't difficult; just step together, step back, then step front. But he had to concentrate. The moment he took his mind off what he was doing to look at another couple and see how they moved together or how they changed up a step, he got confused and stumbled. And then, just as he was getting comfortable, just as he reached the point where he could anticipate Leona's next move, the band threw him a curve ball and downshifted to something slow. It was a sweet lilting melody with an old timey feel. The guitar whined as the leader sang in Spanish.

"This here is my song," Solomon hummed softly. Now he held her hand firmly, pulled her close. So close, that she felt where the front of his shirt was damp from their dancing. So close, she felt his breath on her ear and neck as he exhaled and she smelled his citrus muskiness. But every time Solo moved one way, she moved the other.

"Sorry," Leona said for bumping into him. "Sorry," she said for stepping on his feet.

"It's all right, just relax."

She smiled.

"Besides, aren't you the dance instructor? Or don't they teach women how to follow when slow-dragging up in that fancy dance studio of yours?"

She blushed. "We don't teach slow-dragging." Leona's back and shoulders tightened. She started to sweat. Over and over, she kept messing up and apologizing until finally Solomon pulled his cheek away from hers just enough to regard her.

He caressed her face and gave her a long careful stare. Then, in a calm steady voice said, "Listen to me Miss Pearson, I know you're a strong woman. You're a dance professional and believe me when I say I appreciate it. I really do. But when it comes to this right here," his eyes fell to the lack of space between them, "you need to relax and let me lead."

Leona sighed hard. Her heart stopped. *Let him lead. Let him lead.* Yes. She could do that. For once in her life. Okay, for ten minutes at least. It'd been years, twelve to be exact, since the last time she slow danced with a man in earnest. Her partners at the studio could lead her through a salsa, a merengue, a waltz or even a tango with the greatest of ease, but when it came to dancing with a man who she might consider giving her heart, her boat stayed far away from those shores.

"Trust me, Pearson." Solomon slowly started back into the groove. "I got you."

With those words, Leona's rigid dance instructor mentality melted away. She let go and succumbed to the strong arms of the tall, dark and handsome psychologist whose arms—she wished—would never let her go. "Okay," Leona said, "I'll try."

Solomon pulled Leona close again. Her shoulders relaxed. He pulled her closer still so that his face was right against hers. His chest right against hers. And she felt the vibration of his quiet humming. *Giving him something he can fee-eel. To let him know this love is real. This love is real.* The band played two long slow songs in a row and she tried to let go of everything except the sound of the music and the feel of Solomon's body—solid and strong—moving with hers.

At the conclusion of the slow music, most of the crowd left the floor. The band broke into a slightly quicker tune as anonymous and seductive as an Argentinian samba. For a dance instructor, the tune was her nirvana. Leona threw herself into the rhythm. Solomon tried to follow. The now only half-full floor allowed plenty of room for her to dance. Leona, feeling extravagant and perhaps empowered by their conversation, sprung and moved as if she were a ballerina and there was no one else in the practice room training at midnight on the eve of opening night before her first lead performance. Rugged hips rolled inside his baggy jeans. Solomon was a satellite, unable to match her moves step for step. At best, he was a tall, dark comet caught in her gravitational wake, drifting close in her tail, but never getting close enough to actually be considered her dance partner.

An energetic, muscular, gay-looking man in a too-tight European shirt started to orbit around them, breaking the gravitational pull.

Although Solomon found himself floating to the far reaches of Leona's constellation, he was not ready to allow some other man to enter her atmosphere. With a scowl and balled up fists, Solomon intimated to the too-tight European shirt guy that if he came closer, there would be trouble.

European shirt guy pursed his lips, snapped his fingers and moved on.

The cinnamon woman with the imperfection on her cheek danced like she was one of the greats, moving in intimate harmony with the music as if the rhythm was her lover. Solomon, a voyeur trapped on a window ledge, studied the graceful movements of Leona's body wishing he were the ebb to her flow.

When the set was over and the band took a break, he led her back to their table. He sipped his last Old Fashioned of the evening. He later found out the name of the track from their last dance was titled *Possibilities.*

<hr>

A half-hour later, they parked curb in front of Solo's duplex. Tucked in among the trees, the house hovered in darkness. Two of its four windows emitted squares of soft yellow light. When she stepped onto the freshly stained porch of wide cypress planks, she caught the fragrance of newly bloomed camellias. Red double doors with frosted glass panes sat like flared nostrils centered on the first floor. On either side of the doors, teardrop lanterns flickered quietly. Pale green shutters flanked the soft yellow windows on both sides of the split porch. The door to the left-hand unit an exact match to the right.

Solomon owned both sides, living in one and using the other as a rental property. Leona wondered if Solomon picked the color pallets himself. Or if this was the decorative eye of his deceased-wife.

A kaleidoscope of well-tended, potted plants lined the left-hand porch. On the right-hand porch, a money tree rose from an antique kettle. Three almost dead hydrangeas were scattered about that side. Solomon's porch was on the left.

She felt a pleasing sense of order, and couldn't help marvel in the belief that if this man could take such good care of his property, he would take even greater care of his woman.

When he realized that his house key was where he always left it— in the glove box of his Audi, in the garage at the back of the house; he'd driven the Torino that night—Solomon held onto Leona's hand and made his way down the steps. He followed the stone paver path around the side of the house. But rather than lead her back to the garage, he remembered the hollowed-out fake rock by his back porch where he kept a spare house key. Stopping to retrieve the key he said, "I planted a couple of flower beds along the walk to help make it more inviting. Out back by the garage, you can't see them now of course, by the base of those mimosa trees are a bunch of tulips that have just started to bloom."

She squinted across the dark oasis trying to catch a glimpse of color. Moonlight shimmered on a deep, lush carpet of lawn. Blades of grass rustled softly. Flowed like waves against a gentle breeze. As Solomon rummaged through a small flowerbed, Leona stepped up onto the back porch which, like the front, stretched the width of the house. It was quiet. Peaceful. A fan sat still on his half, another spun slowly on the far half. Another flickering gas light, softly illuminated Leona's face.

"Got it." The steps creaked under Solomon's weight. In the yellow light, the mild wrinkles around Solomon's eyes were more pronounced.

Leona stepped to the side to allow him to open the door. The faint glow shone his eyes a darker brown than she remembered.

Just then, a noise back by the garage captured their attention.

"Stay here," Solomon said. "I'll be right back."

Leona pulled her cell from her clutch. "I'll call the police."

Solomon reached the side of the garage and turned the corner. Immediately he noticed the latch on the wooden gate to the alley was open. The purr of an engine could be heard outside the rear parking pad where, first thing that morning, he and Majac had washed their cars.

Trespassers had pried open the window to the bay where Solo kept his Audi. One of them was inside, and another was standing lookout near the cracked open window. Solo picked up a loose two-by-four piece of wood he placed under his tires so his car wouldn't roll. He approached quietly in the dark of the moon. Without a word, he struck the lookout in the shins like he was teeing off with a five wood at the Masters.

The guy yelled as the pain exploded from his leg. Instinctively, he swung out in the direction opposite the alley, catching Solomon in the head with the corner of his high school ring. Immediately after, pain quickly spread throughout his body as a second and third blow met his arm and back. At the sound of his lookout screaming, the guy inside quickly climbed through the window.

Having backed away from the lookout, now writhing on the ground, Solomon caught the trespasser with a blow to the midsection as he landed outside. From the alley, three more trespassers exited the parked car and came to their rescue. Solomon pushed the window shut and backed around to the side of the garage, disappearing into the shadows. Shielded by the darkness of the hedge that separated the pavement from his lawn, Solomon crouched down waiting for a fight that never came.

After looking around in the darkness, the three from the car pulled the two trespassers back into the alley. A moment later, the five of them sped away without getting Majac's or any of Solo's cars. At the sound of the engine accelerating, Solomon, board in hand, rushed into the alley. A serious car buff, Solo easily recognized the body style of the Dodge Charger. He stood for a moment longer, committing to memory four of the six numbers he was able to identify in the Washington license plate.

Leona finished her phone call with the police inside the house.

She directed Solomon to a kitchen chair and administered first aid to clean up the scratch on his forehead. As he explained what happened outside, she noticed a door cracked ajar in the corner of the kitchen opposite the door to the backyard. "So, what's behind door number two?"

They laughed.

"That would be Solomon's Sanctuary." Solomon smiled.

"Sanctuary?"

"Yes. That's where I go to relax."

"Can I see or is that too private a space to share?"

Rising from the kitchen chair, he checked the lock on the back door and grabbed an ice pack to cool the hot surge of pain flowing through his temple. He opened the door fully and led Leona down a staircase into the basement granting her access to his most elite of man caves. First to grab her attention was a poker table that seated six. Above it on a wall in the corner, was a dart board hidden within a wooden enclosure. Leather-backed armchairs surrounded. A deep red cloth and leather pockets adorned a mahogany, regulation-sized pool table. Washington State University logo pools balls were racked ready for play. Hanging above the elegant pool table was a three-bulb Tiffany chandelier. As she stepped closer, she could make out the word Psyche etched in a cryptic font amidst a rainbow of muted colors.

Two-dozen shot glasses with phrases like *Portland—The Rose City, I left my heart in San Francisco, Disneyland-The World's Greatest Amusement park, Tijuana, Welcome to the Grand Canyon, What happens in Vegas*...and many more sat perched on a single-plank shelf above a wet bar hidden beneath the stairs. Awards and pictures rested atop the twin four-shelf cabinets flanking a sixty-five-inch 4K television. Solomon headed toward the left hand cabinet which held beer glasses shaped for stouts, pilsners, lagers and ales on the top shelf, both red and white wine glasses resided on the second shelf while cocktail glasses, highballs and brandy snifters made their home on the bottom shelf.

The right-hand cabinet served as his liquor cabinet. Distinguished ambassadors from the world of spirits such as Elijah Craig, Johnny Walker, Jack Daniels, Chivas Regal, Captain Morgan and Jose Cuervo flew their colors among friendly neighbors of both Irish and Canadian descent, islanders from the Caribbean and elderly statesmen from England, Scotland, France and Italy. White wines and blushes made their home in the wine cooler beneath the liquor cabinet while a brewery of assorted beers resided in the fridge beneath the beer glasses.

The wall of television and alcohol was the centerpiece of the room. Down a hallway to the left was a bathroom with a shower that adjoined a bedroom in case his Partnas became too inebriated to make their way home. Through a door to the right beneath the rental half of the duplex was an addition to his man cave. He sealed off the rear half of the rental property side from the upstairs. The front of the adjoining basement housed a wine cellar capable of holding 1000 bottles of his favorite vintages.

The five-foot area on either side of the entry housed a foyer separating the wine cellar from a small powder room and a cigar parlor. The cigar parlor was complete with an eight-foot-wide, floor-to-ceiling humidor, negative ventilation that energized on the same circuit as the motion sensing lights and two six-seat sectionals that sat around wooden tables topped with butane lighters, cigar cutters and ashtrays. This was his man cave, and other than his mother and deceased wife, she was the first woman to receive an invitation to breech its hallowed walls.

Solomon maneuvered Leona back out near the pool table. Standing at her side, he placed one palm on the table, the other on the small of her back and leaned into her.

Her mouth fell open instinctively as his lips approached hers. She tilted her head back slightly and shifted her body to a comfortable position so that she could enjoy the duration of his kiss. At that moment, all her thoughts of chastity and fidelity floated away. If she had ever considered making a man wait to explore her pleasures, this was not the time. She wanted to make him pursue her, but the hunter had become the hunted.

Solomon retracted his tongue and pulled his lips from hers.

This chase excited them both.

"Oh don't go now," she said craning her neck to pursue his retreating lips. She sighed when he finally stood up straight. It had felt the same as the kiss they shared earlier. So uncontrived. So unforced. Like it was his inherent right to kiss her whenever he felt so inclined. And she had to admit, she felt he did. Again he flashed that smile, and again she felt moist.

After they toured the man cave, he led her up the basement stairs, through the kitchen and into the spacious open living area. An elegant, antique clock—a wedding gift from his Aunt Carolyn who had died the year before—ticked ever so softly. With every step, Leona felt the stress of the outside world fall further and further away. In the foyer, she marveled at the sepia portraits of his ancestors. When she stopped before a set of French doors, a floorboard creaked underfoot.

Solomon mused, "Sounds like you found my burglar alarm."

"More like your...Booty Call escaping...alarm?" She turned to face him, placing her hands on the French door handles behind her back.

"Busted." He raised his hands in jest.

They laughed.

"What's behind door number three?" She nodded toward French doors.

"My quiet place."

"May I?"

He stepped inside her personal bubble. Eased his hands past her waist, bringing his to rest on top of hers. When she relented, a gentle push of the door handles granted her entrance into his sacred place.

Leona pecked his lips before entering. "Thank you Sweetie."

Inside, a fireplace anchored the outer wall. A poster-sized picture of a beautiful woman hung above the mantel. Long, jet-black hair covered one of her deep-set, almond-shaped eyes. Eyes that floated above the blue powder accenting her high cheek bones. Leona marveled wordlessly at her beautiful Asian features; that was, until the sound of Solomon clearing his throat released her from her trance.

"Yes, that's my wife," he said before she shaped her mouth to ask.

"Her name is Mareschelle Betancourt Alexandré. I called her Schelle."

"She's...very lovely," Leona said respectfully.

"Thank you." A beat later, he reached for her hand.

She accepted, giving a gentle squeeze in the silence between them as she continued to surveil the room. "What, no television?"

"Not on this floor."

"No TV? Oh my God. My niece would fall apart without TV."

He turned, gently pulling her toward the hallway.

She wasn't ready to leave his quiet place just yet, so she stood steadfast, turning her attention toward the wall adjacent the dining room. "And they are?"

"They're my advisors." He was referring to the framed photos hung on the wall like a shrine to every intriguing black person in American history.

Leona marveled at the historically significant photos of politicians, authors and social activists the likes of Thurgood Marshall, Malcolm X, Maxine Waters, Martin Luther King Jr., Marcus Garvey, Langston Hughes Frederick Douglas, Mary McLeod Bethune, Huey Newton, Medgar Evers, Barack Obama, Louis Farrakhan, Madam C.J. Walker, and Andrew Young. Socially conscious musicians, athletes, and comedians included Jackie Robinson, Dick Gregory, Jim Brown, Tommie Smith and John Carlos, Miles Davis, Colin Kaepernick, Muhammad Ali, Josephine Baker, Arthur Ashe and Redd Foxx. "Is that?" She paused as her tongue and brain seemed momentarily disconnected. "Is that Richard Pryor?"

"Yeah, that's Rich."

"I love Richard Pryor!"

"Me too." Solomon wrapped his arms around her waist. "Rich was one of the deepest, most insightfully honest people I've ever heard speak. Everybody is familiar with his raucous comedy, but most forget that he was one of the most inspirational activists of the 1970's."

"Richard Pryor. An Advisor?" Leona bemused. "Ain't that a kick in the head."

"Not just him, but all of them have provided me some inspiration. When I need some guidance or need to cogitate life's conundrums," Solomon continued, "I come in here and pray on it. I sit and think things through. I look up at those faces and they help me figure out how to proceed. I spent a lot of long nights in this room after my wife died."

Leona shifted in his arms so she was facing him. Turned him away from his wife's portrait. "Are they telling you anything right now?"

"They're saying…" Solomon looked over the crown of her head at the wall of influential men and women. He fixed his eyes on Redd Foxx and smiled. "They're saying, 'She gave you a second chance, now don't blow it this time; You Big Dummy.'"

"They must be reading my mind," she whispered.

Solomon went to the front window to turn off the table lamps.

"What about now?" Leona shifted her weight nervously. "They have any other suggestions?"

He regarded her intently. "They're suggesting that I invite you to see the second floor."

A set of eight stairs elevated from the area separating the dining room from the living area, met a landing, turned and led up eight more to the middle of the upstairs hallway. Three en-suite bedrooms were on the second floor. At the top of the stairs was the actual guest room. His master— the bedroom he had shared with Schelle—occupied the rear of the house. Leading her into the guest room at the front of the house, where he'd slept almost every night since his wife's death, Solomon gestured toward a wooden armchair with white cushions. She sat. He knelt before her. Eased her shoes off. Placed them beneath the chair then started kissing her neck.

Leona caressed his bald head. She exhaled and surveilled the room. On a table next to her, she saw a lone piece of jewelry sitting in a bowl. She fished out what appeared to be a men's wedding band, then held it up to the light before slipping it onto her middle finger. She asked. "Is this your wedding ring?"

"Yes."

"Do you still wear it, or does it just stay here collecting dust?"

"Yes, I still wear it. That is except when I'm working out." He rubbed his swollen ring finger, indented from where the ring had pressed into it. He'd left the ring off after he finished cutting the grass earlier. Unlike his, Schelle's ring was on a chain around his neck to always remind him of her. Though in truth, despite the pictures of her around the house, there were times when he struggled to remember expressions on Schelle's face. Those times are when he'd opened the door to her closet, which he always kept shut, and ventured inside where he'd more easily recall her scent in her clothes. He'd sit in there and remember the easy sound of her laugh, and the feeling of being with her in the kitchen as she cooked Sunday breakfast before church. He remembered Marvin Gaye blasting from the ceiling speakers. The handwritten recipe that she'd transcribed from a phone conversation with his mother now splattered with food particles and oil. The counters overrun with flour, eggs and spilled milk as his culinarily challenged wife did her best to prepare his favorite breakfast—cinnamon pancakes. "Okay," Solomon extended an open palm to her. "May I have it back?"

"It's a beautiful ring." Leona twisted away playfully, still holding the ring. "What is it, one-and-a-half; no, gotta be at least two full carats?"

"Please?" Solomon begged stoically.

"I won't lose it," Leona teased. "I just want to hold it for a few."

"Please give it back." The hint of urgency in his voice alarmed her. Leona slid the too-big ring off her finger. Jiggled it in her cupped hands. "Un tel enfant gâté," Leona said under her breath, calling him a spoiled brat in French.

Wary of alarming her, Solomon thought to grab it, but stopped himself. He exhaled and silently counted to ten. She hadn't done anything wrong; he just wasn't comfortable with another woman handling his wedding ring. His heart hurt. He felt like he'd betrayed Schelle when he saw that Leona had placed the ring on her finger.

She closed her fists and pulled her hands upward, cupping them between her breasts.

Solomon took a calming breath and offered his hand. Leona put her chin to her hands then relinquished the ring back to its rightful owner. Solomon slid the ring onto the third finger of his right hand to avoid a repeat performance later in the evening.

Leona exhaled as her eyes travelled about the room. A warm but dim light emitted from the cinnamon sugar scented wax smelters burning on the nightstands flanking the bed. Her eyes stopped on a floor-to-ceiling bookcase standing between the windows overlooking the front of the house.

Almost three hundred books lined the shelves.

Solomon turned his gaze to follow hers.

"I bet you know all of those titles by heart?"

"Most of them."

"Well?"

"Well what?"

"So have you read all of them?"

"I've read about a hundred or so."

"Which is your favorite?"

Solomon paused. He studied her face to see if she was kidding. Kidding or not, now was not the time to talk about the books on his shelf. If she wanted to read; if she wanted him to read to her; she would have to wait until after he settled himself. After she had weathered his storm and ebbed his tide. After she had calmed the beast rising within. He ran his finger along her shoulder and kissed her neck. "I'm not interested in those books right now."

When she felt the heat of his stare focusing on the scar on her face, she held her breath and waited with taut nerves for him to say something about her imperfection. Something predictable and disappointing. Something she had heard before from crass men who weren't intelligent enough to recognize her sensitivity toward her blemish. An intimate situation was the wrong time to remind her of it; but if he did, she was ready to defend herself, ready to pounce if he insulted her, and ultimately, ready to leave.

But he didn't insult her. Instead he leaned closer, gently caressed her point of trauma with his thumb and said, "Tell me a story, Red Velvet."

Red Velvet complimented her. Surprised her. Brought a smile to her face. She smiled, kissed him on the forehead. "There are so many things I'd like to tell you," she said softly, "but I'm afraid I don't know how."

He unbuttoned her blouse. Eased it open and revealed her pretty bra.

"'Cause there's a possibility..." She lifted his head until their eyes met. "That you'll look at me differently."

"Not possible." He smiled. Kissed her collar bone. "Since the first time you spoke my name, I've thought about what it would be like having you in my life."

"I was in a bad place emotionally when we met. I wasn't interested in meeting you that night. I was only there because your friend promised me a great meal."

"Now that you've gotten to know me?" Now he tongued her earlobe.

Leona pressed her hands on his chest. Felt his strong, steady heartbeat. Pushed him away to make him stop kissing that sensitive spot on her ear.

"Now that you've entered my life, the world looks so brand new to me," he said. "I'm not one to believe in destiny, but I know I've changed. The sultry way you called me Doctor; I knew things in my life were destined to change."

"I want to get to know you Solomon Alexandré. But I'm scared that you'll compare me to your dead wife. To be honest, I'm terrified of you not loving me."

"Shhhh." He teased her with quick, closed-mouth kisses. Ran his hand over one of her satin-veiled breasts. Whispered, "So lovely."

She pulled him in for a kiss.

He reached behind her and unzipped her skirt.

She placed her palms on his shoulders, lifted her hips from the chair and cooed as he eased her skirt down to the floor. "I take it you want to get to know all of me?"

"Through all of the ups and downs," he said caressing her thighs. The sound of her pleasure was music to his ears.

She arched her back. Let her legs roam. Leaned her head against the wall and closed her eyes. "And you won't stray?"

Solomon stretched his hand across her taut belly. Traced the sateen remnants of stretch marks beneath her navel. "Gorgeous." He leaned closer still. "I really like." He tilted his head and traced those silky, maternal beauty marks with his tongue. Then ran his tongue over the imperfection where her kidney used to be.

Leona had been caught in the wrong place during a prison riot. Stabbed by the jagged edge of another prisoner's rusty knife. A surgeon tried to save her right kidney, but the lacerations caused so much damage that it had to be removed. And despite that scar, she'd lived a healthy life with just one kidney.

Fearful he'd be repulsed, she tensed when he fingered the edges of the scar above her right hip.

But he wasn't. Instead, he wondered what caused a size-six woman with no children to have stretch marks.

Leona began to dance on magic legs. "Solomon!" was all she could say as tiny bolts of lightning surged through her. Her words didn't matter, because he wouldn't have heard her if she had been able to string the words together.

He lifted her from the comfort of the plush chair. Turned off the ceiling light. Carried her to the bed. Gently laid her on cool sheets then removed the remainder of her clothes.

Cinnamon scented candles on the nightstands emitted a dim glow of light.

He stroked her hair tenderly. She cried and he kissed away her tears. She held him and touched him beneath the sheets. Allowed him to hold and touch her the same way she wanted to hold and touch him. They made sensual, passionate love amid flickering candlelight. Their silhouettes dancing The Forbidden Dance on the walls.

Leona Pearson fell into euphoria as Solomon Alexandré made love in his house—to a woman who was not his wife—for the first time in almost three years. His large, soft hands—hands that earlier tapped off-beat at his sides unable to match her rhythm on the dance floor—now stroked her body in perfect syncopation. And as they enacted this unspoken declaration of their feelings, Leona absorbed his every movement, his every change in facial expression, as though she was translating his actions into words.

He opened his eyes and a look of fear appeared on her face. Solomon paused, despaired at recognizing her fear; wondered about conquering it. Then wondered if what he saw was a fear inside Leona; or a fear reflecting within himself?

But what was he truly afraid of?

Was it the fear of…making a commitment?

The fear of…taking a vow?

Or simply the fear of…falling in love again?

15

Cabin Fever

LIGHTNING FLASHED. THE SKY GRUMBLED. Dark clouds masked the afternoon sunlight. Tessa stole peeks of Majac as he drove his Range Rover Sport north on I-5 at a steady click on a rainy Thursday afternoon. In the months following her move to Seattle, she and Anton had fallen into an inseparable groove. She there for him. Him there for her. They spent all of their free time together—most evenings and every weekend, except for those interrupted by a number of underways on the ship. She thought about the Saturday night she sat on a barstool at the counter in his kitchen watching him prepare their meal, a song on his lips, dish towel on his shoulder, and a glass of wine never more than an arm's length away. Some evenings she cooked for him, but most he cooked for her. They went to concerts, countless nights of dancing, to ball games and she took him on a trip to Mt. Rainier— with this time her acting as the tour guide.

Because he reported to his ship early and had not taken many, if any, days off work since reporting, Majac had accumulated a large amount of leave. Now, several months since they started dating, Tessa managed to finally convince him to take a well-deserved weekend getaway during an extended inport period. Solomon told him about a great spot in Vancouver where he and Désirée were planning a Marriage Quest therapy retreat the following summer, so he called and made reservations for the weekend.

"**Charles, party of two**" Majac exclaimed proudly.

167

Pierre, the desk attendant at the Tofino Resort, beamed a practiced smile and greeted them with, "I trust your ride from Seattle was enjoyable Mister Charles?" He was thin, wiry, and although he appeared to be in his late forties, his shrill voice was that of a teenage boy battling puberty. "Everyone from down your way always enjoys the scenic drive."

Majac and Tessa smiled their concurrence despite missing the scenery for the storm.

Pierre took Majac's credit card and driver's license. He swiped the card then returned them both. "If you're hungry, our restaurant is serving a wonderful Veal Marsala tonight."

"No thank you," Majac replied. "We stopped and ate along the way."

"Very well Sir." Pierre sized up Tessa with contemptuous eyes. The eyes of a jealous woman eyeing another woman's man. He turned his head to Majac, but kept his gaze locked on Tessa. "One room key or two?"

"One will be fine." Tessa bared her teeth in an over-exaggerated grin. Despite an instinct that told her to cuss the scrawny man out, she held her tongue and let him finish his task.

Her focus was on the man standing next to her in a walnut-brown suit with a bright white shirt. Mister Anton Charles: the first man she had ever kissed. The first man she had ever loved. The man to whom she had surrendered her virginity a month before he went and joined the Navy.

Underneath that suit was the body of a man ten years his junior. She noticed he had gained a bit of weight, and although still slender, he was as muscular as a prize pit bull. A body hardened by continuous exercise in preparation to one day be restored to full submarine duty. Flecks of gray in hair that, in another life, sported a high-top fade. A style that was all the rage during his junior and senior years in high school. Tessa recognized him as her yin. Her heart fluttered. She wrapped her arm tightly within his and smiled. "We won't be far enough away from each other to need two." She knew she couldn't persecute people for their thoughts. But if she wasn't so anxious to get to their cottage and start the weekend, she would've read puny Pierre right there in the lobby.

Their cabin was situated at the end of a secluded driveway, a mile or so off the circular road entering the resort. Twenty yards off the back porch was a small lake. Tessa inhaled the crisp mountain air. Marveled at their little slice of tranquility. The clouds parted just enough to let her catch glimpses of the sun setting over the lake. This made the scene even more breathtakingly serene. "This is so peaceful."

Majac grabbed their smaller bags and walked her to the cabin. Its windows were dingy and opaque, allowing little to no view in or out. When they stepped inside the large, yet cozy, one-bedroom cottage surrounded by trees, the interior was rustic and clean.

Tessa saw what she had long imagined as the perfect setting for unfettered romance. No television, no computer; no communication devices of any kind with the outside world. The thought of being secluded with the man she'd dreamed of being with for almost twenty years finally set in.

Majac turned on the overhead light and rested their bags on the dresser. Tucked away in the corner, was a telephone with no numbers or buttons to dial. Tessa picked up the receiver and after a few seconds came the voice of the middle-aged, pubescent attendant, Pierre. "How can I help you sir?" Her eyes opened wide with surprise before she hung up without speaking.

Tessa escaped the confines of her shoes. Waving a butane lighter like a fairy in a storybook novel, she glided barefoot across Brazilian hardwood floors, lighting numerous candles of various shapes and sizes scattered about the room. After she turned off the overhead light, she made her way back to Majac who stood smiling in the center of the now candlelit room.

"Have a seat by the fire, I'll be right back." He disappeared into the bedroom with their bags. A minute later he reappeared and headed to the kitchen in the far-left corner of the room. A bottle of champagne sat in a clear acrylic chiller atop the counter. Majac looked inside the small fridge. Carrying two glasses of champagne splashed with mango juice in one hand and a platter covered by a silver dome in the other, Majac returned from the tiny kitchen and placed his bounty on the small, oval coffee table in front of the fire. He guided Tessa down onto one of the fluffy floor pillows. She sat and crossed her legs beneath her. From behind, he spread her napkin across her lap.

When the dome came off the platter, a generous ensemble of fruits and lavish desserts lie beneath. He scooped a finger full of the decadent filling from one of the cannoli and slowly glided that finger into her mouth. Lightning shot from his fingertip. Surged through her body. Electrified her senses. She closed her eyes and took in a deep, sharp breath as that lightning spread far and wide within.

Majac smiled. "Don't worry about messing up your beautiful figure; this weekend's activities are going to work off all these calories."

Tessa was nervous at first. Actually, they both were. Majac took a seat opposite her, just three feet away. The phrase three-feet-too-far danced around Tessa's mind. Candles flickered at either side of the table as he started dissecting small morsels of dessert for them to enjoy. Almost everything he'd done since they walked in the door felt like seduction, and moreover, felt completely natural. Natural like a man and woman were supposed to feel together in a cozy, isolated space. Natural like sex wasn't even a necessary part of their relationship.

Tessa didn't get the impression that he was trying to relax her just so he could ease her into bed. The feeling was like he genuinely wanted her to be comfortable. Again, thinking three-feet-too-far, she slid her pillow around the table until it sat right in front of his; then she draped her legs across his.

Majac eyed the length of her legs and said, "I thought we agreed we were going to take this thing slow?"

What they agreed upon during the ride up was that they would maintain their personal bubbles while taking in as much about the other in conversation as possible.

"You're right," Tessa said. "I'm sorry. I'll behave."

"And we've been able to behave ourselves around each other when?"

They shared a laugh. Majac took advantage of her mouth being open. He fed her a bite-sized morsel of a white and red cream cheese mixture called cherries-in-the-snow. In all her life, she'd never tasted a dessert that light and flavorful. It was absolutely heavenly. A dimple pocked his cheek as he smiled at the satisfied expression on her face. She regarded the keloid on his neck behind his ear. She'd noticed it a couple of times prior, but never thought it appropriate to ask until now.

"Anton, what happened to your neck?"

His eyes followed hers. His hand touched the place on his neck that had captured her attention. He grimaced before saying, "A couple of years ago when I was in Japan, we were at the gun range. A young sailor on the next line had his gun jam. I don't know for sure, but I guess he grew impatient waiting for the range master to come unjam his weapon, so he decided to try to do it himself. Needless to say, he wasn't successful at clearing the round. What he was successful at was accidentally letting off a round which caromed off the deck and found its way to my neck."

"Oh my God!" she exclaimed.

"I fell to the floor screaming. The only thing I remember after that is the range alarm blaring. When I woke up, I was in the base hospital. The doctor told me how lucky I was. An inch to the left and it would have severed my spinal cord, or even killed me."

"Oh God!" she exclaimed again. Her brow furled. "Where do I get ahold of this guy so I can kick his ass?"

Majac smiled; again those huge dimples. The next bite of dessert he fed her was a chocolate-covered caramel treat that made her want to kiss.

"Ummmm, now that is heavenly." She took a swallow of champagne and said, "Okay, distract me quickly. Ask me something about me."

"All right, let me think. Oh, I got it…If you could have a thirty-minute conversation with anyone—dead or alive—who would it be?"

"Oh that's easy. My grandmother."

"Your mother or father's mother?"

"My mom's mother."

"Why her?"

"Two reasons really. First, because I've never met her. She died when my mom was seventeen. My Mom doesn't remember much about her and other than telling me how pretty she was, which never did much for me because I knew that from her pictures, all she remembers is that my grandmother loved to cook and loved to listen to jazz."

She paused, took a piece of the cherry dessert and fed it to Majac. He licked her fingers clean. The amazing sensation of his thick lips swallowing her fingers increased her arousal. She pulled her hand away begrudgingly. Her tepid skin flushed hot from the heat of his touch. Her pitch went high. She cleared her throat. "The other reason is so my mother would have an opportunity to say goodbye to her mom."

"How is that?"

"When my grandmother died, my mom was away at summer camp."

"Wow, I can't imagine how crushing that was for her to come home from camp and no longer have her mother."

"Yeah, to this day, my mother hates parks, farms, going camping or anything outside the city that makes her think about the country."

"I'm sorry for her."

They took turns feeding each other. Then washed it down with more champagne. The minutes stretched into hours and the hours became endless. All of the candles burned out.

They shared things about themselves that being apart from each other had never allowed them to before. When they saw something on the other's body that they didn't know the history behind, they asked. Anton asked about her torn left earlobe and she asked the stories behind the tattoos on his arm and shoulder. As he explained, he placed her hand on his tattoo and guided it across his chest and along the curve of his bare arm.

Mixed into learning about each other, they ate, drank, talked and laughed. Tickling mixed with affectionate ridiculing of each other's physical imperfections. Joking led to laughing. That night they laughed a lot. After telling him about being left at the altar, Tessa told him that she'd had an abortion when she was twenty-five. Tears came to her eyes as she reminisced about it. A void settled in the pit of his stomach. Her story left him almost in tears.

Majac told her about the injury to his leg that left him disqualified from submarines for four years. His story ran her through a gamut of emotions. First with sorrow about his injury, then with joy about him getting reinstated into the submarine program. She touched her nose to his. She had never been happier than she was at that moment.

Majac flashed her that perfect smile, picked her up, carried her out onto the screened-in porch and laid her on a white chaise lounge. He went back into the room, grabbed their glasses and another bottle of champagne then lay next to her and draped a throw across both their legs. "You all right?" he asked.

Tessa nestled deeper in his arms. "Perfect," she said.

Without much of a breeze, the scattered clouds drifted lazily across the sky. The moon spied on them from time-to-time. Tessa looked at the stars in the beautiful sky and caressed the back of his head. Touching begat caressing and caressing begat kissing. Lots of kissing.

Majac placed his hands on top of hers to slow her down. "Thanks for making me come this weekend, Tess. I really needed this break."

She leaned forward and they delved into a kiss that seemed to know no boundaries. A thousand thoughts raced through her mind—*How far will this go? Is he ready for a committed relationship? What will he be like as a father? Does he even want kids? When her mind slowed, the only thought that remained was, Does he love me?*

"Yes, I love you!" Majac said.

"What?" she asked, wondering how he'd read her mind.

"You asked do I love you. Yes, I love you."

She didn't realize that she'd said it aloud. Then thought it must have been her subconscious willing her mouth to say what her heart was feeling. At that moment she was glad her inner voice didn't stay inner.

Without any other words, Majac leaned in and kissed her for what seemed like an eternity.

The evening proceeded with awe-inspiring precision. The desserts were to-die-for; their sweetness paired perfectly with the semi-dry champagne. Their conversation was everything she'd ever dreamed. He told her his deepest secrets; they laughed and reminisced about friends; and they shared questions and answers about each other that solidified feelings of simpatico. The rest...well the rest was the closest either of them had ever been to bliss without actually having sex.

"Anton Charles." She sat up abruptly. "Promise me something..."

"Anything," he said. His breathing was haggard. His look intent.

"Promise me that no matter what happens, you will always be there to hold me and tell me you love me."

"I promise."

They finished the night in bed with her nestled comfortably in his arms. They held each other with a quiet desperation as if they were compressing time. As if they were distilling the essentials of their history, the good and the bad, the mediocre and the great. Her head rested on his chest. An American flag tattooed on his chest just above his heart. As he drifted off to sleep, Tessa repeatedly traced over the words Old Glory inked above that regal tattoo. She could feel his heart beating. Beating only for her—or so she wanted to think. Beating so strongly that it made her feel like his heartbeat was hers. Silently she prayed that this feeling would never end.

16

That, Ladies and Gentlemen...

FRIDAY MORNING TESSA AWOKE TO the most delectable cup of coffee she'd ever tasted. *This must have come from the same place as those delicious desserts*, she thought. While she wandered out onto the porch with her coffee, Majac went out to the car and toted in their two larger bags. She took a seat on the chaise and watched as small wildlife scampered about the lake. The temperature was a comfortable sixty-four degrees. The overnight clouds now a distant memory.

Joining her on the porch, Majac placed a thermos of coffee on the end table then joined her on the chaise. "I've got a full day planned today."

"Oh really, I thought you wanted to relax?" she asked. "Why can't we just lay around here and enjoy all of the beauty right here before us?"

His eyes turned to her. "I'm going to enjoy the beauty before me everywhere we go."

She blushed. He smiled. "You're right; I came here to relax, but relaxing doesn't necessarily mean being sedentary."

"Sedentary can be good. But trust me; locked up in this cabin with me, you'll be far from sedentary."

Trying to contain the smile on his face, Majac raised his coffee to his lips and took a long swallow. She lifted the lapel of her robe revealing a perky left breast. "Need milk?"

He laughed and a small geyser of coffee squirted past his lips. He choked down a swallow. "Girl, you need to stop."

Lowering the lapel of her robe, she conceded, "Your loss."

Majac put his cup down on the table next to the thermos and leaned over to kiss her. "Got milk?"

After making love on the porch before an audience of forest's locals—three herons, two snakes, six rabbits and an eagle circling above the lake—they took a shower to freshen up. Despite an overwhelming desire to go back to bed, she followed him on a quick two-mile run through the woods.

Following their run, they showered again, dressed and took-in a late brunch at the resort's restaurant. Kart racing followed brunch. Most women choose to be more submissive when it comes to sports and men, but Tessa's competitive demeanor refused to allow Majac to drive circles around her. By the time their helmets came off for the last time, they'd finished three races. Tessa surprised him and won the first. He handily won the second, causing her to spin out when they bumped fenders rounding the final turn. In their third and final race, both of their inner Fast and Furious drivers came out as they continuously bumped and cut each other for the length of the ten-minute race. In the end, Majac practically willed his way to a victory but only by the smallest of margins.

Having satiated their need for speed, they leisurely drove the thirty miles back down the coast. Vancouver, British Columbia had paved roads, but when they left town, they left pavement and asphalt behind.

The view of the ocean was awesome, but the unpaved roads were bumpy and rough. Most had more potholes and dips than the busiest streets in downtown Seattle. Twenty minutes of getting tossed around on a rough road was a long time. They zoomed along the coast, stopping only long enough for him to take pictures of a group of fishermen seated at splintered wooden tables at the head of a long pier. Back across the border, they headed to the Festival on the Green at the Chateau Ste. Michelle Winery where their reservations for a tour and reserve tasting awaited.

To Tessa's dismay, the tour preceded the tasting. And the wait was worsened when the pace of the tour was slowed by the couple ahead of them repeatedly challenging the tour guide, openly disagreeing with the guide and each other through several topics of conversation.

The way they fought and then made up right after reminded Tessa of a music video that ended with the rapper tying his girlfriend to the bed and burning the house down around the both of them. Observing the bi-polar intensity of their interactions throughout the afternoon's journey brought about the vivid image of that video girl suffering through such a terrible demise. If Majac had not been there with unsolicited light touches and caresses to distract her from their annoying antics, Tessa surely would have said something to the couple that was making the tour unpleasant.

Tessa's mood improved markedly when the tasting tour arrived at the wine cellar below the enormous patio on the back of the main building.

The sommelier, a woman of fifty or so, talked them through tasting four bottles of white wine ranging from super sweet to painfully dry.

Sampling the red wines brought the life back into Tessa's handsome date. By the time he had repeatedly sampled all four bottles of reds, his mood was as cheerful as when he got milk earlier in the day. They purchased a case of wine; six reds, four whites and two sparkling, which were boxed and staged for pickup.

The autumn concert series at the historic Chateau Ste. Michelle Winery had over the years brought in major jazz and rock artists like The Moody Blues and the Doobie Brothers. Carlos Santana headlined six weeks prior to their visit. The outdoor amphitheaters' lakeside setting offered a beautiful backdrop to sit back, watch and relax as world-famous artists performed on the winery's 87-acre estate. The opening act for that evening's concert featured a newcomer to the festival—the Earl Johnson Jr. Trio featuring Diana Krall. The headliner was the incomparable Harry Connick, Jr.

Sloping, grassy knolls surrounded the crescent-shaped center stage erected next to the lake. Their early arrival allowed them the opportunity to pick a great spot near a tree to watch the concert. Majac found a spot slightly left of the stage and spread out a blanket. "You want to take a walk on the beach?" he asked, trying to take advantage of a chance to explore the area before the show started. In preparation for their walk in the sand they slipped off their sandals. Majac rolled up his pants legs. Tessa's skirt, which ended just below her knees, was short enough to stay dry as they wet their feet in the warm waters of the lake. At the water's edge, Tessa lost the battle with the soft sand. She moved away from the water's end where the sand was firm and wet while Majac waded ankle deep. The waves followed him, crashing against the shore and breaking into foam. When Tessa stumbled, Majac ran to her rescue. On her knees when he came to her, she grabbed Majac around the waist.

"Always my hero." Tessa wanted to cry.

He pulled her to her feet and they kissed. He'd kissed her plenty of times before, but the sensuality in that kiss was different. Not eager and out-of-control like some lusty, hormone driven kisses, but gentle and passionate like his lips were kissing the words I LOVE YOU onto hers. She was surprised at how aroused she became. An arousal that started in the pit of her stomach. Crawled up and around her shoulders. Then plummeted quickly down to her hips like water from a hot spring matriculating off a waterfall. If they'd been alone in that quiet patch of beach Tessa would've laid him down and made love to her man right where they stood.

When they returned from the lake, The Johnson Trio entered the stage. A gentle southerly breeze swirled soft, seventy-nine-degree air around them. Tessa pulled her skirt up and folded her bare legs comfortably beneath her on the blanket. When she looked up, she found him staring at her long brown legs. She tried to maintain a sexy sort of innocence to the moment, but it was obvious that the view of her bare legs was driving him wild. The generous helping of wine he'd drank that afternoon helped fuel his desire. They sat still and absorbed the pretty twilight as the evening sun warmed their outsides. Their longing for each other—and the wine— warmed their insides.

A man dressed as winery waitstaff stopped in front of them. After waiting for a brief moment to be recognized, he cleared his throat. When they looked up to acknowledge him, he stood holding a wicker basket. "Mister Charles?" he asked.

Majac rose to his knees. "Thank you." He exchanged the basket for a once-folded twenty-dollar bill. When he sat down, he unpacked plates, silverware and napkins, then placed them on the blanket before her. She giggled when he set their plates side by side. Majac emptied the remainder of the contents from the basket; first grapes followed by bananas and sliced mangoes. Next he pulled out two small bags of chocolates— one dark and one milk. Last thing to come out were two bottles of Chateau Ste. Michelle wine. They reached for the mangoes and their hands brushed. Tessa smiled down at her plate. Majac shifted his body closer to hers.

The music was magnificent. Tessa nestled back into Majac's chest and he wrapped his arms around her. They sipped their wine and shared wonderful conversation as they enjoyed the music.

Behind their huddled up bodies, the light sound of waves washed gently against the shore. Majac asked, "So what do you want first? A boy or a girl?"

"Excuse me. What are you talking about?"

"I'm talking about when you have kids. I want a son first." Majac continued without waiting for an answer.

"Oh really?"

"Yes. You should always have a son first to take care of the rest of his brothers and sisters."

"His brothers and sisters?" she inquired mockingly. "How many are you talking about?"

"Not many. Four or five are nice round numbers."

"Wow. I don't know many women who are looking to carry and birth five children. Women care way too much about their figures these days to seriously consider having five children."

"Well, I think women place way too much emphasis on their figures. That's their man's responsibility."

"Yeah, yeah. That is until her figure gets out of control and he starts looking for a woman with a figure like she-used-to-have—four kids ago."

"No," he replied gently bumping his pelvis against her lower back. "That's when he keeps her active enough that she burns enough calories to get back to the woman she was—four kids ago."

They laughed.

"And besides," Majac continued. "I know I ain't talking crazy when I say we both know your mama and my mama want some grand babies."

His words were definitely true for her mother. She could only assume he knew his mother felt the same way. Tessa asked, "Do you seriously want five kids?"

"I don't know. Truthfully, I really don't care as long as they're healthy. But, I would like to have a son. Someone who can carry my name. Someone I can teach sports."

"Someone you can potty train," Tessa chimed in. A gentle laugh shook both of their bodies. She said, "How about teaching him how to treat a lady?"

"Yeah, I guess that's important too," he said, unable to hide his amusement well.

"Pig," she said, playfully punching him.

He chuckled.

Through most of an hour the Trio played a myriad of both upbeat and slower-tempo jazz tunes. Neither Majac nor Tessa were familiar with the group, but she was impressed enough that she thought to look for their CD the next time she was in a music store. There was an intermission as stagehands switched the instruments between bands.

It must have been the morning run and the tour of the vineyard that gave them such appetites because all of their bowls and both plates were empty. By the time the headliner came out to perform, Majac was uncorking the second bottle of wine.

The velvety sky was bright with stars as darkness settled quickly over the southwestern Canadian countryside. Tessa shook off a chill. With the absence of the sun, the evening had grown cooler. Noticing her slight shivers, Majac took his sport coat off the blanket and attempted to wrap it around her legs. When he arrived at her feet, she regarded him oddly.

"No, that's not necessary."

He put the jacket around her shoulders and, using the lapels, pulled her in close. He leaned toward her pert lips and said, "But this is."

As rhythmically as the head of a cobra, she leaned away from him teasing. More skilled than a snake charmer, he lunged quickly in response and kissed her full on the mouth. Feeling her own consumption of wine, she leaned into him and hungrily returned the kiss. "I didn't ask for that," she said when they broke the kiss.

"Well, what if I ask something else?" he replied.

Her brow furled. *Ask what? I know he's not saying what I think he's saying.* She sat up away from his reach for a moment to get a good look at his face. She couldn't read him, but the look on his face didn't appear to be joking. No girl wanted the embarrassment or heartache of anticipating a proposal to only have the man ask something totally different. Hesitantly she asked, "Ask what?"

Wordlessly Majac reached out and tapped twice on the outside of his left jacket pocket. At first she didn't respond. She just looked from him to the pocket and back to him. Majac smiled, amused that although he'd wrapped her in the jacket more than twenty minutes prior, she hadn't felt what he was tapping against. Tessa's eyes locked on his.

"Go ahead," he said. The smile was gone from his face. At that moment in time, Majac's stoic, expression was even more serious than she'd remembered when his father passed.

As if cautiously reaching blindly into a bag filled with venomous snakes, Tessa Ajai eased her left hand into the jacket of her boyfriend of less than six months. The velvet box she pulled out was no bigger than two inches square. Tessa looked intently at the box. She said, "A ring?" Her voice was strained. Majac smiled. She swallowed. "MacArthur James Antonio Charles." Glared hard at him before continuing. "Don't play with me." Tessa watched him carefully, hoping to expose his subterfuge.

"Who said I'm playing?"

Tessa gasped. Held her breath. Unsure of what to do next, she looked rapidly at the people near them on both sides hoping that this was not some type of prank.

"A diamond ring," he said when her eyes once again met his. "That is what every respectable Lady deserves as a sign of appreciation and more important, as a sign of love."

Tessa gasped. Tears flowed down her cheeks like champagne from a wedding fountain.

Majac appreciated Tessa; and moreover, he was definitely in love with his lifelong friend.

"Anton, I didn't…"

Majac decided to be direct. "Will you marry me, Tessa Ajai?"

"Are you serious?" Tears wet her face. Sniffles almost made her question unintelligible.

"Dead serious."

Tessa was stunned. Her head swam. Her heart pounded. She maintained continuous eye contact trying to make sure he wasn't kidding. *Is he playing with me? Is this the wine talking?* She regarded him cautiously. She'd been left at the altar before and was extremely leery about journeying down that path again. Things were going great between them, and even with him confessing last night that he loved her, she couldn't say that she saw a marriage proposal coming. *When did he have time to get the ring? I've been with him all day. Had he brought it with him? Had he planned to propose the entire time? Should I have seen this coming?* Tessa tilted her head to the side. Stared intently at him, waiting for the recantation to come. When it didn't, she raised her brows and asked, "Are You serious?"

"Serious as a heart attack," he smiled.

Challenging him, she asked, "So if I open this box, there's going to be an engagement ring inside?"

Without the slightest bit of hesitation, he said, "Open it."

Tessa almost pulled a muscle in her neck as she fumbled to open the contents of the velvet box. Her excitement instantaneously rocketing to rival that of a kid at Christmas. She paused for a moment. Took several deep breaths. Tried to figure out how over the course of the day with him draped all over her, she hadn't felt the box in his jacket.

Majac shifted until he was positioned on one knee. Her gaze shifted from the ring back to him. When she saw him on his knee smiling, tears escaped from her eyes like runners dashing to start the New York Marathon. "If you're willing to take a chance Baby, let me have it."

Tessa regarded him and the tears shifted into third gear.

Some of the people sitting near took notice to Majac on his knee and refocused their attention. Like a slow-motion scene in a movie, Majac removed the little box held tightly in the palm of her hand. As he eased the box out of her hand, Tessa rose up onto her knees, her face mere inches from his.

"Anton…I…" Her words didn't come, but the tears flowing down her face told him the answer to any question he could have put into words.

He smiled, slowly opened the small blue velvet box and turned the lid to face her. When she saw what was inside the jewelry box, her mouth dropped open in a gasp. Her hand shook as the muscles in her arm vibrated like the tremors of a San Francisco earthquake. A woman to her left gasped in anticipation as if it were her finger being adorned.

Tessa could hear her cheering her on, *Say yes Girl. Say Yes!*

Majac removed the diamond engagement ring from its satiny cradle. Tears leaked from his eyes as he slid the ring onto her quivering finger. In the gentlest voice to ever cross her ears, Majac said, "If you're willing to give me a lifetime to love you, I promise I'll spend every day of the rest of my life doing everything it takes to make you happy." Her waterworks shifted uncontrollably into overdrive. He continued, "So if you're willing to take a chance on a lifetime with me; Yes my Love, I am asking… Tessa Ajai will you marry me?"

Tears muffled her answer. Her lips mouthed the words, *Yes. Yes. Yes.*

Again, he tugged on the jacket as he leaned in to kiss her.

Cheers erupted from the crowd nearest them as if he'd just scored the winning touchdown in the Super Bowl. Across the microphone came the voice of Harry Connick Jr., "Now that ladies and gentlemen, is how you propose to a woman."

Over the years they'd had sex several times as consensual lovers. But that night, in their small, secluded, cabin at the resort, they made love passionately and repeatedly. Without abandon or inhibition. And most important, as newly engaged fiancées. The fresh country air of the Vancouver countryside was like an added aphrodisiac further igniting their desire for one another. Their hunger for each other soared to new levels of intensity, urgency and satisfaction.

17

Surf's Up

TESSA WOKE TO MAJAC'S KISSES Saturday morning. There was a fire warming the cabin. "I have some fruit for breakfast if you'd like," he said escorting her from the bed to the bearskin rug. Saying *some fruit* was an understatement. On the table in front of the fireplace was a tray of strawberries and raspberries, a pot of warm tea and an assortment of warm breads and pastries. They sat facing each other, Indian style—Majac in silk boxers, her in a satin bra and panties beneath a matching silk robe; a set her mom had given her six months prior for her birthday. She'd saved it for a special occasion, and last night, was the occasion she was waiting for.

Tessa marveled at her ring as she took the first bite of an orange cranberry scone. A smile crossed her lips as she relived Majac's proposal. That smile grew wider when her next thought was how she'd never had a man take total control of her the way he did the night before.

When they returned from the concert, Majac briefly disappeared into that little corner of the room known as the kitchen. He returned, removed her shoes then commenced to give her the worlds' best foot massage.

Five minutes later, the sweet aroma of chamomile tea filled the air. He left her again. Disappeared into the bathroom. The gentle sound of running water made its way to her ears as he drew a bath. He returned and continued with her massage, this time caressing her ankles and calves.

"Ohhh Anton." She whispered his name through sips of tea as gently as if it were the first word she'd ever spoken.

Majac put both cups of tea on a low table when the sound of the tub filling grew quieter then led her into the bathroom. The Brazilian hardwood was cool on her feet. Feet that felt so good from her massage that it heightened the cooling sensation of the floor. In the bathroom, they paused on a plush area rug next to the tub and stared out of the plate glass window overlooking the lake. The night sky was clear as a bell; much clearer than any she'd ever remembered in Pennsylvania.

Tessa was totally submissive as he undressed her with strong, gentle hands. The steam from the hot tub of waters generated a moist vapor in the air. She watched as he undressed himself then turned her around to face the window and stood close without pressing against her.

"You know I love you, right?" she said. "Always have." She took a deep breath and tried to remain calm. "I won't ever ask you to do anything except love me as intensely as I am going to love you."

With that, he turned her around and kissed her for what felt like an hour. When they finally came up for air, he said, "Fair enough!" His simplistic tone made it sound like the easiest request in the world.

In the tub they talked about everything from cartoons and politics to Kama Sutra positions, the latter being their precursor to a night full of intense lovemaking. A night that she silently hoped would never end. After their bath, she sat upon the small chair next to the tub as a still naked Majac rubbed her with oils from neck to toe. Moonlight piercing through the window illuminated his well-defined muscles, inciting her to capture some small pleasure of her own while briefly taking him into her mouth. She grazed upon his ample bounty, trying to raise his manhood to a height that would fill the depths of her during intense, yet intimate congress— their own private filibuster. She released him, exhaling a mellow sigh.

He opened his eyes, glanced down at her smiling face and their eyes immediately connected. For a long moment he stood before her, knees trembling, recovering as she relished his taste. It was so quiet; they could hear each other breathing.

Teasing, she swiped away the drop of his essence and licked her finger.

Majac regained his composure; caressed her shoulders and the nape of her neck then sank to his knees. Caressed her back with gentle hands, then wrapped around to her front and upward across her pert breasts. He kissed her lips. Then kissed each nipple; his tongue lingering only until each was taut with anticipation.

She tensed, recoiled, then saw the love in his eyes and relaxed. She squirmed and wriggled her hips as her pulse pounded in that place between her legs. A pulse that grew stronger as he oiled her feet, then her legs and finished with her hips.

He put his hands on her waist. Effortlessly lifted her from the small perch and carried her out to the bed. Lighted her on the riser surrounding the bed and kissed her, their tongues intertwining rapidly, passionately. He stepped up on the riser to meet her. Softly ushered her back onto the comfortable bed. Hovered inches above her, their eyes open, each looking deeply into the others.

She caressed the back of his head and ran her fingernails down the center of his back. Their moans grew louder. Majac leaned down, his lips pressed gently against hers. Again, they kissed. This time deeper than before. He took her gently into his arms. Her wetness came down. A dew-covered flower opening for him in the morning sun.

He entered her slowly; exasperated with how wet she was for him. He prolonged his entry. Savored it. Eased his full weight down upon her and went deeper. Then deeper some more.

Tessa held her breath, marveled at the feeling she'd gone so long without. Or, at least it seemed so long since the morning. Those moments where she saw Heaven seemed like temporary forevers. He helped her discover things about herself sexually that she'd never known. The better his effort, the wetter her treasure. His erect stature continually reflected his eagerness to please. She shifted her hips, rolled him over and eased down on top of him. Eased him into that limpid pool. Sweat trickled down her back, breasts and stomach as she rode off into her own ethereal paradise.

Hours passed like minutes. His extended foreplay between orgasms helped time reach five the next morning. They made love until the sun began to shine its golden light from the horizon, jutting across the mountains and through the frosted glass of the balcony door.

When he began to tremble, she knew that she was truly going to enjoy the feeling of his submission. She lowered herself until her mouth covered his, savoring every moment, making her desire for him grow and losing control as multiple spasms erupted from deep within. She came to meet him and after they arrived, they both lay spent, covered in the glistening dew of perspiration, still connected, but now both completely relaxed.

Majac had helped her reach sensitivities previously unattained. Given her what was better than better. Taken her to heights that piqued her nature and expressed the highest form of admiration from a man whose goals were to exceed any and all measures of physical pleasure.

Sated beyond belief, and believing, Tessa folded herself down into his arms and drifted off to sleep.

As they sat on the bearskin rug finishing their Sunday breakfast, Tessa overjoyed in the news that the day's activity was surfing lessons. Surfing was something that she'd always wanted to do since watching Hawaii Five-O as a child. When she mentioned surfing a couple of weeks before the trip, Majac didn't seem too excited, but agreed to try.

Three hours and forty-five miles later Majac and Tessa stood watching the waves break on the beach at Nootka Island. A place described by the natives as the best surfing in Vancouver. Walt, a lifeguard and their stocky powerhouse of an instructor, proceeded through a half hour surfing lesson before allowing them to venture out past waist deep water. In her first six attempts to stand up, Tessa fell off the board each time. On her seventh unsuccessful dip in the water, a wave passed overhead. Her board came loose from her ankle and surfaced some twenty feet further from shore. Majac swam out to retrieve her board as Walt helped her safely back to shallow water.

Tessa stood in ankle-deep water and watched, applauding, as her hero securely strapped the board to his ankle and started to swim back to shore. Several strokes later her clapping halted. Majac appeared to be struggling. Now that it was wet, the shiny material of the teal bikini glistened in the sunlight. Majac marveled at how it accentuated the depth of her sexiness and the maturity of her curves.

Tessa didn't know it, but her board was caught in the undertow, and was now dragging Majac under. Before she could call for help, a wave crested. When the wave fell, Majac was dragged down, caught completely in the undertow and was now out of sight.

"Help!" Tessa screamed. She couldn't see what was happening, but beneath the water's surface, her board was being dragged farther away from shore until it finally dropped over a fifty-foot underwater cliff. The two boards attached to Majac's ankles held him underwater for almost thirty seconds. When he realized that he couldn't swim hard enough against the motion of the two boards, he turned and swam down to grab them. The next wave brought him up.

"Walt!!!!" Tessa call for the lifeguard to help, but it was too late. Seconds later she watched in terror as Majac went down again.

Dashing back into the water, Walt spotted Majac when he resurfaced. Blowing his whistle to get the other lifeguards' attention, he pointed at the water and took off running to Majac's rescue. Walt dove into a cresting wave as Majac went under for the second time. Majac was a strong swimmer, but the force of the undertow on the surfboards was more than he could overcome. Unable to free himself from Tessa's board, Majac was pulled back under as Walt splashed his way toward the cliff.

Another minute passed. Again the great blue sea overpowered Majac and sucked him down past the underwater cliff. Anticipating the next wave to ride in and force him back to the surface, Majac rode the ebbing current down to the surfboard dragging him under.

He grabbed hold of the board and, as the current shifted, he turned the board to allow the force of the wave to push him back to the surface using the same force that dragged him under.

Walt swam hard in the general direction where Majac had gone under. When he looked up, he was unable to make visual confirmation of Majac's location over the incoming waves. Two lifeguards rushed past Tessa and entered the water, swimming like dolphins in Walt's direction. Walt swam, spinning in circles, waiting for Majac to surface.

Like a cork in a tub, Majac bobbed to the surface just before Tessa's heart exploded from terror. She exhaled a huge gasp of relief. An all-out waterfall of tears followed that gasp. She was scared to death. Didn't know if he was alive. She pined for the lifeguards to save him. Screamed at the top of her lungs. Jumped up and down. And pointed in the direction where she saw her fiancée of less than a day. Walt heard her screams and initially looked back to the beach. When he caught the direction in which she was pointing, he turned and rapidly began paddling in that same direction. The other two lifeguards followed Walt back into the sea.

The unrelenting ocean retracted for a third time, using the force of Tessa's surfboard to drag Majac under. This time, however, he wrapped his arms and legs around the board, pointed the board toward the head of the current and allowed the water to rush by him more so than push him down over the cliff. The roar of the water and the rage of the ocean absorbed every ounce of his energy.

The first time the mighty ocean swallowed him whole, Majac plunged greater than a hundred feet below the surface. The second time under, he gained control of the board around the forty-foot mark, bottoming out no deeper than seventy-five feet. This third time, riding the board with the current, he was pushed no more than fifty feet below the lip of the cliff before the ebb subsided. As the current turned and the force of the ocean relaxed in preparation to drive its energy back toward the eroding beach, Majac released his legs from the board and shifted the board once again to allow the incoming current to push him back to the surface.

When Majac broke through the surface for the third time, two of the lifeguards were less than ten yards away. They rushed to his aid before the ebbing current could return.

Majac collapsed as the lifeguards lassoed him and guided him and both boards back to shore. Once in waist deep water, the first lifeguard harnessed Majac with his floatation device and attempted to pry his arms from around the board. A second guard dipped beneath the water's surface and freed the board from his ankle. Tessa's tears streamed down her face as the board floated quietly away with the retreating current.

The two lifeguards carried Majac back to shore and laid him in the sand. Tessa fell to her knees at his side. Frantically she reached for his face. Panic stricken; the worst of thoughts ran through her head. Majac was unconscious. Immediately, she started to blame herself. She knew he had arranged the surfing lessons, but she wanted this trip, not him. She had wanted some time alone with him and had all but forced this vacation on him. It was all her fault. She would never forgive herself if he wasn't all right. The first lifeguard grabbed her. Moved her out of the way. Walt checked his breathing. Tessa pushed herself free. A second lifeguard tried to wrap a blanket around her. She fought hard, but couldn't free herself from his grip. He held her out of the way while others performed CPR on Majac. He wasn't breathing. But he did have a pulse. One lifeguard started resuscitation. Again, her tears came. This time wails of her distress filled the air for all to hear. Crocodile size tears pelted the sandy beach as she cried a river at the thought of Majac never waking up.

Cough–cough escaped Majac as Walt restarted his lungs. *Cough–cough* forced half a gallon of the Pacific Ocean out of his body and onto the sandy beach. Coughs continued as Majac slipped back into consciousness and eventually opened his eyes. The sight of his eyes opening evoked another surge of emotion in his bride-to-be. A sight that incited her to cry larger, faster tears.

Finally, the ambulance arrived. Tessa retrieved their belongings. The lifeguards helped the EMTs place Majac on the gurney. As the ambulance whisked them away to the local hospital, Tessa used Majac's phone to call his best friend. By nightfall, Jaz and Crystal had joined them at the hospital. They visited for a while, again bringing Tessa to full out waterworks as she recounted the horrific story of the worst day of her life. Crystal comforted her, rubbed her back and cooed to her like she did with her own girls until Tessa was once again calm enough to be considered coherent. Somewhere during that comforting, Crystal noticed the engagement ring. Her shriek captured the attention of almost everyone in the almost silent room. Almost, but not everyone, as Majac was sedated and sound asleep.

As visiting hours ended, Tessa handed Crystal Majac's key card and offered them the cabin. The shift nurse had brought Tessa hospital scrubs to replace her bikini and a blanket to keep her warm after the ambulance departed. Crystal promised that they'd return in the morning with clean, dry change of clothes for both her and Majac.

Tessa hugged Jaz and Crystal, told them how much she appreciated them rushing up there and again started crying as they left.

Alone in the room with Majac, Tessa pulled the single guest chair up next to the bed and watched her future husband sleep. She looked him full in the face—staring for moments on end as if seeing him for the first time—wondering what dreams were occupying his mind.

Over the course of the next two hours, she twice heard him faintly utter his father Manny's name. Later, the name of his ex-girlfriend from San Diego, Celeste, came to her ears along with someone named Marissa. From the painful look on his face, traumatic memories were interfering with what should have been peaceful rest under heavy sedation. Tessa called his name. Tried to wake him from his nightmares, but he stayed asleep. As much as she thought she wanted to know at the time, Tessa would never know the story behind a dream that was strong enough to disturb his sedation. On the other side of that restless sleep, Majac was working his way through the nightmare of a wonderful love making session gone horribly wrong on the night his girlfriend conspired to trick him into cheating on her with her sister.

Tessa barely slept, spending what was supposed to be their last night of a fabulous weekend getaway, in a semi-private room at the local hospital. The doctor said he had to keep Majac for 48-hours to observe for dry drowning. Although less than 100%, Majac was released from the hospital Tuesday afternoon. The Stevensons decided it would be best if Tessa rode back to Seattle with Crystal. Jaz, driving Majac's car, followed right behind.

18

Making the Call

MAJAC'S FULL RECOVERY FROM HIS surfing incident took about two weeks. For the second time in his military career, and in as many years, he would require a medical clearance to return to full duty. And for his ship and crew, the timing couldn't have been better. That weekend would see maximum liberty for the crew of THURGOOD MARSHALL because ten days later the ship would get underway to participate in the Rim of the Pacific Exercise called RIMPAC. After six weeks of the world's largest international maritime warfare exercise, all ships involved will embark in San Diego where the Pacific Fleet commander will host a weekend full of ship tours and sports competitions to celebrate the conclusion of the multinational exercise. The exercise finale would be the Admiral's Ball on Saturday night. Sunday would offer a day of rest from all of the excitement and grandeur before the crews got back to work on Monday to begin preps to get their ships underway on Tuesday and Wednesday.

When Majac arrived home Wednesday night after his first full day back on the ship, the entire property looked deserted. Both his and Solomon's sides of the Hang Suite were unusually dark. He couldn't remember if he'd left any lights on, but he knew his neighbor always did. He had decided to drive around the Sound vice taking the ferry across so that he could swing by Tessa's apartment, pick her up and take her out to dinner. When she declined, citing that she had plans with Leona and her sister Jennifer Fleming, Majac brooded through the remainder of the ninety-minute drive from Bangor to North Seattle. As a consolation, Tessa promised to come by his place late Saturday morning to make him brunch. She'd surprise him with tickets she'd picked up to a one o'clock performance of the musical Stomp. They could have brunch, take in the show and still have time to grab a bite for dinner before their counseling session that evening.

The couple shared mushy farewells—an *I Love You Bunches* followed by a counter *I Love You More*—then exchanged air kisses over the phone before hanging up.

Home alone with no plans for the night, Majac grabbed a beer and began unpacking his briefcase. On one of the flyers the ship Ombudsman had left for approval was a list of the foreign ports the participants in the exercise would be visiting. This list would be provided so that family members who chose to travel could meet their sailors and vacation while the ship was in port.

The exercise commenced with a one-day ceremony at Pacific Fleet Headquarters in Hawaii. Among the port visits on the list were Okinawa, Japan; Dunedin, New Zealand; Sydney, Australia; Santa Elena, Ecuador; and Puerto Vallarta, Mexico. Six weeks later, all of the participants arrived in San Diego for the closing ceremonies.

As Majac rifled through the paper in an attempt to unclutter his briefcase, the phone rang. "Hello?"

"Hey Partna, how was the first day back?"

"It was cool. The junior officers were glad to see me. Don't know that I can say the same for my Department Heads. Apparently my XO and Department Heads were power tripping in my absence."

Jaz laughed.

"So, what's up?" Majac asked. "You back in town yet?"

"Yeah, we flew in earlier this afternoon. Tomorrow night we start a three-game home stretch before we head east for seven games. I hate east coast road trips."

"Yeah, I feel you. We're getting underway for six weeks come start of next week."

"You need me to check on the crib for you while you're out?"

"Nahh, I'm good. Between Tessa and Solo, everything should be cool around here."

"Wait a minute. Six weeks? Does that mean you're going to be gone for Christmas?"

"Nahh."

"Cool."

"I know, right. Being away from home for the holidays sucks. Not so much for me, but for the married guys and the guys with kids. The mood is always so miserable on the ship when we miss a big holiday."

"I can't imagine. The only holiday I've ever had to miss was having to play a televised away game on Christmas. But when we do, the owner usually charters a plane and brings all of the families."

"The players' families? That's cool."

"No, I'm talking everybody's families. Players and staff. He damn near buys out the hotel. Rents rooms for everyone and after the game we have a big team family feast on him. I love working for the Brights. They know how to take care of their people."

"Yeah Partna, if everything goes as planned, we should slide in here just in time to get everybody home for the holidays."

"Good. Because you know the girls would go crazy if Uncle Majac wasn't here for Christmas."

They laughed.

"I caught the game last night. Looks like you guys need a shooting guard. That kid for San Diego was wearing you out. I don't think he missed in the second half. What he have; 28 – 30 points?"

"Try 38. Made me mad enough to want to lace my shoes up in the second half."

"Yeah, San Diego would've loved that."

"Hey, speaking of loving something in San Diego, guess who swung by the table at the team dinner last night?"

"I don't know. Where did you eat?"

"We ate at Seau's. You've gotta try their ribs."

"Umm, I don't know. Who? Tony Gwynn? LaDainian Tomlinson? Oh I know, the kid who lit you up for 38? He came by to pick up the check for letting him have his way with you guys all night?"

"Nahh, he ain't that crazy."

"All right, well who then?"

"Does the name Celeste Devereaux still ring a bell?"

Majac went silent for a beat. His anxiety went from zero to sixty in two words. Six years prior Celeste Deveraux had left him high and dry. Had let him propose only to find out that she was pregnant by her ex-boyfriend, despite being Majac's current girlfriend. Had walked out on him after he got arrested for fighting the man who interrupted his wedding proposal. He hadn't thought about her since Tessa moved to Seattle and much less, didn't consider that, after all of the drama with him, her ex-boyfriend, and her maniacal sister, she would choose to stay in San Diego.

"Maj, you still there?" Jaz called against the silence.

Silence answered him back.

"Maj, you all right? You ain't drop dead on me, did you?"

Through the receiver Jaz heard a heavy breath of wind break through the silence on the other end.

"Why you telling me? I ain't seen or heard from her in five—six years."

"Well, you may not have seen her, but she would sure like to see you."

"Yeah? Well then why hasn't she called me?"

"Come on Maj. I know she used to be your girl and everything, but that chick is way too bougie to pick up the phone and reach out first. You know how uppity she is."

"Well if she didn't ask about me, then why you bringing her up?"

"I didn't say she didn't ask about you. After that stuff her crazy ass sister pulled with Crys, you know she ain't got no reason to just come up to me making small talk. She saw I was in town and found me so she could find you. Stop playing like you didn't know."

"So get to the point. What did she say?"

"Not much. Asked if I remembered her. Asked if we still hung out. When I told her that we still kick it when we cross paths, she pulled out a business card and handed it to me. Asked me in a real sweet voice if I would forward you her number. Told me to tell you that you're welcome to call anytime…day or night. After I took the card, she beamed a smile around the table at everybody watching her like the groupie she is, said thanks and left."

Again the line was silent for a beat.

"Maj I didn't lose you again; did I?"

"Nahh Partna, I'm good."

"So you want it?" Jaz asked. Majac and Jaz had been Partnas since middle school. Jaz knew Majac wanted her number. He knew how deeply in love Majac had fallen with the beautiful Cajun. Knew that despite knowing she cheated on him and was stupid enough to get pregnant by another man, Majac still thought of her now and then, even if he never said so. But he didn't have to. Jaz was his best friend, and best friends know unspoken things like that about their boys. Jaz admitted to himself that Celeste was fine. Downright gorgeous. Not that he was interested in her, because in his eyes, she couldn't hold a candle to Crystal Porsche

Stevenson, but nonetheless, Celeste Devereaux was a beautiful woman. Crystal and Celeste hometowns were less than fifty miles apart. *Must be something in the water down there on the Gulf Coast.* He broke the silence with, "Or should I just toss it?"

Sailing the seas taught a man many lessons, and chief among them was patience. Before answering his best friend, Majac inhaled, and then exhaled deeply. Calmly he pulled a pen and a slip of paper from his briefcase. He blew air into the telephone, and, as calmly as he could, told Jaz, "Yeah, Partna. Let me have her number."

Three hours after Majac hung up with Jaz, thoughts of his time with Celeste Devereaux flooded his mind. He ordered Chinese food, drank four beers, and was sleepy now. He called Tessa before getting into the shower. Her phone went to voicemail. Now, as the water rained down on his head, two years' worth of memories about his time in San Diego courting the beautiful and exotic Celeste Devereaux consumed his thoughts. He was unsure why he was reliving and remembering all of those feelings. He tried to listen to the television, but thoughts of the beauty from his past oozed into every moment of silence.

Before he had hung up, Jaz told Majac, You know you're my Partna. I know you and Tessa got a thing going on right now, but if you ever found out that she had given me her number and I never gave it to you, you would be mad at me. I ain't telling you to call her. But at the same time, I ain't telling you not to call. She was a part of your past. And I don't know anybody who has ever broken up over a phone call.

"Think about it. She's a thousand miles away. I didn't tell her where you are, just that we keep in touch. Keep the number and call her. Throw it away and don't call her. You're a grown man. Make a decision and live with it. That's all I'm gonna say about it. Hit me up in the morning if you wanna go to the gym."

Celeste Devereaux. If the mere mention of her name sparked feelings, what would happen if he saw her? He chalked her memory up to experience. Hadn't seriously thought about her in years. A complicated, confusing memory that he buried and tried to block from coming to the front of his mind as much as sanely possible. Why did her name have to come up now? Now that his relationship with Tessa was in full bloom?

Majac gazed at Celeste's phone number for a moment, thinking about his Partna's advice. Finally, he told himself that he was secure enough in his life to have an innocent phone conversation with a woman three states away. Majac's hand shook as he picked up the phone and dialed the number. He felt a twinge of melancholy when he heard Celeste's voice on the answering machine. And then he felt a sharp anxiety mixed with fear. *What if she was married with children? What if she was sick and just didn't want to tell Jaz?* When the message ended, Majac hesitated for a moment. When the silence after the beep got to the point right before the machine would stop recording, he left a message, "Hey Celeste Devereaux, this is Anton Charles. Jaz gave me your number. I'll be in San Diego for RIMPAC and I…I…umm…and I…don't know…maybe…" At that point it seemed as though his voice had vanished. He couldn't speak. Before he could conjure the words to continue, his time expired and the machine cut off…*Beep.* The line went dead.

Majac hung up. After a moment he looked at the phone and muttered to himself, *What am I doing?*

19

Before Saying "I Do"

Anton Charles, Tessa Ajai, I'd like you to meet the Reverend Lawrence Didier. Pastor will be joining our session today. Marriage counseling is a newer part of my practice," Solomon said as the quartet stood in his foyer.

The only other time he'd held a session at his home was an emergency when a woman, who was separated from her husband, showed up at his door insisting that she didn't want to go home because she thought her husband was waiting there to kill her. Today's concession was made because his patient was his next-door neighbor. Solomon's business office was twenty-one miles to the south, and afterwards, he and Lawrence had plans to head north to attend a private pay-per-view boxing party hosted by Lawrence's brother, Kenny.

A wave of skepticism washed over Majac's face.

"I earned my Master of Science in marriage and family counseling just over a year ago," Solomon offered the couple in reassurance of his qualifications, "and although you two are only the second couple I've seen in my practice, I've sat through more than fifty sessions."

Tessa also noticed the look of angst on Majac's face. She held her fiancée's hand and said, "You have a lovely home Doctor Alexandré. A person could easily get comfortable here."

Lawrence led the way to the office. From the rear, Solomon said, "Through conversation, I've learned that Majac is a religious man, but you don't yet have a church home. Since most couples are accustomed to ministers performing the marriage counseling, I invited Reverend Didier to join us."

They sat around a circular, four-foot wooden table. The prospective couple sat facing each other. The two counselors doing the same. Solomon did most of the talking through the first twenty minutes, then he handed a composition notebook to both Majac and Tessa. "From now until the wedding, every time you have any type of question about each other that you less than 100 percent certain of the answer, I want you to write it down in that notebook and ask your partner the next time you see them."

"But what if we're together when we think of the question?" Majac asked.

Solomon chuckled. "If you're not together when you think of it, write it down. If you're together, by all means, talk to each other."

Tessa opened her notebook and began to write.

All three men shifted their eyes to her.

"If you have a question Tessa, please ask it now," Solomon said. "Unless it's too personal for us to hear, you don't have to wait until you're alone. I encourage you to get things out in the open. Counseling is a judgment free zone."

Tessa continued writing as he spoke. When she finished, her eyes went to Majac's. "Not a question Doctor, just a reminder."

"Fair enough," Solomon said. He turned his attention to Majac. "When did you first know, or think, that you loved Tessa?"

Majac turned and looked away before Tessa could catch his smile. His mind immediately journeyed 3,000 miles east to Tuskegee, Pennsylvania and thoughts of his Pops.

~

As they pulled in front of their house, Pops reached up and pressed the button to open the garage door. As they exited the garage and made their way through the small backyard toward the back of the house, Majac felt awkward. Pops bopped ahead of him in his usual cool way like he was walking on air. When they got inside the house they found that Momma and Angel were gone. Perfect. Now he could talk to Pops in private about his angst in approaching Tessa.

"She definitely got something," Majac said as Pops eased down into his perfectly broken-in recliner. Majac loosened his tie and hung his jacket on the back of one of the kitchen chairs. Gym bag, keys, wallet, lunch box, all on the kitchen table.

Then he put one of the food containers in the microwave for Pops. The cheer team was selling fish dinners as a fundraiser and Majac convinced Pops to buy two for dinner. Tessa was the girl who took Pops money. Pops masked his smile as he watched Majac trying to act cool when she handed the boxes to his son.

"What you mean she got something? You ain't talking about diseases are you? We need to get you a shot?"

"Nahh, Pops. Come on, Man. You know me better than that," he snapped, already a little emotional about the girl. "Not a disease. Just. Like a good thing, Man. It's hard to explain; she's just cool. She's got a crazy swag thing about her. You know?"

Pops nodded, trying to refrain from laughing at his son's crush. When he was his son's age, he knew that he would have been crushed if his father had laughed at him when he told him he liked a girl. Fortunately, Majac's father had much swag—and understanding.

The microwave dinged. Pops lurched forward in his chair then eased to a stop trying to play it off all smooth so that Majac didn't see his momentary fit of crazy.

Majac smiled, stood and walked all smooth into the kitchen, over-exaggerating his father's cool walk. When he popped open the microwave door, a cloud of steam carrying the smell of recently fried fish came bursting out. He took a deep breath. Yelled across the kitchen and into the living room "Sure smells good, Pops. Hungry as I am, I could probably eat both plates."

"And you better enjoy, because it'll be the last meal you eat on this earth," Pops returned quickly at the same volume.

Majac set Pops food on a tray then added a knife and fork, and a glass of tea. He pulled a clear seasoning bottle with a handwritten label from the cupboard. 'Anton's Everything Spice' was written in his handwriting on the makeshift label. He sprinkled the spice on his rice and beans, then on Pops', before carrying the tray into his dad. He warmed his plate next.

After saying a silent grace, Pops picked up a large hunk of the fish and took a bite right out of the middle of it. It was hot, and he hung his mouth open, panting to cool off. Then he moved his fork to the middle of the plate, dragging it through the rest of his food to make a valley. On the left, a mountain of church rice; on the right, a hill of seasoned green beans.

"Umph boy," Pops growled with his mouth closed, food trapped in his puffy, trumpeter cheeks as Majac re-entered the kitchen, "This food is slamming."

"Your girlfriend cook this?" Pops asked. "If she did, then I get why you're bugging—as you kids say." Pops smiled with his mouth closed. "She cooks better than you."

"She's not my girlfriend," Majac barked. "And no, she didn't cook it."

"Not Yet!" Pops chimed, shoving another forkful of the wonderful food into his mouth.

"And," Majac interrupted, "It don't taste better than my food."

Pops took another spoonful of rice. His face lit up. "Okay, so maybe you're right about the food." Pops guffawed. "But she's definitely your girlfriend."

Majac didn't say anything in return. Pretended he didn't hear him. Let him go on inhaling his food. But he couldn't help thinking about the possibilities of Pops being right. Of course, he was right. Pops had more experience with the opposite sex than his son, and, he was married. Majac carried his tray of food and tea into the living room and joined his father.

Pops put down his fork. He had already finished his rice and beans.

"Now Son, back in my senior year when I was your age; And I'm talking long before your Momma and I got together, I used to kick it with this girl in my class named Colleen Reed. Now believe me when I tell you, she was a certified winner. Colleen was so fly that a bunch of the older dudes at Hammond U. was trying to get at her. That was until they found out she wasn't yet eighteen. And even then, some of them still tried to get at her. But during football season, Colleen was all mines. And she was absolutely cool to hang out with; at home, the malt shop, drive-in movies and especially at the games. Nowadays, your generation would say she was 'the bomb'."

Majac laughed.

"Later on, during basketball season," Pops continued, "I kicked it for a while with Donna Haines and Lana Douglas at the same time.

Now Donna, she was a little geeky. But in a cute way," he gestured with his hands like he was wearing glasses.

"And Lana was a cheerleader. She had that whole pretty smile, long hair thing going on. She was in shape and was always cheery all the time. Something like that girlfriend of yours at the fish fry." Pops stuffed a fork full of fish in his mouth, chewed, swallowed and washed it down with two swigs of tea before continuing. "Now here's the catch. The two girls knew about each other because I was up front and told both of them the truth. Crazy thing is they didn't even care. You see, other brothers in my class were jealous of me. I would hear them talk behind my back about how they didn't understand how I was getting the ladies. You know, the Superfly brothers who knew their stuff didn't stink. My secret, and the one thing they didn't understand, was that I was nice to them. I was honest with them. I had a part time job, so I always had new clothes. That was a major plus. I could tell a joke, and most people thought my jokes were funny.

"And the key to it all was that I was a Momma's boy. Other guys were too, but it was different for me. Unlike most guys who had their dad or their mom's boyfriend to make their mom blush and feel all fuzzy, my mom had nobody but me. Your Grandpa died when I was in eighth grade and after that Mom never had a boyfriend. Said she wouldn't date until after I graduated from college. So since I was gonna be all she had, I spent a lot of time figuring out what it was about my dad that made my mother smile. What made her feel special. Your grandma worked in the school library, and when girls saw me waiting to walk her home from work and checking on her during the day, that pretty much made me the smoothest dude in school. So now," Pops declared with a big exhale, "just tell me the truth. Do you like her?"

"Yeah. She's real cool."

"She like you?"

"I hope so."

"Does she flirt with you?"

"I think so; but, she's hard to read."

"Does she look you in the eye or try to make eye contact when you think she's flirting?"

Majac thought about the bus ride back from the game and how each time he stole a glance in her direction that she seemed to be talking to one of her girls.

"Nahh, I don't think so, Pops."

Pops leaned back in the recliner and stared at Majac. He was witnessing his son figure out how the female psyche worked.

"What Pops?"

"Come on Boy, you're the smartest kid I know. And the dumbest."

Before Majac could answer, the living room telephone next to Pops' recliner started ringing.

He looked away from his son to answer it, expecting it to be his wife calling to tell him that she was on her way home. Pops caught the phone before the third ring. "Hello?" His eyes glistened as he turned toward Majac. "May I ask who's calling?" The look in his Pops eyes told Majac that it was the girl who had served Pops the dinners at the fundraiser. "Yeah, he's here. Who, may I ask, is calling?"

~~~

A long beat had passed since Solomon asked the question. When Tessa cleared her throat, Majac followed with, "Well now that I think about it, I would have to say that I fell in love with Tessa Ajai the first time she met my Pops."

The answer caused a looked of wonder to creep onto Tessa's face as she remembered the late, elder Mister Charles. She was fond of both of Majac's parents. But as she sat in that room, the memory of her first meeting with Majac's Pops escaped her.

Seeing that Tessa wasn't at the same moment in time as he, Majac offered two words, "Fish dinners."

Tessa erupted in laughter. The earnest look of joy on her face confirmed for both Solomon and Lawrence that her memory was now synched with his.

"Tessa, can you tell us when you knew you loved Anton?" Solomon asked once she stopped laughing.

Lawrence saw the smile that crept across Tessa's face as more telling to than any words she could string together. He'd smiled that same smile the day he saw his bride in her wedding dress on their wedding day. Although he'd never before met Tessa, her smile convinced Lawrence that her love for Majac would last a lifetime.

"I've been in love with MacArthur James Antonio Charles since the first day I met him in high school. I've felt like I've always loved him, but I've known that I've wanted to spend the rest of my life with him since my birthday last year. You see, I was packing my suitcase for my first trip to Seattle to meet my sister—a sister that I never knew I had—when Anton texted me out of the blue. Exchanging those words on that phone with him was the best birthday present I ever had. I didn't tell him that I was on my way to Seattle. And he didn't tell me that he had just arrived in Seattle. But the words in his texts told me that of all the women in the world, I was the only one he was thinking about. The only one he wanted to be in touch with. The only one in his heart." Tessa smiled at him.

All three men sat silent.

"I've been obsessed with my first love since the day he left me and joined the Navy, but because of the time we've been apart and the altercation last time we'd seen each other, I was uncertain of how to proceed. I was afraid of getting hurt."

"Hurt how?" Solomon asked.

"I wished he wanted me as much as I wanted him. If he could only understand the things that he does to me. I can't explain what it is about him that always makes me want to run back to him." Tessa paused for a moment, staring into Majac's eyes for understanding. "Seduction has always come easy for me, and I used to settle for the physical to pacify my desire for companionship. It was easy to find someone to play with and it didn't hurt that men found me attractive despite being such a geek. When you're lonely, almost anyone will do to fill your idle time. But finding that incredibly special someone to share all your dreams is hard.

"I remember one guy telling me that because of my quirky personality, he didn't think I was that cute at first, but I became better looking the more he got to know me."

Majac smiled hard. He remembered calling her quirky.

"I guess when all is said and done, I love the way Anton can make me feel like I'm the only person in a room filled with hundreds of people." Majac returned the smile Tessa beamed across the table. "I hope that's the answer you were looking for," she said, turning to Solomon.

"I wasn't looking for a specific answer. I was looking for the honest truth."

"Do you mind if I say a couple of things?" Lawrence asked.

"Uh oh," Majac giggled, "it's scripture time.'

"Time for chapter and verse," Tessa added.

They hoped Lawrence would smile with them, but he did not. When it was apparent that their humor was lost on the Reverend, Majac nodded and pulled out a pen. Lawrence turned to Solomon, who nodded his permission to engage the couple.

"At some point in your marriage, you're going to ask yourself, *Do I want to leave my marriage?*" Lawrence said in a deep baritone. "You're going to realize that getting married was a monumental mistake and now that you're there, you have buyer's remorse?"

Majac and Tessa regarded each other in wonder. The matching

expression on their faces told that they questioned their counselor's tactics. Neither one knew whether to, or how to answer, so they remained silent.

For the next ten minutes, Majac and Tessa recorded numerous book, chapter and Bible verse numbers as Lawrence recited one passage after another regarding the sanctity of marriage, commitment, and the duties and responsibilities of husband and wife. Each time he asked a question, he continued with the biblical answer before the couple had a chance to offer their opinion of his inquiry. His tone was that of a minister; in character for his profession, but without all of the pomp and circumstance that accompanied delivering a Sunday sermon.

"Tell me what marriage means to you?" Lawrence said, his voice trailing off as if his sermon had concluded. "Not now, but write it down in your notebook. I want you to record this part separately. Keep your thoughts to yourself until your next session.

"Whew," Majac huffed.

"What's the matter?" Solomon asked. "Are you all right?"

"Yeah Doc, I'm good. I just didn't think that marriage counseling was going to be this deep."

"And what did you expect it to be?" Lawrence asked.

"I don't know to be honest. I guess I expected to be told that marriage is more than just hugs and kisses. That it's going to take a lot of work, but neither of you said any of that. I guess more than anything, I thought you were going to talk about the stuff in the wedding vows. You know, love, honor and cherish, and then after all of the love, we'd touch on sex in the marriage. I didn't...I just."

Then Lawrence smiled, broad and wide.

"Awe shoot," Majac said, realizing the diabolic intent that lay behind that grin. "Go ahead pastor; get it off your chest."

"Well since you asked," Lawrence started. "There's a portion of the vows that go, I don't know, something like 'and forsaking all others, be faithful only to him or her'. Before you get any further down this rabbit hole called engagement, hoping everything is going to be all peaches and cream when you pop out on the other side called marriage, you should be certain that all of the other chapters in your life are closed. You want a fresh start, and in that, you need everyone from your past to know that they are just that. Your past."

Majac and Tessa stared silently at each other. Contemplated how the other was digesting the pastor's words. When his cellphone buzzed in his pocket, Majac almost jumped out of his skin.

"You all right?" came at him from three different directions.

It was as if the devil himself was making his cell phone ring at that particular moment because he had called Celeste Devereaux instead of throwing her number away. *Damn you Jaz! Why'd you give me her number? Why didn't you just throw it away after she left?* The thought of it being Celeste calling caused Majac to break into a sweat.

"Do you need to answer that?" Tessa asked. "It might be the ship."

Her words made perfect sense. Murphy's Law was a force to be reckoned with. And despite having only left a voicemail, he knew that if he pulled out his phone in front of her, that there would be a 619 area code on the display. Majac wiped his brow. He reached into his blazer and tapped the screen to silence his phone. Exhaling deeply, he looked at the session timer and said, "The ship is all the way in Bangor. Nothing I can do that won't keep for the next ten minutes. I'll call back when our session is over."

The look of bewilderment on Tessa's face spoke her worry. "Baby, what's wrong?"

"Nothing," Majac said. "It's our time for us right now. Let's just get through the end of the session and then I'll check on it."

"Are you sure?"

"I'm certain."

"Anton, if it's an emergency, we can take a break," Solomon said.

"All good, Doc," Majac said. His words more compelling than his face.

"All right," Solomon said. "Well, since we're almost finished anyway, I just want to say that if you read all of the chapters Lawrence referred you to, you will see that everything you just mentioned is in there. As far as the sex...I mean, as far as the love making..."

"Lovemaking is a sacred art," Lawrence interrupted forcefully.

"Sleep with your spouse, but only with profound love in your heart. Merge your bodies, minds and spirits, and you'll effectively be offering yourself to them on a silver platter. Always remember that the metaphysics of lovemaking goes way beyond the physicality of having sex."

The room was quiet for a beat. Eye contact was shared between all four, but the room remained devoid of spoken words. A moment later, a beep-beep-beep signaled the end of the session. Lawrence was the first to stand. For the last half hour, he'd needed to use the restroom but didn't want to seem rude by exiting the session. "It was nice meeting you Tessa. I wish you and Anton the best," he said, turning to exit the room.

"Nice meeting you as well. Maybe one day we'll make it to service at your church?"

"You're always welcome," Lawrence said then turned and disappeared into the hallway.

"We really appreciate you making time to see us at your home on a Saturday," Majac said to Solomon as they made their way down the hall towards the foyer.

Tessa paused. Her purse jingled as a series of three text messages registered on her cell phone. She pulled her cell out of her purse.

Majac pulled his cell out of his jacket to see his missed call as Tessa read her messages.

Their sighs came simultaneously. Hers, a sigh of frustration. His, a sigh of relief.

"Something wrong?" Majac asked.

"There goes dinner," Tessa huffed. She answered the questioning look on Majac's face by saying, "Gang shooting on 21st Street. Looks like I'll need to take a raincheck on dinner."

"I'll come with you," Majac said. "Afterwards, we can grab a bite."

"I appreciate that Honey, but I don't want you sitting around waiting on me. Besides, there's no telling how long this is gonna take."

"I don't mind waiting for you."

"That's sweet," Tessa said, kissing him gently on the lips. "Why don't you let me take you to brunch tomorrow to make up for dinner tonight?"

"After church, I suppose?" Lawrence asked from behind them.

"Yes Pastor. After church," Tessa laughed. "Please send Anton the address. We'll be there."

"Good," Lawrence said with a chuckle. He shook hands with the couple as they made their way onto the porch.

Returning her phone to her purse, Tessa stretched her arms wide and pulled Majac close. "Come on," she said, pressing her nose to his neck. "Let me smell you."

Lawrence and Solomon averted their gaze while the lovebirds kissed.

"Hey Majac, do you like boxing?" Solomon asked when he heard the pair talking again.

"Haven't really watched it since Tyson retired."

"Well, why don't you come hang with us?" Solomon offered. "Des always has plenty of food at Kenny's parties, and there's no reason for you to be alone. Especially on a Saturday night."

"Thanks, Partna," Majac said. "Count me in."

20

Belle of The Ball

ON AN UNSEASONABLY WARM DECEMBER AFTERNOON, eight weeks after departing Hawaii, the RIMPAC sailing group arrived in San Diego to celebrate the successful completion of the exercise. That Thursday evening, after all of the ships were moored, the admiral hosted a social for the officers from all of the wardrooms. On Friday, an all-day Admiral's Cup sports competition was hosted on Seal Beach. Almost a thousand sailors from ships representing four countries enjoyed a beach cookout where they played volleyball and sand soccer, participated in obstacle course and swimming relays, and tug-of-war competitions throughout the day. On a dazzling, mid-sixties, Saturday evening, clouds and stars dotted an endless, dark-blue sky as the officers and crew of the nine ships descended upon the Coronado Convention Center to attend the Admiral's Ball: the culmination of the RIMPAC exercise.

The deep, rich burgundy colors of the paisley carpet in the foyer offered a warm welcome to its guests. The round-faced woman at the receiving table with short hair and black, horn-rimmed glasses asked everyone their name upon arrival and presented them with a plastic poker chip notating which table they'd be dining. Groups of sailors and officers huddled in pockets about the foyer, mingling, exchanging stories, and absorbing the beautiful architecture of the historic building.

At seven o'clock, the doors to the dining area slid open allowing the crowd access to the main ballroom. A circular bar was the centerpiece of the massive dining area. Dozens of round tables set with plastic, sea-creature centerpieces dotted the room. A dance floor took up two-thirds of the east wall and was big enough to host American Bandstand.

The arched, exposed-wood ceiling gave the room character and grace. Majac was talking to the Captain of an Australian Destroyer when she entered the ballroom. She was by herself in an attention seeking dress— custom-designed, maroon-hued Dolce & Gabbana gown with a circular, open back —which, doing its job, engaged the attention of every man in the place. When he recognized her, he lost his voice. All of the women were dolled up. Most were attractive. Some were very pretty. She was absolutely gorgeous.

Puzzled with why he stopped talking, Majac's Aussie counterpart turned to see what—or better yet, who—had derailed his attention.

"Do you know her?" the Australian Destroyer Captain asked, now staring at the same woman.

"If she is who I think she is," Majac replied, "she's an old friend."

When he saw she was facing their direction, the Australian waved to get her attention. The smile stretched across her face indicated his success.

Celeste Devereaux approached the two men with a confident swagger in her step. Heads turned as if sucker punched, trying to get a better view of the woman whose body belonged to that of the Gods. Two seconds after she passed, the intoxicating aroma of her Gucci Rush perfume whispered look what you just missed, to the Australian. She gave Majac a warm hug hello and a kiss on both cheeks. The Australian noticed the extra-long hug, thinking it odd, considering he said she was just a friend. Instantly feeling ignored, the Australian cleared his throat.

"I'm sorry," Majac said. "Ms. Celeste Devereaux, this is Terry Watts, Commanding Officer of Australia's Destroyer Ginsburg."

Celeste offered her hand and the Australian kissed it. She smiled and said, "I hope you don't mind Terry, but I am going to steal this one a way for a moment. It's been awhile and I'd like to catch up."

"No problem. Maybe I'll get to talk with you after dinner. Where are you sitting?"

"Appears I am at table twenty-one," Celeste said peering at the chip bearing her table number.

"Nonsense," Terry said. "My second chair is open. You can join Captain Charles and me at table four."

"Table Four. That's front row. Are you sure that's okay?" Celeste asked, shifting her gaze between the two men in uniform. "I don't want to mess up anyone's seating arrangements."

"If it's okay with Terry, then it's fine with me," Majac cosigned. "Besides, what's the point in being a CO if you can't pull rank?"

"Great then, it's settled," Terry said, joining Majac in a laugh. "While you too talk, I'm going to fill this empty glass in my hand. Can I get either of you anything?" Terry said before turning and walking towards the bar.

"Well don't you look great?" Celeste said. "Commander, huh? Looks good on you."

"Not half as good as you look," Majac replied. "That dress is telling a story."

"And just what story is that?"

"That you are still the baddest woman in all of San Diego."

"Well thank you, Sir," Celeste said smiling so he could see all of her perfect teeth.

"Why don't we get that drink and find our table?"

Majac found Terry at the bar, bought Celeste a drink then escorted her to his table where, for the next twenty minutes, she listened intently as he caught her up on where he'd been since leaving San Diego five years earlier. When the Admiral's Chief Staff Officer invited everyone to dinner, Terry Watts joined the table with more drinks in hand.

For dinner, Majac and Celeste both enjoyed a great piece of prime rib with baked sweet potato and sautéed spinach. Celeste had a couple of glasses of Bordeaux while Majac had iced tea. They ate, talked about the recent rash of basketball players getting into trouble over women, the upcoming NFL playoffs and surprisingly to him, she did not mention anything about her job, her sister, or how she came to be at the dinner.

After a short speech acknowledging the success of RIMPAC, the Admiral invited everyone to enjoy their dinner, enjoy the rest of their weekend in San Diego, drink responsibly and enjoy the live band because they were a favorite of his. He stepped away from the mic for a minute, then returned quickly, encouraging everyone to "Make sure you tip your terrific wait staff generously. They've done a terrific job tonight." He left the podium to a tremendous applause.

Having eaten all that her tight dress would allow, Celeste announced that she was ready to dance. Captivated by how magnificent she looked in her dress, Terry slid his chair out before Majac had a chance to answer, grabbed Celeste's chair and jokingly said, "I thought you'd never ask."

She shrugged her shoulders and shared a laugh with Majac as Terry escorted her to the dance floor. Majac had twice visited Australia. He knew how upbeat the Australian's could be when it was time to party.

Terry, despite his position as Captain, threw all caution to the wind when he hit the dance floor. For the better part of a half hour he jerked, spun, bounced, moon-walked, and hopped with arms flailing and hips gyrating as he danced circles around Celeste—who did not move much in her tight dress. When the music finally slowed, Majac picked up Terry's drink and made his way to the dance floor to rescue the barely dancing diva from further distress.

Exchanging Terry's cocktail for the lady in the cocktail dress, Majac took Celeste's hand, spun her gently then wrapped an arm around her and gracefully pulled her into him. While they danced, Majac made every attempt to not let his hand wander from where it set on the curve of her hip. Had it been earlier, when they were together, he would have pulled her close enough to wrinkle the delicate material of her fancy, delicate gown. Instead, he slow-stepped her around the dance floor for a couple of songs, expertly guiding her motion with his hand caressing her skin through the circular, open back of her gown.

After putting their dancing shoes through the ringer, Majac and Celeste made their way out onto the balcony overlooking the San Diego Harbor. From their vantage point, they could see the lights outlining the ships moored at the base. She turned to him, pointed across the water and asked, "So which one is yours?"

Majac put his hand above his eyes and looked off into the distance toward the base. "I think we are somewhere down there to the right."

"How can you tell as dark as it is over there?" she asked.

"I really can't," Majac said. "I just guessed based on what I remember from when we came up the river." They laughed. He said, "We're here for another two days. Now that I'm the Captain, would you like to see my ship?" When he was the Engineer on USS TUSKEGEE, he'd invited her to the ship several times, but she'd always declined.

"I have a full day Monday, but maybe we can squeeze it in tomorrow afternoon. That is of course if you are willing to come back across the water and get me."

"No need for that," he said. "I'm spending the night on the island."

"Not on the ship?"

"Not tonight. Each of the Commanding Officers have a room here at the Hotel Coronado."

"What a coincidence," she said, feigning wonder, as she placed a hand to her chest, covering her exposed cleavage. "I live right across the street at the Westin."

"Really?" Majac said incredulously.

"Yes, Mister Charles." Her mouth straightened into a line. "Really."

At that point, he wasn't certain of her intentions, but he was certain that she was intent on him seeing her place, no matter what it took.

"The Westin, huh? Isn't that interesting?" He wondered how much coincidence could there be in her, a civilian with no true military ties, having an invite to the ball and living right next door?

Celeste had never been the conniving or devious type of woman when they dated, but nevertheless he had experienced a relationship with this woman, and he knew that her words did not always reflect the intentions of her actions. Unlike her crazy, younger sister Marissa, she was not a bad person; she just hadn't been openly truthful with him about things when they were together. But that was years ago and tonight was extremely pleasant so far. She hadn't mentioned their past and neither had he.

They were living in the present and she seemed to be over him the same way he was over her. Or at least the way he thought he was over her.

"What happened to your house?"

"I sold it about a year ago. Would you like to see my new place? I'm really enjoying our conversation and if you don't mind, there's something personal I'd like to talk to you about."

"Personal?" Again his tone was incredulous. He looked down at her stomach, remembering that she was pregnant the last time he saw her.

"Yes, personal," she said sternly. "If I remember correctly, when we dated, we not only used to be more than friends, but we were also friendly. I haven't seen you in years and I'd just like to talk without so many eyes and ears around. Someplace I feel comfortable. And besides, my condo has a nineteenth floor view of San Diego that is to die for." Celeste invited Majac over because she hadn't seen nor heard from him in more than five years. When she heard his voice on her answering service, she practically jumped for joy. Now with him standing before her, she exerted every ounce of self-control to prevent herself from acting like a schoolgirl with a crush on the prom king. They hadn't discussed the current state of their relationships, but from the absence of a ring on his finger, she assumed he was still a free man.

When she'd given her phone number to Jaz during his visit to San Diego, she inquired if Majac was still in the Navy. Jaz told her that he was and being the proud friend that he was, told her that he was now the Captain of his own submarine. With little convincing, he was also forthcoming with the name of his ship. Celeste's company partnered with the Navy League to sponsor the RIMPAC cookout, so when she saw his submarine's name on the list of attending ships, she was well aware of when Majac would be in town. And for the most part, she knew where he was going to be based on her involvement with the planning for the RIMPAC Cup competition and Admiral's Ball.

Saturday afternoon, Celeste took a long bath. She moisturized with a honey, jasmine and lavender lotion with enough pheromones to attract any mammal with testosterone in his blood for a hundred miles.

She then put on some of her fancy satin and lace panties with a matching garter. Her dress was so form-fitting that she almost passed out holding her breath trying to slide into it. Hair, nails and makeup perfected to match her dress, Celeste took her company invitation and proceeded to find her Majac man at the Admiral's Ball.

They stood next to each other on the balcony across a ringing silence. Below them, waves washed gently onto the beach. Sailing the seas taught a man many lessons, and chief among them was patience. He looked out over the bay and sipped some more of his Long Island Iced Tea.

After a beat passed, Celeste took another sip of her wine. "So Captain, you have time to make sure a girl gets home safe?"

Majac smiled, checked his watch and said, "Sure, I've got a little time."

Majac and Celeste walked the long block to her hotel in silence. She gazed at Christmas trees that looked like they were winking at her and knew what she had on her mind. When they arrived at the Westin, he stepped back in a gracious manner when the elevator door opened and motioned for her to enter first.

She thought back to how he had always opened doors and let her enter first. Always treated her like a queen. Feeling naughty, and wanting to sneak a peek at his butt in that crisp white uniform, she smiled at him playfully and insisted that he go first. They walked into her suite and were greeted by classical jazz. "I have got to get out of these shoes," she said.

"Whoever convinced women that open-toed heels were cute never had to spend an entire day walking miles in the same pair before being able to take the dreaded things off. Let alone dance in them." Right then, she wanted someone to rub the swollen feet left behind by those 'cute' shoes.

"Make yourself at home. There's some flavored, sparkling water in the fridge. The bar is in the dining room to the left of the kitchen. Don't worry, nothing in here will bite." she said with a smile as she disappeared into a back room to change clothes. She didn't see it, but Majac wasn't smiling.

Celeste had bitten him once, playfully she thought, while making love one afternoon. He'd cried out upset and pushed her away for a second, when she returned to him, she tried it again, only softer. He'd surrendered to it because it felt better than anything he'd ever felt before. He recalled that she slept with one arm curled beneath her head and the other resting on her full breasts. He always woke first. He attributed that to his military training needing him to rise early. You know the *We do more before nine a.m.* mantra from the television commercials. He lived that early riser philosophy, even on his days off. Sometimes he'd stay awake late in the night so he could watch her sleep. The sound of her breathing comforted him. He loved the sweet smell of her hair. Sometimes he'd wake her by gently pushing his knee between her thighs and she would roll onto him without a word. Her body ripe for his body, their tongues would fill each other's mouths. Often he'd wait until morning so he could see her face as the slatted light entered through the blinds of her apartment. Then he'd find her with his mouth, and she would moan softly or sometimes laugh outright at his audacity that he wouldn't consider her bladder was full after an entire night's sleep. Back then he was truly glad to be with her despite Crystal's warnings about the bad voodoo vibe she gave her. Celeste Devereaux. Celeste Devereaux naked. He stood there amazed. Despite their awful ending, and being engaged to Tessa, he still wouldn't mind seeing Celeste Devereaux naked again after all these years.

Majac poured himself a glass of White Hennessy and looked around. Celeste's penthouse was fabulous. It looked like something out of Lavish Living magazine. There were Roman columns, a majestic fireplace, marble floors and oriental rugs. Besides the vainglorious picture over the fireplace, there was artwork everywhere. Pieces from all over the globe. Everything looked in its perfect place, without looking cluttered. She still had excellent taste, he thought.

Celeste changed into a wide-bottom, black skirt and a long, loose-fitting blouse the color of flaming coals. She walked back into the living room barefoot and saw Majac looking out the large picture window at the San Diego skyline.

"San Diego's still as beautiful as I remember it," Majac said as he turned around with a smile full of white teeth.

She saw that he had unbuttoned his collar and top button of his jacket. Simultaneously, she was turned on and intimidated. "It's all right," she said, detouring into the kitchen to get a beer from the fridge.

"You must be doing well for yourself," he said, waving his arm at the collection of finery throughout her condo. "Tell me again what you do?"

"I am the Director of Product Marketing for Qualcomm," she said, joining him in front of the large window.

"Qualcomm?" he asked. "Like the communications company that owns the football stadium, Qualcomm?"

"Yes, Anton," she said laughing. "As in the football stadium, Qualcomm."

They laughed and touched glasses in a salute to her success.

"Did I mention that I was taking some law classes at San Diego State? I'm thinking about starting my own Sports Agency."

"Wow, you're going to have more degrees than a thermometer. Where do you find time to run a marketing department, start a business, and go to school?"

"I go to bed late and I get up early."

"Well I'd tip my hat to you, if I was wearing one," he teased.

When Majac and Celeste met, she was a financial assistant at a local bank and a cheerleader for the NBA's San Diego Cougars. They dated for almost two years. Majac was about to propose when he found out that her ex-boyfriend wasn't completely out of the picture. A couple of months later, Majac would leave San Diego, but not before finding out that Celeste was pregnant. Until Jaz told him that he'd run into her a couple of months back, Majac hadn't heard from her in more than five years and had never confirmed that the baby was his, her ex-boyfriend's, or if she even gave birth.

Majac looked at the pictures on the wall trying to see family members, special events, and most important, any pictures of Celeste with a child young enough to maybe be his. There was no evidence of a child where he could see, but that didn't mean she didn't prepare for his arrival and rearrange her place so that he wouldn't see what she didn't want him to.

She never did say what she wanted to talk about. Getting him alone in her condo would be the perfect place to spring a child on him. "So what did you want to talk about?" Majac asked.

"How's your love life?" she blurted out. "No, I'm just kidding." Although it was one of the things on her mind, it wasn't the subject she was referring to when she asked him back to her place. As long as he was there with her, she didn't really care what his love life was someplace else. She was in the here and now. That was all that mattered to her.

"That's what you want to talk to me about?" Majac asked.

"What? No! I mean…" His direct questioning caught her off guard and she wished she could turn it back on him.

"Then what?" he asked, removing some of the bass from his voice.

"I don't know, exactly," she said. Celeste started fanning herself, stalling for time. "Is it warm in here to you?" His brusqueness had thrown off her seduction. He was supposed to just relax, have a drink, get a little tipsy and let her seduce him. Why did he have to go and ask real questions? She stepped away from him and checked the thermometer. It indicated 72 degrees.

Majac turned back to the window and asked, "So whatever happened to your baby?"

"I don't want to talk about that," she said bluntly. The memory of the abortion clinic came into her thoughts, but she quickly pushed it away.

"Why not?"

"I said I don't want to talk about that."

"Then what do you want to talk to me about?"

"What if I just wanted to enjoy your company?"

"That's cool," Majac said as he looked at his heavy silver watch.

"Why didn't you just say that?"

"That's the second time you've looked at your watch tonight. Does the Admiral have you on a curfew?"

Majac turned and shot her a fierce look.

"Just joking," she said raising her hands in self-defense. "Take a pill."

Majac shook his head and sat down on the sofa. After a minute of toying with the thermostat, she sat down next to him.

"So how's your sister?" He hated asking the question the minute the words left his lips, but he wasn't quite sure what else to ask. During Majac's time in, her sister Marissa was a terrible person. An outright psychopath.

"My sister?" Celeste asked. The confusion in her tone seemed like she had no idea who he was talking about.

"Yes. Your sister. I think I remember her name being Marissa?"

"Mari. Yes…she's good." Her mind went blank. She didn't know why she had invited Majac to her room. Or did she? "I'm sorry, you caught me off-guard. I didn't think you would want to talk about her." Her attempt to get his fine body next to hers again was failing. She missed Anton. She went to the Ball just to see him and share a little friendly conversation. Find out a little about what he'd done and where he'd been the past five years. That was before she saw how good he looked. Before the memories of their relationship came flooding back. Before she had a couple more glasses of wine than she should have and started to think with something other than her brain. Anton wasn't a stranger. They were familiar in the biblical sense. She could rationalize enjoying uninhibited sex with this man. Could he still be interested in her? He must have some curiosity. After all, there wasn't a ring on her finger and he came to her place without a lot of provocation.

There was only one way to find out. She knew she couldn't count on Anton to make the first move no matter how bad he may have wanted to get with her. "Excuse me one more time," she said, placing her beer bottle on a coaster on the table. "Tiny bladder." She shot him a soft smile before leaving the room. "You remember."

"Sure. Sure." Majac smiled. "Take your time."

She noticed how easily he smiled, and felt herself melting like butter on hot toast. She wondered, *Is that the kind of smile that comes with being comfortable with yourself?* She went into the bathroom and pulled off her blouse, then dropped her skirt. She looked in the full-length mirror and noticed the glaze of excitement in her eyes. When she noticed her wetness, it was clear that her womanhood was obeying no master but its own mind. Surely Anton would remember that her body was built for sex. If he weren't interested in rekindling their relationship, he could at least give her a night of pleasure. She brushed her teeth, mussed her hair and sprayed parfum directly below her navel at the silk mesh fabric of her underwear hiding the landing strip of short, neatly manicured hairs. She took a close look at her perfectly made-up face, ran her hands along her sides and said, "Let's do this."

For a few uncomfortable seconds, then confidently, and all but nude, she exited the bathroom. Smooth as melted chocolate, she glided through the door and padded into the living room with the majesty of a Persian cat.

Majac sat reading a magazine. When he looked up and saw her nearly naked body, he jumped back like he was afraid of snakes. A second later, the snake between his legs looked too. He remained seated.to hide his arousal. "Celeste? What's going on?"

"You tell me," she smiled shyly and walked toward the window overlooking the city. She could feel Majac stealing glances of her ass. When she turned around, his eyes weren't looking at hers.

It took everything within him to look away. A panicked irritation swept across his face and he said, "I think I need to go."

"Why? The party is just getting started."

She was gorgeous at the party; but now, standing before him, the remarkable beauty of her hair, face and body were beyond compare. "Celeste, why are you doing this?" he asked. His voice was low, husky, and full of confusion.

Celeste looked in his eyes, but they were unreadable. There was a long tense silence. Her body covered in a thin nervous sweat. She finally broke the silence to ask, "What if I did want to get with you? Are you game?"

After a beat of silence, Majac spoke in measured tones. "I'm flattered Celeste, but I mean, I don't just hop in bed because some good…I mean great looking woman wants to. I mean, I used to, but…I…I…I only make love with someone I'm intimate with. We don't have that anymore. I'm engaged and getting ready to get married. I mean, you're beautiful and still incredibly attractive, but why would I risk causing this woman that much pain?" He started to tell her about the wedding plans, but figured the less he said, the better. "We haven't seen each other in years," he said. "You don't know anything about me anymore."

"I know you're here in my apartment." She paused long enough for him to speak, but he remained silent. "Does she?"

"I'm not talking about that part of my life. This is about you and me."

"You wanted to marry me at one point in our lives. That should matter?"

A pit of anger settled in his stomach. He could remember everything about their last night together. The view from the floor as she walked away from him. The details of the back of her. What she had on. What she looked like. What she smelled like. How her hips moved when she walked. How her lips moved when she talked. How she had thrown pounds of sensuality into the Macarena when they danced. What her body felt like against his when they slow danced. The emptiness he felt when she walked away after being that close to accepting his marriage proposal.

"If you don't want to get with me, that's cool," Celeste yelled. "There are plenty of men that would love some of this," she said, all of a sudden feeling uncomfortable about being next to naked. She grabbed one of the curtains and stepped behind it.

Majac wondered if she was playing some type of game. Did she want him to just rush in and take the ass; or did she want something more? He wasn't looking for a relationship. He was already in one. The second serious one in his life. Celeste was his first serious relationship, but that was half a decade ago. He had never been a man to recycle a relationship, and he wasn't about to start now. "Celeste, I think you're a great girl. And if I weren't engaged, I would definitely consider doing this with you tonight…"

"Engaged," she scoffed. "Humph. Well congratulations."

A beat of angry silence passed between them.

"But if I'm going to be totally open and honest with you," he continued. "I can't be involved with a woman who might think it's all right to one day want to drop an infidelity bomb on my relationship. I want someone who honors a relationship, no matter what the relationship." He recalled the image of her walking naked into and across the room. "You've got a slamming body, but I can't."

"Then leave!" she said curtly, shifting her body behind the curtain. Tears fell from her eyes.

Majac stood. "Are you going to be all right?" When she didn't answer, Majac repeated more forcefully, "Are you going to be all right?"

"I'm cool," she said, and felt how ironic the popular saying felt at that moment. She was anything but cool. She was a little more than half-drunk, horny and almost naked, and her bare ass was plastered against a window for all of San Diego to see. No, she wasn't all right, and unless he took his clothes off and got naked with her, or left her place right away, she wasn't going to be all right.

Majac started fumbling in his pocket. He walked to her, pulled something from it and said, "I want to leave you with something." He reached out his left hand and held it to her.

"What?" she asked, opening her palm like a kid about to receive candy.

Majac noticed sweat glistening on her face, and when she spoke, her voice took on a certain childlike innocence. "This." He placed in hers a gold coin embossed with his ship's emblem.

"What is that?"

"My command coin. It's a memento that signifies my tour as commanding officer on my submarine. Remember me every time you see it. It gives me a lot of confidence. Commanding sailors gives me the ability to look myself in the mirror and be proud of the man that I've become.

"I want you to have this and believe that it will give you courage to make the right decisions about your life. I want you to be totally happy when you look at yourself in the mirror, even if there ever comes a time when you don't have a perfect body."

She gazed at the coin and then into Anton's eyes. Inside them was a look of promise and comfort. His thoughtfulness seemed sincere, but she couldn't speak, so she closed her hand with the coin in her sweaty palm and pulled the curtain up to her neck.

"Maybe one day the coin will help you the way it helps me. Maybe one day you won't need it anymore. I hope when that day comes, you will pass it on to someone who needs it." Majac took a handkerchief from his other pocket and wiped her tears. "There will always be someone who'll need it. Who knows, I might need it again."

Her blank eyes roamed the room in silence. The silence brought a chill. The emptiness of the luxury apartment engulfed her.

Majac wiped her tears again. "I'm going to leave now, but I'll call you tomorrow afternoon if you're still interested in taking a tour of my boat."

When the door closed behind him, Celeste threw the coin across the room. She picked up her beer and emptied the bottle, then picked up his glass and drank the last of his White Hennessy. Then she turned out all of the lights in the suite. In her expensive lingerie, she stood in front of the plate glass window overlooking the brightly illuminated San Diego nightline until she saw his tiny form emerge from the building onto the sidewalk below. Tears streamed down her face. She was lonely. Had been rejected. Whatever pride she'd had exiting the bathroom— painted, naked...and horny—had vanished. Now, standing alone in the darkness, she felt tarnished...and ugly.

21

Scratching A Riff

SOLOMON ARRIVED AT LEONA'S DANCE studio just before one-thirty. He hurriedly parked his '68 Mustang and, taking the steps two at a time, bounded up to the second floor. A muscular man stood just inside the studio door. Solomon excused himself as he entered. The man faced Solomon, but didn't move so he could enter. The two six-foot behemoths exchanged glares for a beat. Solomon saw Désirée waving him over. Unfamiliar with the man or his story, Solomon humbly said, "Excuse me, Brother. I'm running a little late." Begrudgingly, the man turned his body. Solomon passed sideways, then climbed over a few people to join Désirée.

"Cutting it close, I see," was what she offered as a greeting.

"You know how traffic can be."

"Don't even," she said, twisting her lips at him. "Traffic?"

Solomon was the epitome of professionalism when he was in the office. His downfall, however, was that he was a bell tapper. He was notorious for sliding through the door just-in-time for the next thing. He was rarely late, but never early.

"Anyway, thank you for coming," Désirée said. "Leona's been raving about her class's graduation dance for weeks."

The lights dimmed and the drummer began to scratch a riff. The strum of the guitar string hummed a siren in stark contrast to the booming kick of the bass drum. Roombas rumbled. Bass notes rolled then stopped. At the edge of the stage, legs spread wide, feet turned out, Leona Pearson stood posed with her arms outstretched, fists balled like palmed grenades, head cocked back. The music paused, then fired again, the high-hat jerking like someone sprayed it with bullets. The shock of the rhythm took over and she high-stepped into the middle of the room where she doubled over as the rhythm took her down to her knees. Then she leapt, undeniable, as if the drum roll launched her forward and flung her towards the sky to dance. All of this while the guitarist and the drummer doo-wopped sweetly. She stopped and the music paused again. When it returned an octave higher, Leona's dance students entered from the opposite side of the stage to the uproarious applause of the crowd.

Leona's timing, tone, agility and breath control were astonishing, but more than that, she had an immaculate understanding of rhythm and tempo. Exercising the impeccabilities of an exotic dancer with a pair of perfect breasts, she used these gifts to tease the dance until the audience became enslaved. This was the secret of the great dancers like Gregory Hines, Alvin Ailey and the Nicholas Brothers. They could seduce the dance and have it produce emotions held secret from everyone, including its choreographer. Behind her, the troop of seven teenage girls, led by one tall, strikingly pretty girl, mimicked her every move. If those girls weren't professionals, then Leona was simply a good dance teacher.

The audience, a sellout following the rave reviews Leona received from Kendra Morrison on Good Morning Seattle, was as strongly excited by the dance as Solomon was vibing Leona following her flawless evolution from captive to conqueror with the intensity of a cheetah mauling a gazelle in the African savannah. When the motion of the dancers and the music stopped, Leona stood center stage bowing and smiling while Solomon joined the rest of the audience in enthusiastic applause.

His special connection to Leona filled him with pride. Looking around, he spotted the man who didn't want to let him enter standing in the back clapping harder than anyone else. His narrow jaw and slight chin drew a strong resemblance to that of the strikingly pretty girl in the dance troop.

After the performance, Solomon and Désirée stood at the end of the line of parents and family members who waited to take pictures with Leona and their girls. After the group photo and all of the individual pictures had been taken with the girls, then with the girls and their parents, Leona retreated to a table in the lobby to sign pictures and sign up potential new students. Four couples ahead of Solo and Désirée, the man from the door approached Leona's table. Without looking up, Leona reached out to receive his picture.

The man said something neither Solomon nor Désirée could hear causing Leona to snatch her hand away and quickly stand up.

"Oh, so now you don't have time for me?" the man said loudly.

"Get out," Leona ordered, crossing her arms. Her harsh gaze shot daggers towards the man.

He stared back at Leona with the same intensity. He reached in his pocket and pulled out a cigarette lighter. He raised his arm and stared at her as the lighter danced over and under his knuckles. That was his nervous habit. The thing he did, but didn't realize he was doing when he was nervous and didn't know what to say.

"Get out," Leona ordered again, this time much louder.

That's when one of the fathers, a broad-chested man of medium height, pushed back his blazer revealing a badge. He placed his hand on his service weapon and identified himself as a police officer. "Is there a problem, Ms. Pearson?"

The man with the lighter averted his gaze from Leona to the police officer. Seeing the badge, the gun, and the bulky size of the stout policeman, the man stopped twirling the lighter, palmed it, and raised his hands in retreat. "My bad officer," he said, returning his gaze to Leona. "Just a case of mistaken identity. No problem here."

The officer pocketed his badge and walked with his hand firmly on his pistol until the man with the lighter was out the door. He re-entered the lobby when the man was down the steps and out the door.

When the commotion settled, Leona went back to signing pictures with her girls from the dance troop. In the presence of the other parents, her entire dance class and Désirée, she did the unthinkable...she leaned across the table, rubbed her hand against his face, kissed Solomon on the cheek and said with authoritative nonchalance, "Would you wait for me?"

Their eyes met. There was a silence that hung in the air as the temperature between them soared through the roof.

Seeing the look of disbelief in her therapist's eyes, Leona recovered in an instant. She laughed, fanned herself, and made a joke about the heat. Solomon and Désirée laughed as well.

The question was so unexpected. The mood so light. Leona Pearson was a brilliant dancer, but she was unpredictable. For the first time in her life, she had feelings for a man to the point of exposing herself in a way she'd never done before. Being completely open and honest was something Solomon always admired in Mareschelle. And as others around him took to their feet and began to mill about before exiting the dance studio, Solomon asked for all to hear, "Leona, would you like to have dinner tonight?"

Three hours later, Leona Pearson sat on a bar stool at the island in Solomon's kitchen with her legs crossed and her clutch in her lap.

"So is it always that packed at your recitals?" he asked.

"Not normally. Usually only the parents come. Today's crowd was unusually large. I'm not certain why."

"Well, it was so packed in there, that I could barely get by this guy standing inside the door when I got there. I almost thought he was a bouncer. From the way he looked at me, I thought I was going to have to fight him just to get inside. At the end of the recital when I saw him clapping so hard, I figured he must've been related to one of your girls."

Leona had also noticed him clapping extra hard. Her eyes sank for a moment.

Solomon noticed.

"Do you know that guy?"

Leona exhaled a deep breath. The look on her face told that there were words bottled up inside her that couldn't quite find an exit.

"You all right?" he asked.

"Yes," she whispered.

"So, is he like an ex-boyfriend or something?"

"Or something," she murmured.

"Hey, if you don't want to talk about it, I won't press it."

"No, it's all right." Leona shifted in her seat and took a swallow from her glass. "After all, he's the reason I have to see Doctor Crittendon." Leona went on to explain that the man was the guy who had framed her, causing her to go to prison. She told how he tried to pimp her out and that he raped her. She didn't tell him about that rape resulting in her pregnancy.

"Wow. I'm sorry," Solomon said. "I didn't know." He reached his hand to hers, but reflexively, she pulled away. Solomon slowly retracted his hand.

Leona averted her eyes. She noticed a pleasant aroma coming from the oven. She forced a smile and asked, "WHAT…is that heavenly smell?"

Solomon sniffed at the air, but pretended not to notice the wonderful aroma wafting from the oven. "Oh that," he joked. "That would be my world famous baked chicken ala Alexandré. I also have spinach, carrot soufflé, baked macaroni and cheese, yeast rolls; and for dessert; drumroll please…"

Leona smiled as she drummed her hands rapidly against her thighs. "Peach cobbler."

"Homemade?" she asked excitedly.

"Using these two hands right here." He regarded her. "I guessed that it was your favorite."

"Yeah, but how did you know?"

He shrugged. "It was an educated guess. I remembered you saying you liked any and all things peach. Peach roses. Peach dresses. Peach desserts. And once you taste my cobbler, it's going to be your new favorite peach."

"Well Doctor Alexandré, if we were downstairs at the pool table, I'd tell you to put your money where your mouth is."

Again that devious smile returned. With his back turned to her he said, "I'd rather put my mouth where your money is."

When he turned back to her, Leona looked confused. When his eyes dropped to her clutch, she laughed out loud. "You are horrible."

He stepped inside her bubble, kissed her cheek and gave a wicked grin. "And you even taste sweet like a peach."

"Thank you." Still seated, she laughed, grabbed her skirt and curtsied. "Darn it," she cried, releasing her dress.

"What's wrong?"

"I broke a fingernail," she said, picking at the nail hanging from the middle finger of her left hand. She extended the lone finger towards him and asked, "See?"

"Funny," he said.

"Do you have a file or nail clippers?" she asked when they finished laughing.

The oven timer chimed. Solomon opened the door and saw his macaroni bubbling. "Yeah. Give me a minute and I'll go grab it for you," he said, rushing to pull the hot, bubbly pasta from the oven.

"Just tell me where it is. I can get it."

"Upstairs; back bedroom. Top bathroom drawer, next to the sink."

"Thanks," she said exiting the kitchen. "I'll be right back."

"Don't get lost, Carmen San Diego."

"Don't burn the macaroni, Chef Boyardee."

While he tended to the pot of baked pasta, she made her way upstairs. The last time she'd been up here, they'd made love in the bedroom at the opposite end of the hall. From the looks of it, the back bedroom was his master suite. *He probably sent me come up here by myself so I could accidentally stumble across the whips and chains, and mirrors on the ceiling*, she thought.

His bathroom door was wide open so she went right in. After finding the clippers and effecting a temporary nail repair that would hold until her manicurist, AJ, could make it right, she exited the bathroom and headed towards the window overlooking the backyard. Stopping at the armoire, she perused his watch and Cologne collection. She saw a two-thirds empty bottle of Invictus by Paco Rabanne and picked it up. She was impressed. It was one of her favorite scents on a man. She squirted a single puff onto a shirt draped across the valet stand in the corner near the window. After taking a deep breath of the fine aroma, she returned the bottle to its resting place, turned off the light and made her way out into the hallway.

When Leona returned to the dining room, she saw Solomon set their dinner plates on the table. "Now didn't you just ask me if you could cook for me before we left the recital?"

"Yes."

"That was at four o'clock, correct?"

"Yes."

"And now it's seven o'clock, correct?"

"Right again." Solomon took his chair and admired her silently. He knew where the conversation was going. Despite the facial imperfection, the time in jail, going M-I-A for five years, and the way she moved on the dance floor, she was simply the girl next door. As much as he tried to deny it, her mysterious past woke up something inside him. He was on the way home to a problem. A crisis to deal with. Ran into her and became distracted. Meeting her made everything else going on in his life, everything bad that had happened, seem irrelevant and small.

"So in the span of less than three hours, you expect me to believe that you went to the store bought all this food, brought it home, and just whipped this up? Baked chicken, macaroni and cheese, and homemade peach cobbler? And on top of that, had time to shower and make sure your house was clean?"

"Yes inspector, that's what I'm telling you."

"I want to lean toward saying impossible, but we all know that nothing is impossible if you put your mind to it. Nevertheless, I will say that I need the name of your maid service and your caterer before I leave."

Solomon leaned back in his chair. "All right, you caught me. The yeast rolls are courtesy of Golden Corral. Half-dozen for five dollars, you can't beat that."

"Ah ha," she spouted. "I knew you were a fraud."

"But the rest of it is 100% courtesy of Chef Alexandré," he said, ignoring her character assassination.

"So you just assumed that I would be willing to come to your house and break bread with you? How do you know that I didn't want the safety of dining in a public restaurant?"

Solomon flashed a wicked grin.

Leona felt a muscle in her left eye twitch and had to make a conscious effort to keep her knees together.

"I was hopeful," he said.

More like confident, she thought, continuing to admire his perfect smile. And he had every right to be. She really liked him. And she was sure that he could tell. As heated and open as she was at the moment, he could probably smell her attraction the way a wolf could smell fear.

Again, he chuckled.

"What?" she asked.

"I was just thinking that we have had some long dates. All day affairs."

"Yes, that thought has crossed my mind before." She studied his face. "I sense a complaint coming?"

"Are you growing tired of me already?"

"Well, I think you're a pretty smart guy."

"And I think I like you inside and out."

"You want to put some of that smartness in me and turn me out?"

"I want to study your brain. Get all up inside your head."

"Get up in my head…while I give you brain?"

"A fair exchange," he started.

"Ain't no robbery," she finished.

They both laughed out loud at how silly they were being. Solomon cleared their plates then returned with dessert and more wine. Despite their combined apprehension, they found comfort in each other. Found it easy to relax when they were together. She knew what he did and how he did it, and despite her being a patient similar to his, only twenty feet away in another office, she admired and respected his work.

She opened up to him while he stuffed cobbler in his mouth. Told him that her mom married when she was sixteen. Gave birth to Jennifer when she was nineteen. And that it would be another ten years before she came along. Told him that the obituary photo was the only picture she had of her mother. That other than the stories Jennifer told her, she retained no personal memories of times shared with her mother and father.

After dinner they retreated to the front room. Solomon changed the music from the classic jazz that had played through dinner, to the smooth sounds of that Me'Shell woman with the hard to pronounce last name. He sat on the sofa and patted the cushion for Leona to join him.

She ignored his invite, choosing instead to wander around the room sipping her wine. A picture of a woman sat on his mantle. The looks of people and décor in the background suggested that the picture had to be more than 40-years old. Back when the woman was probably in her twenties.

"Who's the Diva?" Leona asked.

"My mother."

"She favors your receptionist."

"One in the same."

She appeared to be at a nightclub, maybe working as a hostess or a singer but definitely not a waitress. Her face was flawless. Makeup perfect. Her shiny dress appeared to be covered in sequins and was way too expensive to be worn by a waitress. She held a cigarette in the tip of her fingers on one hand and a glass of clear liquid, probably vodka, in the other. Leaning on the sofa, looking as frisky as she could for the camera, she smiled gaily and appeared to be the absolute life of the party. A diva in her prime, she was a far cry from the cranky Bible thumper who sat in his office pretending to be his secretary.

After taking a good look at everything she didn't remember seeing during her first tour of his living room, Leona finally came to rest on the sofa next to him. Her glass was empty. When he offered to refill it, she declined and pulled him into a kiss. Twenty minutes later after they'd both worked up a glimmer of perspiration from the intense making out, Leona stood, took his hand and walked him up the stairs.

As she stood in the doorway of his dark master bedroom, he entered, turned on a dim light near the headboard and pressed the power button on the stereo. He turned the volume up, but kept it low enough that they could hear each other talk. He went back to her, indulging in the perfection of her curves and edges highlighted in the silhouette cast by the light from the hallway behind her.

She pulled him close to her and he gave, their bodies continuing until they were fastened together. He clasped one hand on her butt and the other in the center of her back searching for the clasp of her bra. Her words *Show me something naughty* slipped out of her in the form of a groan, and, recognizing it for what it was, he wrapped his hands around her waist.

He kicked the door shut and lifted her off the floor. She wrapped her legs around his waist. Solomon was nowhere near the dancer she was. However, he was a confident man who knew how to move when a woman was in his arms. Their dance incited another kiss as he plunged his tongue into the warm and welcoming space between her lips. Shivers shot through her as her arms went around his neck and tightened. The sharp tips of her breasts pressing against his chest told him that she wanted him as much as he wanted her.

Even though Mareschelle had passed more than three years ago, Solomon knew he still wasn't ready for a serious commitment. Although he didn't want to be known as a womanizer, he wasn't averse to a casual relationship where the woman understood that he was satisfying her physical needs and she was satisfying his.

Following two solid minutes of intense kissing, his manhood hardened and began pressing against her. Excitement shot through her. She pushed her skirt into him with the heated warmth of her soft mound. Visions of what was to come had her writhing and twisting against him as her mercury screamed past boiling, anxious to experience the pleasure of an overdue orgasm. After he freed her bra, she unfastened the two buttons that closed her blouse, exposing her high, rounded breasts.

He lifted her higher, sucked her left nipple into his warm mouth and squeezed her butt harder. When he came up for air, his words, "Mmmm… I never—" were garbled.

Before he could finish, she planted her mouth to his. Slid her tongue deep inside. A deep moan filled his ears as she struggled to unbutton his shirt. Lighting her on her bare feet, he slipped her skirt to the floor—she wore no panties. Her eyes grew with excitement and anticipation.

He scooped her up roughly. Strong arms carried her as they kissed. He sat her hips on the back of his plush reading sofa. He broke the kiss and gently pushed her, holding her hips as her shoulders and back splashed softly onto the cushion of the comfortable chair. Her smile was delirious.

His smile was devious in return. He pushed her knees together and went to turn up the stereo. Turned the volume up loud enough for his neighbors to sing along to Maxwell's *Bad Habits*, even if they didn't know the words.

Leona laid upside down on the back of the sofa anxiously awaiting his return; her feet fluttering, her legs bent at the knees dangling like a toddler.

He returned, knelt before her, raised her feet toward the ceiling and plunged his tongue into her. She exhaled like she'd been punched in the stomach. His strong groans matched her loud cries. She made barbaric, unnatural, sounds he'd never heard before. He shifted his hands from the back of her knees to the front of her hips. As if transformed into a marionette, her legs hung in the air of their own accord. She howled as he worked. As she neared orgasm, her hips twisted, her legs dropped and her ankles locked across his back.

He paused and took a deep breath.

"Nooo!" she screamed, fearful that he was going to stop.

He chuckled, and after a short breath, he went back to her, his tongue slowly moving in and out of her. Her wetness came down and she felt his desire as his fingers caressed the back of her legs. She loved the way he squeezed and gripped them making her legs fan and shake. She cooed as he tongued and teased her, sliding his fingers up across her stomach, then stopping on her breasts. His strong hands squeezed and massaged her breasts then fanned across her chest and came back down to her belly, his palms gripping the front of her hips. His tongue sped up, and he played that chord in a different way, double chopping instead of strumming her chords. She hummed a joyful noise. Her hands landed on top of his and as the music came to a crescendo she screamed, pressed her hips against his face and bucked hard through orgasm.

When she pressed her thighs together and moaned, he pulled away from her and fell back into a squat. For a long moment, a silence hung in the air. As the music shifted to the next song, the only sound in the room was her heavy breathing.

When she regained her sense of sight and sound, she sat up to face him. He stood up, and she noticed that he had somehow produced a condom. She smiled, and took it from him. She untied the cord in his linen pants, pushed them and his boxers to the floor then slipped on the condom. Once again, she leaned back over the sofa as he dipped himself gently into her. Once her feet were settled on the sofa back, she immediately began pumping like her libido had shifted into the next gear. He gripped her waist and quickened his pace.

Her nerve endings burned. She pushed her palms against the cushions and raised her body to him with such force that she nearly threw him off her. He smiled, reset his feet and shifted his base. She rose, the muscles in her stomach rippling as she came to him. She kissed him hard, pulled him down onto the sofa and rolled him onto his back. She shifted with him until they were both comfortable, then she arched her back, held him still, tilted her head to the ceiling and rode him mercilessly.

He sped his pace and took her breath with a forceful upward stroke. Her nostrils flared and she panted heavily. He lingered there for a moment, his tip touching her bottom. Her knees were spread wide, her hands planted firmly on his taut abdomen and her eyes were shut tight. His hands travelled from her hips up and across her collarbones, gripping her neck.

Her body spasmed as he pulsed deep inside her, quickly thrusting his hips into hers. She cried expletives and spoke in tongues as he lowered his hips and her hands slid off him and onto the sofa. He sucked a nipple into his mouth, planted his hands firmly on her hips and shifted her to and fro, pumping with all he was worth until his orgasm exploded like a hot spring.

She screamed and sank into a vortex of oblivion until her pleasure erupted again. Her arms buckled and she lowered herself to hover above him. He held her close, her palms across his chest, rocking into her with a tambour that couldn't match her sporadic breathing. Aftershocks pulsed through them both. His rhythm was a two; hers was a five. When he finally eased into a down stroke, she caught her breath. As his hips came to rest, she contracted, squeezing him as he stayed inside her, taking pleasure as his face contorted with the pain and pleasure she caused his sensitive member.

"Oh my God!" he said, allowing her body to collapse atop his.

"What?" she gasped softly in his ear.

"I never knew a woman could come that hard," he said.

"Me neither."

22

Touch and Go's

FIRST SESSIONS WERE THE WORST. Instead of heading straight to his mother's house, Solomon exited the I-5 freeway a few miles south of his normal Lynnwood exit in the Mountlake Terrace section of North Seattle. He headed west towards the Sound, then parked after making two left turns and a right. The smell of fried foods in the air and the din of a radio in the distance banging a rap song reminded him of warm spring days back on the quad on the campus at Washington State.

A blue neon light outlined the blacked-out windows of the non-descript storefront. An oval, flashing *OPEN* sign welcomed those who might dare to enter the barely noticeable massage parlor. Inside, the scents of fresh cotton candles, jasmine incense and chamomile tea permeated the air in each of the ten rooms built for two.

After a six-minute wait in the lobby decorated with knockoff oriental artifacts, he was escorted down a narrow, dimly lit hallway to the fourth room on the right. The modest room was adorned with a massage table, a clothes valet, and an end table that held a portable stereo, two glasses and a pitcher of ice water. Alone in the space barely bigger than a jail cell, he turned on the power, inserted a Roy Ayers CD and pressed play.

He undressed, folded and neatly hung his clothes on the wooden valet then wrapped himself in a Turkish towel before making his way to the padded massage table in the center of the room. After the day he'd had, all he wanted was to lie down and relax his mind. He put on large, noise-cancelling headphones, pressed a button on the side of the table to energize hidden heaters and the leather-topped table instantly warmed. He laid face-down on the starched, white sheets, inhaled the soothing aroma of jasmine and forced his eyes closed.

Two minutes passed before his masseuse, a petite Filipina named Ginny, entered the room, dimmed the lights then washed and oiled her hands. She rubbed him familiarly on the back of his bald head to inform him of her arrival.

When Solomon didn't move, she lifted the headphones from his ears and unplugged the cord, allowing the relaxing sounds to fill the room.

He'd been a customer since pulling a muscle in his back three years prior. He'd experienced other masseuses, but of the six on staff, Ginny had established herself as his favorite. Her efforts routinely relaxed him in both mind and body, but today's angst would put her skills to the test. Solomon turned to face her, smiled, then returned his head to the face hole in the table and closed his eyes. Ginny smiled, grasped both ears with her fingertips and rubbed vigorously.

She did that for a long minute. Then she moved to the bottom of the table and grabbed a warm, moist towel. She toweled off his feet, then applied warm oil to his feet and calves. When she wove her fingers between his toes, he groaned into the face hole. The long fingers on her small hands brought instant pleasure as she massaged the balls of his feet. She worked oils into the back of his legs and extracted groans from deep within as she used both hands and elbows to knead the long muscles of her client's hamstrings. She barely disturbed the placement of his towel as she eased her hands beneath it and applied acupuncture-like pressure to the muscles in his hips and butt. From there, she removed her shoes. With the help of a stepladder, she stepped onto the table. "You okay Doctor A?"

He didn't answer at first.

Placing her knees on either side of him, she adjusted his back with a tilt to his shoulders, releasing a series of pops that relaxed and comforted him. He sighed heavily. She oiled his back until it was slippery as an eel. She placed her hands just outside his shoulders for leverage and hoisted herself onto her feet. Grabbing two handles permanently mounted on the ceiling, she lifted one leg then the other and glided onto Solomon's back. He winced, cooed, moaned and groaned as the heels and balls of her perfectly pedicured, size-six feet sank into the tense muscles of his back. Like velvety cat paws on a frozen pond, she glided across his body with the grace of an Olympic figure skater, soothing the muscles across his back and shoulders bundled by stress. Twenty minutes into their session she climbed down and gently tapped him on his head. When Solomon opened his eyes to meet hers, she wordlessly flipped her hand over twice. She stepped back towards his lower half, and maintaining a professional posture, she averted her eyes toward the ceiling for the sake of his modesty, then lifted the towel covering his private parts.

Solomon pushed up on his elbows. Rolled over onto his back. He placed his hands under his head. Spread his elbows wide. When he no longer sounded like he was moving, Ginny lowered the towel to cover him.

She started with his feet again, massaging oils into the front of his legs, then upwards across his stomach and the wide expanse of muscles spread across his chest and arms. Solomon laid still and absorbed the physical nirvana bestowed upon him at the hands and feet of his rented concubine.

Ginny sensed the intensity of his stress in the tightness of his muscles. Frustrated that she couldn't relax him after more than a half hour, she decided to go beyond her normal service to ease whatever thoughts were troubling her favorite customer.

Solomon heard her catch her breath in surprise when she removed the towel covering his middle. He smiled, knowing that his exceptional gift of nature was the cause of her shock.

Since he'd never before revealed himself to her in that department, he raised his head from his hands and asked, "Everything all right?"

"You not okay. You extra tense today," she said in a clipped tone. "You relax. Ginny make special good for favorite Doctor."

Most customers didn't tip after every massage, but Solomon did, and better than all of her other customers.

He never complained, never asked for more than what the service warranted. His generosity over the years had helped Ginny out a couple of times when life situations found her in need of additional funds. His prior generosity had earned him special treatment during this session. It wasn't a service offered at the parlor, and it wouldn't be her norm, but it would be her gift to him today because she felt he needed it. Solomon raised his eyebrows, but didn't speak. He shrugged his shoulders, laid his head back on the table and closed his eyes.

She changed the cd to Phyllis Hyman then lit another incense.

"Ginny give Doctor A special massage today." She waved her hand about to disseminate the smoke. "Relieve all tension or massage is free."

She added more oils to the residual on her hand, shifted the towel to cover his stomach and held her hands in front of the air-conditioning vent for a beat before gently embracing Solo's flaccid manhood.

"Wow!" His body tensed. His head raised up off the table and their eyes met. He exalted a deep guttural moan as his body went rigid in reaction to her attention.

"SSShhhhh," Ginny hissed softly as she eased his head back to the table with a soft palm to his forehead. Her hands spun opposite each other in a circular motion and applied gentle pressure with warming oils to awaken his arousal. Ginny, comfortable with him in her hands, said, "You relax Doctor A. Massage make all better."

Putting his trust in her expertise, Solomon relaxed, closed his eyes and fell out of rigidity on the warm table.

Ginny tenderly massaged his thighs. Put her hands inside his knees. Wedged his legs apart until his feet dangled over the sides of the table.

He could hear her bare feet pad on the hardwood floor to the end of the room and return a moment later. He felt a hand on his knee, then the towel moved and her cold mouth was on his manhood. He was instantly fully erect. His body began to tingle all over. Muscles contracted, his back arched, and for a moment, his shoulders were the only part of him still laying on the table. Her hands roamed sensually over his body. Aroused sensations he'd never experienced.

Everywhere she touched became sensitive. His sensibilities were ablaze with passion. His nerves became raw, and tingled with unheard of pleasures. He felt like screaming, but held back in anticipation as she widened her lips and released him from the vacuum of her soft mouth.

He sighed heavily and relaxed on the bed.

Over the next ten minutes, small, warm, velvety hands stroked, kneaded and massaged him well. The warmth of a hundred delicate kisses inspired a complimentary happy ending to Solomon's special session.

At the final moment, he grabbed her hair then released it. She turned her chin and a voluminous flood of his tension released onto the towel with an intensity rivaling the spray of the geysers at Yellowstone National Park.

Ginny cleaned him with damp, hot towels, then wiped down everywhere she'd kissed or rubbed with the warming oils. She covered his middle like it was when she entered. She laid the palm of her small hand on his chest. Solomon opened his eyes. She pointed to the clock. Ten fingers to indicate how long he'd have the room. "No more stress for favorite customer." She flashed an innocent yet conquering smile before he closed his eyes. She kissed the top of his head before exiting the room.

When she returned to clean the room, she found that her generosity encouraged her favorite customer to gift her with his normal Benjamin Franklin tip...along with three of Ben's twin brothers.

〜

Tension in the car was thick during the ride home from Club Me Saturday night. Tessa was upset with Majac for dressing down Crystal at the club, yet he seemed to give Jaz a pass when he showed up late acting a fool. As if it were yesterday instead of months ago, Tessa time-lapsed back to the time outside the club and gave him the business about the way he treated the old man in the parking garage, finishing with, "I can't believe the man I love, who considers himself an officer and a gentleman, could be so cruel and heartless to a homeless veteran." When he parked in front of her condo, she unlocked her door, grabbed her clutch and said, "and don't call me until the jackass is out of your system," before rushing out of the car and into her building. It was the first time in over four months that they'd not spent a Saturday night together that he wasn't out to sea.

Majac decided to give her the forty-eight hours that consummated Saturday night through Monday night as sufficient time to cool off. When she didn't call him before work Tuesday morning, he called her during her lunch hour Tuesday afternoon to invite her to the Boxing Smoker later that night. When she didn't answer, he left a message. He called again during the ferry ride home. She answered, but was still a little salty. She avoided the personal. Kept the conversation professional.

"I'm sorry Mister Charles, but I have to work tonight. My office is hosting a Town Hall meeting on gang violence in the Renton District and fortunately that's more interesting, and more important to me, than some stupid boxing match. But you're welcome to come."

After a long moment of silence, Majac said, "Well, I miss you, and I'll call you tomorrow,"

"Okay," was Tessa's one-word answer.

The lights by the garage came on as the line went dead. Majac stared out into the darkness of the backyard. He pursed his lips in indecision, then hung up just as Solomon stepped onto the back porch.

≈

Relaxed by the magic of Ginny's oils, hands, and mouth, Solomon rolled the windows down, turned the radio up, unaware that Bluetooth had not connected his car to his cell phone—the battery was dead, and took the surface streets home. He inhaled the crisp night breeze as an instrumental cover of the hip-hop favorite *Summertime* played on his favorite jazz channel. The music, Ginny's unsolicited favor and the fresh air made his stressors less aggravating than two hours before. *Tomorrow has to be a better day*, he thought, watching one street after another pass by.

At home, he noticed the red, flashing number indicating he had three voicemail messages. He pressed the white *play* arrow.

> Message One: *Good morning Mister Alexandré, this is Bugs Be Gone Exterminating calling to inform you that Joel will be at your property on Thursday morning between nine and eleven. He will need access to the basement and the garage. Please call us at 847-4739 if this time is not convenient. Thank you for being a Bugs Be Gone customer and have a good day.* Beep
>
> Message Two: *Solomon Alexandré this is your mother. Where are you boy? And why aren't you answering your cell phone? I don't know what in God's name you are out doing with what skank this time, but if you care at all about your mother's life being threatened, then you will find time for me before I end up dead on the 11 o'clock news.* Beep

Solomon grabbed his cell phone out of his jacket pocket and pressed his fingerprint on the home button to unlock it. Nothing. The battery was dead and he didn't know it. Frustrated, he dropped the cell phone on the counter and called Vivienne from his house phone. "Ma, are you all right?"

"Well it's about time. I have been calling you for hours. Why in Jesus' name can't you call your one and only mother back?" Her deep voice was husky as if she'd been too long without a drink.

240

"What?...Who?..." he shouted. "Calm down, Ma." A knock came at the back door and trailed him into the kitchen. A face poked in and he saw it was Majac. Wordlessly, he motioned for his new neighbor to enter. "What?" Solomon said again, raising his voice in the phone. "Slow down Ma, I can't understand what you're saying." A moment passed in silence as Solomon listened to his frantic mother's fearful recollections.

Vivienne's doorbell rang twelve times before she made it to the door. When she answered, ready to flame spray the culprit, she found two boys standing outside her locked screen door. A shorter, stocky boy with a bushy, platinum-blonde on top, dark on the bottom, honey-badger style afro was holding two puppies. The taller of the two boys had a Mohawk with shoulder-length braids adorned with red and green beads. The sides of his head were completely shaven. He said, "Hey Lady, we got these cute puppies for sale and an old lady like you who lives alone needs a dog for protection."

"I ain't got time for no dog. And I damn sure don't trust no pit bulls."

"Come on Lady, we're only gonna charge you a hunnet dollars." His lip piercing immediately repulsed Viv. "That's real cheap."

"Go bother someone else, boy?" Vivienne exasperated. "What makes you think I got a hundred dollars to spend on a puppy?"

"C'mon old lady. We seen that expensive car your son drives," Mohawk said. "We know you got money."

"But that's my son's car. That ain't got nothing to do with me, boy."

"Well then get your son to pay for it."

"You two need to get off my porch and leave me alone."

A moment after she slammed the door, a rock crashed through her living room window. Vivienne screamed. Outside, on her small front lawn, the Honey Badger yelled, "You need to understand lady, the Haves have to pay. And you, are a Have."

Vivienne screamed fiercely, "I'm calling the police."

"We'll be back," taunted honey badger as they dashed away

Before she shut the door, she glared out at them like an Amazon about to spear a rival warrior. She lived alone. She had heart palpitations and was subject to panic attacks.

"And when we come back, you'd better buy a puppy or else." The boys were out of sight before the 911 emergency operator answered.

Vivienne told Solomon, "Several of my neighbors have called the police and complained over the past couple of weeks, but there've been no arrests. Tillie Jones asked for protection but because there was no crime there's no protection."

Solomon's heart raced. In a voice two octaves higher than normal, he said, "All right Ma, calm down. I'll be right there."

"And hurry up." Whenever she got mad at him, Vivienne was often quick to remind Solomon that he had ruined her. That she was only twenty-eight when his big head destroyed her womb from the inside and caused her to have a hysterectomy after only giving birth to one child. The boys at her door were not his fault, but him not being there to protect his mother when she needed him was. "I could've been killed—dead and buried—and you would've been nowhere to be found. You don't love your mother."

"What Ma?" Majac started to talk, but Solomon silenced him. Then to Vivienne, "Yes; go to Ms. Menzy's house until I get there."

"What's wrong Partna?" Majac stood just inside the kitchen door.

"Somebody broke into my mom's condo. I gotta go."

"You need me to ride with you?"

"Nah Partna, she's on her way to a friend's house. Besides, I don't know how long I'm going to be there." Solo called Kenny. He answered after the second ring. Without a greeting, solo said, "Yo, it's me."

"What's up, Partna?"

"Call your boy Alphonse. I know it's late but I need to holler at him."

"You need to holler at Alphonse? Hold up. That brother is ruthless. People like you don't have no reason to holler at him."

"Just call him. If he ain't free tonight, tell him I need to see him by noon tomorrow."

"Hold up Bruh, I need an explanation if you need to holler at grimy ass Alphonse?"

"I got some things on my mind right now."

"Enough that you need to talk to Alphonse?" Kenny said, a whirl of intrigue in his voice. "Damn all that. We need to talk. I'm on my way."

"I'm on my way to Viv's," Solo said angrily. "If you wanna talk, meet me there." Solo loved Kenny, but was more focused on getting to his mother's house than explaining. "Look Partna, I appreciate the concern, but can you get me the appointment or not?"

"No worries, Doc. If you're for real, it's as good as done. Let me throw some shoes on and I'll meet you at Mom's."

By seven o'clock Tuesday night, more than three hundred mothers and fathers, aunts and uncles, sisters and brothers, and grandparents gathered inside the Boxley Fellowship Hall at Jabez-Christ the King-Church of God. Anticipation buzzed through the standing room only crowd of gatherers waiting to hear what Tessa's supervisor, the Seattle Director for the Deterrence of Gang Violence, had to say.

Reverend Lawrence Didier opened the meeting with a short prayer. "Let us bow our heads. First let us say a prayer for the sick and the suffering. For the hard working and hustling because they need prayer too. Sometimes more than most. These are the people you came up with. The people you've known all your life. Some of them may not have had the fortune that we have had. May not have had the favor, but they need the love. They need the prayer. They need you, me, and everyone within the sound of my voice caring about them through their trials. Grant them safe passage and the courage to do the right thing when faced with adversity. Bless everyone here among us tonight. Open their hearts, minds and ears so that they can hear what is being said then take that message with them as they go back to this community that so desperately needs your mercy. In Jesus' mighty name we pray, Amen."

Next, a short, balding, white man in a dark green suit stepped to the podium and shook Lawrence's hand. Although Lawrence had just used it, he tapped the microphone with his index finger to check that it was on. "Thank you Reverend for that inspiring invocation." The shoe leather on his black wingtips was dull, but despite looking like they'd travelled to the edge of time and back, there weren't many scuffs.

"I'd first like to welcome you all and applaud you for your attendance," he told the restless crowd. "We have a tremendous turnout this evening, and without the support and cooperation of people like you in our communities, we City Officials would not be able to combat the problems that plague our neighborhoods on our own."

"We are not a plague Mister Whatever Your Name is," a lady yelled from the fourth row.

"No ma'am, you certainly are not. But the problems in our neighborhoods are reaching epidemic proportions which is why I used the term plague. I apologize if my choice of words offended anyone."

"No need for apologies," she replied gruffly. "Just say what you got to say." A dull roar of shared hostility bounced through the crowd.

The speaker's eyes washed across the crowd like a greyhound chasing a mechanical rabbit. "Well if you ain't got nothing good to say, then get off the stage," came from a gravelly voiced man in the front row.

Hearing that, Tessa sprang to her feet and joined her boss. "Good evening," she said. "My name is Tessa Ajai and I am the Deputy Director for the Deterrence of Gang Violence." A murmur washed across the room. The black woman who was brave enough to stand up and push her boss out of the way so she could talk, had the complete attention of every man, woman and child in the room. "We want you all to know that the City has several projects in the works to improve public safety in our communities. We've devised an implement strategy for our plan, but before we do, we've come here tonight to listen to whatever ideas you all may have that may help us provide safer neighborhoods for you and your families." Again a murmur waved across the room. "We have seven new initiatives summarized in the flyers that were handed out tonight. The details are documented on the website at the bottom of the page. Please read the flyers, and if a program interests you, go to our website…"

"I ain't got no computer," a man yelled from her left, "so I ain't never gone see it no how."

"For those of you without ready access to computers, paper copies are available at the Renton Library, the Self-Help office at the Lee-Hines Community Center or at our local office just across the street. If you leave your mailing address with the young man to my right," a nineteen-year-old, brown-skinned boy raised his hand on cue, "then the complete package will be mailed to you."

"Well, how long we got to wait for y'all to do something about the crime that's going on now?" called a man standing against the back wall.

"Our budget can support three of the seven programs the city wants to implement. The purpose of us coming here tonight is to start a conversation with you about what programs you think would best serve your community. We understand that everyone has different needs and concerns, but from a community standpoint, we would like to get a consensus about what you, the community, want done with the funds that are available for these programs."

"We want them little punks off the streets," said a lady of about forty, seated in the second row. She held a baby in her lap. "I shouldn't have to request second shift so I can walk my twelve-year-old son to school, then turn around and use my lunch break to walk him home from school just so he can be safe from the harassment of all those boys on the streets. Y'all put three security guards in the school this year, but that don't do nothing for my boy when he leaves the school yard and has to fend for himself for the six blocks he has to walk home."

Tessa's eager intern was busy scribbling down notes even though she had directed him to record the meeting on the digital recorder she gave him. He'd pressed record, but was also trying to capture key talking points so that he knew where to focus his efforts when he transcribed the minutes.

"Ma'am," Tessa started, "Please leave your name with my intern." The bright faced boy raised his hand. "We'll get you a copy of tonight's minutes and all of the programs being considered. If you can come in for an interview, at your convenience, we will capture all of your concerns."

The crowd seemed antsy. Contentious comments were muttered throughout. In the back of the room, four boys stood and kicked their chairs to the floor. The small ruckus grabbed the attention of the crowd. One boy with a bushy, platinum-blonde, honey-badger style afro shouted, "Neighborhood don't need protecting. People like you who stick your noses in the neighborhood's business are the ones who needed protecting."

When the two policemen who'd drawn security duty for the event started to walk their way, the honey badger and two other boys ran out the back-door shouting, *F#ck the Police*. After they left, the policemen posted themselves inside the back door to prevent their return.

During the final forty-five minutes of the session, Tessa fielded comments from older citizens about the lack of police presence in the neighborhood. Younger citizens complained of police harassment. She did her best to maintain some sense of order as angry citizens raised one-after-the-next tough, almost unanswerable question about selling drugs on the corners, slow or non-existent police response times for 911 calls, playground safety, and gun violence.

After handing out more than three dozen business cards to concerned citizens, Tessa and her intern walked to the parking lot. He walked past her trunk toward his car parked three spots away as she unlocked and opened her car. When her phone rang, he stopped, but she waved him off as she answered. "Hey Leona, what's up?" she said as the boy drove away. She stood in the open door of her car and waved as she noticed that her car appeared to be leaning towards the passenger's side.

"Not much," Leona replied. Tessa began to walk around her car to inspect it. "I stayed late at the studio and since I knew you were downtown tonight, I wanted to know if you wanted to meet me to get something to eat? That way you can tell me all about your talk with our people in the hood."

"That's cool," Tessa said. "Where do you want to eat?" Her right rear tire was low, but it wasn't flat. She knew it was too late to get it looked at, but if it wasn't completely flat in the morning, she'd drop it off at to the shop on her way to work in the morning. "That sounds great," she said, agreeing with Leona's dining choice. "Twenty minutes sound good to you?" Tessa asked.

"Perfect," Leona confirmed. "Talk to you later."

Tessa kicked her tire before ending her call. "Yeah, it'll be all right until the morning," she said to no one. She made her way around the back of her car and noticed what appeared to be two male figures walking rapidly in her direction. Tessa hurriedly made her way to the driver's door, but stopped at her rear bumper when she saw a young man dressed like the boys who caused the commotion and cussed her before leaving the meeting. She looked over her shoulder to see that the other two boys were definitely coming right at her. Tessa stepped out of her heels into her bare feet, preparing herself to run.

"Look, if it's money you want, I got about fifty dollars cash," she said, letting her purse slide down her arm so she could reach inside.

"I don't want your money lady," the young man standing in her car door said. "You was talking all that crap about us inside and you don't even know us. I bet your bougie ass ain't never been down here without your boss and the police. How you gone talk smack and you don't even live here?"

Tessa pressed the talk button on her phone, but kept it hidden in the palm of her hand. Leona knew where her meeting was held that night, and if her sister heard she was in trouble, Tessa hoped that she'd either come to her rescue, or if the call went to voicemail, she'd call the police to come check on her. Either way, Tessa let the call go through. As the quartet of loud footsteps stampeded to a halt announcing that the two boys behind her had reached their destination, Tessa screamed like a banshee, threw her purse at the boy standing in her door and rushed him just as the other two boys reached out to grab her.

The foursome crashed into her car door. Momentum pushed Tessa and the boy in her door inside as the other two pulled at Tessa's back trying to extract her from the car. In the struggle, her phone dropped onto the floor of the car. Her call to Leona had gone through and Leona was yelling her sister's name on the other end of the line, but her pleas were oblivious to the quartet brawling inside the car. Tessa fought back hard. Refused to give in. Refused to let her car, her chastity or her life be taken by these boys. The rumble in the parking lot continued for upwards of ten minutes before the boys finally overpowered the incensed Tessa and were able to drag her from the car, the contents of her purse spilling onto the ground in their wake. As they pulled, Tessa punched, bit and kicked the first boy who was pressed beneath her by the weight of the other two. Outside on the macadam, the three boys taunted, chastised and threatened her about coming to their neighborhood and starting trouble. When a set of headlights turned into the parking lot, they grabbed Tessa's wallet and ran in the opposite direction leaving Tessa lying on the ground, bruised but not broken, in a pool of sweat and blood. Two blocks later, the first boy threw her wallet in a dumpster. He was smart enough to know that they could be tracked if they used her credit cards. But he did take all of her cash.

23

Hunting

MAJAC AWOKE WEDNESDAY MORNING ANXIOUS to talk to Tessa. He couldn't wait to tell her that members of his crew had won three of the eight matches at the Naval Station boxing smoker. By noon, he had called both her cell and her desk number five times each with no answer. Instead of calling her desk phone a sixth time, he called the common office line. The receptionist, who didn't know about the previous night's incident, didn't tell him where she was, just that she wasn't in the office.

During the ferry ride home, he called Tessa again. Leona answered. Although he liked Leona, his tone morphed from determined to irritated. He knew Tessa had been upset with him Saturday night, but four days later, she still wouldn't take his calls. How long would this woman hold a grudge? "Hello?" he said curtly. "Hey, um, is your sister available?"

"Hi Anton. I'm good," Leona said. "You sound well. Is everything all right with you?"

"Yeah. Everything is everything." His retort was curt.

"Not with that attitude it isn't."

"Look. My bad. It's just that your sister hasn't spoken two sentences to me since the club Saturday. I asked her out last night and she turned me down. And today she hasn't answered or returned my calls. On top of that, I get called to the Admiral's office this morning because my Engineer showed up at squadron headquarters out of the blue and told them he wanted to quit on me. So excuse me if I'm a little bent right now, okay." Following a firm scolding from the Admiral in charge of the squadron Majac's ship was assigned to, all of his officers and chiefs spent the entire afternoon and early evening at squadron being counseled on leadership by squadron staff and a command climate specialist. It was after dark when the leadership of his crew was finally released for the day.

"Humph," Leona breathed into the phone. "Anyway, I wanted to call you earlier, but today has been hella crazy. I got caught up with calling Tessa's boss, the follow-up call with the doctor and then with all of the questions we had to answer for the detective, I just lost track of time."

"Doctor? Detective?" Majac blurted out. "Why the hell did you need to talk to a detective?"

"It's cool, he was a really great guy. Oh my God he had the sexiest voice, and anyway, I'm certain this will all be resolved as soon as..."

"Doctor? Detective? Great Guy? What's resolved? What the hell is going on Leona? Where is Tessa? And why are you answering her phone?"

Majac skipped the ferry ride from the base to his house in North Seattle and drove around the Sound at a NASCAR pace towards Tessa's condo. He called Leona as he parked and she unlocked the door so he could come right in. Inside, Majac immediately saw Tessa lying on the sofa sleeping. The living room of her condo looked like a gang of teenage girls had a sleepover on a rainy weekend. The narrow, impeccably decorated living room was a mess. Magazines were thrown across the leather recliner. The sofa pillows were flat and tossed on the floor like discarded toilet paper. An apple Jacks cereal box and two empty microwave popcorn bags were turned on their sides atop the glass and stone coffee table. Empty Starburst candy wrappers were strewn all over the floor.

The chime of the alarm system notified Leona of Majac's arrival. She held her finger to her lips and motioned him into the kitchen. "I'm glad you're here," Leona said. "Now I can keep my date tonight."

"You want to tell me what's going on? What's this about a detective?"

Over the next half hour, Leona recapped for him what she was able to dissect from the ramblings of a first hysterical, then highly sedated Tessa Ajai. She told him about the detective who had met them at the hospital and that he was supposed to come back in a couple of days once the medication wore off and Tessa was in a more lucid state to answer questions about the boys who attacked her.

"Why didn't you call me earlier?" Majac asked angrily. "I've been calling her all day. I knew she was mad at me, but I didn't know all this was going on. I should've gone to that damn meeting with her."

"I don't know your number, and her phone has a password, so I couldn't use hers to find your number."

"Why didn't you call Solomon? He has my number."

"He pissed me off. I'm not talking to him right now."

"You and your damn sister mad at the world."

"Whatever." Leona sucked her teeth at him.

"Well, I'm here now," Majac huffed. "Thank you for looking after her, but I'll be here until she wakes up and is ready to talk to the police."

"Look at you," Leona laughed, "being her golden knight?" After giving him Tessa's medication schedule and doctor's name, she gathered her stuff and left her sister in the care of her soon-to-be brother-in-law.

Wednesday's fiasco with his Engineer quitting, followed by the butt chewing from the Admiral and the counseling session for his crew meant that Majac staying to care for Tessa on Thursday would probably cost him his command. Tessa wasn't his wife, so any extenuating privileges that could be extended to a married sailor didn't apply to her; and despite having a deeply credible rapport with squadron leadership, now was not the time to test the length of his leash. Tessa's boss insisted she take the remainder of the week off to recuperate. Majac left work early Thursday, then spent that night and all of Friday spoiling Tessa. He gave his XO orders to release the crew no later than noon on Friday following field day.

Starting with a takeout order of her favorite Indian food including two servings of a delectable salted caramel dessert, he fussed over her every waking moment for the next two days. When she'd nod off to sleep, he'd find things around the apartment to clean or straighten up until she awoke and called for him. He loved her place. The eggshell walls were adorned with small, wood-framed paintings, mostly outdoor scenes, African masks, and plants that dangled from pots and somehow clung to the paintings and masks. He'd sit on the floor in front of where she lay on the sofa while she watched one sappy Hallmark Channel movie after the next.

Since the incident, she'd been sleeping erratically, up at odd hours of the night alternating between watching the TV and it watching her. In case she needed him through the night, Majac pushed the coffee table across the room and made himself a sleeping pallet on the living room floor. As much as he hated it, the television remained on all night providing background noise to stave off the nightmares brought on by the silence and darkness.

By the time Saturday morning came, he felt that same sense of being underway since coming to her Wednesday night. She'd been in bed for three straight days and Majac thought it was time to get her moving again. He encouraged her to leave the house with an entire weekend of pampering planned to keep her mind off her tragedy. He decided to start with a big breakfast followed by an outing in the afternoon. When he returned with groceries at ten Saturday morning, he was excited to find her still asleep.

"Come on Tessa, we're going to be late," he called from the foyer after they had finished breakfast. He'd made some appointments for them that morning, and if they didn't leave in the next fifteen minutes, their entire schedule would be thrown off.

"I'll be out in a minute," she called from deep within her bedroom. "Just finishing my hair and makeup."

"You don't have to get 'all dolled up'. Today's going to be a casual, relaxing, stress-free day."

Hating to be late for anything, Majac paced to occupy himself, clasping his hands behind his back to prevent from continually checking his watch. Near the door was an ancient upright piano and next to it, a miniature Italian water fountain made of faux stone. The earthy, relaxing quality of Tessa's personal space seemed at odds with her sharp business-like demeanor. No doubt she needed this calming vibe to protect her spirit.

Majac wore loafers, black shirt and slacks, and a grey blazer just in case she went super chic on him. When she finally emerged from the bedroom, she wore black pedal pushers, a red cashmere sweater and casual open-toe shoes. Her hair was pulled back, tucked up and captured in a clip allowing the last six inches to bounce wherever the sashay in her hips guided it as she walked. "I hope I'm not overdressed?"

"Oh no," he said, his eyes gravitating to the three-inch crease of cleavage that separated her breasts and ran from the bangles in her necklace to the round top of her blouse.

"So it was worth the wait?"

"Yes," he said, his smiling growing uncontrollably with the utmost admiration, "definitely worth the wait."

He opened the sunroof and let the brisk morning air flood his car with the scents of autumn. As they headed east on Route 18, he admired her perfectly pedicured feet and the depth of her dimples when she smiled.

Tessa was lost in thought considering how the compilation of her soon-to-be husband's possessions would marry with hers. Neither of their places were large enough for all of their possessions. *Yes,* she thought, *we are going to need a bigger place. I'll have to ask him when his lease expires.* They'd been riding for a half hour when she asked, "Where are we going?"

"It's a surprise. Can't you just go for a ride with your man?"

"Well, it better be nice."

The first house they looked at was a partial brick Tudor-style home set on a well-manicured lot. The front door resided a good eighty feet from where they parked on the street. It boasted a corner lot with a wrought iron fence encompassing the back yard. The two-car garage offered two separate doors, loaded from the side street and was hidden from the front view. Inside, there were three bedrooms upstairs—she had hoped for four—and two bedrooms down. Sunlight came in through the two grated windows that flanked the front door, falling perfectly on the sculptural construction of lines and planes of the tile and slate foyer. As they exited the living room, he grabbed her hand in his and pulled her towards a back staircase. At the base of the steps, he placed his mouth over hers and gave her a kiss complete with the delicious spice of a cinnamon-flavored tongue dancing over her lips. All of the anxiety left her. Her body and her spirit trusted his touch, breaking down the harsh demeanor she'd worn since Tuesday.

Tessa thought of how much she needed that relief. She thought of how he liked to squeeze the little bit of fat on her hips, then she reached for his hand and placed it there. Indulging herself because none of her other lovers had reminded her of her softness. Anton's hands were on her now. The touch. The squeeze. The glancing pat. Then just the slightest shimmer. He raised his head brazenly, allowed his eyes to travel from her thighs back to her face. She met his gaze, but did not surrender the wonder of his smile. "Thick like I like it," Majac murmured as he touched and squeezed her again. She pressed her face against his chest and laughed. And he felt her laughter pulsating through his heart. Then he began to laugh too. And they laughed and held each other until the stairway lamp made Tessa think of the something that she wanted to forget—the assault in the parking lot. No longer wanting to laugh, she jerked, gave him a sharp shove.

Unaware of what had happened, he let her go and backed away.

The real estate agent returned from the yard. "So what do you think?"

"I think I'd like to see something a little more contemporary," Tessa made her way through the kitchen and out into the side yard. They drove to the second house in silence, each following the trail of their own thoughts. "Tessa," Majac said breaking the silence, "Are you sorry you came to Washington?"

She was surprised at such a forthright question. She shook her head and replied, "Not at all. You don't need to worry for a moment Anton. I do not regret my decision in the slightest. Quite the contrary. I thank God each night for bringing you back into my life. And when we get married and move into our new house, I am going to love our home. The home we share as man and wife."

"I just want our house to be like the one you dream about," Majac said.

Tessa laughed. "I rarely remember what I dream about," she said, leaning across the center console. She looped her arm through his, leaned against him and rested her head against his shoulder. "But if I did, I'm fairly certain that I would remember dreaming about the house I'm going to share with the handsome Navy Commander who will soon be my husband." She looked up at him in time to see him nod his head with a satisfied smile on his face. She squeezed his arm, confident that she had conveyed all that was in her heart.

The exterior walls of the second house had vertical wood siding. They were painted grey and had casement windows. Thirty or forty years ago when the place was new, that design must have been the latest thing. As they walked through the 3,500 square-foot Victorian home set on a half-acre of land overlooking Shadow Lake, Tessa thought of the things she wanted to see in their house—little kid toys, cabinets full of a wide array of cereals, crayons and butterfly barrettes stuck in the sofa, report cards, smudges by the light switch, a place where their children could learn the lessons of their grandma. She turned to Majac and asked, "What do you think we need a place for in our house?"

"Over there we can put the kids' art class drawings. In the library I want a bookshelf with textbooks, and a large family room with sports magazines on the coffee table."

"Sounds good to me," Tessa said and squeezed his arm tight. She knew that in order for her to make all of that come true in that house, they would need to spend a fortune remodeling.

The realtor parked near the walkway that connected the sidewalk to the front porch of the third and final house they visited that morning.

Majac and Tessa pulled up behind her. Something about the inside of that house frightened her. Maybe it was the smallness of the rooms. Maybe it was the cobwebs and thick layers of dust. Maybe it was the blood-red carpet throughout the upstairs. To Tessa, the medieval mini-mansion was more like a mausoleum; a house for ending life, instead of a home for starting the life of her new family. When a chill swept across her neck, ran down her spine and settled in her hips, Tessa froze. The childhood memory of being locked in a closet in her neighbor's grandmother's dirt basement scared her. She let go of Majac's hand and slowly backed out of the living room into the hallway until something invisible stopped her. "Not this one," she said then turned and rushed out the front door.

Around two o'clock they stopped at Haller Lake Park for lunch. Majac spread out a blanket he kept in his trunk. The sun was bright in the western sky. It was hot, but it was a perfect late autumn afternoon for a picnic lunch. Tessa sat closer to Majac than she normally would or maybe he was sitting closer to her. She unbuttoned the top button of her sweater before she leaned down to slip off her shoes.

"I'm your Man." He grabbed one of her fingers and held it. "Do you know what that means?"

"No...*My Man*," she said turning to face him. "What does it mean?"

A nearly inaudible murmur came from either the bushes or the trees behind them.

"It means you've got to be good to me."

She squeezed her thin hand between his elbow and his side. "Well, Mr. Charles, I sure am going to try."

"More than you've tried with anyone else in your past?" Pigeons strutted along the walks and throngs of adolescents roamed up and down the pathways of the park. "I'm going to be better to you than any woman you've ever known." They exchanged bright, earnest smiles. "Especially that witch you brought home for your father's funeral."

"Be nice," Majac said, squeezing her hand a little tighter. "And if she hadn't been with me, what do you think would have happened when I saw you with Greg Spires?"

"I would've forgotten his name right there on the sidewalk!"

They both roared with laughter, rolling back onto the ground, hugging each other.

"So, what ever happened to you and him?"

In the months following her sidewalk encounter with Majac's

California girlfriend, Tessa grew apart from Greg. He was a spoiled, privileged, white boy from the suburbs—no, from the country—who she felt could not understand her situation. Her relation to her people. Her dedication to the young black boys in her community whom she vowed to do everything in her power to keep out of jail or the cemetery despite their own best efforts to thwart her. She didn't see herself coming home to Greg's insincere placations at the end of a hard day. She couldn't live a lie in her own home.

One summer morning, there was a gang-related shooting in the J. Z. Robertson projects. A fourteen-year-old girl jumping rope with two of her friends caught a stray bullet. She died before the ambulance arrived. Tessa invited Greg to meet her for lunch. She needed to talk to someone about it. Needed to vent her anger. Needed to decompress. When their food came, she didn't pick up her fork or spoon. Greg stuffed some spaghetti in his mouth. As he chewed the wad of pasta, she tried to explain to him her mental state about the shooting. He grunted a couple of times, never once looking up from his plate to make eye contact. When his plate was halfway empty, he finally put down his fork. The clattering of the metal on china brought about Tessa's silence. Where Tessa expected her significant other to console her, having heard the horrific story she'd just relayed and the way it made her feel, she received in its place an explanation of why he was so hungry—he missed breakfast; and he was tired of his job—his boss had given him a new employee to train, then turned around and asked him to finish his presentation two days early for a client.

"Did you hear me Greg? I said that girl is dead."

"Yeah I heard you. Another innocent, young, black girl got shot in the projects while minding her business. It was probably her own brother who shot her. Why are you letting it bother you?"

Her eyes fell into her lap. The desire to be with him fell along with it.

Outside raindrops started to splatter the glass. "And I don't have an umbrella," Greg said, stuffing more pasta into his mouth.

"It's okay," Tessa assured him, "I do. Let me go get mine." And once she got it, she got in her car and drove away.

That was the first of a series of fruitless relationships for Tessa. A month later it was the custodian at the courthouse who asked her to dinner while walking her to her car one night after hours. He relayed to her that one day he would own his own company and no longer have a boss. Although ambitious, the delinquent child support payments for his three children would prevent his dream from ever getting off the ground. She accepted his dinner invitation, but when he complained incessantly about the bill, she knew that a second date would not be on the menu.

Next there was the attorney who was trying to find his O.J. Find that client that would take him to the legal stratosphere of defense attorneys. Make him famous; a nationally recognized name that would allow him to move to New York or California and land some big-name clients. When he stood her up for the second time without calling, she knew the jury of her heart and mind had to return an unfavorable verdict of not guilty of caring for her and set him free. When he called her three days later to apologize, she simply told him "Sorry Counselor, but please lose my number. All of your appeals have been exhausted."

The list went on and on: the single father with a six-month old daughter whose drug-addict mother died during child birth; the barber who bred would-be show dogs, but couldn't produce the proper paperwork to verify their lineage; the garage owner who only opened on weekdays—his brother ran a chop shop out of the garage on the weekends. She would date these men for a spell. All nice guys at the beginning.

The worst of them was Benny Carson, a chemist for a pharmaceutical company. She dated him the longest—eleven months. "He wasn't one for long term," she said. "Those weren't his spoken words, but his every action told me he wasn't. We both pretended it could work, but I remember exactly when I found out.

"I felt good. Benny was doing well in the program and was sober for almost a year. At first, we were just friends. Both of us in a good place. Drake had just graduated. My mom was celebrating her cancer being in remission. He didn't know what happy was when I met him. It was like he was trying to make up for something. He needed fun in his life; he needed to have some sober fun. We had good, sober fun. I loved him is what I'm saying, and the love I had for him made him want new things.

"After I convinced him to move from Baltimore to Tuskegee, I spent more time with him. That's when he got comfortable and started disappearing. First for a night, then for a day or two. When I confronted him, he refused to look me in the eye when we talked. I knew he was using again. I allowed him to run over me. I'm not proud of how I acted.

He couldn't stay clean in a new environment with a new job, new friends and a new lady. When I told him about the pregnancy, he was high. He told me to get a paternity test. In my heart, I knew that he knew he was the father. I was monogamous. It was his child. I knew it was the drugs talking not him. I wasn't going to allow him to run over me anymore. And I wasn't going to have a baby with a man that I couldn't trust to stay clean and sober no matter how much effort I put into him.

"We argued something terrible that night and he hit me. Hit me with the back of his hand hard enough to split my lip. I fought back and he punched me in my stomach. Knocked me to the floor. When he realized what he'd done, he started to come near me. I raised my hand to stop him. We stared at each other without saying anything for a long minute. I don't know who started to cry first, him or me. A minute later, he turned and ran out my back door.

"The next morning, I woke up in a pool of blood. The doctor assured me that the baby was all right, but when I left the hospital two days later, I made an appointment and terminated the pregnancy.

"Two weeks later, he came knocking on my door about ten o'clock one night. With the chain latched, I cracked the door open far enough for him to see my face. He stood on my porch and made some confessions that rocked me to my core. I cried as I listened to his story. I wished him luck with his problem, told him he didn't have to worry about the baby and shut the door in his face. He never knocked on my door again."

Tessa had the hardest time trying to figure out why Benny had to wait until after she found out that she was pregnant to tell her that he had a wife and three kids in Ohio. His betrayal would have hurt less had it come earlier. He confessed that he was working in Maryland because his company had closed their Ohio office and transferred him to Baltimore as the only alternative to laying him off. Benny started off selling a handful of prescription pills to friends on weekends, but nothing of significant volume. Three weeks after his confession, Benny went to a party with his new girlfriend. There he met an undercover narcotics officer who arranged to buy 200 prescription pills from him. A week later, Benny was arrested for possession with intent to distribute.

"Two weeks before I moved to Seattle, he was released from prison," Tessa said.

"How long was he in?"

"Eight years."

"Dang."

"I said all of that to say that after I saw you had chosen that woman you brought home, over me, that for years I dated anyone who would take me. And somewhere along the way I ran away from my reality."

"Or maybe you just lost your way?"

"That too."

"Where were you going?" Majac asked.

"Right here, I guess. I guess I was going right here. They say you always end up exactly where you're supposed to be."

"Do you miss home?"

She shrugged. She missed her mother; or better yet, she missed being able to get to her mother easily. It sent her into a frenzy whenever she called and her mother didn't answer the phone. "Worrying about my mom is about the only regret I have about moving."

"Do you think you're missing out on something by being here?"

Tessa smiled. "The only thing I ever missed out on was being with you. I don't feel like I missed out on much else in the romance department. Even though they weren't the most romantic of relationship experiences, they were very educational, growing-up experiences." She held him close. "And now that we're both here, I'm never going to miss out on that again."

Clouds covered the sky and the air grew chilly. Majac got his jacket for Tessa who was sitting with her knees bent. He didn't drape the jacket on her back like a cape, but put it on the front of her like a blanket. When he sat next to her, he put his hand beneath the jacket, bringing it to rest on her thigh, at the side of her knee. A half hour later, the sky was swirling. They were lying on the ground and Majac was talking about his Navy travels: Guam, Thailand, Australia, and the Philippines. Drawing a map on her with his finger, he traced a line from her thigh to her chest. "I want to make travel plans with you," he said.

Tessa pointed at the sky and explained to him what formation she saw in the giant puffy cloud.

"We'll go from here," he said. Her belly button was Mexico. "To here." Somewhere near her hip bone was the Panamanian coast. He drew circles within circles on her middle, making her browner and browner still. Eventually his finger came back to her belly button. "I've never done it here before."

"Mexico?" she asked.

"You're funny."

"Yeah, I know," she said, placing her hand on top of his.
Majac noticed the time on his wristwatch. "Oh no, we're late."
"Late for what?"
"Jaz's basketball game."
"But Jaz is retired."

24

Mama's Boy

VIVIENNE PUT HER CARDS DOWN. "What's wrong, Baby?"

"You think this is all a bad idea?" Solo said in reply.

She screwed up her face. "I have never in all my days heard of someone making of list of exes to see if they should go back to one of 'em. What I am thinking is why I'm not screaming at you. Or maybe I should be thinking 'When did my son go crazy?'"

"So I take it you don't like what I'm doing, huh Viv?"

"The only part of these shenanigans that I could ever consider liking is the fact that you're making the effort to find someone instead of continuing to drag around moping over that uppity heifer you married when you were young and stupid."

"Mom, don't you bring Schelle into this. She has nothing to do…"

"She has everything to do with it," Vivienne interrupted. "That high-yellow…"

This time Solomon interrupted. "Watch your mouth, Mom. You KNOW it ain't right to speak ill of the dead."

Vivienne fell back against the chair and stared at her only child.

Solomon returned her stare. Intense silence held center court for a long moment. Solomon slid his chair out from under the table and stood. The sound of wooden chair legs feet scraping across the tile floor violated the silence. "You want something else to drink?"

Vivienne blew air in response.

"Suit yourself." Solomon retrieved another bottle from the fridge.

"What do you know about that little beauty pageant girl from Spokane anyway?"

"Really, Viv?"

"Okay, okay, I'm sorry."

"Look, I didn't chase Jordyn. I didn't interrupt her life. She didn't have to give me her number. She didn't have to come down here to see me. She doesn't have to agree to see me when I went up there. It's all been her option. She's a grown woman and she's gotten this far in life making up her own mind and doing what she wants to do. I don't have to force her to DO anything."

"Just seems like she came out of nowhere. Doesn't sit right with me."

"Well, it feels right to me, Viv."

"Any piece of tail feels right if you're horny enough."

"You know what, Viv..." he cleared the cards from the table. "I'm through. Correction, you and I are through with this conversation. I like her. That's the end of it for now. I ain't trying to rush into more than I want to handle right now. I ain't asking her to marry me. I just like her and I enjoy spending time with her. Is that too much for me to ask?"

"Okay, already." Vivienne raised her hands in surrender. "Don't let me be the one to stand in the way of your happiness. Gees, I was just offering a little motherly advice and see what I get in return, hostility. I didn't pop you out into this world for you to just take up space. I've always wanted you to make a good life for yourself. If this beauty pageant woman half your age helps you to do that, then I'll be quiet about it."

"Now you and I both know that not only do you not know how to be quiet about it; you have no intention of being quiet about it. Not now, and not later. You may not speak your mind right this moment, but whatever you're thinking will eventually be heard."

"I mean it son," she said brightly. He walked around the table, leaned down and hugged his mother. When he released her, she said, "I'm just surprised that my son is starting his mid-life crisis in his thirties. Most men wait until their forties."

"Viv!" Solomon exclaimed.

"I'm just saying," she said.

"There's the problem," he said. "You're always just saying."

Before he could finish his thought, she asked, "So what's going on with you and that scar-faced woman? I haven't seen her sniffing around much lately."

"Her name is Leona. You know that. I haven't heard from her in a while. It is what it is. She'll call me when she's available."

"Maybe she ran away again," his mother said. "Didn't you say she ran away before? Young people think they can run away from their problems. Life is too hard. Nobody wants to take responsibility for their mistakes. News flash people, Life is and always will be hard. Been hard since they brought us over here on them damn ships, and as long as they," she said using air-quotes, "are in charge of this country that they founded for themselves, life as we know it is going to be hard for the rest of us. Ain't no running away from it."

He'd heard the *nobody wants to take responsibility* speech a hundred times and knew in the back of his mind that she was referring to his father running away from the responsibility of their family. But now was not the time to rehash that age-old tragedy, so he stayed with what he thought to be the current subject. "I haven't heard from her in a while, but I'm pretty certain she still runs up this way. I'm hoping if she's free next time I see her, that I'd be able to take her to dinner."

"If she's anything like I 'spect her to be from what Désirée writes in her files, her fast ass has probably forgotten all about you and moved on with some other unlucky guy."

"What made you ask about her?"

"I don't know. Anyway, unlike Miss I'm a Beauty Queen, Little Miss Scar Face isn't a couple too many years too young for you, and other than needing to see Désirée for her anger issues, she seemed to have a good head on her shoulders. And," she continued despite the look of consternation on her son's face, "she was prettier than the rest of them hussies that keep ringing your phone, despite whatever that is she has going on with her face." Vivienne waved her hand near her cheek to emphasize her point.

"Well, at least you thought she was pretty," was all Solomon could bring himself to say.

"You probably ran her off," Viv continued. "You know how you shy away from strong independent women like me and Désirée."

"Like you and Désirée? Mom, don't bring Des into this."

"Yeah, she's too good for you anyway."

Solomon laughed. "You're probably right."

"Ain't no probably. That girl's the best thing ever happened to you."

"But Désirée never happened to me, Viv. She's my business partner. It's best we keep it that way. And besides, she has Lamont."

"Another useless nigg ..."

"Viv!!" Solomon shouted, stopping her mid-sentence.

"Look Honey, I know that we all have our types, but I just want you to stop chasing useless women. If you find a decent black woman and you honestly like her, then let the relationship come slowly and stop hopping in bed with every split with a clit."

"Where do you get this stuff? I don't know who you are." Solomon laughed. "You are amazing."

"I know that," Viv said. "But we're not talking about me. Focus boy, I'm trying to school you."

Solomon popped the top off another beer and leaned back in his chair.

"You have to make sure that you like the woman she is. And make sure that she loves the man you are without trying to change you the way all of these young women think it's their job to do nowadays. Back in my day when your father was courting me ..."

"I know Viv," Solomon said cutting her off again. "My father was a real man and real men back then didn't need a woman to show him who he really was. Men in your day knew how to handle their business."

"Damn right."

"Right up until he abandoned us." That hard truth drew Vivienne's silence. Solomon got up from the table and quietly filled the dishwasher absorbing the words from his mother's rant. He washed the pots and pans, then took out the trash. Solomon loved his weekly dinners with his mother, but with all of her trying to tell him what he needed in a woman, he couldn't help but think that she needed a man. When he left, Viv rode with him to the church multi-purpose hall for bingo. When she was finished, her neighbor, Missus Wright, brought her home.

~

An hour later Solomon had made it home, showered and was on the phone talking to Kenny when his call waiting beeped in his ear. He looked at the caller ID. Recognizing the number, he told Kenny they'd talk more when he got there.

"Hey, how are you?" he said after he clicked the call over.

"I'm good, handsome. How are you?"

"Everything's good, just trying to finish getting dressed," he told Leona. He had called her earlier in the afternoon before heading over to have dinner with his mother, but his call went to voicemail. "Look, I don't know what's on your calendar, but I'm going out with friends tonight. Do you want to hang?"

"As wonderful as that sounds, Sexy Man, I can't. Unfortunately, my calendar is full for the evening."

"Oh." The dejection in his voice emanated through the phone.

"I'm sorry," she said. "Bad timing."

"Yeah, no worries." His attention shifted when he heard the sound of a car's engine outside his window.

Then Leona's doorbell rang. "Hey, that's my ride. Can I call you …"

"Yeah, that's cool," Solomon interrupted. "Don't have too much of a good time without me."

"You too," Leona said. "I'll talk to you soon."

25

Bad Sushi

University of Washington Airlines Arena was where Jaz Stevenson joined NBA Hall of Fame Guard Gary Payton as celebrity guest coaches for the Washington state girl's high school all-star basketball game. In front of a crowd of almost 5,000 screaming students, parents and more than three dozen college scouts, Jaz's team lost a nail biter of a game.

After the game, Majac and Tessa attempted to follow Jaz and Crystal to Nijo, a sushi restaurant, but construction and Jaz running a couple of yellow lights put their arrival for dinner ten minutes behind their friends. A host of exotic cars were valet parked in front of the restaurant, but he parked his Range Rover on the third level of the parking garage a half block away. They took the stairs instead of waiting for the elevator. On the street level, they passed the elevator door heading for the exit. Majac reached to open the door leading to the street and a homeless looking man appeared out of nowhere.

His grungy, tattered outfit brought immediate alarm. Tessa squealed. He wore combat boots, a woolen skullcap and a tattered army fatigue jacket. U.S. A-R was above the left pocket—the M and Y were missing. Only K-L-I-N was above the right. He wore a nine-inch salt-and-pepper mane of hair and a scraggly, gray goatee surrounding his mouth. The peaks above his temples were starting to recede, elongating his face more towards a six-head than a fore.

Majac flinched in his direction. He jumped backwards so hard that he slammed himself into the latticed brick of the garage wall.

"What?" Majac yelled then pushed the door open for Tessa.

She stared at the man as she exited the garage stairwell. What held her gaze was his eyes—oval, pecan-shaped, hazel colored eyes. The same eyes she saw when she looked in the mirror. Except his were dour, pained. The feeling she felt radiating from his eyes was that of hopelessness.

Eyes wide, the man remained against the wall as Majac let Tessa exit. Majac placed his hand on her lower back and ushered her out onto the street, leaving the man with her eyes alone in the stairwell.

At the front door of the restaurant, a group of ten or twelve crowded the door waiting to enter. As they waited, the older man in the dirty Army jacket, passed them carrying a backpack. He had a noticeable limp. The youthful spryness of his prime had long since abandoned his gait. Majac and Tessa noticed him, but the rest of the crowd ignored the man as if he were nothing more than a shadow extending from a dark alleyway.

A moment later, there was a slight commotion twenty yards to their left. From what Tessa could see, a group of teens were harassing the older man in the Army jacket. "Hey, stop that," Tessa yelled, her inner gang enforcement officer coming to life. She grabbed Majac by the arm and started to move toward the commotion by the alley. The shortest of the three boys turned and pushed back a mop of platinum-blonde afro to see who was yelling at them.

Tessa stopped cold when she recognized them as two of the boys who had assaulted her in the parking lot.

"Hey, you heard her; leave him the hell alone," Majac yelled in a strong, commanding voice as they neared the entrance to the alley.

The tallest of the boys smiled, exposing a silver lip piercing before he shoved the man to the ground. The red and green beads on his braided hair jingled when he took off running.

When they finally reached him, she leaned over and touched the foul-smelling man's cheek.

In return, he stretched a creaky arm back to her. His body was aching in just the wrong places to make it impossible to sit still. He remembered the strange feeling of being both conspicuous and peripheral. People didn't look at him as he moved toward them. They didn't seem afraid; they were all too self-absorbed with their own trivial conversations to pay him any attention. He didn't matter in their world. They just didn't think he was important to look at.

"Are you all right, Sir?" Tessa asked as Majac helped the raggedy old guy to his feet and dusted him off. Again she noticed that she had his hazel colored eyes, although hers were a shade lighter. His held a tint of green, but the hue of their color was like looking at a mirror-image of yourself in an undisturbed lake. Tessa blinked first.

"Thank you for the help, but if you'd have given me another minute, I could've taken them," the man said, tipping his hat. He was tall, over six feet, but shorter than Majac. The way the old Army jacket hung on him, you could tell that sculpted, taut muscles hung beneath. The street messiah smiled at her and long, deep lines crinkled his face.

His teeth were all there. Yellowish-ivory-colored, but healthy and strong. Except for those hazel and green eyes, he wasn't what she considered a handsome man, but his eyes gleamed with pure sincerity when he smiled. With one brief smile he captured her heart.

"Yeah. You had them shaking in their boots, Old Timer?" Majac said.

"Anton," Tessa huffed, punching him in the arm. "I know Momma Charles raised you better."

"If he's ready to fight then I guess he's all right," Majac said.

Tessa tightened her mouth.

"My bad," Majac said. "You need a couple of bucks, Pops?"

"Uggh," she exhaled, appearing angry enough to cry. She wondered how many times in the course of a day she'd encountered people who looked like her; normal-looking, well-dressed people who might be one paycheck away from being homeless; or may have no food in their refrigerator or their family goes to bed hungry. The thought chilled her.

What frightened Majac more than her growl was that she looked like she wanted to slap him. And she did. Not for the money comment, but for being a jerk who thought he was better than the next man. Without making eye contact, she held out her hand and said, "Let me hold your wallet."

"What?" Majac asked.

Again, her eyes said she wanted to slap him. Cautioned by her stern look, he eased his wallet out of his blazer pocket and handed it to her.

She rooted through his cash. He had just over $100 in paper bills. "Here, Love," she said removing $40 and handing it to the man in the tattered Army jacket. She said 'here' the way your big sister, or your mother, or your grandmother would have. She said it a way that let you know that it was hard earned money but, also, that you needed it more than she did. And that she loved you and you didn't have to beg her for it. The love in the way she said it that meant that since you didn't have it and she did, then 'here' you are welcome to it.

He slowly reached for the money without meeting her gaze. He didn't immediately say thanks. She didn't do it for that. He held her hand for a beat before letting go—the money still wrapped tightly inside. Motionless, he stood listening as Tessa leaned into his personal space. Her words remained private as she spoke to him. When he let go, he kissed her hand and smiled, then tucked the money in the breast pocket of the old jacket. "Bless you child," was the last thing Tessa heard him say.

The man in the Army jacket went out the way he was accustomed, down the alley behind the businesses where the light was dimmer and the trash stank. Down where there were fewer people who weren't like him. Down where he knew where to hide, if needed. Down where he felt safe.

When they finally made it inside Nijo, Jaz and Crystal were seated at one of ten tables in a glass-enclosed patio that bordered the active sidewalk. Across the street from the restaurant was a boardwalk overlooking the Sound. Three blocks to the south was the parking lot where three boys had attacked Tessa five days earlier.

Jaz ordered a bottle of sparkling Rosé and the sushi sampler platter as an appetizer for the table. Tessa and Crystal bantered about the neighborhoods and houses they'd seen that morning. Crystal sharing in his fiancée's excitement brought a smile to Majac's face. Ten minutes later, the sushi came. While everyone else ordered their entrees, Crystal divvied up the platter ensuring that they each had at least one sample of each kind of sushi. The table grew quiet as the hungry quartet sampled the colorful assortment of sushi. Majac couldn't help notice that several diners at nearby tables recognized Crystal and Jaz's celebrity, but fortunately for them, people were considerate enough to let them enjoy their meal without being those annoying fans that came over and asked for an autograph or to take pictures just as your stuffing food in your mouth.

When dinner arrived, the conversation pleasantly bounced around the table, all four of them trying to avoid the elephant in the room. Majac and Tessa did their best to keep the conversation light and centered on them, their house hunting and the wedding. She inundated Crystal with details when she wasn't actively eating, or when Crystal had food in her mouth and couldn't talk. With their meal finished and the waitress' dessert suggestion on the way, an uncomfortable silence filled the air.

"I could use a cigar," Jaz said injecting words in the air.

"Good for the rest of us they don't allow smoking," Crystal quickly barbed, hating the smell of cigar smoke. Her stare shot daggers at her estranged husband. His stare returned the like.

"Well after being cooped up in the house for almost a week, I could stand to do some dancing," Tessa chimed.

"That sounds cool," Majac cosigned.

"Some of us have danced too much lately," Jaz's tone was sour.

"You have some nerve Jared Stevenson," Crystal spat.

"Me?" Jaz replied. "I wasn't the one shaking my ass with some stranger like I wanted him to take me home and dance at his place."

"No," Crystal fumed, "You were just stalking me in the background when you were supposed to be home spending time with your daughters."

"Stalker?"

"Yes, Stalker. If you weren't stalking me, then you would've come out of whatever corner you were hiding in and been the husband that I needed taking care of me. What about you buying me a drink instead of letting some stranger send me one? Or better yet, what about dancing with your wife who you know loves to dance?"

"But you know I'm not a big dancer," Jaz said.

"I don't need you to be Michael Jackson, Jared. I just need you to care enough about me and my needs to come out on the dance floor and move next to me a little bit while I dance." She slid her hand on top of his. "And if you had come to me, I would have sent him, and anybody else who wasn't you, packing!"

Jaz pulled his hand from beneath hers. "Well your dance card was more than full. And from where I was standing, it looked like you didn't mind his hands all over you."

Heat surged through her and her eyes flamed red. "You wouldn't do it, so somebody had to." She didn't mean that last statement, but she was angry, and it came out so fast that she didn't have a chance to stop it."

Just then, the manager appeared out of nowhere. "Is...everything all right?" he asked wearily

"FINE!" Jaz and Crystal said in concert. Jaz and Crystal's flare up came just as Majac and Tessa doused the flames of their last argument. Crystal flopped back in her chair. "So am I to understand, that instead of coming over to your wife and letting her know you are in the same place she is, you would rather stand in the shadows and let some other man bring her the pleasure that she wants from you, just because you have this fixation with not embarrassing yourself in public?"

"Yeah," Jaz intoned. "Everybody you pass nowadays has their cell phone ready to take pics. I ain't going out there to make no fool of myself so the world can see. I don't particularly care to embarrass myself."

"You're not embarrassing me."

"I still ain't doing it with you."

"Well in that case, I'm not doing it with you either."

Majac and Tessa regarded each other, uncertain if the conversation had changed course.

"You know what," Crystal said, "I'm ready to go home."

"Well, I'm not," Jaz said.

"Well I don't care where you go," Crystal exclaimed, "as long as I don't have to go with you."

An angry silence engulfed the table. After an extended beat, the group collectively exhaled. Muted consent told that the meal was a bust. When the waitress passed, Crystal pointed at Jaz and told her 'he's ready for the check' then got up and walked to the bathroom. Her exit prompted Tessa to suggest that Majac should ride home with Jaz, and she would take Majac's car and give Crystal a ride home. "Call me later. I'll meet you." Tessa took his car key and dashed to the bathroom to console Crystal. Majac recognized that the look in her eyes was much more inviting than a week ago when she didn't invite him in back to her place.

From the garage, Majac texted Tessa that he and Jaz were going to the Train Station for drinks and cigars. She responded with a red lipstick kiss emoji. Majac smiled as Jaz sped out of the garage heading south.

26

Viv's Got A Gun

IT WAS DUSK ON FRIDAY when the would-be puppy breeders came banging on Vivienne's front door. From inside, they heard a woman's voice yell, *Go away.* They banged again. When there was no answer, they kicked the door until it came off the hinges and opened. Bum rushing the door; they were greeted by the business end of a gun. They didn't have a puppy with them. When they realized it wasn't the same old lady they had threatened before, they turned to run. Solomon fired the gun. He hit the short one in the leg. He screamed and fell. His partner in crime pushed past him, slamming the shorter one into the broken front door.

Solomon sprinted through the battered doorway. Running across the lawn in front of Vivienne's townhouse, he shot twice at the taller boy, the second shot hitting him in the arm. When the boy fell, he stopped shooting. Solomon reached the boy in three steps. He grabbed him by his bleeding arm and dragged the boy back inside. At the front porch, he pointed his gun at the shorter boy, yelling, "Get your ass back inside."

As his mother came into the living room from the kitchen, Solomon ushered both of the boys back into Vivienne's living room.

Outside a crowd started to gather. Where there was no one before, the sound of gunshots drew people to pop up like dandelions.

The shorter boy crawled across Viv's floor. Solomon, annoyed by how slowly he was moving, kicked him in the thigh. Again he screamed. The bullet had entered his hamstring, right below his butt. "Get your ass over in front of the couch." When the boy reached his destination, Solomon used the sole of his boot to again push the boy until he was face down on the carpet. The shorter boy turned his face to Solomon.

Solomon pointed the gun at him while twisting the arm of the taller boy standing next to him. "Now lay your ass right there. Move a muscle and I'm going to shoot you in the other ass cheek. Say anything and I'm going to shoot you in the other ass cheek. Do anything except lay there and breathe, and I'm going to shoot you in the other ass cheek. You feel me?"

Tears streamed from the boys' eyes, but they nodded.

"Come here Viv." Solomon's mother came closer at her son's request. The six-foot woman in her late sixties stood eye-to-eye with the taller boy. "This him?" her son asked.

"Yes. These are the young men who threatened me."

Enraged, Solomon tightened his grip on the tall boy's arm and hit him across the head with the gun.

Seeing that her son had a firm grip on the boy's arm, she started in on him. "I can't believe the children of this generation. You young people have it better than anybody who as ever come before you and all you want to do is take from people. You're too lazy to go out and get your own like everybody else. Lazy and shameful. Lord Jesus help these lost children. Purify their souls, Lord."

"Viv!" Solomon yelled, interrupting her diatribe.

"What?" Vivienne's glare turned to her son. She wasn't used to him raising his voice at her and despite the situation, she wasn't having it now.

"Slow your roll, Viv. I got this."

Vivienne huffed. Took a deep breath to calm herself. She glared at her son for chastising her, but remained silent.

The taller boy laughed. Solomon punched him in the temple with the butt of the gun again.

"That's right," yelled Vivienne. "Keep talking young man. He's got a lot more where that came from."

"Viv!"

"All right." Vivienne glowered at the young boy but stopped talking.

Now that she had identified them as the two who had previously threatened her, Solomon knew what he had to do. He engaged the safety and handed Vivienne the gun he was holding. The gun he had used to shoot both of the infamous intruders pretending to be puppy salesmen. "Point that at him so he won't move," he said.

"Now close your eyes Viv, you don't want to see this."

Vivienne raised the gun until it was pointed at the taller boy then closed her eyes.

Still holding the taller boy by his bleeding arm, Solomon grabbed the boy's wrist and swung.

"What are you going to…"

Before she could finish her question, Solomon used the boy's hand to strike Vivienne in the face. "Lord have Mercy," she yelled. The blow hit her just beneath her right eye. Because of her large size, Vivienne stumbled back in surprise, but did not fall.

The look of awe on the boy's face paralyzed him. "Yo Homie, what the hell you doing?"

Quickly, Solomon punched the boy in his face, knocking him to the floor; Then he kicked him in the ribs. "Get over there with your boy."

Before Vivienne had time to understand his next move, Solomon turned, pulled out a second gun and shot at her. The bullet grazed her right shoulder. Instantly blood stained her blouse. She started screaming. Screams that drew an ever-growing crowd outside on Vivienne's lawn. She dropped down in her recliner and called for God and Jesus to save her.

Solomon rushed to where she sat. Just for good measure, Solomon wrapped his hand around his mother's and took the gun from her as she cried hysterically, praying for mercy. Seeing that he had barely nicked her, Solomon didn't bother to get anything to cover her wound.

He spoke loudly so she could hear him over her own cries. "Viv look at me." When she wouldn't stop, he yelled in a louder, more commanding voice, "Vivienne Marie Alexandré, stop all that noise and listen to me."

A second later she was reduced to sniffles.

Solomon said, "Look at me Viv." She was quiet, but her eyes remained closed. Again he demanded, "Look at me Vivienne."

Vivienne opened her eyes. Tears ran down her cheek.

Focusing his gaze on her, he said "It's all right Viv, I got this."

Silently Vivienne nodded her head.

Solomon put the safety on and then used a handkerchief to wipe down the gun that he used to shoot Viv. He called 911, reported shots fired at Vivienne's address. He handed Vivienne the gun he had shot the boys with, told her to point it at the boys, and keep her finger on the trigger until the police came. He knelt; emptied the bullets from the gun used to shoot Viv. He put his knee on the tall boy's neck, and told him to take the gun. After the boy put his fingerprints on the gun, he told her loud enough for both of them to hear him clearly, if either one of them moves a muscle, shoot first and ask questions later. He moved toward the front door, then turned around to make certain his mother had the situation under control. "Vivienne Alexandré, look at me," he demanded. When she made direct eye contact with him, he asked one last time, "You all right?"

Her eyes were locked on his now. She stiffened, sniffed twice then said, "I will be once they get this trash out of my house."

Solomon jammed the gun he used to shoot Vivienne underneath the broken front door, wedging it into the carpet. Then he ran outside, down the porch, around the left side of the house and disappeared.

From the crowd gathering outside, the boys could hear cries of *Everything all right in there?* And, *You okay Miss Vivienne?*

Despite the overwhelming urge to take their chances at running, the boys remained on the floor. The taller boy's eyes met Vivienne's. She strained her arm toward him as if willing a bullet to escape the barrel of that gun. Her eyes dared him to move. When he saw the disgust and determination in her eyes, he acquiesced. The thought of fleeing before the cops arrived fled from his body and he lowered his head back to the floor. While she waited for help to arrive, Vivienne quoted scripture, prayed, lectured the two puppy salesmen about their sins and cursed them for breaking down her front door. She asked them their parents' names. She asked them what their grandmothers would think if they knew they were out in the streets robbing old ladies. Neither of the boys spoke. By the time the police arrived, Vivienne had damn near preached a full sermon. The two boys were to the point where they wished Solomon's bullets had been kill shots instead of mere flesh wounds.

Moments later a police squad car hit the brakes in the middle of the street at the back of a crowd. A street that was devoid of people when Solomon started shooting. One of the officers jumped out of the vehicle and pushed his way through the growing crowd. A crowd that stood gaping through Vivienne's doorway at the bleeding boys lying on her living room floor. Making it to Vivienne's front porch, a Hispanic policeman called into the broken front door identifying himself before entering the home. Vivienne yelled that she was okay and that the policeman could come in. Inside, he saw Vivienne still pointing her gun at the boys. "Put the gun down, Ma'am" he yelled, pulling his own firearm from its holster.

His partner, a white man, followed him through the front door.

Vivienne did as she was instructed. The first police officer grabbed her gun and stuck it in his belt. The second officer pointed his gun at the boys bleeding on the floor. And just like that, Vivienne went into hysterical victim mode; crying, screaming and telling the pretend story Solomon had her rehearse before the boys showed up. Somewhere in the annuls of Hollywood, an Academy Award had slipped this great actress's grasp.

The cop checked the boys lying on the floor. The shorter one was having trouble breathing. He rolled him over and found him lying in a pool of blood. The police called for backup and an ambulance. Two more police cars had arrived before an ambulance eased its way down the now crowded street before backup made it to the house.

When Ms. Menzy appeared at the door, Vivienne went into full hysteria. She was trembling when they put her into the second ambulance. She would live, but her arm would be in a sling for a month longer than necessary to heal and the ugly scar from where her son grazed her shoulder would be with her for the rest of her life.

The Hispanic officer who arrived first on the scene asked a fifty-something looking man standing ten yards from the front porch, "What happened?" From the calm look on the elder man's face, the policeman was certain he knew exactly what had transpired.

Before he could answer, a white lady in the crowd yelled one thing.

A white man by her side yelled something different.

A teenager said there were six of them.

A tall, black man drinking a beer said there were only four.

A guy in a wheelchair said he saw the whole thing, but he wasn't gonna say anything until the news cameras came.

Seven different people standing in the crowd gave seven different accounts of what they saw. The fifty-something man the officer first identified, never offered his account of what happened.

The police officer asked the fifty-something man, "Anybody else live there?"

"No Officer. She lives alone." He and Vivienne had lived across the street from each other for more than two decades. She and his now deceased wife became friends the day she moved in. He was on his porch working on a Sudoku puzzle twenty minutes before the boys arrived at Viv's and didn't move off the porch until the crowd was more than twenty people deep. The man kept a stoic face as he said, "As far as I know, Ms. Vivienne is the only person to ever live there. And I've lived on this block for twenty-eight years."

"Did anybody see anybody else go into or come out of the house?" the policeman asked to the gaggle of witnesses.

"Nope!" the fifty-something man said firmly. "Ain't seen nobody but her in that house in at least four—five days."

27

All Aboard

During the daytime on Monday through Friday, the Train Station was a tavern-type coffee-house where people sipped overpriced cafés and teas with complicated names beneath a pre-programmed playlist of soft jazz and smooth R-and-B as they used the free Wi-Fi to search the internet on their laptops for whatever tickled their fancy. On Tuesday and Wednesday, they closed at 6pm. As evening fell on Thursday and throughout the weekend, the computers and hot beverages were replaced with people sipping mixed drinks and listening to live rhythm and blues falling from the speakers mounted on, and painted the same color as, the black walls. As day turned to night, the modestly decorated tavern transformed into an old school, blue-light-in-the-basement party spot billed as an after work party set for mature professionals where some of the hottest unknown and soon-to-be-known bands on the West Coast did their utmost to impress an eclectic crowd of listeners.

Solomon was at the Train Station with Jordyn, his friend from Spokane. His personal *Equalizer* episode had concluded hours earlier and the police hadn't yet come knocking on his door.

When Jordyn couldn't decide what to eat, their waitress recommended the appetizer sampler. Solo remembered her saying in the car that she hadn't eaten all day, so he ordered two of the biggest steaks on the menu. When their food came, he ordered water with lime for himself and a pink pomegranate martini for her. "Better make it two, I need to loosen up her dancing shoes."

On the dance floor, he was a polite dancer. This was new to her because most guys she dated were all over her when they danced. He knew how to lead and moved his hands to points on her body that made her comfortable enough to allow him to control her motion. His hand and body movement was all-around smooth, barely needing to touch his body to hers as they swayed to the beat. Upbeat songs found him swinging and dipping her with the fervor and intense motion of the best Lindy dancers from the forties. Slow songs left her breathless under the warmth and comfort of his powerful hands holding her close, his hips and shoulders guiding her motion as if she floated on clouds. At one point she leaned in soft, kissed his cheek and made a sound from the bottom of her throat that was part moan, as if she was saying, *Damn, this feels good*; part song, as if she wanted to serenade him. She turned to face him, a thin film of perspiration glistening above her eyes; those crystal blue eyes being her most prominent feature. She moved her mouth to his and paused an inch away. Their eyes met, searched each other trying to define what was happening. He knew he needed her permission and the only way he'd get it was if she'd come that final inch. Again she moaned, this time her tongue escaping her mouth to lick her lips and keep them from going dry. Softness, more delicate than normal, overcame her eyes before they closed. She leaned into him and covered his mouth with hers, evoking a soul stirring moan that let her know he enjoyed the kiss.

When they got back to the table, Kenny was waiting for them.

"Hey Frat, you remember Maurice Powers from Crossing the Line right? He was either a senior, or recently graduated, but he couldn't have been more than four years ahead of us."

"Not really," Solomon said, searching his memory bank to place a face with the name. "Refresh my memory."

"Corny, muscle-bound, dark-skinned brother with a big laugh?"

"Nope." Solomon said.

"Rugby player."

That brought about the recognition Solomon needed. "Yeah. Wow, I forgot all about that cat."

"Well anyway, he passed by here while you were out wearing out them dancing shoes and we chatted it up for a bit. Turns out, he's CEO of his own Sports Agency now. He said he's got a private table up in the VIP and invited us Frats to come join him."

"Cool," Solomon said, then regarded Jordyn. His expression apologized in advance for abandoning her while they chopped it up with their old fraternity brother. "Let me cool down for a minute then we'll go give Frat a quick shout."

Jordyn and Kenny both recognized the look of remorse on his face.

"Go ahead," Jordyn said before either of the men could form their words. "Me and Pink will be right here when you get back." She smiled and lifted the glass of light-red aperitif.

"We'll be right back,' Solomon offered, apology still dripping from his words.

"Nah Bruh, we ain't leaving her by herself," Kenny said. "You know how we get down. I'm certain Frat won't mind if she joins us for a bit."

When Solomon, Kenny and Jordyn, her hand tucked inside Solomon's elbow, entered the exclusive VIP lounge, he saw Maurice Powers standing on the seat in a booth. Five or six others were seated around him. From his vantage point, Powers, the obvious Fat Cat of the group, storytelling.

Even though he was only a couple of years older than Solo and Kenny, he had a white soul patch, white temples and the beginnings of a perfectly round, salt-and-pepper afro. His weathered face held piercing, light-brown eyes. A pronged cane which aided his walk, leaned against the side of his chair. His well-tailored, vested suit was tweed and strictly fifties style. He had the stance and presence of a Poitier or a Belafonte. Having finished his story, he took a seat right before they arrived.

From the side, Solomon immediately recognized the brown-skinned woman sitting on Maurice's lap.

"Unh, umh." Kenny cleared his throat to garner the Fat Cat's attention.

Leona looked up to see the man she, the dance instructor, thought she was dating. Solo made eye contact, but did not speak. Leona cleared her throat, raised an eyebrow, shifted in her seat, and returned his silence.

"Maurice, you remember Frat? Doctor Solomon 'Solo' Alexandré?" Kenny said uncomfortably.

"Sure do." Maurice unleashed a booming laugh that seemed to sway the curtains and shake the walls. Without standing, he reached his right hand to shake Solomon's; his left hand firmly attached to Leona's waist.

"What's up Frat?" Solomon said as their hands came together. He did not despise him. He had no thought for the man at all.

"Nothing but the living?' Maurice replied.

Leona said she couldn't accompany Solomon and Kenny out that night. She forgot to tell him that her previous engagement was being hired as an escort for the evening.

"I'd stand," Maurice said, "but as you can see, this gorgeous lady has me locked down at the moment."

"No need," Solomon said trying to calm the rush of thoughts roiling through him. He averted his eyes toward Leona, while they finished their fraternity handshake. Her beige beauty, smooth lips and slender face made him wonder...*What if?* His words were directed toward the Fat Cat, but his eyes remained focused on Leona. "I see how you do."

Trying to measure her breaths in Zen fashion, Leona shifted her eyes to the beauty queen whose arm was tucked inside Solomon's. Inhale. Some stares are mesmerizing. Exhale. Some are intimidating. Inhale. Leona's burned. Burned and bore a hole right through Solomon's soul.

A cute, brown-skinned woman with a small waist and firm thighs escorted Majac and Jaz to one of the little round tables near the front of The Train Station where the standup comedians would be performing. Majac recognized two of the three names scheduled to appear and thought, *this show is going to be raunchy.* That made him glad that Tessa and Crystal decided not to join. Neither Majac nor Jaz drank as much as they used to in their twenties, but they ordered some beers just to cover the clubs two drink minimum. With time to kill before the show started, Jaz got up and made his way over to some of the women he recognized from team parties. Majac found it odd that Jaz would do that when he just finished a knock-down drag-out fight with his wife. It was as if Jaz had to be reminded that he could still pull women at will, but chose not to because he was married. As far as Majac knew, Jaz never took it past flirting. Nevertheless, once he'd arrived in Seattle, Crystal hadn't let Jaz go out to a club unless he took Majac with him. That was their unspoken deal since the Los Angeles thing. Jaz could go wherever he wanted, as long as Majac went along. Other than that, he had better be home before dusk. That was, of course, prior to him moving out. In the months since moving into his own place, Majac couldn't say for sure that Jaz didn't do this more often.

Tonight, Majac just hoped that Jaz didn't take it upon himself to bring any women over for him to meet. Before Tessa, Jaz was good for doing that. Majac sometimes thought that Jaz obsessed about Majac's love life, or lack thereof, more than he did. Despite his best friend's thoughts to the contrary, Majac had had more than his fair share of no-strings-attached loving. Like any straight man, he liked the feeling of a woman in his arms, maybe even more than some men, because if anything, he tended to over romanticize the idea, which lead him to trouble in San Diego. But three years ago, during his first year at the Pentagon, he'd he met a female named Katrina and that experience forced a change in his outlook on women.

She was a Lieutenant Commander who worked in the Intelligence office, situated across the hall from his. Originally, he felt they were as different as night and day. Katrina was from one of the roughest neighborhoods of West St. Louis. While he was from the safe environs of little old Tuskegee, Pennsylvania. When she wasn't in uniform, Katrina was flashy, loud, brutally honest, and would curse you out without thinking twice if you crossed her. Whereas Majac tended to be restrained and polite, she was the most overtly sexual woman he'd ever met. In fact, the only reason he talked to her, was that she approached him first.

After a month or so of passing each other silently in the passageway, Katrina decided to find her way across the hallway and come talk to him in his office. In the months that followed, they'd gone to baseball games, movies, Baltimore's Inner Harbor, clubs in both DC and Northern Virginia, or sometimes just walk the banks of the Potomac. Majac remembered times when that in itself was an adventure.

Katrina dressed provocatively yet tastefully. Her figure was so fitfully curvy that men would openly gawk at her even when she was walking with another man. She was fine, knew she was fine, and didn't mind letting you know that she knew. Apparently, she was too fine to succumb to Majac because she forestalled every attempt he made to sleep with her. Since he had taken so long to make his first move, Majac feared that Katrina had tagged him with that most dreaded of labels—a nice guy. Like Jaz always said, calling a man a nice guy is equivalent to the sexual kiss of death.

Women want their children to play—nice. They want other women to look at their living room furniture and say—nice. When they shop, they want salespeople to be—nice. The last place a strong confident sister wants to see niceness is in their men. For a woman with Katrina's ghetto origins, Mister Nice lives a little too close to Mister Weak, who lives right next door to that most dreaded of neighbors, Mister Punk. So, whenever Majac got the impression that a woman thought he was nice, or just a friend, he knew that his chances of getting laid quickly diminished.

That was okay when all he wanted was friendship, but if he wanted sex, he would sever ties. He had difficulty being around a woman in the capacity of friendship if he was attracted to her. Particularly if he had made a play and she knew that he wanted her. Once a man lets a woman know how he feels about her, and she says no, every time she looks at him he'll see a smug self-satisfied, condescending "you can't help wanting me" expression on her face. Even when he no longer does. At least, that was Majac's theory. While he knew he hardly qualified as an authority on women, only having four actual girlfriends and one fiancée, the one thing he was certain of was that women choose men, never vice versa. Some are simply clever enough to let the man think that he has chosen her.

So after Katrina let it be known that he simply wasn't getting any, his visits became less and less frequent until he stopped visiting altogether.

Jaz returned with two more beers, and no women, just as the emcee for the night took the stage.

"Toot-toot," the emcee shouted into the microphone. "Time to get onboard ladies and gentlemen, The Train is about to take off. Let me hear you make some noise."

The emcee waved his arms up and down encouraging the audience to get louder. "Now that's more like it," he said as the roar of the crowd came to a crescendo. "Good evening and welcome to The Train Station.

I am Devon Kirkland and I have the honor of being your host for the night. I hope you're all having a good time." A round of applause confirmed his inquiry. "Well, it appears that a mechanical failure has prevented our scheduled acts for the night from arriving, but we won't let that ruin your evening. The manager has waved his magic wand and with some of the local talent he's discovered in the building, tonight's comedy show is now an Open Mic Night."

A murmur swept across the room. It was quickly obvious that some of the crowd was unhappy about the change of events and from the growing din of background comments, it was possible that some might get ugly.

"Now before we go any further, the owner has said that he will return your cover charge if you decide to leave before the show starts," Devon said. "But, rest assured, we have some musicians, an amateur comedian and a spoken word artist who are set to rock your world tonight. You may not have heard of them, but they've performed locally before and if I do say so myself," Devon said bouncing his head from side-to-side, "they are pretty...damn...good." Devon laughed, and the crowd laughed with him. "Now, the show is going to start in ten minutes, so if y'all want to break camp and get your money back, now is the time to do it, 'cause once the first artist takes the stage, the refund window is closed. But in the meantime, support your waitresses' college fund, order another drink and get ready to rock it at The Train Station."

Fifteen minutes later, the accepted equivalent of ten minutes in CP Time, the spotlight illuminated the stage and Devon returned to the mic. "All right Train Station, let me hear you make some noise!"

The clapping was so meager that it could barely be called noise.

"Dang, y'all," Devon said. "Now you know if it was you about to get up here, you wouldn't be happy to give it your all for no weak ass greeting like that. Come on now, I know y'all got more energy than that."

Devon paused and waited. Another meek round of clapping ensued.

"Oh, I know what it is, I forgot to tell y'all. During our little intermission, the owner decided to raise the stakes a little for tonight since he doesn't have to pay our comedians. So, our open mic night is now an amateur talent contest. Grand Prize is five-hundred dollars for first place. Winner take all. No second place. No third. At the end, we'll bring everybody back and let you determine our winner. So, come on Train Station, make some noise."

The audience clapped, hollered and whistled like they were at a football game and the Seahawks had just scored the winning touchdown.

"All right Train Station, now that's what I'm talking about. Now that we're ready, please give a warm Train Station welcome to our first performer of the night, jazz trumpeter and Seattle's own, Cary Bryant."

The trumpeter carried his horn the way the Count of Montecristo wielded his sword. He grinned like Louis Armstrong, then played like Miles Davis. Cary's selection was a cover—a hip, jazzy rendition of *The Way You Move* by Outkast. The crowd showed him some love, but it was apparent that they weren't moved by his performance. On a scale of 1 to 10, he earned a solid six.

Next, a brother, who was introduced as Terrible Teddy, called himself a comedian. He told jokes for his five-minute session. A few were funny, a few were lame and one was totally hilarious. Terrible Teddy earned a mixture of half-hearted claps and murmurs from the crowd as Devon introduced the third act.

Behind the curtain, to the left of the stage, Solomon stepped up and stopped next to Leona. His cologne, the same that she'd sprayed during her visit to his bedroom for a band aid, silently introduced him. She knew she'd never forget that scent.

"All right Family, I'm told this next brother is a Doctor by day and bad ass pianist by night."

"Pianist, hunh?' Leona said to the man who had stopped next to her. Curiosity creased her brow. He remembered how she used to do that and how attractive he found it.

"If his music ain't no good, maybe his doctor side can heal some of Teddy's broke ass jokes," Devon continued.

The audience roared.

"Yes," Solomon said, "a pianist." During the pause offered by Devon's outburst, he had time to compose himself and put his thoughts in order. "I'm sure I told you."

"I guess that explains why you work so well with your hands." Despite him turning his entire body to face her, she kept her gaze straight ahead.

"Okay Train Station give it up for Seattle's own, Doctor Solo."

Solomon made his way to center stage, swung his suit jacket away from his shoulders the way Superman flips back his cape and sat on the bench. And the music that came from that piano contained a spirit that sprinkled a lyrical blessing all around the room. He had begun playing the piano at age three. He'd brought tears to the eyes of the women at bible study. By age twelve, he was playing symphonies. The next year he discovered the jazz band and immediately fell in love with the rifting melodies and fantastic rhythms that converted his passionate keystrokes into sensuous sounds.

Solomon began to play, two octaves below the songs normal register. The notes spoke to Leona's heartache at the loss of her parents. Burned with honesty and talked about the poverty her eyes had seen as she travelled abroad, the sorrow her lips had cried, and the courage her heart had felt. In the middle, he curved two notes, going up then down the scale. Next were the edgy notes; they represented life on the street, made men sway, made women hum along, some even cried. Profanity translated into sharp notes punctuating his expression, but still all-in-all, riveting. Solomon finished playing. As the piano died off, the crowd cheered, whistled and woofed for Solomon. He stood, gave a bow and made his way back to the side stage.

Leona was moved to tears. "That was beautiful," she moaned.

Solomon looked straight out onto the stage and glowed. And because of the way she said it, and her expression afterwards, so mousy and so geeky, Solomon laughed.

Devon laughed a little louder before agreeing with her. "Solo, My Man, you got skills. Mad skills." Devon gave Solomon a fist bump, then made his way back to the microphone. "Now that was some funky piano playing right there," he said. "If doctoring don't work out, Brother, let me know, because I can sang," Devon mused as laughter followed from the crowd. "Nahh, for real. I can." His comical tone drew more laughter. "All right Family, the final arteeest of the night," he said rocking side-to-side with a J.J. Evans from Good Times swagger in his voice, "is a pretty young thing that is hotter than fish grease and has a stage name to match. Please give a warm Train Station welcome to Miss...Decadent Red."

Leona emerged from the side stage without acknowledging the meager 'Good luck' Solomon offered as she walked away. She paused at the microphone for a moment. Allowed her eyes to adjust to the light. "Good evening Ladies and gentlemen. The piece I'll be performing for you tonight is called *The Taste of You*. It's something I first tried out on my Sensual Intelligence podcast. I hope you enjoy it." She closed her eyes and bobbed her head as the band started to play a cover of a slow, lazy tune by Jill Scott entitled *Slide*.

> *Are there limits to my fingertips?*
> *And borders to your skin?*
> *I think the thoughts you have are mine,*
> *Because I feel them from within.*
> *The taste of you grows longer and stronger*
> *With every measured dip...of my head.*
> *Effortlessly I slide up and down, the fullness of your staff,*
> *Your hips...rotate more and more in synch with my lips...*
> *As the length of you presses where I once laughed.*
> *That sliding velvety rhythm.*

Then she squinted against the bright spotlight, smiling and swaying to pass time. An extended trombone slide drove her neck to crane through the elongated rhythm. The tambour of Decadent Red's voice was beautiful. Lilting above the room, objectifying the essence of her innermost desires.

> *Strong hands strain against the back of my neck...*
> *As the sensation of Overload...takes effect.*
> *Body hitches, muscles tighten, breath is hesitant, mouth*
> *agape.*
> *Low, groans from deep within rise and rip the air;*
> *You...tremble with release and then you quake...*

> *I...relax, curled lips inside my mouth, savor...The taste*
> *of you!*

From the back of the room came, "You can taste me anytime, Baby!"
Solomon marveled at how the curve of her mouth formed the shape of
an unfinished kiss after each syllable.

Near the bar a man shouted, "Whoooooooooo! Give me more."
Decadent Red took a long, slow breath then gave another verse.

> *There are no limits to our fingers...nor borders to our*
> *skin;*
> *We are not sure where one ends...nor where the other*
> *begins.*
> *For it seems that in our shared touch...*
> *Are common thoughts of you and I;*
> *As you start a journey that ends down south,*
> *Wrap arms of steel around my thighs.*
> *Shoulders support my caramel thighs;*
> *Time for you to taste what's mine;*
> *Grab my ass strong and tight;*
> *No gentle pinch back there this time.*
> *Hips writhe hard and fast...and cherish your tongue;*
> *I open wide, use you shamelessly...freak until I cum.*
> *Would you flip me over... and spank me back there?"*
> *Yes, pleeeeaaassseee flip me over... and pull my hair?*
> *She dropped her head, exhaled and then begged,*
> *"Would you?*

"Yes, Baby," came from the darkness of the crowd. "Yes indeed."
Before she continued, she ever so slightly raised the corners of her
mouth in silent acknowledgement of her boisterous volunteer.

> *Would you slap my ass then enter me...slowly;*
> *Giving me a little taste of you...only?*
> *Then grip my ass...and spread my cheeks,*
> *Watch my pleasure...as you enter.*
> *With every inch...you go...oh...so......deep?*
> *Again that long pause. "Would you?*

Leona opened her hazel eyes, put a hand atop her brow and peered into the crowd for her distant lover. Solomon watched anxiously from the wing. Every fiber in his being beckoning silently for her to look his way. When she didn't, he put two fingers in his mouth and let loose a long, loud, piercing whistle that silenced the rest of the crowd. Leona's neck twitched in his direction as if about to face him, but her neck refused to allow her face to turn and give him the satisfaction. Instead, she closed her eyes and gave the audience her flavor, her tempo rising with the music, her intensity reflecting in her face. When she had control, she finished with:

> *Do we know where my body ends?*
> *Do we know where yours begins?*
> *The heat of our passion radiates...*
> *And I dip slowly before you...*
> *Heels on, ass high, head stopping at your waist;*
> *My tongue it circles...then up...then down...*
> *Firm grip with both hands...then taste...the crown;*
> *Then take you in...inch...by...velvety...inch.*
> *Warm hands twist back and forth;*
> *Fall to my knees before my King,*
> *And savor you...for all your worth.*
> *Past lips and tongue you slide your might,*
> *Nails pierce butt flesh...I gently bite.*
> *In fear and amazement...*
> *You watching Me...*
> *Me watching Too...*
> *As you gift me with...*
> *The Taste of You!*

Those words and a thunderous drumbeat took the spotlight dark. The room was stock-still. A moment later, the light came back on, and she opened her eyes to absorb the crowd's jubilant response. The entire Train Station audience, men and women alike, were on their feet clapping, screaming, whistling and shouting at the top of their lungs. The overwhelming applause left no room for interpretation of who had won. Leona took a bow and walked off the stage as Devon appeared from the darkness.

"Give it up for Decadent Red," he said although the crowd still hadn't stopped applauding. "I don't know about the judges, but I'm sorry fellas, I for damn sure know who my winner is." Devon released the microphone, stepped back and clapped until the audience quieted down.

"That was pretty good," Solomon said when Leona reached backstage. "I didn't know you did poetry."

"Now you do." Just like before her performance, she stood next to him, not facing him.

"Maybe I could hear a little more some time?"

"Depends…"

"On?"

"On how long you plan on doing Barbie," Leona barbed in return.

Solomon went straight into defense mode. "She's a friend."

"Okay Biz-Markie."

Solomon took a second to compose himself. He was impressed with her comedic timing. If Terrible Teddy had half of the delivery Leona had in that one line, he may have had a chance at winning. "She just showed up on my doorstep right before me and Kenny headed out. She lives in Spokane. I couldn't just walk away from her since she'd come all this way." He watched the surprise on her face and believed instantly that it was real.

"All this way just to see you?"

Solomon was silent.

"Just a friend?" Leona grunted. "Humph."

"If memory serves me, I called You and invited You to be my date tonight, but you already had plans with the Fat Cat in the white suit whose lap you were sitting on when I got here."

Before she could reply, the air in the Train Station was filled with the chant…*We want Red, We want Red, We want Red.*

"Decadent Red," Devon hailed her. "Your audience awaits!"

Leona turned to face Solomon. Before she could utter a word, he said, "Appears I'm not the only one who can't get enough of you."

She stared at him for a beat. Inhaled deeply, then walked back onto the stage sans conversation.

Trying to sound like a verse from a popular rap song, a man in the crowd yelled, "Can we get an ennn-core? Yes, we want more."

An eruption of cheers, cat-calls, and a deafening applause left no doubt in the judges' minds that *Decadent Red* was their winner. Leona Pearson, the beautiful, curvaceous woman with the edgy personality and perfect facial imperfection, beamed with pleasure before the crowd.

Devon addressed the audience. "Give up for tonight's champion,

Decadent Red." Before he exited the stage, he handed Leona an envelope and said, "Hit it DJ." Then the room went dark and the spotlight hit Leona.

"Before I start, I just want to say thank you everybody. This means a lot to me. And if you ever want to hear more, please visit my podcast, *Sensual Intelligence*." She took a breath then softly blew air. The spotlight dimmed and smooth music once again started to play. With that, Leona morphed into Decadent Red to give them another taste of her alter ego.

> *Tonight he lays in his bed, alone, but not lonely.*
> *The only person in the room, but definitely not by himself.*
> *He closes his eyes. Recalls her visit last week.*
> *Seven days ago, almost to the minute,*
> *When he laid in her bed, pretending to watch a movie.*
> *Wondering how to initiate an incredible love making session*
> *With the most beautiful woman he's ever known.*
> *One week before, almost to the minute, before she took him in;*
> *Her tongue's sweet honey inviting his essence to rise.*
> *Before she took him in her arms;*
> *Spread herself wide and let him enter her essence.*
> *When he held her close; the length of his torso draped on hers.*
> *Held her extra tight. Rocked her slow and steady.*
> *Stroked her warm...taut...beautiful...sex;*
> *Slow and sensual...until her Phoenix rose.*
> *Her nirvana bloomed.*
> *Her ecstasy came.*
> *That beautiful face arrived.*
> *Relished in the knowing that her pleasure was brought by his heat deep within her sugar walls.*
> *Touch me.*
> *Tease me.*
> *Taste me.*
> *Talk to your man while I pleasure my woman.*
> *Tell me everything this man needs to do...to make you scream.*
> *He tasted her sensuality.*

Wished every nerve ending in his body was a taste bud.
Savored her nectar as she reached that next mountain top.
The next peak; higher, sharper, more intense than the first.
Her sex...now wet and warm as a mid-August puddle;
Showering him with her lust.
Manhood taut, yearning high, the first drop of his dew escapes.
Thoughts of her sprint from mind to loin.
Boxers strain as his desire aches to find her welcoming.
Aches to plunge deep inside her intense heat.
Lingers at the opening of her desire.
Then dives in with an engorged fullness.
Massages that softness as her love squeezes...holds him in her;
Until...her tsunami crests and she explodes...around him.
Until pressure busts pipes and he explodes...within her;
The release she desired finally quenching...
Her Fire...her Desire...her Love.
But she too is alone in her bed, her fingers restlessly flutter;
Longing to wrap themselves around his manhood;
So eager.
So thick.
So filling.
She dreamt of him a moment ago;
And woke in desperate need of release.
She touched herself.
Lonely hands attempting to squelch that ache
To feel him deep within.
Rebellious hips squirm and press back at her;
Remembering the heat of his lips.
Thrusts, moans and her vision of his memory;
Escort her impending release.
Decadent Red is what he called her.
The Decadent sound of her that flooded his consciousness.
The Red undertones of her face that met his eyes.
His lonely hands finally squash his own desperate ache.
That ache grown from deep within.

Goodnight Fair Maiden are the words
That accompany their star-crossed dreams.
Beautiful, intoxicating dreams of his filling her...
With the sensually intelligent memory...
Of their not-so-distant love.

The stage lights went dark.
Decadent Red exited the stage.
The crowd erupted in applause.

Leona was walking on sunshine when she reached the side stage. Behind her, the crowd was still clapping, whistling and chanting *Red* over and again. She kissed Devon on the cheek then practically leapt into Solomon's arms. He held her there for a moment as she squeezed her joy into him. "Ahhhhhhh!" Leona screamed. "That...was...so...Awwe-some!"

Behind them, Kenny and Jordyn rounded the corner. They figured they'd come see where Solomon disappeared since he hadn't returned to their table. As if she'd been struck a violent blow on the head, but hadn't fallen, Jordyn stood stock still. Her eyes open, stricken with disbelief.

Kenny took a deep breath and grabbed her hand when he saw his best friend and Leona embraced in a bear hug. "You want me to kick his ass," he deadpanned while glancing at his best friend.

"Dammit!" Jordyn said loud enough for all five of them to hear.

Leona met the angry gaze of Solomon's date as he loosened his grip on her and turned to find Jordyn's voice.

"I guess I should've known by the way you couldn't take your eyes off of her upstairs," she said.

Solomon was caught in a bad place. Although he hadn't initiated the hug, he didn't stop her from hugging him. And she felt so good in his arms, he did not hurry to let her go.

"I knew coming-k here was a mistake," Jordyn spat. She stared at him the way a scorned woman could stare right through a man—long and hard. Could burn a hole through his heart and soul. Make him want to turn away, when he knows he can't. "I should've figured that out when you dropped me off at the hospital and never came back." Jordyn snatched her hand away from Kenny. She was a lioness in a cage, mentally pacing back and forth, wanting to break free. She rushed toward the club entrance.

Solomon hurried after her. Called her name several times. She was distancing herself from him, but for her, it was neither fast nor far enough. On the sidewalk, she searched left and right, frantically looking for a taxi or some type of ride service to facilitate her escape. "Where the hell can I get a cab," she turned and asked the bouncer.

"Jordyn wait." Solomon emerged through the door in full stride. "Please, let me explain."

"Nothing-k to explain Mister Lover Man." She avoided his eyes. "It's obvious you want to be with whoever that is. It was obvious upstairs and it was obvious backstage."

Solomon touched her hand. She pulled it away. "Don't you touch me."

Solomon raised his hands in surrender as the bouncer and a dozen people waiting to enter the club watched the sidewalk drama play out. He watched her face go through a range of emotions. Her eyes showed uncertainty, then apprehension, then anger.

"What does it take to get a flipping-k cab in this town?" she asked to no one. Her eyes grew vacant as she stared into a past that sometimes crept up on her in quiet moments.

When he saw her expression move from anger to pain, he tried his best to wipe that pain away. "Look Jordyn, she doesn't..."

"Don't you dare say she doesn't mean anything-k to you. I don't know how long you've known that woman, but I'm grown enough to know that there's something-k between the two of you." Jordyn spoke with the fatalistic languor of an innocent woman on the verge of signing a confession to a crime she didn't commit.

"Jordyn, come on." His tone exasperated. "I didn't mean to sound..."

"You sounded like how you felt," she said, cutting him off. "Like I was annoying-k you. Oh, I'm sorry. Maybe I misunderstood. How did you mean to sound?"

"The hug was innocent. She was excited and it just happened," he said. "It had nothing to do with you."

"Obviously," she snarled. "From where I was standing-k, it had a lot to do with your past with her. Whenever that ended. If it ended."

"Some of it was, and some of it wasn't," he said. "Most of it was not though. She was excited about winning and some of our familiarity probably made her comfortable enough to hug me."

"Just some, hunh?"

"Look, nothing happened. It...was an innocent hug between friends."

"If you're such friends, why didn't you introduce me to her upstairs?"

"It wasn't the place. She was with her crowd and I went upstairs because Maurice invited me."

"And because you knew her, and you were with me, you didn't see any need to introduce me. Let me tell you why. Because you have a past with her, plain and simple. If she was just a friend, like you say, you would've had no problem introducing-k me to her."

"That may be true but," he said.

"No buts about it. You have a history with her, and because of that history, you waited backstage hoping-k I wouldn't see you with her."

"The fact remains," Solomon said forcefully, "that I am sorry."

"All I ever wanted to do was please you," she sobbed. "I tried to show you a good time in Spokane and you abandoned me. Then, being-k the idiot that I am, I come all the way to Seattle hoping-k to make up for whatever you think I did wrong and end up being-k treated like dirt again."

Solomon stepped closer.

She turned her back. "Taxi!"

He spoke to her back in a more subdued tone to prevent their impromptu audience from any continued eavesdropping. "Jordyn, I'm sorry for what you thought you saw. Leona and I are friends. I didn't introduce you to her upstairs because it wasn't the place or time. If that was wrong, then I apologize. I'm glad you're here and I'm glad you cared enough about me to come all this way to see me, but if you want to get away from me, let me get my car. I'll take you back to my place to get your bag and then I will drive you anywhere you want to go," he said dejectedly, having grown disgusted with the flavor of her capricious words.

"No, you can mail my stuff to me," she spat venomously. "I don't ever want to see you again!"

28

Roasted Alfresco

SEATTLE HAD A MILD WINTER. Unseasonably warm temps resulted in a record low number of days below freezing. The three snowstorms amounted to snowfall totals four inches below the region norm. Now that Spring had sprung, the citizens of Seattle were once again enjoying warm afternoons, brilliant blooms of foliage for Mother's Day, longer days, and of course, that greatest of American pastimes—baseball.

Since both of their mothers and their extended family still lived on the east coast, Majac and Tessa agreed to have their wedding back home in Pennsylvania. She had always wanted a June wedding, and in fourteen days, on the first Saturday in June, she and Majac would become man and wife. Finally, her lifelong dream of becoming Missus MacArthur James Antonio Charles would come true.

Under normal circumstances, a rehearsal dinner and the bachelor and bachelorette parties would take place the night before the nuptials, but since the wedding was on the other side of the country, Jaz and Solo rented out Woody's for a private dinner celebration with friends.

Denesha, Woody's General Manager, oversaw the party. Jaz and Crystal along with Solomon and Leona were the official hosts. In the month following Jordyn's explosion at The Train Station, Leona and Solomon had been distant. Their close proximity to Majac and Tessa in the months leading up to the wedding gave them plenty of opportunities to be together. Now, they were pretty much exclusive.

Desmond, there as a guest, not as the owner invited Sharet as his date. Luke and Jennifer Fleming came, but Luke apologized as soon as he finished his dinner and excused himself without reason. The tension on Jennifer's face told that she was pissed about her husband's unexplained departure, but she maintained her composure and brought back a smile when Leona told her that the talent at the bachelorette party would make her forget all about him being an ass.

Pastor Lawrence Didier was there with his wife, as well as his brother Kenny. Sylvia and Ben Lockette, and Désirée and Lamont Crittenden rounded out the guest list, along with the department heads from Majac's wardroom—the Executive Officer, Navigator, Weps and Engineer— and their wives.

At the conclusion of the dinner, the party collected their jackets and purses from the coatroom and gathered in the foyer.

"Your attention please." Solomon said from atop a chair. "There are a dozen professional chauffeurs waiting outside for us. Everybody find the driver holding a card with your name. We anticipate that by the time tonight's festivities conclude, none of you will be in any condition to operate a vehicle, so we've hired them to take your car keys and drive your vehicle home."

They emptied out onto the sidewalk where the chauffeurs and two Hummer limousines were waiting. As the key swap commenced, Crystal wrapped her arm in her husband's and led him back inside Woody's where Denesha was supervising the cleanup. Recognizing the seriousness on Crystal's face, she quickly ushered the two bus boys into the kitchen, giving Jaz and Crystal the entire dining room to talk.

"Jared, you know I love you. I love Anton and even though I don't know Tessa as well, I'm going to love her like even more of a sister once she becomes Anton's wife."

"Cool," Jaz said.

"But with all of our troubles in the past, I'm having a hard time with this bachelor party thing."

"Crys, I…" he interrupted.

"Please Jared, let me finish."

Jaz pursed his lips and stared hard at his wife. "I'm listening."

"I know that there are going to be strippers there. That doesn't mean I don't trust you, but I…"

"I don't get it," he said. "I know where you girls are going. I know that there's going to be strippers there too, so what's wrong?"

"No, you don't get to…"

"See that right there," he said. "That's why I can't talk to you."

"What?" she asked. "I didn't do anything."

"You did. Everything always has to be whatever Crystal say goes."

"That's not fair. I try to keep you in mind too."

"No you don't. It's all about what Crystal wants. It's Crystal's way or no way at all. What about me? You don't listen to me."

"That's ridiculous."

"You don't listen to nothing I…"

"Of course I listen to you," she interrupted.

"Look at that. You hardly ever let me finish. You always start talking before I finish."

"I am listening to you."

"Then stop talking when I'm talking."

"I'm listening to you, dammit."

"Stop loud talking me."

Crystal took a deep breath and blew air. She exhaled a second time then said in a calmer voice, "Okay, I'm listening. Talk to me?"

"Then stop loud talking me."

"Please Jared, just talk to me?"

"I would, but you don't respect me anymore."

"I…" she nodded a couple of times then shook her head, trying to make her words match her thoughts without exploding. She dropped her gaze, searching for her words.

"All I'm saying is that whatever you want to do, you do it," he said. "If we're together, it's your way regardless of how I feel or what I say. I admit, my wrongdoings started this, but dammit, your roses stink too."

She raised intense and weary eyes at him. "What the hell does that mean?"

"It means that your shit stinks too."

"I don't know what you're talking about Jared."

"Look, we are going to separate parties. Bachelor parties where men and women will be looking at other naked men and women. We're all grown. And we're married." Jaz had angry tears welling up in his eyes.

"We know what we are supposed to do and what we're not. We should trust each other despite our track records."

"Yes, Jared; we are grown and we are married," she said, her tears forming as well. "I don't know what all of this roses and manure mess means, but I do hope you know that you better not make me regret letting you throw this party for Majac."

Jaz cocked his head, opened his eyes wide with surprise because Crystal never referred to Anton as Majac.

"You know how much I love my brother, but don't let this further ruin our marriage."

Jaz grabbed her hands, lowered his forehead against hers and for the next three minutes, he and Crystal stared at each other as tears rolled down both of their faces. As if in some Mexican Death match, where the first to blink or wipe their face was declared the loser, neither one bothered to wipe the tears away.

Feeling his wife's disappointment in her slackening grip, he pulled his wife into an embrace and kissed the top of her head. Crystal held onto her husband for dear life. The sharp scent of his masculine, citrus-scented cologne pulling her further into the comfort of his chest.

Five minutes later, Jaz and Crystal emerged from inside Woody's. Her face was dry, but her makeup was a mess and his eyes were bloodshot. As they neared the curb, Crystal reluctantly released his hand. "Maybe I can meet you somewhere later and we can talk some more?" she said before she turned and walked to her limo.

Jaz watched her, thinking about what they'd just said. "Crystal."

She turned and regarded him.

"I love you," he mouthed silently.

For the first time in a long time, she had to force herself to respond. "Me too," she said with a sad grin.

He wanted to believe what she'd said, but there was no life in her voice. No emotion in her words. And no joy in her smile. For the first time in his life, he felt that it was possible that she might not love him.

The look in her eyes said she wasn't even sure if she loved herself.

Majac and his eight disciples for the night were already piled into the navy blue stretch Hummer limousine parked curbside. All except Solomon that is. He was standing in the open limo door. Leona clung to him, kissing him with all the passion that had grown between them since she jumped into his arms that night at the Train Station. A chorus of banter, ranging from cheers to catcalls to overtures of *Save that for later* or *Don't waste it all on her* to *Come on Man, there's plenty of that waiting for you where we're going*, was shouted from inside the limo.

Blushing from all of their rhetoric, Leona stared into Solomon's eyes when she finally broke the kiss. She loved eyes. They said things that mouths never would. And despite how much she loved Solomon's eyes, his were no exception. Every time they were alone, his eyes filled with lust, then uncertainty, then curiosity, as though several personalities inside him were all weighing in on if there was a future for the two of them.

Before she released her grip on him, she wiped hints of her lipstick from the corners of his mouth.

Solomon held her hands wide and stepped back to take all of her in. Her strapless number was held in place, or better yet suspended, by the youthfulness of her perky breasts. He enjoyed her look. Her flawless skin tone perfectly accented by soft hazel-brown eyes and a short pixie haircut. Whether she was dressed casually, to the nines, or down and dirty, she slayed every look with her easy natural beauty.

"You better stop," she said, then pushed him in the limo. "There'll be time for that later. Right now, you go play with your friends."

Before closing the door, she leaned inside and said, "Now you boys have a good time, but don't do anything you didn't learn from me."

Those who didn't know her, looked confused. Those that did, laughed out loud.

Leona stepped back out of the limo door and exchanged fake silent smiles with Jaz before dancing off to meet the other women waiting in their identical pink stretch Hummer.

From Woody's grill, the massive party SUV transported the guys to the Thunderbird Marina where a 60-foot yacht waited to take them to Mercer Island. Ten bikini-clad women wearing Mardi Gras masks greeted them onboard the big white boat.

As dusk fell on Lake Washington, the yacht rounded the southern tip of Mercer Island. Solomon was on the deck forward of the bridge with Majac and Jaz, toasting with a bottle of Louis XIII cognac. When Jaz asked him for a moment, Solomon headed below to the fantail where Kenny was schooling Majac's department heads about how their personal finances could benefit from starting an investment club. Those who weren't involved in Kenny's teaching, were inside in the main cabin dancing and drinking with the hostesses. Solomon took a seat on the waterproof, white leather bench. A moment later, a perfectly tanned woman in a green mask sat on his lap and lit his cigar.

Above them on the bridge, another masked woman with brilliant, red hair lit cigars for Majac and Jaz then left to find them a bottle of champagne. Majac gently slapped the bare skin on her bottom not covered by her bikini. Surprised, Jaz laughed then gave him a fist bump.

"Yo Partna," Majac said. "This is…Amazing."

"Amazing? Wow." Jaz guffawed and took a swig of champagne. "I expected you to praise me for this, but amazing never crossed my mind."

"What's so funny? I think amazing is perfectly fitting."

"The way you said amazing, is exactly the same way Crystal said that exact word when we first found out you were moving out here."

"Oh she did?"

"Yeah."

"So what else did my wonderful sister say—exactly?"

"That she'd bet me her car that you would be engaged in a year or so after you got here."

"Which one, the Jag or the Mercedes?"

They laughed.

"She talked about how you always hang around us to get that sense of feeling," Jaz said without answering his friend. "In her mind it was time for you to get serious about women and settle down. She said once you were back here with us you'd tire of living vicariously through us and find a wife of your own. Don't get me wrong; she wasn't criticizing. She's one of your biggest fans. It's just that she knows how much you love family and wanted you to find a woman who would make you happy."

In his head, Majac was searching for a snappy reply. When nothing came, he laughed dismissively as if those comments hadn't scratched an open wound.

"You all right? I didn't hurt your feelings did I?"

"Nahh Partna, we good," Majac said, half lying. "But I was wondering what *you* thought. Don't get me wrong, I love Sis, but right here in this moment, I want your open and honest opinion. Not Crystal's words. I'm a big boy. I can handle it."

They both let loose full, hearty laughs. "Partna," Jaz started, "If you're ready to take that leap, it's cool with me. I've been a civilian for a dozen years now. You're the one, technically for the next two weeks at least, still out there in combat battling all of those female assassins and their warrior sidekicks. The best I can do is vicariously enjoy the memories of all the beautiful honeys that threw themselves at you over the years.

I don't know if having a wife is going to work out for you, but the way that girl was looking at you at dinner, you're sure to get plenty of sex—and who can hate that?"

"Sounds all right to me." Majac took a long toke on his cigar, leaned his head way back and exhaled smoke rings straight up into the evening air. *Jaz was right*, he thought. Amazing was truly the perfect word for the night they'd had so far.

"Hey, where did you and Tessa decide to go for your honeymoon?"

"We're spending a week on the Polynesian island of Niue. Our flight leaves D.C. Monday morning."

"And where the hell is Niue?"

"It's some little island Tessa found down off the Australian coast near the Somoas. I knew she wanted to go tropical, but I just figured we'd end up in Hawaii. And it's just as nice as all them other far off Pacific islands."

"Yeah, Hawaii's cool. Crys and I have been twice."

"And you didn't take me? I'm hurt."

"Next time Uncle Maj; when we take the girls."

"That's a bet. And the best part about Hawaii is that you don't need a passport"

"And the people speak English!" Jaz said before they touched glasses.

"Amen, Brother." Majac took another toke on the expensive cigar then popped up board-straight when one of the masked beauties sat in his lap.

"Rumor has it that you are the guest of honor?" she asked.

"And who might you be?" Majac replied.

"You can call me Ginger?"

"Ginger?" he asked as a grin stretched across his face. "That's a rather unique name for a black woman. That moniker is normally reserved for pasty white women with bright red hair."

She smiled. It was her usual response before fielding inquiries about the origin of her name. "Well, my Korean mother told me that my Jamaican father was a huge fan of some movie star named Ginger on an old TV show he used to watch. According to Daddy, if he had a daughter, she was going to grow up to be a huge movie star. Hence, when I was born, he insisted that I be named Ginger."

"Well, nice to meet you Ginger." Majac smiled. Her appropriate use of the word hence surprised him.

She pulled a shell from the plate she was holding and offered to feed it to him.

"No thank you," he said, "I don't eat oysters. They make me sick."

"Awww, sad face," she said. "You know they're an aphrodisiac? You never know when you'll need one."

"No thanks, I'm good for now."

"But what about later," she asked.

"I think I'll still be good then too."

She sat gleefully wearing a more for me look on her face. Since he hadn't eaten the oyster, she slurped it down then brought her hand to rest inside his thigh. "I bet you will." She slid her hand up his thigh. He jumped, reached down to stop her. "I can't wait to find out how good."

"Damn, you're something else," he laughed. "But I doubt that's going to happen."

"I'm sorry, I thought you were the guest of honor."

"No you're not. Sorry that is," he said in the lilted tone he used when he talked with people he disliked. "And yes I am."

Before she could respond, the yacht's engine slowed. A moment later, the pilot announced, "Welcome to Mercer Island ladies and gentlemen. I hope your ride aboard *My Fair Lady* was as good for you as she was for me." A round of applause was his answer. "Give us a minute to get tied up and I'll have you all on your way to the rest of your evening."

The women from the boat were picked up from the pier and departed five minutes before the guys. A second limousine picked up Majac and his entourage, and slowly winded its way around the curvy roads on the bottom of the island before delivering them to their destination.

Six-foot adobe walls surrounding the brick and cobblestone courtyard provided security for the Peacock Mansion. A subtle mixture of Spanish architecture and bright colors made for a pleasant curb appeal. The entry to the courtyard was enclosed behind an arched gateway with a massive, motorized gate—two twelve-foot lengths of iron, each standing eight-foot tall. Inside the mini-fortress, the circular drive surrounded a stone fountain. When the silvery water fell, the never ceasing spray provided extra privacy against unwanted onlookers by obstructing said passersby from obtaining a clear view to the front door.

Wide galleries ran all around the sidewalls portraying a picturesque scene of a far off, ancient, Mediterranean land where grapes and olives grew in large vineyards along rolling hillsides. Arabesque arches and ornamented pillars made one imagine a gentle breeze of sea spray washing across a Spanish, Greek or Italian coast.

The guys exited the limo and ascended the wide marble front steps to the huge glass front door. As Solomon clapped Kenny on the shoulder, he looked past his friend and noticed a black Lincoln. The car had specialized Washington license plates. They read S-19. The letter "S" represented Senator and the number 19 represented the Senate district. Those S-19 license plates belonged to Luke Fleming, Jennifer Fleming's husband who inexplicably made an early departure from Majac's dinner party. Now Solomon knew why.

When they entered the foyer, the open vastness and wide, clean rooms portrayed the appearance that nothing was happening nor was there any prospect of happening in the future. Statues both miniature and life-size stood rigidly in place. A huge chandelier hung from the ceiling. Paintings clung to the wall so still that the images inside looked to be holding their breath.

Skye Reynolds, their host for the remainder of the evening, greeted them in the massive foyer. The masked women from the boat stood posted like Price-Is-Right models on every other step up two grand staircases flanking the foyer and leading to the second story. A sharp-dressed man stood next to Skye holding a box that appeared to be a humidor. He opened it when she began to talk.

"Gentlemen, if you wouldn't mind leaving your cell phones with Reynaldo, we'll get your evening started right away." The gesture was an indication that her clients' confidences, and property, would be safe. Following their compliance, the guys were requested to escort the masked models upstairs so they could prepare for the party.

First they were provided white shorts and plush towels. After twenty minutes in the steam room they were treated to full-body massages. Then they retreated into separate bedrooms to shower and change. When they emerged dressed in black-tie, the masked ladies from the yacht, having switched from bikinis to evening gowns, escorted them down to the foyer.

Before they could join the party, they'd have to wait for Majac, whose escort had been instructed to delay his return until last.

In the main living area, six women who were not on the yacht entertained the newly arrived guests. Majac's male entourage had now grown to a total of two dozen, including the junior officers from THURGOOD MARSHALL; officers from WILLIAM PENN; and, despite knowing most of them by name only, several of Jaz's teammates, including one celebrated rookie who'd been recently acquired from Las Vegas.

29

Village People

WHILE THE FELLAS YACHT SLOWLY floated across Lake Washington towards the southern tip of Mercer Island, the pink stretch Hummer boarded a ferry to take the ladies across Puget Sound to their party destination—the Casino at Tulalip Village. Jennifer and Crystal had reserved the lounge for the night and invited two dozen of theirs, Leona's and Tessa's closest lady friends to watch the exotic dancers from Chocolate City perform for the bride-to-be. At the casino entrance, passersby strained their necks trying to see who would get out of the large pink truck while the women waited until the limo stopped in front of them dropped off the dancers. When the back door of the pink limo finally opened, a popular dance track by the Queen Bee flooded the parking lot with sound as the half dozen women in Tessa's party bounced out of the truck onto the casino's front porch. Leona and Tessa were walking to the door with their arms entwined, but stopped when they heard a deep voice call Leona's name. They looked left. There stood Winston Montgomery.

Leona introduced him to Tessa and told him why they were there. The other women had already entered the casino, so Winston escorted them inside Big Willie style, with Leona on his right arm and Tessa on his left. He was such a frequent karaoke regular at the casino that you'd think he was a celebrity the way people in the lobby greeted and fussed over him. The only thing missing was the red carpet and the paparazzi.

As they headed to the lounge, it didn't take long for the night to become interesting as some Pretty Ricky in a loud Bill Cosby sweater stopped dead

307

in their path. He stood before them like they were the Red Sea and, like Moses, he was waiting for them to part.

From the way his arm tightened around her hand, Tessa could tell Winston's machismo had awakened. He raised his eyebrows at the man's brazenness. She raised hers in a similar manner, anticipating the peacock's explanation for standing in their way. But before the cockfight started, Leona released Winston's arm and lurched toward the pretty man.

"Hey Keith," she spat emphatically, giving him a quick, co-worker-style hug. "I didn't know you were going to be here tonight." She appeared to be genuinely surprised to see him as she stuck her hand inside his arm the same way it had been inside Winston's a minute earlier.

Tessa watched quietly as the real-life 'B' movie clip played out.

Winston was silent. His increased blood pressure driven by the uncertainty of contemplating if he would have to knock this man out.

Tessa was silent too. She knew Keith's name from conversations with her sister, but she didn't want to miss a second of Leona's performance in this situation. Hopefully, her sister's methods would prove better than her own, when Tessa, once upon a time, wound up in a cat fight with the tramp Majac brought home for his father's funeral.

After Winston popped his eyes back into his head, Leona turned to Keith and said, "Keith, this lovely lady is my sister Tessa. She's getting married next week and we're here tonight for her bachelorette party."

Tessa offered her hand and with his glare still locked on Winston, Keith kissed it.

"Winston this is my friend Keith," Leona continued, ignoring the men's bravado. "Keith this is my friend Winston." Like two gamecocks on opposite sides of a cock-pit, the two men puffed out their chests, exchanged silent head nods. Their unfriendly glares spoke volumes.

After the introductions concluded, Leona went back to Winston's arm. "Well, you enjoy yourself tonight Keith," she said, letting Keith now that he was to in no way interrupt her evening. "I know I will." Her dual-purposed words ended the conversation and dismissed Keith all in one.

They stepped around him, then Winston departed his dime-piece duo when they spoke of needing to use the bathroom. When they were out of sight, he entered the Diamond Bar where he'd spend most of the next three hours up on stage karaoke singing as much as possible.

"So tell me about this umm Winston and Keith situation," Tessa requested as soon as they were alone in the bathroom.

"I met Winston about four years ago when he showed up at the Commodore Club one Thursday night for karaoke." Leona checked her makeup. "Not the prettiest man I've ever dated, but he was the most fun."

"How did I not know you liked to karaoke?" Tessa asked.

"I'll have to invite you sometime," Leona said. "You'll have a blast."

"It's a date," Tessa said. "I love to karaoke."

"Anyway, Winston's a certified public accountant, who, when he isn't running his own business, loves hunting, fishing and…that's right, karaoke singing.

"Pretty boy Keith really is a model. He was the first guy I met when I got back from overseas. Most of his portfolio is catalog work and magazines. Now he *is* the prettiest man I've ever dated and the most self-absorbed. Too much of a diva for me."

Through the remainder of the powder room conversation, two other women entered the bathroom. Tessa learned that although happily single, Leona had been casually dating four different guys during her time with Winston and Keith. She said that they all had different qualities that she liked and if she could roll up the best of each into one, then she might have considered settling down with the collective him.

"Together they would be the perfect man." Leona checked her lipstick in the bathroom mirror. "But who wants perfection? Too hard to measure up to." She told her sister that she was not ready for a committed relationship back then, and was just enjoying herself. She said they knew each other existed, but other than openly dating, she had shared no details with them about each other.

After powdering their noses, Leona escorted Tessa inside the green, black and gold decorated main lounge. The Run-DMC remix version of *Let's Get Married* by Jagged Edge was blaring on the sound system. Gold strobe lights swerved around the room in random patterns. The DJ announced, "The bride is in the house," and Leona marched her sister past the tables and straight up onto the main stage. Crystal joined them, and after Leona pushed her sister down into the wooden chair, the two ladies tied Tessa's wrists to the arms of the chair with silk scarves.

"Aww, yeah, it's party time." the DJ announced. "All right ladies, give it up for The Black Ranger and Pronto."

Crystal and Leona exited the stage as the DJ called for the first two Chocolate City dancers to take the stage. A cowboy and an Indian emerged from backstage. Their costumes fit their monikers. The Black Ranger twirled a lasso around his head as he chased Pronto to the end of the stage. They jockeyed back and forth around Tessa, pretending to fight. The Black Ranger threw his lasso toss at Pronto, but Pronto caught the rope and dropped it around Tessa. The Black Ranger pulled the rope until it was snug around her shoulders then proceeded to wrap her up in the rope as he chased Pronto, who was doing a war dance in circles around Tessa. When the rope ran out, he reached across Tessa and pulled Pronto to him, making Tessa the meat in their cowboy and Indian sandwich.

The ladies in the crowd howled, shouted and squealed as the cowboy's gun rubbed up against one side of Tessa and the point of the Indian's tomahawk poked her other.

Tessa shouted her laughter to the point of tears as the well-built dancers gyrated all over her cliffs, occasionally landing in her prairie of a lap, falling between the peaks of her legs and pressing their strong, oiled chests into the summit of her face. By the end of the song, Tessa's makeup was smeared, her face was shiny with dancer oil and her stomach ached from laughing so hard.

The DJ announced, "Give up for The Black Ranger and Pronto," before adding, "Now who else wants to be a part of their posse?"

Ladies at every table in the room stood, whooping and hollering, as The Black Ranger and Pronto descended from the stage and made their way into the gulf of the Wild West.

The song changed to *Fire* by The Ohio Players and the strobe lights changed from green and gold to yellow and red.

"Aww shucks ladies. That can only mean one thing, Captain Caliente, the hottest firefighter in all of Washington, is in the building."

When the curtain opened, a light-skinned Latino with a ripped chest and sculpted arm muscles burst onto the stage amidst a sprinkle of fine mist. He was barefoot, wearing a fireman's hat, red pants, and nothing but red suspenders above his waist. Sewn to the right leg of his fireman pants was a light–colored, foot-long, firehose shaped appendage.

The first thing Captain Caliente did after bursting through the fine red and yellow rain was to plant his foot on Tessa's chair right between her legs. He smiled, moved his hips like he was dancing a samba and rubbed his hose from top to bottom. Thrusting his hips to-and-fro, he unwound the rope The Black Ranger had lassoed around Tessa.

When she finally stopped screaming, Tessa looked dead into Captain Caliente's eyes. She thought she knew him. If she remembered correctly his name was Jandel Altuve, or something like that. Jandel, a trash truck driver for the city of Seattle, was the one of the first guys she met while hanging out with Leona during her first visit to Seattle. She'd been skeptical about why Leona was dating him. That was until her sister gave her the details about how he was so well-endowed, and, how, when he came to visit, he satisfied her every sexual need. If this really was Jandel, she was going to kill Leona.

Tessa screamed again; partly in recognition, partly in delight, partly in fear of what Jandel had inside the foot-long hose that danced in front of her face like a king cobra mesmerizing its prey.

"Captain Caliente," the DJ announced, "that hot little mama looks like she might need that big hose of yours to cool her off."

In tune with the beat, The Captain dropped to his knees, removed Tessa's red-bottom high heels, a wedding gift from Leona, and tossed them into the crowd. The handle of a thin firehose dropped from the ceiling. He grabbed the hose and began dancing around Tessa.

"Ladies, do you think The Captain can help our guest of honor cool off?" the DJ asked.

Shouts of 'Cool her off' repeated in a chorus throughout room like the wave at a football game.

"No!" Tessa shouted.

"Yes!" the women roared.

Captain Caliente urged the women in the crowd into a frenzy as he straddled the hose he'd pulled from the ceiling, pointed it at Tessa and began to stroke its length.

"No!" Tessa shouted again.

"It sounds like she needs saving Captain," the DJ said playfully. "I think you better let her have it."

Tessa Ajai, Crystal Stevenson, Leona Pearson and every other woman in the room screamed as Captain Caliente twisted the nozzle on the hose hanging between his legs and showered the bound bride-to-be with a fog-like spray of water tinted red and yellow by the ceiling strobe lights.

Tessa screamed in exhilaration as the chilly water doused her body, her clothes and her hair. The crowd cheered, and when Captain Caliente stopped the water, Tessa was hands down the winner of a one-woman wet t-shirt contest. She took long breaths, her chest heaving as she laughed along with the crowd. When she finished laughing, she leaned back fully in the chair and hung her head back, her eyes focused on the invisible depth of the black ceiling.

"Uh oh, looks like she might need some CPR!" the DJ said as Captain Caliente dropped the hose and ran off the stage into the crowd. "Quick, is there a doctor in the house?"

The horny women who weren't pawing at or stuffing dollars into the sling-back G-strings worn by The Black Ranger and Pronto immediately swarmed to Captain Caliente. As the three dancers disappeared, engulfed into the mob of horny women, the DJ rapidly announced, "I think we have a Code Black. Code Black, center stage. Doctor Goodlove please report to center stage."

Again the curtain flew open.

"Doctor Goodlove please report to center stage," the DJ said, slowly pronouncing each word.

The music shifted to a persistent dial tone as *Operator* by Midnight Starr introduced Doctor Goodlove, a chocolate-brown man with curly black hair. Running onto the stage wearing a lab coat and surgical mask and displaying the bed-side manner of a seasoned midwife, he took hold of Tessa's wet mane dangling behind the chair and checked the pulse in her neck; first with his fingers, then through the mask with his tongue. Playing for the audience, he stood, dropped his mask and shrugged his shoulders indicating he couldn't find a pulse.

"Calvin?" Crystal said to no one. Even if she had expressed the inquiry loud enough to be heard, nobody was listening. Calvin McConnell, a weatherman for WSTL, was known in TV circles as the pretty boy of weather. A trust fund baby of one of Silicon Valley's original millionaires, Calvin was born with a silver spoon in his mouth. When it came to lavishing women with whatever they desired, Calvin spared no expense. He knew he wasn't looking to marry, so his vanity did not allow him to care that women only spent time with him for his money. Calvin always showed up to every industry event with a dime-piece on his arm, but no matter how fine or stuck on herself a woman was, he kept them at bay with his own high-maintenance attitude. Once she was certain it was him, Crystal joined the cheering.

At the urging of her horny friends, Doctor Goodlove turned to Tessa, grabbed the back of her chair and laid her down on her back.

Feet flailing, Tessa screamed as her sexy physician immediately dropped to his knees, lifted his surgical mask, planted his mouth on hers and gave her what was probably the hottest kiss the Tulalip had ever seen.

Pretending that the mouth-to-mouth did not seem to revive her, Doctor Goodlove broke the kiss and shifted into EMT mode. First he paraded a lap around Tessa's chair, then threw down his lab coat, exposing his black satin boxers. He straddled her stomach. Drumbeats boomed from the speakers. The music changed to the club version of the 1980's classic groove *Heartbeat*. While his hands hovered over Tessa's heaving breasts like magnets alternating between repulsion and attraction, he rocked his hips up and down. In rhythm, the Good Doctor leaned in and pretended to start chest compressions. In exaggerated movements, he bounced on his knees to the beat of the music as the women in the crowd screamed *Please, Me Too, I'm next* and some other, much more vulgar remarks.

When a woman appeared to pass out in the crowd, the DJ said, "Doctor Goodlove, it looks like your needed on the floor."

The Good Doctor left a revived Tessa lying on her back laughing uncontrollably while he rushed down into the pool of women eagerly awaiting his assistance. Fortunately for the bride-to-be, she wouldn't be abandoned for long. A lumberjack, with a cloth axe sewn to his costume similar to the fireman's hose, was coming to her rescue.

"Hey Jack," the DJ called. "She looks a little thirsty to me."

When Jack turned to face the DJ, Leona was standing at the side of the stage with a Long Island Iced Tea in her hand. She handed the drink to Jack the Lumberjack, then reached for his axe.

Instead of falling Leona's tree, he kissed her cheek then took the drink to her sister.

Jack up righted Tessa, delicately poured half of the large, highly-alcoholic drink down her throat, danced for her, then made her finish the rest of the huge glass before he finally cut her loose.

Tessa stood, rubbed her wrists and gave the lumberjack a kiss on the cheek before he, and his giant axe, dived into the forest of women.

"Excuse me Miss Thang," the DJ proclaimed as the lumberjack swung his axe in the forest. "Don't run off too quickly. I think your ship has finally come in."

Thinking that the night couldn't get any more interesting, Tessa remained on the stage, stood in front of her seat and watched as the curtain slowly opened for the sixth and final dancer.

Anchors Away, the Navy fight song, started playing before the curtain opened to reveal a masked, six-foot man in a Naval Officer's dress uniform. "I don't know Miss Tessa," the DJ barked into the microphone, "The Admiral looks like he wants to board your vessel."

"Oh hell yes!" Tessa yelled. She covered her mouth and looked out into the crowd for her sister. Her Anton was walking quickly towards her. The other dancers were fun, but she had no idea that her Anton would be dancing for her too. The officer approached her in his bare feet, white pants and officer hat. He unbuttoned his jacket as he approached her and pushed it all the way open to reveal a thick, hairy chest and a six-pack of rock-hard, bronze abs.

Tessa turned to the crowd, bent over and mouthed WOW. The excitement in her face dimmed when she realized that the masked officer was regrettably not her fiancée. Her Anton was his same color bronze, but he did not have the model's chest hair. Nevertheless, Tessa squealed as the bronze god of a man padded quickly towards her, his bare feet splashing in the small puddles left behind from the fireman's entrance.

The music faded and a mic dropped from above as he stopped in front of Tessa and saluted. "Request permission to come aboard, Ma'am," purred the sailor behind the mask.

"Permission granted." Tessa offered him a mock salute in return.

Bad Habits by Maxwell started to play as The Admiral knelt and swooped Tessa off her feet. All of the women lost their absolute minds. Like Debra Winger at the conclusion of *An Officer and A Gentleman*, she took the hat off his head and placed it on hers then wrapped her arms around his neck as he carried her towards the back of the stage where a dancer's pole was mounted. He placed her down in front of the pole, pulled a handcuff key from his pocket and placed it between his teeth.

Then he pulled out handcuffs, slapped one on her left wrist, wrapped his free hand around her waist and pulled her close. He grinded on her real slow while the music boomed, his free hand holding the handcuffs behind her back. The Admiral dropped it like it was hot then came back up to meet Tessa's face. He pressed his mask against her neck, his free hand on her shoulder and let his mask take a journey south, over her mountains and toward her woods, until he came to a stop at her belly button. His free hand was now on her free wrist. As he kneeled, blowing his heat into her belly button through the fabric in her dress, Tessa buckled in anguish.

Without her noticing, The Admiral clasped the second handcuff onto her free wrist behind her back, leaving Tessa handcuffed to the dancer's pole. He stood, bared his teeth and dropped the key into Tessa's bosom.

The women shouted their approval as Tessa struggled with the cuffs.

For the next couple of minutes, The Admiral commenced to perform the most erotic dance Tessa had ever seen. When Maxwell ended and the DJ started *Scandalous* by Prince, The Admiral bumped, grinded, pawed, poked and prodded his body against Tessa's while the roar from the ladies tore the roof off the building.

"All right fellas," the DJ said halfway through the song, "I think The Admiral needs all hands on deck to wish Miss Tessa a Bon Voyage!"

The Admiral circled behind the bride-to-be, whispering in her ear, running his hands up and down her arms and pressing her hands against his body as one-by-one, his fellow dancers made their way back to the stage and each took a turn dancing their hard body up against a still handcuffed Tessa Ajai. *Scandalous* boomed loud in her ears. Her knees buckled, her head swam and her shouts came one after the next as each man offered his own scandalous flavor of bump and grind. When The Admiral was the only dancer remaining on stage, he came back around and faced Tessa, removed his mask, pulled at her cleavage and dipped his tongue between her breasts to retrieve the key.

Every woman in the room screamed like they had just been proposed to, or had won the lotto or had experienced the best orgasm in her life!

The Admiral dropped the key in his hand, leaned his chest against Tessa's and pressed his closed lips against hers.

When the song ended, The Admiral walked behind her, unlocked one handcuff and left the key in the other. He saluted, tossed his hat into the crowd and disappeared behind the curtain.

Tessa leaned back against the dancer's pole and slid to the floor. She sat back on her haunches, aroused, exhilarated and exhausted, her hands dancing uncontrollably by her side.

30

A Dozen Rainbows

MAJAC WAS THE LAST GUEST to descend the stairs and join his entourage in the foyer of the Peacock Mansion. When the high-C note of a champagne glass clanging in the background had sufficiently captured their attention, Skye waved her hand like a homecoming queen at the crowd milling about. On cue with the grandiose gesture, Reynaldo opened the set of French doors at the back of the foyer.

"Gentlemen," Skye said inviting Majac, his guests and their escorts into the back of the main ballroom. "Welcome to Majac's Night in Vegas."

Inside, the party was in full swing. There were roulette wheels and poker tables. Two fully-stocked bars were centered against the right and left walls. A dozen loveseats and a variety of wide chairs were scattered throughout. Majac's guests were in every corner of the room seeking the attentions of their favorite flavor of scantily-clad, exotic woman. When the DJ noticed Skye enter with the baker's dozen in tow, he dimmed the lights.

A spotlight set on Majac. A second model took his empty arm and helped escort him to the short, wide stage at the front of the room. A brass, ten-foot tall, stripper pole set in the center of the stage.

The threesome shuffled, bumped and grinded their way to center stage as the *gotta get that money* chorus from a popular dance song boomed from the speakers. The crowd clapped and cheered their approval. Never one to disappoint, Majac danced enthusiastically as he assumed the filling position in the three-person Oreo cookie sandwich. When the first model's back pressed up against the pole, the train stopped.

As Majac gave his all for the crowd with the model in front of him, the second model danced her way behind the first. She pulled Majac's arms toward. With the stealth of a seasoned magician, she produced a pair of handcuffs and slapped them on Majac before he realized what happened.

When the first model recognized the look of surprise on his face, she opened her legs in a split; slid her back down the pole. She rubbed her face against Majac's zipper, licking and biting playfully at the front of his pants. She screamed, eyes wide, pretending to be afraid that she had awakened the monster hidden behind the zipper. Then she rolled away from him like a professional break dancer.

Majac struggled with the cuffs.

The crowd roared.

Majac roared louder.

Solo and Jaz roared loudest.

After the initial shock subsided, Majac stopped jerking the cuffs and started dancing again, now playing to the chorus of cheers from the crowd.

The two models who were the wafers to his human cookie sandwich, once again danced in front and back of him. The second model stepped back and produced a handcuff key. Majac pressed himself against the brass pole, straining to reach her. The model teased the guest of honor for a moment, holding the handcuff key just out of his reach. When she pretending to accidentally drop the key into her bra, the DJ played the game show noise note that indicates a contestant has lost. Dunt-Dunt-Dunnh!

Majac smirked a look of defeat.

The crowd gave a massive round of applause.

The two models moved to the end the stage. They encouraged everyone—guests and models—to join them in a conga line. The first model who was part of Majac's cookie sandwich patted Majac on the butt as she passed.

"That's right everybody," the DJ encouraged the guests. "Let's all give the groom-to-be a little congratulatory pat on the ass to wish him well."

Each passing member of the conga line patted Majac on the butt. Some of the ladies let their hands linger on his butt long enough to make him blush. Most of the men who weren't Majac's close friends or senior officers, gave him a gentle love tap. Jaz, Solo and Majac's XO—a college classmate—all reared back their arms and gave Majac all the love of a fraternity master-at-arms wielding the frat paddle at line crossing.

"Damn fellas!" the DJ shouted. "Save some of his ass for his bride!"

After the conga line, Jaz returned to the stage with a glass of beer.

Right after Majac accepted the glass and started drinking, Jaz grabbed the back of Majac's head, pushed the bottom of the glass up and spilled the remainder of the beer up Majac's nose and all over his face and chest.

Majac tried to break free and punch his friend.

Jaz ducked, snatched the glass and ran off the stage laughing.

Majac cursed and kicked at Jaz. Called him every foul name known to man. He vowed to kick his ass once he was free, but then stopped fussing when he noticed out of the corner of his eye, a dancer slink onto the stage and start crawling his way.

"Aww yeah." The DJ scratched the record then started playing *Sex Me*; one of Majac's favorite songs. "Come on fellas; give it up for Heaven!"

Heaven snaked her way towards Majac, and just like that, his half-hearted desire to fight Jaz evaporated. The singer from Chicago crooned his almost explicit lyrics as Heaven enacted the scenario in her dance.

Heaven stripped down to nothing but a thong as the DJ mixed in a song called *Freak Me*. She grinded her front against Majac's front. Danced circles around him. Pinned the much larger man against the stripper pole and rubbed her front against his back. She raked her hands down his front and opened his shirt. When his chest was bare, she slithered in between him and the pole.

Majac jerked when another dancer ran on the stage, poured baby oil on them, then dashed back into the crowd just as quickly as she came.

Heaven squeezed her hands in the slit between her body and the front of Majac's, freeing him from his pants and letting them fall to the floor.

All in the name of having a good time at his bachelor party, Majac kicked off his shoes, then kicked his pants from around his ankles.

For the next five minutes, Heaven mimicked the words in the song while playing body tag with Majac. She danced close, used every part of her except her hands to spread the oil all over his body. When Majac seemed as though he was about to explode in ecstasy, Heaven pressed her lips on his, slithered down his body, then crawled off the stage like a cat.

The crowd went bananas! Cat calls, whistles, and shouts of *I'm next* and *me too* escorted Heaven off the stage and into the darkness. As the lights and music dimmed, The DJ shouted, "Now that's what I call a slice of Heaven!"

Another scratch changed the music to the up-tempo *Black Velvet* by Alannah Myles as Precious, a curvaceous, dark-skinned woman in stilettos pranced onstage. She pressed her back against Majac then squatted until her butt rested on her heels. Fleshy pink skin where her panties should have been winked at the boys seated nearest the stage.

"Oh shit!" yelled one of Jaz's younger teammates.

Precious smiled; took off her top; revealed almost perfect breasts. Showed nipples the size of gum drops and slightly darker than her skin. She grabbed, tugged and played with them, then got down on her hands and knees and humped the floor, exciting the men even more.

An Ensign from the THURGOOD MARSHALL rushed to the stage. Precious slid to the edge, slammed her knees together, took his head and pulled his face to her crotch. The crowd went wild. The young man, a native of one of Boston's upper crust, predominantly white neighborhoods and had never seen a naked black woman in the flesh, had found heaven. She raised his chin to her chest, put her nipple near his mouth and smiled mischievously as he attempted to suck her warm breast.

High off lust and drunk off vodka, he extracted a wad of five dollar bills from his pocket and stuffed them into her garter. When dollar bill number ten rubbed her thigh, she kissed him deeply, rubbed his face between her breasts and left him begging for more as she slid away. Precious crawled between Majac's legs, stood, produced a key and freed Majac from the confines of his brass pole captivity. She escorted him, offstage then skipped back to center stage as her second dance song, *Black Betty* banged to life.

Somewhere deep in the mansion, a clock chimed marking midnight, but unlike Cinderella, Precious didn't run away. Instead, she grabbed the pole and swung her legs open like scissors, giving Majac and the boys in the front row a full frontal shot of her precious gift. For the next three minutes she twirled in several full 360 degree circles. She flipped, slipped, climbed up, and slid down the brass pole offering a naked exhibition the likes of anything those men had ever seen before. By the time the song ended, the stage floor had grown a carpet of green cash. She made her dismount as the music faded, then strutted off the stage across the top of her money to a standing ovation.

A howl came from a far corner as a copper-skinned Mexican named Guadeloupe pushed Majac's Engineer down into a plush wing chair. She unbuttoned her dress, unsnapped her bra, and in just her heels and panties, proceeded to give him a lap dance he wouldn't soon forget. Her long black hair and deep brown eyes entranced him. She pulled his head into her breasts, playfully slapping the side of his face with her generous double d's then shoved one in his mouth before he could resist. Not that he would have.

Near the bar on the west wall, a model called Shy Towne, who was by no means shy, took off her barely-there dress, her lace bra and strutted around in a white, lace G-string proudly showing off the long, lovely legs on her six-foot frame. Perfect C-cup breasts with areolas the size of silver dollars adorned a slim 32-26-36 figure. Her well-shaped butt, which jiggled when she strutted, caused the XO's head to turn like an owl's. He blushed when the junior officers laughed at him, then he, feeling like the gauntlet had been dropped, quickly recovered, walked to her and gave her a wet, sloppy kiss.

When the brave sailor came up for air, Shy Towne showed the XO who was really boss. The Chicago native pushed his head down to face the tattoo around her navel. She tousled his hair, gripped his ears hard, held him in place and made him kiss that too. Then she pulled him back up her body; stopped him at the deep valley of cleavage between her breasts; rubbed his head in that cavern like she was trying to smother him.

XO flexed, turned and briefly managed to snag a nipple in his mouth.

Shy Towne challenged him. "Is that all you got, Big Boy?"

Inspired by the courage of cognac, he accepted her challenge. The XO wrapped his arms around her waist and stood straight up. Lifted her off her feet. He pressed her against the wall then pushed both breasts together and proceeded to suckle both nipples simultaneously.

As good as his tongue play felt, Shy Towne also refused to back down. She pulled hard at the XO's hair as he kissed, licked and sucked her breasts. She wrapped her legs around his waist and started grinding her hips into his.

It was half past midnight when Majac came from upstairs. He'd taken a half hour to shower off the baby oil and dress in fresh clothes. As he passed Shy Towne and XO going at it, he pumped his fist and twice chanted "Go XO, it's your birthday!" The crew followed Majac's lead and urged XO on.

A moment later, when Shy Towne had kept his head buried in her chest so long that he struggled to breathe, the XO conceded as he and Shy Towne tumbled onto the carpet. She propped her feet on the floor and released his hair. When they broke their embrace, Shy Towne told him, "Now that's how you handle a Chicago woman."

The guys from MARSHALL cheered on their XO.

"Remember boys;" XO caught his breath, "a bachelor party is no different than Vegas, or a port of call; what happens here; stays here!"

The Sailors all laughed, raised their glasses and cheered a hearty *Oo-rah* to their second in command.

As Majac stepped clear of his crew, a swarthy, 5-foot-9 Puerto Rican in six-inch stilettos approached him carrying an empty basket. "Are you the groom to be?" Her accent was as thick as her thighs. Dimples accentuated her light freckles. Long swirls of jet-black hair draped her chest and ended at her silk teddy's hemline just below her navel.

Majac nodded.

"Hey girls, over here." Her call summoned a dozen reinforcements dressed in a multitude of pastel nighties. They encircled Majac like a pack of sexy lionesses. "I think our guest is overdressed."

"Fellas, can y'all help a brother out?" Majac called while being undressed by his sexy baker's dozen.

No one answered, but they all watched.

"Yo, what the?" he fussed but didn't fight being stripped to his boxers.

As the lionesses ravaged their prey, Miss Puerto Rico blew a whistle to summon the DJ who responded with, "Aww Yeah, looks like the Majac hour has finally arrived."

On cue with the whistle, Reynaldo rolled an armless swivel chair into the room. The DJ started Nelly's *It's Getting' Hot In Here* and invited all of Majac's guests back to the main stage for the grand finale. Jaz and Solo helped Reynaldo lift the chair onstage.

Encouraged by the crowd chanting *It's Getting' Hot In Here... So take off all your clothes*, the Puerto Rican model handed Majac her basket. She turned around, and with knees locked, slid out of the silk panties that matched her nightie. More unwilling than unable to resist, Majac tapped her ample ass with an open palm. It shook like set jello before she stood, grinned devilishly at him, then dropped her panties into the basket. The pack of lionesses followed suit, each bending over in front of Majac and letting him pat their ass before placing their panties into the basket. Once finished, each took their place alongside the main stage.

Jaz grabbed the DJ's microphone. "Come on Partna." With a drink in his hand and a smile on his face, he encouraged his best friend to come rest in the plush seat. "Last chance for free romance."

After the parade of pretty underwear concluded, Majac returned the basket to Miss Puerto Rico, pranced his way to the stage with a little Dion Sanders shuffle and took a seat. Miss Puerto Rico handed Solo the basket filled with a rainbow of pretty lace and satin panties then made her way to the stage and made thirteen.

"King for a day has taken his throne." The DJ turned up the music. "Welcome, back Mister Majac. Get ready for the best night of your life."

A spotlight shone on Solo and Jaz. Solo raised the basket above his head and Jaz blindly pulled out the first pair of colorful undies. The color was teal. The crowd shouted like madmen as the first model, a 5-foot-8, half Japanese, half African-American woman named Hayami stepped onstage. The translation of her name meant rare and unusual beauty. Her trademark was a long, whip-like braid of hair with which she playfully whipped Majac as she danced.

For the better part of the next hour each woman approached the throne and paid their five minutes of homage to the king for a day. Majac's party guests ate, drank and watched in awe as each of the first half-dozen scantily-dressed women performed the most intense, erotic and exotic dances, on, with and for Majac. One at a time, they rubbed their bare-bottomed bodies all over the brass pole; over his face, his chest and groin.

Miss Puerto Rico performed sixth following a Fijian woman named Jasmine—whose beauty matched the cartoon character from Aladdin. Jasmine had followed an Ethiopian named Cleopatra. Guadeloupe, the Mexican with high cheek bones, danced before her. Rayne, a taller version of the Bajan pop singer Rihanna, danced after the Hafu princess.

Miss Puerto Rico ended her performance by serving a cold beer to a sweat soaked Majac. As two of the models passed out jello shots to the guys in the crowd, the DJ commented in the background that they wanted Majac fresh for the second half of the show.

Red was the seventh color chosen. The shapely, olive hued, redhead named Fyre fit the bill. Wearing an aptly hued, satin nightie, she rushed to the stage under cover of flashing red and white lights as the DJ restarted the show with the rap song *Fire* by Busta Rhymes. A handful of moments later, once Fyre had sufficiently heated Majac back up, Solo chose black panties from the basket and a well-tanned blonde in a black nightie walked on stage. Fyre made herself comfortable in Majac's lap as the six-foot blonde in clear plastic heels balanced on one foot and swung a lengthy leg over Majac's head. She squatted facing Fyre. Majac imagined the look of what he could feel but not see, as smooth, hairless skin lighted on his chest.

The DJ boomed the rap song *Pump It Up* through the speakers as the blonde bounced her beautiful bottom up and down on his chest.

Chants from the crowd of kiss her, kiss her rose to a crescendo. Eager to oblige, the women leaned forward and kissed. The crowd went bananas.

As if pre-rehearsed, the DJ made the record skip and injected the pounding rhythms of *Pony* by Ginuwine. The lyrics *Jump on it, Get to it, Ride it, My pony* soared through the room as Fyre and the blonde kissed lips, touched bodies and grinded their pelvises atop Majac as if they were they only two people in the room. If Majac had not been so entranced by the magic of the clean-shaven blonde's butt jiggling on his chest, he'd have been awestruck by the passion of the kissing pyramid mounted atop him.

The blonde and red head rode Majac hard like a mustang racing a Camaro. Just when it looked like they were about to put him away wet, Solo waved a pair of pink panties at the DJ.

The DJ scratched the record a few times. Wiki-wiki-wiki-wiki screeched through the room. Then LL Cool J started mumbling something about *Pink Cookies in a Plastic Bag Getting Crushed by Buildings.*

The spotlight shifted from the pyramid of three to illuminate the front wall. And there, in all of her barefoot, six-foot-one glory, stood Precious. The Atlanta native, by way of a failed attempt at acting in Hollywood, only danced part time to pay her tuition at the University of Tacoma. But when she danced, it was a sight to remember. She sashayed across the stage and reached Majac, pleased to find the red head and blonde gone. Having earlier acclimated herself to the groom-to-be's sturdy physical form, she lured Majac out of the chair. She bounced down then back up and the loose-flowing, pink nightie exposed her beautiful, dark-skinned frame. Her 36-24-44 measurements were the curviest at the mansion.

On cue, the DJ scratched the record and *Drunk in Love* boomed loudly. Reddish-brown hair reached half-way down her back and swung freely as she danced. As if entranced if not intoxicated, Precious enacted the most erotic, most sultry dance Majac had ever been a part of. Keeping with the lyrics, she staggered about the stage bumping into him with random parts of her body. Her hips gyrated, legs swayed and ass twerked all over Majac like only a true down-home Georgia peach could.

As Precious enacted her best reproduction of the video by the curvy singer from Houston, Jaz grabbed a beer and a shot of bourbon from the bar then made his way to the open space behind the last row of chairs. He listened from Ben's blind spot as his guests commented on the show.

When the lyrics *surfboard, surfboard* repeated several times in the song, and were forcefully echoed by the crowd, Precious maneuvered Majac to the floor and pretended to wave ride him like the famously imaged scene in the song.

By song's end, the crowd was drunk…out of their minds.

Majac was drunk…in Precious's love.

Ben Lockette and Majac's XO were drunk…in the third row of seats and enjoying themselves as much as the younger sailors and ball players sitting in the rows in front of them. It was during *Drunk in Love* that Ben's ears perked up to the continued rantings of the new booty, hotshot rookie.

"Yo, that bitch is fine; but she ain't as fine as this reporter I was with in Vegas during summer league." Lance Braeburn was a good sheet to the wind past the other drinkers. Although traded from Vegas, it was quickly becoming apparent to the older men in the room that he had not yet adopted the *What happens in Vegas, Stays in Vegas* mentality.

After a half-heartedly *Down in front*, Ben kept an ear on the front row.

Lance bumped a teammate in the arm and said, "I'm pretty sure she said she was from Seattle. Old girl was a closer. And now that I'm here, I'm for real gonna have to get at her and close that deal." Lance fist bumped the player next to him then signaled a waitress to bring more drinks for the front row.

Ben kept Lance's words in the back of his mind. He knew Crystal Stevenson was a sports reporter from Seattle. He knew that if she was in Vegas, it would have been to cover the WNBA, not the NBA rookie tournament. But he couldn't help wondering what the odds were that they might have crossed paths? He knew the rookie tournament was held in July in Vegas. He remembered that last July's WNBA All-Star game was also in Vegas. He couldn't immediately recall Seattle having any other female sports reporters, but he imagined that she couldn't be the only one.

The rookie clambered on about how sexy the woman was when they were dancing; about how she was all over him while they were drinking champagne at his birthday party, and about what he wanted to do with the woman if he ever got her alone. When Ben yelled, *I said shut up, Rookie*, Lance and the others turned to regard Ben. He cast a scornful eye that the others knew meant business. Following the lead of the boys in the front row, Lance quieted down.

Ben turned to locate Jaz. When they made eye contact, Jaz seemed to recognize the look of concern in Ben's eyes. Ben wondered if he was close enough to hear what Ben had heard. If Ben were wrong, the point would be moot anyway. Jaz frowned what Ben took as a look of concern. When Jaz didn't speak, Ben shrugged it off. He offered a halfhearted thumbs up to his team co-captain, which Jaz returned with a non-committal thumbs up of his own. Ben resolved to check out female sports reporters in Seattle and see how many there were…tomorrow. When the drinks for the front row came, Ben signaled for another refill.

Blue was the tenth color picked. The room quieted down as the DJ announced the color. A moment later, jungle sounds preceded the voice of local Seattle hip hop artist Sir Mix-a-Lot booming through the speaker rapping *My anaconda don't; my anaconda don't; my anaconda don't want none unless you got buns, Hun.* The younger guys went wild, jumping out their seat, dancing by themselves and slapping high fives.

In tune to the upbeat tempo, Shy Towne strutted onstage like the fierce, high-stepping, runway supermodel, Naomi Campbell. A shape-hugging, hip length, light-blue nightie seemed to hover above her smooth, muscular, perfectly round ass.

From the back row came a forceful, *Down in Front*!

The Chi-Town stepper cat-walked to center stage in a satin cloth the hue of a clear blue sky. For half a dozen minutes, she mesmerized both Majac and the room full of reptiles as *Anaconda* by Nikki Minaj sparked the room's energy. Then for another six long minutes, her wicked ways encouraged them to vigorously lend their amateur vocals as Bruno Mars begged her over and again to tease him, then turn around and please him. When Shy Towne bent over, her bare bottom left nothing to the imagination. Lance jumped to his feet and screamed, *Please me, Baby*!

"Sit down, Rook. You're killing my buzz."

Lance continued singing in the direction of the stage.

"I ain't gonna tell you again," Ben stood. Pushed his way past the empty second row seats. Leaned against the back of Lance's chair. "Sit your ass down, Rook. We all wanna see the show."

Lance turned around. Told Ben, "What's your problem, Old School? It's a freakin' party. I'm trying to get my freak on with this bitch."

"Either move or sit your ass down. I ain't gonna tell you again!"

"Why you trying to blow my high, Old School?" Lance stepped towards Ben. "If your old ass can't hang, go home."

Before another word was spoken, Ben punched Lance square in the face. Lance fell backwards. Ben moved to pounce on the annoying rookie, but Jaz and the XO grabbed him.

The DJ stopped the music.

Lance crashed to the floor.

All eyes shifted to the ruckus.

Ben glared at Lance. Strained towards him. Silently dared him to move.

I'm gonna knock you out. Mama Said Knock You Out boomed through the speakers.

Failing to restrain a smile, Jaz shook his head at the DJ. The song stopped mid-verse amidst a flurry of murmurs floating through the room.

Again, Reynaldo appeared on cue. Jaz met his gaze and nodded towards Lance. Reynaldo picked Lance up as if he were a child's doll. Sailors and ballers alike pushed chairs back into place as Reynaldo ushered Lance from the room. The rookie's nose was broken. Despite needing medical attention, he continued to curse at Ben as Reynaldo led him out the front door and into an awaiting car. "I do not want to see him back here." Reynaldo's instructions to the driver were clear and concise: Take him to the hospital; wait for him to get his nose looked at; take him home once released from the hospital. "The hospital first, then home," he urged.

The driver nodded and drove away.

Jaz made eye contact with Majac. The best friends nodded at one another. Then Jaz regarded the DJ and spun his index finger in a circle indicating it was all right to restart the party. The lights dimmed and the DJ scratched a tune.

"You all right, man?" Jaz asked Ben at the bar once the music started.

"Men don't call women bitches," was Ben's only reply.

Skye ushered Ben through a side door to get him some ice for his hand.

Jaz replayed what he had heard of the exchange between Ben and Lance. After some thought, he surmised that Ben's comment wasn't about the dancer.

Once order was restored, Solo reached into the basket and pulled out the final pair of panties.

"Our final color of the night is white," the DJ announced emphatically. The spotlight was narrowed to a tiny stream and directed onto a mirror ball rotating slowly in the corner. A million tiny flashes of light danced from wall to wall. In his sexiest baritone, the DJ slowly introduced the final two dancers. "I know first-hand that our final dancers are no Angels, but these Amazons are about as close as we'll ever get to one on this side of the grave. Give it up for the lovely Brazilian twins...Heaven...and Star!"

A melodious, up-tempo remix of the O'Jays *Stairway to Heaven* flooded the room as the exotic, twelfth and thirteenth dancers slowly sauntered onto opposing sides of the main stage. They stopped mid-stage, each grabbing the brass stripper pole. Star held a short, leather whip in her free hand. Heaven dangled a pair of fuzzy handcuffs from her free pinky finger. As Star playfully whipped the signature dominatrix tool back-and-forth across her sister's flat middle, Heaven seductively curled her index finger toward Majac in a come-hither motion.

Having already journeyed down Handcuff Road, Majac feigned a harrumph.

The crowd of anxious voyeurs erupted into encouraging cheers.

Inwardly ecstatic, but outwardly regretful, Majac silently marched the Green Mile toward the brass stripper pole, his head hung low, hands held out in front of him ready to be arrested and face whatever horribly delightful punishment awaited the lucky Groom-to-be.

As the twins handcuffed Majac to the pole, a sexy, Indian model named Misty exited the ballroom through a side door with Jaz. Tall enough to see right over her head, Jaz regarded his arrested and handcuffed best friend. He whispered in the girl's ear; glanced down at her curves; patted her on the butt before she disappeared through the door. He put his finger to his lips and poked them out. Made an inaudible *shh* sound to let Majac know that he understood, *What Happens in Vegas...Stays in Vegas.*

31

Sumthin' at the Hang Suite

MAJAC WATCHED CLOSELY AS TESSA padded barefoot around the kitchen Wednesday night, sipping her wine, the spaghetti strap of her satin, pajama short set occasionally slipping from her shoulder. When she smiled he could see her slight overbite. Very slight. He liked the way a few strands of the hair draped across her shoulders stuck to her lipstick. She tasted the food as she prepared it, her fingers—covered with the fruits of her labor—unknowingly seducing him each time they disappeared into, then slowly reappeared from her mouth.

They'd decided to spend the rest of their final night in Seattle as an engaged couple binge watching the episodes of her favorite show that she'd missed. She'd been working late hours the past couple of weeks to bank credit hours to support time off for their honeymoon, and since they'd finished packing before dinner, the rest of the evening was clear. She made a green salad with shredded carrots, chickpeas and a mango chutney dressing. Brick chicken with roasted beets was the entree. The wine Solomon bought had notes of plum and oak, and a finish of smooth vanilla, and they drank it slightly chilled, the way the sommelier recommended.

Bellies full and the dinner dishes cleaned, they retreated to the sofa with dessert and climbed beneath a blanket to let the binge watching begin. Toward the end of the second episode, Tessa slid her hand under the blanket and squeezed his knee. "Anton, I think I would like some more of that new wine." Without making eye contact, she slowly ran her hand in circles up Majac's leg until it came to rest on his inner hip. "Would you please pour me another glass?"

No fair, Majac thought. *She's wrong and she knows it. Toying with a man like that simply isn't right.* What's more, he had the sneaky suspicion that she knew he was in no position to stand up and get anything without revealing the state of arousal that her hand on his leg had caused.

"And more of this cobbler and ice cream. It's delicious." She handed her almost empty bowl to him. "If you don't mind?" she added innocently.

A little too innocently for his taste. So he played dumb too.

"Well, actually, I do mind. I was just getting really comfortable," he said as he attempted to hand her bowl back to her. "You know you're at home. Mi casa es tu casa, remember?"

She tucked her bare feet under the blanket and wriggled her body to show him that she was settled in also. "Will you please get it for me, Baby?" she asked, batting her long, gorgeous lashes at him.

She's good. He'd give her that. But if she thought he was getting up so she could see his pup tent impersonation, she was crazy. "Well, once you're rested, the wine glasses are in the third cabinet from the refrigerator. The corkscrew is in the drawer directly adjacent to the ..."

"I have to get my own?" she said, sounding offended. "And you call yourself a gentleman?

"I am, but you know I had a long day."

"Oh well, the least you could do is get up and…point me in the right direction." No longer able to contain it, she burst out laughing.

Majac waited for her to calm down before he spoke. "So you take pleasure in ridiculing others, hunh Babe? In making sport of the infirmed?"

"I don't know what you're talking about," she said wiping away a tear.

"I think you do." Their light-brown eyes were like mirrors, his never leaving hers.

"I know I don't," she giggled, using his words against him. "And that thing," she said letting her eyes drop to his waist, "is by no means infirmed."

By now his erection had begun to subside, so he picked up her plate and stood. As he disappeared into the kitchen to refresh her dessert and wine, he thought he saw her sneak another peek at his groin, but if she did, she was too sly to get caught.

Toward the end of the last episode, the couple found themselves curled up in each other's arms, his left arm wrapped around her, right where she placed it, thoughtlessly holding her right breast. A husky moan smoothed into a velvety purr when he put his mouth on her neck. To maintain her balance under the weight of his hot, heavy tongue assault, she reached back and gripped his ear. In their time together, he'd learned that this meant for him to slow down. Her legs widened as heat rose from between them.

He shifted his hips against her backside which pushed back at him in acknowledgment of his bobbing against her. He teased her like that for a while, hot tongue on her neck, hot length on her butt. He kissed her collarbone and turned her around, his tongue tracing a map to the nape of her neck. His eyes left hers and her gaze went to the ceiling. He dipped and pushed her shorts to the side. Her leg shook with anticipation. His head touched her warmth. She arched her back, lifted her butt and welcomed him. He entered her a little at a time. Her moisture came down and welcomed his full length. She winced when his broad girth stretched her wide and brought pain. Pain that, by the third stroke, melted into pleasure.

⌇

Solomon parked Fay Francis, his 1938 Cabriolet Saliot, in the middle bay of the garage then walked around and opened the door for Leona.

"Chivalry will get you everywhere Doctor Alexandré," she said, locking her hand inside his right elbow.

"I think I was twelve," he said, continuing the story he started telling in the car, as he escorted her out of the garage and across his back lawn. "His body was never recovered, so the government listed him as MIA."

He was telling her about his father. They'd stopped by his mother's house after the play to take her some allergy medicine and Leona had noticed a picture of a man in an Air Force uniform on his mother's mantle. A Bronze Star was in a case next to it. She didn't say anything at the time, thinking of her own father who had also served in the military, but she'd broached the subject in the car right before they pulled into Solomon's neighborhood.

"If you let Vivienne tell it, Wastrel is still a prisoner of war somewhere in Iraq. She hopes it more than knows it's the truth"

"Who's Wastrel?" Leona asked, I thought your father's name was Curtis?"

"It is. Wastrel, as my mother calls him, means a good-for-nothing person. I don't know where she learned the word, but by the time I was ten, I actually thought that was his real name. Anyway, she says he's not

MIA, he's just out there trying to earn the medal for bravery that he forgot to earn by being her husband."

"What does that mean?"

"My dad left me and my mom. She thought he was going to work one day, when in actuality, he joined the Air Force without telling her. According to Viv, he couldn't handle being a husband and a father so he ran away to the military and never came back."

"And you haven't seen him since?"

Nope, Curtis Franklin is nothing more than a figment of my imagination."

"Franklin?" Leona inquired. "Don't you mean Curtis Alexandré?"

"No, I mean Franklin. When he didn't come back, my mother changed our last names back to her maiden name, Alexandré."

"So for all you know, he could be alive and walking around Seattle and you wouldn't even know it?"

"Never thought of it that way, but yeah. He could."

"Wow, that's sad," Leona said, leaning her head onto his shoulder. The light above his back door came on when they reached the top step of the porch. She said, "My father's last…" but stopped and gasped when she saw a silhouette on the far side of the porch. "Oh my God." She pointed across the banister separating the two halves of the porch and said, "Solomon, there's someone there."

Instantly alert, Solomon eased her behind him and turned to face the intruder.

There, in the dark, on a swing at the opposite end of the porch, was the outline of a man. His head was lowered and Solomon couldn't tell if he was awake, asleep or pretending. From the way he was slumped to the side a little, Solomon's worst fear was that he was dead. "Hey," he shouted and stepped closer to the shadow. He took a closer look then asked, "Majac, is that you?"

Majac slowly raised his head and looked in the direction he heard his name called. He yawned, stretched and then stood up. "Hey Partna."

Leona wondered what was going on to have him sitting on the porch in the dark on such a gorgeous night. Then she thought, *And where is my sister? Why isn't he out with Tessa, wining, dining and dancing with her until her feet are sore? Then taking her home and rubbing the soreness out of her feet while he tells her stories about all of the fabulous foreign ports of call he'd conquered.* But he wasn't. Instead, he was there in the dark of the new moon, perched on a swing, staring out over an empty yard. "My God, you scared me," she said.

"My apologies," Majac said.

"Everything all right?" Solomon asked.

"Yeah Man," Majac said, extending a hand to shake Solomon's. "Rough day at work, but nothing to trouble yourself with."

"What are you doing sitting out here in the dark?" Leona asked.

"It's a beautiful night," Majac said coming to life. "Just thought I'd come out, get some fresh air, surround myself in some peace and quiet and rest my mind."

"And where's my sister?" Leona asked. "I could've sworn she told me that you two were spending your last single night in Seattle together."

"We did," Majac said. "She's inside. She fell asleep about twenty minutes ago so I came outside to get some fresh air."

"You're not getting cold feet, are you?" Solomon asked.

The guys shared a laugh. Leona didn't.

"Do I need to go inside and check on her?" Leona asked.

"No, Little Sis," Majac said. "Big Sis is all good. Like I said, she's just asleep. Dessert and four glasses of wine will do it every time."

Again, the fellas laughed.

"All right Majac," Solomon said, "if I don't see you before then, I'll get up with you after work tomorrow night when the shuttle comes to take us to the airport."

The two men bumped fists. Majac retreated to his perch on the porch. Solomon escorted Leona inside.

When Majac went inside a half hour later, Tessa was still asleep on the sofa. He leaned down to kiss her but paused and watched for a moment as her closed eyelids danced intensely under what looked like duress. Unconsciously, she was. Her nightmare had just progressed to the point where those boys from the parking lot had just shoved her into her car. He touched her just as that awful scene flashed in her mind. She shocked Majac when she jerked away and screamed, "NO!"

When he reached for her, she kicked her feet and slapped at him. In her mind, he was one of the boys from that night and she was fighting him off. Breathless and panicking, her eyes unfocused and barely open, she kept kicking as she shuffled towards her escape at the back of the sofa.

Majac took a couple of steps back and gave her room. He watched with his hands raised, palms toward her to show he was harmless as Tessa rapidly blinked her way into consciousness. "Hey Babe..." he said in a voice barely above a whisper once her bloodshot eyes finally popped wide open. "...You all right?"

Wordlessly Tessa looked around the room trying to set her bearings. Her chest heaved. Her breath came quickly. The memories of being attacked in the parking lot brought her to the edge of terror.

"It's okay Baby. It's me, Anton," Majac said softly. "Take your time. I'm right here. Nobody's going to hurt you."

A half dozen deep breaths later, Tessa, now in tears, raised up onto her knees and reached for him. Majac stepped to her and wrapped his arms around her shoulders. Tessa hugged him around his middle, holding on for dear life, trying to squeeze out the terror of her nightmare.

Two months after the attack, all four boys were brought to trial. Between the camera footage retrieved from three businesses across the street from the parking lot, Leona's testimony about what she heard while Tessa's phone was laying in the car during the struggle and the confession of one of the boys who settled for a plea with the D.A., all were convicted and sentenced. Those teens would be well into their mid-twenties before the next time they walked the streets of Seattle.

"It's okay Baby," Majac repeated, gently stroking her forehead. "I got you."

"Forever?" Tessa asked.

"Forever," Majac promised.

After their hug, she stood and kissed him. After the kiss, he picked her up, carried her up to his bedroom, laid her on the king-sized mattress that they would share as husband and wife and made love to her until they fell asleep.

Over in Solomon's half of the Hang Suite, they rented a movie Leona was dying to see, but when the opening scene contained an intense love-making session, Leona and Solomon found themselves making out more than watching.

"I really think I could love you Solomon Alexandré," Leona panted.

He hovered over her. "I think I could love you too, Leona Pearson."

Her cheeks flushed. Her ears became warm and her heart thumped like the bass from a kick drum as it slammed against her chest. His *I think… I love you* was deafening.

He bent down, kissed her, hugged her friskily and lifted her in the air. She playfully kicked her feet, her tip toes reaching for the floor beneath. With her face to his, her chest pulled close and her legs wrapped around him, her mind shifted to the memory of their mile-high adventure.

They'd spent their Valentine's weekend together in a four-star suite at the MGM Grand in Vegas. On the flight there, Solomon bared his soul to her about Mareschelle, Jordyn and his inability to commit. Leona in turn, gave him an open kimono explanation of her escorting side hustle. By the time the plane landed, they had agreed to have a longer conversation about exclusivity.

Their unforgettable Valentine's celebration was jam packed with great food, great shows, great sex all over the thousand-dollar-a-night-suite, and roulette winnings topping forty-eight thousand dollars, part of which he used to charter a private plane for their flight home so he could induct Leona into the mile-high club. Once they progressed past the extra-curriculars and were sipping champagne on the white, leather sofa, Leona asked Solomon, "How serious are you about a monogamous relationship?"

"Dead," was his one word answer.

Leona inhaled deeply, exhaled hard, emptied the recently filled glass of champagne and said, "Then I guess I'm out of the escort business."

When the bottle was empty, and they were both full of food and drink, Solomon entered her end zone as the plane made its touch down.

Now, their smiles were broad as they gazed into each other's eyes. Lush, lashy, doe-like eyes looked up at him. Gazed at him the way Eve must have stared at Adam in those first moments. The energy between them was so intense. So sincere. They felt like the two happiest people in the city… in the state…in the world.

A half hour of their foreplay passed before Leona jerked, gasped and let out an "Uggh" that brought Solomon to an all stop. She seized up and temporarily lost voluntary muscle control. Her movements similar to a praise dance, the way people move when a preacher's sermon touches deeply and they catch the spirit.

"You all right?" he asked.

"Just a little kink in my back." Her eyes teared. "Nothing to worry about."

"Come on," Solomon said, taking her hand and climbing off the sofa.

He paused the movie that was watching them more than they were watching it, turned off the TV and told his digital home assistant to *play Decadent Red playlist.*

"My own playlist?" Leona giggled. "Oh, I want to hear every song."

He led her upstairs, her hand still in his, as Maze serenaded her ears. "A hot bath will have your back straightened out in no time." He directed her towards his closet to change into what he'd laid out, while he filled his jetted tub with Epsom salt. Solomon sat on the tub ledge and waited for her. Two pain pills and a glass of wine were next to him.

Steam had fogged the mirror by the time she joined him wrapped in a thigh length satin robe. "You're still dressed," she said, disappointed that he had only taken off his socks and shiny, blue dress shoes. "I was hoping that we were getting in together."

"Maybe next time." Solomon sidled up behind her, untied the knot in the belt, opened the robe and traced her skin from waist to chest, his knuckles grazing across her taut nipples when he removed her robe by the lapel.

Leona shed the delicate garment like a butterfly emerging from a cocoon. Her body firm and taut like that of a teenage girl.

Solomon's eyes reverted back to those of a teenage boy. He marveled over the soft curves and delicate edges of her naked body as if it were his first time seeing her.

"That's not what your eyes are telling me." She looked down. "Him neither," she said with a buttery smooth laugh.

He lowered the robe in front of his waist. "Just get in the tub already."

Leona dipped her hand in the water to check it. "Perfect." She moaned a deep sigh as she submerged into the heat and scented bubbles.

Solomon echoed the perfect sentiment in his mind as he laid the robe over the standing towel rack then lit a scented candle. He put the lid down on the commode then sat down on top of it next to the bathtub. The fragrant smoke mixed with the steam and filled the bathroom air with the warm, welcomed aromas of jasmine, lilac and cinnamon.

"My goodness. This feels so good," she said. "I didn't realize how much I needed to relax." She closed her eyes and drifted lazily, trying to forget the pain in her back. She didn't open them again until she reached for the glass of South American wine Solomon sat on the shelf of the tub next to the faucet. The slightly less than room-temperature liquid slid down her throat with a velvety smoothness that further eased her mind, causing her body to sink lower into the steaming cauldron of fragrant water.

"This is perfect," Leona said luxuriating. She placed the glass back on the rim of the tub when Solomon pressed a button energizing six jets below the water's surface. Hot, pulsating water massaged her from various angles.

The bath had soothed her back and continued her arousal. So much so, that she wanted to forego wearing his satin pajamas. Solomon had laid them out for her in his closet. After he finished undressing, he headed straight to the bed wearing only his boxers.

Watching him undress, confirmed how much she wanted him. Even more now than downstairs; but she cared deeply for him and didn't want to just walk into the bedroom naked. *Where's the fun in that?* she thought. She knew they hadn't made a long-term commitment, but they were enjoying each other's company. They'd been a couple for just over three months and if nothing else, they had an amazing sex life. And even if he hadn't said it, she knew his feelings were just as strong.

As she applied her moisturizer, she decided that having him exert some effort, even if it was only a little bit, was better than just falling naked into the bed. Wearing only the pajama top, satisfied her own desire of feeling wanted. Feeling sexy. Still, she put on the pants, slipped back into her high heels, then joined him in the bedroom, stopping at the foot of the bed.

He placed his hands behind his head and stared up at her. "Why are you standing way over there?"

"Maybe I want you to beg me to come closer?"

"I take it the bath cured your sore back?"

She twisted her shoulders a bit. "I think it can handle a twist or two."

He smiled, pleased that she was ready to play.

She unbuttoned her shirt and propped her hands on her hips offering him a good look at her rock-hard nipples and board flat stomach.

"And the heels?"

"I had a desire to be as tall as you tonight."

"I can work with that."

She began loosening the drawstring in the waist of her pants.

"I like where this is going," he said. He groaned when she turned around and slowly eased her bottoms down to her ankles, bending all the way over until she unveiled the red thong that was hidden by the ample curve of her bottom.

Now he was in agony. He began to grovel, got up on all fours and crawled towards her.

"No, no, no" she commanded playfully. She stepped back, away from his grasp when he reached the foot of the bed.

"Please?" he begged, extending his arm further.

"Be a good patient and get back up there. It's my turn to play doctor."

"So, do I get a complete physical, Doctor Pearson?" He returned to the center of the bed and laid on his back.

"You can call it what you want." Leona lit four candles and turned off all the lights. She gently removed the stitch of red cloth he called a thong and stepped up onto the foot of the bed. Then as if her back spasm had been miraculously cured, she touched the ceiling for balance, walked across his mattress in those heels, grabbed the headboard with both hands and planted her heels outside his shoulders. She hovered over him, seductively swaying to the beat. Languidly wagging her bottom over him.

Solomon's heart was beating so hard in his chest that it drowned out all other sound in the room. Dying to reach out and touch her, he took short, deep breaths as her body lowered closer to his with each sway of her hips.

"But I'll just call it…" She bent her knees into a full squat—a butterfly lighting on a lily pad—her sex making a perfect one-point landing on his eagerly awaiting tongue. Her body convulsed. A deep, guttural moan escaped in the form of the word, "…Therapy."

Solomon was nowhere around when Leona drifted back into consciousness. He had gone downstairs to get them something to drink. Their lovemaking session had left them with wet bedsheets and dry throats. She called his name, but he didn't answer. She stretched, rolled over onto her back, listened to the soft sounds of nature coming through the window. She yawned and fought the drowsiness that hadn't yet released her.

She pulled the dank sheets to her face, inhaled their mixed scents and then fist-pumped the air like Tiger Woods. She peeked at the door, and since the coast was clear, she shrieked into the sheets giddily, legs and arms flailing, her whole body shaking in the revelry of how awesome she'd felt making love to him.

Then she heard it. The piano bounced crisp notes that danced on the ceiling. Notes that slowly wafted down on her body. Then a mezzo tempo found its way beneath her skin and manumitted her from her temporary state of euphoria. She jolted upright, climbed off the bed and padded quickly toward the hallway, hardly able to feel the bottoms of her feet, bare and slightly damp, as they left ghostly impressions on the cool hardwood floor behind her. She almost floated down the stairs. Her heart was in her throat, crowding her vocal cords; freezing them solid like a cold Vancouver breeze. By the time she reached the room from which the sound came, her eyes were filled with tears.

Standing there in the living room with all of his mentors in their frames was Solomon with chamomile tea on the table, grinning at her. "Surprise."

Leona drew her hands to her lips. The second song on the movie's soundtrack started with a long wail of her mother's voice. It swirled around her as the first tear slowly began to fall from her eyes.

"What's the matter?"

She shook her head, unable to speak.

Solomon rushed over to her. Held her. "Why the tears? Do you want me to turn it off?"

"That's my mother."

"Yes. That's your mother. I remembered you told me your mom was a singer. Your birthday's coming up soon, so I was at the music store and I had Joe look her up for me. This was the only album in the system and I wanted to get you a copy as a gift."

"That was the last album she made before her..." Leona paused. "Her accident."

"Your mother has a beautiful voice," he said picking up the album cover. "And she was a beautiful woman. Come on, sit down." Solomon said leading her to the sofa. "If you'd like, I would love for you to tell me about your mother."

The best listeners listen with their hearts. Solomon, wearing boxers and a t-shirt, sat behind Leona on the couch, her legs curled beneath her. Her face was wet with tears. Her hair laid softly against his broad chest. Her nose was two shades of Rudolph red. She sniffled twice before sipping the herbal tea. They listened to the entire album, the last song twice. Then Leona told him about her mother, her father and other things too. And Solomon listened with his ears, his mind and his heart.

32

A Hot Lunch

TESSA TURNED OFF THE CEILING lights in the bathroom. Her head was throbbing. Sour acid was on her tongue and lips. She hoped Anton couldn't hear the vomiting that got rid of the spinning. Neither water nor toothpaste could rinse the taste away. She spat. Spat again. Gargled with mouth wash and dropped eye drops to help conceal her bloodshot eyes. She turned on the water in the shower and stepped in before it got warm. Then she started sweating. She was sweating—and she was dizzy. She pointed the shower head to rain on her forehead then slumped on the floor in a seated position.

"Good morning," Majac murmured. He opened his eyes and rolled over in the bed only to find himself alone. He wanted to hug her, but there was no trace of Tessa to be found. Rising, he padded towards the bathroom but it was dark inside. Not there. He started downstairs. At the end of the hall, staring out into the lush backyard, his only thoughts were on his fiancé and how she had reminded him how to love. He thought, *Why would she run off? Did I do something wrong? Why didn't she tell me she was leaving?* The recent showers had left the city looking damp from too much rain. He stood in front of the window and glanced warily at the morning sky as the sun attempted to punch its way through soft, puffy clouds.

When a boat whistle blew somewhere on the Sound, he thought about the morning before when they were on the ferry. They'd close on their new house Tuesday afternoon and she was so anxious to join him in crossing the threshold of the house they would share after their wedding that she stole 48 hours away from the demands of her job. And for that small act of theft, he was grateful.

341

From the moment Leona and Tessa had surprised him with their switcheroo at brunch, what seemed like a million months ago, he discovered that they shared so much in common, including the theatre, detective novels, historical fiction, long walks on the beach and their love for the Lord. He loved the sound of her laughter. The way she cocked her head to one side when she was trying to explain something. In her, he'd truly found his soulmate and he loved everything about her. Eight months ago, he proposed and she accepted. In two days, they'd be man and wife. And Majac, staring out at the Sound and thinking about marrying his Girl Next Door, couldn't imagine being happier.

~

"**Good morning**," Leona said groggily. Solomon was sitting on the settee at the foot of the bed tying the laces on his running shoes. "Running off already?" she deadpanned.

"Yeah, I've got a lot to do today before we get on that plane, so I was going to head out and get a couple of laps in before I do what I gotta do."

She looked at the clock. "Dang, it's early." It wasn't even seven yet.

"Yeah, I know. I started to wake you when I got up at six, but you were sleeping so soundly and your little snoring was so cute," he said as he stood up and reached for his running jacket. "I figured you must've really been tired."

"I guess I needed it," she smiled. She rolled over and rested on her belly, her legs fluttering restlessly beneath the sheets. "Thank you for putting me to sleep."

He removed his driver's license from his wallet, put on his activity watch to track his workout and checked the calendar on his smart phone.

"Well now that I'm awake," she said, making snow angels in the soft sheets, "why don't you come back to bed and get in a couple of laps over here—then you can...go do what you gotta do."

"As awesome as that sounds..." Solomon kept his distance from the bed. He and Leona had been up until almost four o'clock making love. He knew if he got close enough, round seven would be guaranteed.

"You sure?" she scooted over to the edge of the bed. The sheets rose up her thighs, completely exposing the entire length of her legs. "Okay..." Her tone was elongated and whimsical. She balled the sheets around her hands and plunged them between her legs. "...your loss."

Solomon turned and grinned widely at her unmistakable attempt at seduction.

They exchanged a little more back-and-forth about their plans for the day then he went back to the bed and kissed her like he was leaving for the war. He planted one last kiss on her forehead then headed for the door. When he reached for the door handle, Leona called him. He looked back at the Bohemian beauty who had now unrolled herself from the covers and was sitting on her ankles, the sheets fallen to her waist leaving her topless. She grinned shamelessly. He exhaled and shifted in his pants, but held his ground while checking his watch. A look of uncertainty shrouded his face.

She knew that she needed to let him make his escape. Without sounding desperate, she pulled the sheet up to cover her bare chest and said, "So what time will I be able to catch up with you later? Maybe we can do lunch."

Solomon didn't know if it was supposed to be a question or a statement. "I've got some things to do this morning, and I need to check on my Mama later, but hit me on my cell. I'll be around."

Majac found a note taped to the mirror in his bathroom and called Tessa.

"Hello Honey," Tessa sang her greeting.

"I just wanted to let you know that I was awake and about to get dressed," Majac said. "After I eat, I'm going to make my way to the gym out on Mercer to meet Jaz for our workout."

"Great," she replied. "Will you be done in time to catch my lecture?"

"I don't know if I'll be there for the start, but I will definitely try to be there before you finish."

"Great. We can go downstairs at the Coffee shop after my lecture and get some lunch."

"Cool," he said. "Love you."

"Love you too, Mister Charles," Tessa purred. "Can't wait to see you."

Jaz was about a mile from the Mercer Island Health and Fitness Center when his phone rang. "Well, good morning beautiful," he answered when his phone automatically picked up after the third ring.

"Good morning." It was Crystal calling him back. "Sorry I missed your call."

"No problem," Jaz said.

"I got up early," she continued, "and headed out to burn some calories. I didn't take my phone because I needed some alone time to stop thinking about all of the craziness. Needed to clear my head. You know, try to relieve some of the stress in my world."

"I hear you."

"It was a good walk. I went six-and-a-half miles in 75-minutes."

"Well maybe we can work out a time in our schedules so that I can go with you. I don't mind getting up early. I know you said you do it for alone time, but we can talk…or not. I'm good. Two-way convos; one-way convos; or walking in complete silence. Whatever you need, I got you."

"Sounds good Jared. If I get to a place where I am comfortable with that, I'll let you know."

"Cool," Jaz said. "Hey, he's here already."

"Who's there? Where?"

"Maj. I just pulled into the health club parking lot."

"All right, well I'll let you boys have your fun. Oh, and can you come by around five? The girls would like to stop for burgers before we go to the airport."

"Five it is Missus Stevenson. Talk to you later. Love you."

"Love you. Bye."

Majac sat down on the bench in the gym's locker room. He was just about to text Jaz when his best friend burst through the locker room door. They exchanged greetings, and unlocked full-length lockers on opposite sides of the same aisle. At six-foot-six, Jaz had four inches on Majac, and probably outweighed him by forty pounds. Although a season removed from the league, he wasn't quite twenty pounds over playing weight. By no means fat, neither would be getting any call backs as underwear models.

"You ready for tonight?" Jaz asked. He was referring to their flight back to Pennsylvania. "Last two days as a free man. You sure you want to spend your last free day in Seattle in the gym?"

"Yeah, I'm ready. I think that bachelor party was enough to get it all out of my system."

"No last goodbyes you want to shout out to anybody?"

"Nahh I'm good. Last goodbye shout found me in a twentieth-floor condo, standing face-to-face with Celeste Devereaux in her birthday suit."

"Yeah. You still should've hit that one last time for old-time's sake."

They changed into their gym clothes, filled their water bottles and grabbed complimentary hand towels the ritzy gym left out everywhere for all of their patrons.

"Yeah, she did look good, but she was on some we can get back together mess. And I wasn't even about that drama."

"Yeah, I don't blame you. Those Devereaux chicks are wild." Jaz knew firsthand that Celeste Devereaux and her sister Marissa held the patent on crazy.

"Anyway Partna, thanks for the party last week," Majac told Jaz. "I had a great time."

"To tell the truth Bruh," Jaz said as they exited the locker. "I can't remember the last time I had that much fun."

"Hopefully not too much fun." Majac was referring to the time he saw Jaz at the party before he disappeared behind a door with a dancer.

"Don't worry about me Partna. Everything is good over here."

"You straight?" Majac asked.

"Straighter than six o'clock," Jaz replied.

"All right then, let's get this in."

"Hey, just so I'm certain," Jaz said, stopping Majac's progression toward the stairs. "Are you absolutely sure you're ready to get married?"

"One hundred percent." Majac said.

"No doubts?"

"None whatsoever."

"All right then, you said it," Jaz said. "Let's get this in."

They headed upstairs where, overlooking the court was a three-lane, hard-rubber surface, eighth-of-a-mile-long running track. Outside the track's perimeter to the left were three rooms with hardwood floors and thousand dollar stereo systems where classes such as the fast-paced Katana, high-impact step aerobics, hot yoga and the always packed, standing room only, ever-popular, Zumba classes were held. To the right of the track were two rooms with hard rubber floors that housed the free-weights and cardiovascular equipment.

Unlike the small, grimy, cell of a room with all the charm of a prison yard at the base gym, the weight room at Mercer Island resembled a high-end car dealership showroom. No rust on the chrome of the barbells, no rust on the black of the weights and plenty of cool white led lighting throughout. Members dropped more than a Benjamin a month to sweat in these high-class digs. And despite the pomp and circumstance of the hoity-toity gym, it was still a good place to work out.

Jaz wore Temple basketball shorts that stopped above his knees and a charcoal-grey muscle shirt with a huge Temple 'T' on the front. Majac's shorts were navy blue with gold Isosceles triangles pointing to his hip. His gold t-shirt had the word NAVY in a reflective typeface printed across the back. Following a five minute warm-up jog, they elevated their pace. They jockeyed back and forth, each assuming the lead for varying lengths of time as they internalized winning what always became a race. What started as a friendly jog to warm themselves up for weightlifting turned into a sprint to the finish as the two behemoths completed their two-mile run a quarter shy of fourteen minutes.

"Good run, Partna. Glad to see you still got it in you," Jaz said between breaths as Majac took a long, slow drink of water.

"Whew," Majac exhaled when he came back up for air. Jaz leaned over to get some water as Majac said, "I don't know what you're talking about old man. I'm not the one who's retired."

They recovered from their exhaustion during their walk to the weight room. Jaz set up weights in the power rack so they could work shoulders first. After shoulder and chest presses, squats and deadlifts, they checked out gloves from the front desk and proceeded to the heavy bag.

Jaz held the bag for the first three minutes while Majac pounded the pretend side of beef. A one-minute intermission was all they allowed while switching places before Jaz commenced pounding out his frustrations on the smooth rawhide bag. Ten repetitions of this dance would culminate with Majac and Jaz dancing in a pool of sweat. As Jaz punched through his final set, he pounded that bag with such fierce desperation that Majac required all his remaining strength to prevent the force of Jaz's blows from knocking him to the ground.

"Time," Majac called for the final time, then released the weight of the bag that leaned heavily against his chest and bent over.

Jaz's knees buckled. He was exhausted. He crumpled to the floor and landed on all fours. Sweat streamed down both their faces, chests and backs. A minute passed before Jaz climbed to his feet, placed his gloves atop his head and walked in circles, inhaling deep gulps of cool gymnasium air. As Majac recovered from Jaz's vicarious punishment of the bag, Jaz stopped his pacing and leaned back into the window overlooking the swimming pool area. The sweat soaked t-shirt squeaked on the glass as he slumped to the matted rubber floor. Arms, legs, back and shoulders burned from exhaustion. His forearms came to rest on his bent knees and his head hung low. Sweat pooled beneath him as Majac mopped the floor beneath the heavy bag before joining his Partna by the window. "Hey Bruh, you all right?"

Never felt better." Jaz regarded Majac and exhaled deeply.

Majac pulled Jaz up so they could return their gloves to the front desk.

Intent on completely reaching the point of exhaustion, Jaz insisted they suffer through three reps of chest flies and leg extensions and then two hundred crunches before heading to the steam room.

"Boy I feel good," Jaz said. "She worked me good this morning." He was referring to how well his back felt after the masseuse had tweaked the soreness out of a muscle in his back. He and Majac had showered, finished their post-workout massage and were in the locker room about to get dressed.

"Yo Partna," Majac said. "I need you to listen to something for me." He took a slip of paper from his pocket and unfolded it. "It's my wedding vows. Tessa and I decided to write our own."

"Did you and Tessa decide?" Jaz joked, continuing to get dressed. "Or did Tessa decide and you just gave in?"

"Look Man," Majac started, "I just need you to listen and give me your honest opinion. Can you do that?"

Jaz nodded, slipped on his boxers and pants then sat barefoot and topless listening to Majac read.

"In you, I've found a match made on earth. Most would say they want a match made in heaven, but I don't want to wait that long to have the perfection that I've found in you. Living without you would be like living without the sun in the sky. Without your light, my heart would surely shrivel up and die. Beauty and grace only begin to describe you. Dedication to family and friends make you a wonderful person to be around. Your vibrant personality brings a smile to the faces of everyone lucky enough to encounter you. Your spirit is a gift to be treasured by all who are blessed enough to be considered a friend. Hearing your name makes me smile uncontrollably. I could talk about you all day and only begin to describe how magnificent you are. My love for you will forever live in my heart and I'll make every day the best day of the rest of your life."

Jaz sat quietly, his eyes rolling around contemplatively.

"What do you think?" Majac asked impatiently.

"A little long. I think she'll like it more if you shorten it."

"So you don't like it?"

"I didn't say that. All I said is that it's a little long. I mean, I hope you can remember all of that. 'Cause if you pull that piece of paper out, standing up there in the pulpit, I will slap you into next week."

"You're a funny guy," Majac said. He wasn't laughing.

"Then," Jaz continued, "I'm going to reach over your shoulder and snatch that mess right out of your hand."

"So you don't like it?"

"It's cool Partna. If that's how you really feel, I love it. And Tessa is going to love it. I just think it's too long."

"Aiight, then check this out."

Majac shoved the note back into his bag, then reached into a different pocket of his backpack and pulled out two ring boxes. Before he transferred out of San Diego, Majac had taken the ring he bought Celeste back to the jeweler for a refund. She didn't want to marry him, so he saw no reason to keep it. The ring left behind on the table by the guy who had interrupted his proposal to Celeste, before being dragged off by the police, Majac kept and pawned. Using the money from both rings, he bought Tessa a chocolate diamond wedding set. The two-carat, princess cut, engagement ring had twelve small diamonds, set like soldiers, with six on either side of a one carat, princess diamond. The one-and-a-half carat wedding band was set with six small, rectangular, chocolate diamonds. Majac handed Jaz the rings.

"Wow Partna." Jaz opened the boxes and whistled. "This is crazy."

"Tessa's not the flashy type," Majac said. "You think it's too much?"

"It'll suit her perfectly," Jaz said. "Just perfect."

As he crossed the bridge from Mercer Island back to Seattle, Majac called Tessa's cell phone to let her know he was on his way. It went to voicemail. *Must still be in her lecture*, he thought.

Earlier, when he came down to the kitchen, she'd left him a note on the island asking him to meet her at the Performing Arts theatre on the University of Washington campus. She said she was nervous about talking before an audience because of how aggressive the audience was the last time she spoke, but her boss had the flu, so she had to do it even though she was on leave and flying out later. She said that since she couldn't get back to sleep, she was going to go into the office to make changes to some of the slides before the ten o'clock presentation.

Underneath the note was the envelope with two tickets to the one o'clock performance of *Rhythm Live* by the Junior Theatre All-Stars.

⌁

Since Leona was meeting Tessa for lunch, she parked on the street at the far end of the block that housed her studio vice in the garage. Despite the cost and hassle of filling the meter hourly, she figured parking closer to work would minimize her travel time to get to the U-Dub campus.

The temperature had risen into the upper sixties and since rain was in the forecast, she emerged from her studio carrying an umbrella.

Across the street, her Sentinel rushed into motion and bolted into the intersection. His stiff joints ached from the quick start, but that mattered less than did moving swiftly across the intersection in pursuit of his charge.

When a Hummer H2 ignored the red light and barreled into a right turn, the Sentinel was almost struck in the intersection. With the alertness and agility of a man half his age, he dove back onto the sidewalk to avoid his demise as tires screeched their warning and the large SUV escaped down the street into traffic, never attempting to make a stop.

Leona turned when she heard the commotion and made her way toward the origin of the disturbance.

"You alright, Buddy?" one of the men in business suits asked.

The elderly man in the Army jacket got to his feet and broke free without answering. He lurched away from the men helping him and accidently knocked a passing teen off his skateboard in the process. After ensuring the boy was all right, he turned to continue his pursuit of Leona and found himself face to face with the lovely lady he'd vowed to protect.

⌁

Conveniently nestled on the ground floor of the student union building, the Huskie Café was an open, airy coffee shop with five red booths along the window and a long counter with twenty stools. The faint, sweet aroma of exotic cafés and fresh-baked cookies wafted through the air. Ten tables between the booths and the counter, all three-foot squares, formed a checkerboard from the entrance at the front to the restrooms at the back.

Tessa's cell rang as she entered the Huskie Café. "Hey Sis, I was…"

"Hey yourself," Leona replied. "You are not going to believe what just happened to… You know what, never mind. Where are you?"

"I'm at the Huskie café waiting for Anton."

"Stay there. I'm on my way," Leona beamed into the phone. "Oh my God have I got a surprise for you."

Tessa tried to say, "Call me when you get to campus," but Leona had already disconnected.

Tessa sat her jacket and briefcase down on a chair three tables from the back at table number eight.

When she placed her order, she ordered an extra coffee for Majac and two sandwiches. Back at her table, she noticed she had no napkins, so she retrieved some from the counter. She jumped when her phone rang. A three-year-old girl sitting at the table next to her with her mother laughed at her then put her fingers together and made a heart symbol. A slight sense of relief came over Tessa. "That was so sweet," she said to no one as she raised her phone to her ear.

"What did you say?" Majac asked.

"Nothing," she said. "Don't worry about it." She nodded her head back at the smiling toddler, then sat down. "Hey You."

"Hey back-at-cha, soon-to-be Missus Charles."

"How far out are you?"

"I'm close." He had made it onto campus and was in the parking lot closest to the student union building. He saw a parking spot next to the sidewalk, but waited to allow a lady carrying two back packs to pass in front of him. After she passed, he started to enter the spot but skidded to a stop when a car coming from the other direction cut him off and snaked his parking spot. Two guys got out of the car. The driver made eye contact with Majac, raised his arms and mouthed, *What*? Two against one weren't good odds and Majac was in such a great mood after the night before with Tessa, after his workout this morning, and knowing that in a couple of hours, he was getting on a plane to go home and get married, that he let it go without another thought and drove to find a parking spot two rows back.

After stealing Majac's parking spot, the two men walked into the lobby of the student union building. Majac entered the building a moment later and made his way into the coffee shop. Tessa waved when she saw him enter. He joined her, kissing her on the cheek.

While they ate and drank, the couple talked about the remainder of their day and the things they wanted to do the next day once they got back to Tuskegee. Twenty minutes later, Majac picked up Tessa's briefcase and helped her on with her jacket. Neither of them seemed to notice when her compact umbrella slid out of her briefcase and onto the floor. Majac opened the coffee shop door to the lobby and gestured for Tessa to exit. But before she could get through though, the two parking spot thieves hurriedly pushed their way through, the smaller of them bumping shoulders with Tessa as she tried to exit.

"Yo, Partna," Majac snarled at the guy. "What the hell?"

"What?" the taller, heavier of the two said.

"How rude!" Tessa said, as she grabbed Majac's arm.

"You feel froggy, jump Kermit," the taller one growled.

The three seconds that followed felt like three hours to Tessa. Her eyes went wide as she remembered fighting off those boys in the parking lot. "Forget it Anton," she said tugging harder on his arm. "Let's just go."

"Yeah, you heard her punk," the heavy one said. "Just go."

It took every ounce of restraint for Majac to restrain from engaging in that battle, even if he weren't sure he could win that war. He relented to the sound and touch of Tessa, in his ear and on his arm. Majac wished with everything in him that Jaz was there. He knew in a fair fight, he and his Partna would have whipped both of their asses.

Tessa and Majac had just about made their way to the front door of the building's lobby when she noticed that people entering the building were wet. She reached into her briefcase but didn't find her umbrella. "I must've left it in the coffee shop," she said, rifling through her bag. They turned back and were ten feet from the café when a man came through the door and called Majac by his full name. He turned and saw Solomon entering the building. After a quick greeting, Majac told him that Tessa forgot her umbrella in the café and said he'd be right back.

"No sweetheart," Tessa stopped him. "You guys get the elevator; I will go get it." She kissed his cheek, handed him her briefcase and moved toward the café before he could rebut.

The fellas watched Tessa's departure, not moving towards the elevator until she disappeared inside. "Hey Man," Solomon started, "now that you're moving out, I guess it is alright to let you know that I'm your landlord." Surprised, Majac listened intently as Solomon continued.

Inside the coffee shop, Tessa found her umbrella under the chair that had held her briefcase, knelt down and picked it up. The vibrant woman in the bright green skirt once again caught the attention of the playful child. She turned and saw her tiny giggle partner watching her again. Her smile warranted one last wave goodbye.

Majac and Solomon were laughing loudly when the elevator arrived. Before the elevator doors opened wide enough for its passengers to safely exit, Leona emerged like a train exiting a dark tunnel. She appeared to be dragging the guy with salt-and-pepper braids wearing an Army jacket in her wake.

"Where is she?" Leona asked in a fever pitch.

Solomon and Majac looked from Leona to the Army vet. Solomon's recognition of the man opened his eyes wide. Majac's recognition of the man as the guy he and Tessa had seen in the parking garage and then later rescued outside Nijo brought about a curious scowl. Before either could utter a word, Leona barked her question again.

"She's in the café," Majac pointed. His eyes still glued on the vet.

Leona looked in the direction Majac was pointing. She slipped one arm inside the old man's Army jacket and slammed a hand over her mouth to conceal a squeal.

Majac turned to see what gave Solomon pause. "You alright, Partna?"

"I think I've seen a ghost," Solomon said blankly. "It can't be..."

Inside the café, Leona released the Army vet's arm and rushed to Tessa.

As they hugged, Tessa asked, "Are you okay? You scared me on the phone. What happened?"

Leona released her sister and turned to face the door. "Look who's over there," she said nodding toward the man with the imperfect Army jacket. The black and white edges of his unkempt hair hung sharply about his head and shoulders.

Tessa gawked curiously for a moment. Looking hard, she noticed that he looked familiar. When she settled her nerves, a second glance confirmed that he was, in fact, the unfortunate man she and Anton had scared in the parking garage and then later rescued from those horrible boys. She asked her sister, "What's...going on, Leona? Why is he here? And what happened to you on the phone?"

Leona jumped when Tessa touched her arm. She gasped, drew one deep breath and then another.

"Leona, what's wrong?" You look like you've seen a ghost." Having been through the trauma of her parking lot mugging, Tessa didn't know what to do.

"Oh my God Tessa, do you see him? He's standing right there."

"Yes, I see him." Tessa's confusion was genuine. "But why is he here with you?"

Leona pointed straight at the Army vet and in a breathless whisper uttered, "Because he's our Daddy!"

"What?...Who?...What?"

"There. It's really him. I saw him almost get hit by a car when I came out for lunch and when I went to see if he was alright, I looked him in his eyes and knew he was my Daddy."

Tessa had seen pictures of him in Leona's condo from a long time ago, but now standing eight feet away from him, she did not recognize him as the man from the pictures. She craned her neck trying to look past the long hair, grime and age. When their eyes met, the look on his face told her that Leona was telling the truth.

"Oh my God. Oh my God. Oh my God. Is it really him?"

Rarely speechless, Leona's words were replaced by her tears.

Tessa called to him timidly. "Daddy?"

The Army vet's smile confirmed Tessa's recognition.

Tessa asked, "But where?...How?"

"God works in mysterious ways," Leona said.

As if walking on air, Tessa left Leona's side. She took three steps toward him but stopped short when gunshots rang out in the cafe.

The two men who had pushed their way past Majac had drawn the attention of the two policemen who were sitting at the bar. The police asked them for identification and without warning the shorter man drew a gun and fired two shots.

The mother seated with Tessa's toddler friend screamed. The other gunmen turned and sent four shots in the direction of the scream. The spray of bullets missed the screaming lady and most of the coffee drinkers in the crowded room but did manage to shatter the window to the left of the door.

Majac heard the shots and turned around. Solomon dropped to the floor. When he saw his neighbor standing, he pulled Majac to the floor with him.

The Army vet swooped across the coffee shop and tackled the screaming lady and her daughter, pushing them to cover as other customers started screaming, running, and falling to the floor to evade the barrage of bullets. After, checking that the lady and her daughter weren't hit, the Army vet backtracked to his daughters, covered their heads and pushed them into a booth, causing Tessa's next breath to leave her body in a hurry as their three bodies jammed onto the faux leather seat covering.

The short gunman fired twice more.

"Tessa" Majac shouted, looking up from the floor. He saw blood squirt against the window to the right of the coffee shop door.

People pushed out the door into the lobby, trying desperately to escape without being harmed or worse. Another campus policeman stood in the doorway simultaneously ducking and playing traffic cop. He yelled, trying to herd customers out without anyone getting stomped in the stampede.

Majac hopped up and raced back towards the coffee shop shouting Tessa's name. Solomon got to his feet and followed. Arriving at the bow wave of the mass exodus, they tried desperately to push their way through, straining to get a view of anything happening inside. Their adrenaline was flowing; Majac's military training inured him to anxiety during calamities.

The campus cop rushed them when he saw them going the wrong way. Solomon backed away from the cop with his hands raised a la 'hands up, don't shoot'. The cop turned his attention back to the door. That was all Majac needed to see. He ran toward the other side of the door. The security officer ran behind him, yelling for him to do something that Majac knew that he would never do. The officer shouted, "STOP!"

Majac ignored him like he was the squad leader he hated freshman year at the Naval Academy. Signs and lights and people shot past him in an unending spectrum of color and sound. The officer's voice faded as his footsteps trailed in the distance.

Like a salmon trying to swim upstream against the current to spawn, Majac barreled into the crowd. He pushed hard. Almost knocked over a stroller. Then, as if he were Moses miraculously parting the Red Sea before him, people moved out of his way and he emerged from the other side of the sea of people, nearly falling down again. He righted himself, ran as fast as he could and jumped through the broken coffee shop window to the right of the door.

It seemed that everyone was watching him. The cop who had been directing traffic out the coffee shop door, was now focused on him inside on the coffee shop floor. The people who had rushed away from the melee slowed down to watch the crazy man who was rushing towards the bullets.

The Army vet peeked out and saw the tall gunman standing over the two campus cops at the bar. He cringed when the gunman looked them dead in the face, squeezed the trigger from point blank range and executed one of the two campus policemen.

When the tall gunman stopped shooting, the army vet scrambled out from underneath the booth table and charged the counter. Using a chair to help him leap across the counter, he lunged at the tall shooter and knocked him down. The gun fell and they fought like Greco-Roman warriors.

With the mass exodus concluded, the shorter gunman climbed over the counter and hit the Army vet in the back of his head with the butt of his gun. The vet fell to the floor; stunned, but still conscious. The short gunman helped the tall gunman to his feet and the two of them made their way toward the exit at the back of the coffee shop.

Campus security officers entered the building lobby with guns drawn. They pushed people toward the exit, as some scuffled to get a view of the man running towards the gunfire.

Majac pushed himself off the coffee shop floor. The last of the coffee shop patrons had rushed out. "Tessa!" he shouted.

"Anton!" Tessa screamed a horrified reply. She was laying in the booth holding her mid-section. One of the errant bullets from the second shooter's gun pierced her belly just to the left of her belly button. When she saw Majac, she tried to slide out of the booth, knocking a half-empty glass of milk onto the floor.

Majac's heart leapt when he heard the glass fall. He looked in that direction and heard the worry in her voice. He saw Tessa's olive-green dress knelt in front of the red lounge chair and started to panic.

The Vet made it to his feet and followed the gunmen towards the back door. When the short gunman started shooting again, the Vet took cover.

Majac ducked bullets as he rushed to Tessa, trying frantically to lay worrisome eyes on the face of his beautiful bride-to-be. A bullet hit him in the right shoulder. He fell to the ground in slow motion.

Tessa felt light-headed. Began to slowly fall to the floor. Falling.

Falling. None of her thoughts had weight. Her head felt lighter and lighter as life snatching flames of fire swirled all around. She landed on Leona, who had been caught in the rush of the crowd exiting and was lying on the floor unconscious. She wasn't bleeding, but she was breathing.

Majac pulled himself to his knees with his left arm. Called Tessa's name again then stumbled toward her.

Tessa was silent. The room wobbled up and down. She tried to look through the smoke that was clouding her vision. Her arms were weak. Her heart pounded. Falling. She called out her fiancée's name. Falling. As she fell the last few inches onto the field of black beneath her, two hands caught her like a ballplayer making a shoestring catch.

Majac grabbed Tessa's shoulders and rolled her over. He saw her eyes close and exhausted his last ounce of energy when he shouted, "somebody call an ambulance." He lay huddled around Tessa's shoulders, holding her in his arms, her head against his stomach. The only sound he could hear was the beating of his own heart. His lips moved slowly as, almost inaudibly, he repeated the words I love you over and over again. If he was going to die, he was going to die with her in his arms.

And just like that, the coffee shop was quiet. The air was still. The gunmen fled out the back door before Security breached the front. Two cops and two other people lay dead. Six others, including Majac, Tessa, Leona and the Army vet, who struggled to his feet but fell and eventually passed out from exhaustion, lay wounded in the melee. Outside behind the yellow tape stretched across the building entrance, dozens of onlookers took videos with camera phones and gawked anxiously inside.

~~~

The only sound Majac heard as he regained consciousness kneeling next to Tessa on the coffee shop floor was the sound of his own breathing. He no longer heard the sirens. No longer heard the crowd outside the door. Tears blurred his eyes and then he heard nothing. He crumpled to the floor holding his lover.

Sometime later, he felt tears run down his cheeks, but there was still no sound. A moment later it started. Unrecognizable at first, the sound got louder the harder he tried to hear his own thoughts. Then, the distant echo of gunshots bouncing off the walls shocked him back into consciousness.

"Is the ambulance here?" he shouted as police rushed through the door. Solomon entered right on their heels.

"Not yet, sir," an officer said. "EMTs are on their way."

Solomon knelt over Leona and slapped her cheek trying to wake her. After six or seven slaps, she started to blink her way to consciousness. When she groaned, Solomon leaned down and kissed her.

To an anxious, worried, covered-in-blood Commander Anton Majac Charles, being told nothing more than *the EMTs are coming* wasn't getting him the help he needed fast enough.

A red spot grew in the center of Tessa's green dress. Fear grew in her eyes as she struggled to look up at him. He knew if he waited for EMTs and an ambulance, Tessa might not survive.

He leaned down and kissed her. Held her close. Felt what he thought was her trying to put her arms around him. Blood saturated his arms and shirt. "Don't worry, Baby," he said in a husky whisper. "I got you now. Nobody will ever hurt you again." He turned to the campus cop at the door. "How far is it to the University hospital?"

"About a ten-minute drive from here."

Majac picked Tessa up and carried her out the coffee shop door. Solomon helped Leona to her feet and followed.

"Sir, you can't." Although adamant, the cop did not stand in his way.

"Watch me."

"Sir, where are you going?" This was the campus cop who had earlier prevented him from entering the coffee shop. "You gotta wait for the ambulance. She might die if you don't."

"She'll definitely die if I do."

"Sir, please." He placed a hand on Majac's shoulder.

"Get off me," Majac growled and pulled away from the officer. There was no way he was going to let his bride-to-be lay dying on a cold tile floor when he still had the breath in his body to try to save her. He trudged through the lobby, out into the pouring rain toward his car.

Campus police followed in his wake, begged him to wait for an ambulance, urged him to stay until the professionals arrived to care for her.

Solomon and Leona followed Majac as he ignored the cop's pleas and pressed forward. When he reached his car, he gently laid Tessa in the front passenger seat, buckled her seatbelt and then jumped in without buckling his own. Solomon helped Leona into the back seat then slid in beside her. The only thing that mattered to Majac was getting Tessa to the hospital.

He was on campus, so travelling at speeds necessary for a seatbelt never crossed his mind.

As he put the Range Rover in gear, a campus cruiser pulled up and waved for him to follow. Lights flashed and sirens sounded as the two vehicles sped out of the parking lot and turned onto the campus's main thoroughfare. A sense of dread shot through Majac as he drove through the brown brick campus gate posts. As of its own compulsion, the car slowed a moment later as it passed the chapel. "Don't let her die, God." He blinked past tears and the headlights from the approaching car. Tessa's eyes danced behind closed lids. Tears etched valleys across her cheeks. Her small, brown face looked stressed, but alive. "Don't let her die."

Tessa coughed.

"Come on, Baby, you can do it."

She gasped. Coughed a few more times. Gulped in a breath of air.

"That's it, Baby. Stay with me." He gripped her hand tightly in his, thankful for the sign that she was still with him. "We're on our way to the hospital, Baby."

She opened her eyes into shallow slits. "I wanted to wait and tell you on our honeymoon," she said groggily then coughed four more times. "But I think it's better I tell you now."

"You don't have to tell me anything, Baby?" Majac said as tears streamed from his eyes. "Just rest. We'll be there soon."

Her eyes closed and her head fell limp again.

Shock appeared on Majac's face. He shook her arm trying to roust her again. "Stay with me, Baby. Wake up."

Tessa opened her eyes but didn't look at him.

"You will not die. Do you hear me?" Majac whispered as the police officer turned onto Huskie Boulevard. "We're getting married in two days. We're taking our honeymoon on that island with the black sand beaches and you're going to wear that little string bikini I bought you so every other man on the beach will be jealous when he sees you on my arm."

Tessa opened her eyes a bit wider. Strained to focus. "I...I..."

"Yes Baby, I'm right here." Anxious, Majac pounded on the steering wheel. He restrained from blowing his horn as he followed the slow-moving campus police car.

Tessa was quiet again. In the back, Solomon sat quietly holding Leona.

As they entered the north side of campus, the sun peeked through the clouds onto the rows of sugar maples in full bloom that lined nearly every street of center campus. Students dodged raindrops, hurrying down the shaded, rolling hills of tender grass to seek shelter at the soccer stadium on their right or the mammoth library on their left.

"I'm…pregnant…Anton." A cheer rose from the soccer stadium like water spewing from a geyser and startled her awake. "We're…having a…baby."

"A baby?" Majac gasped. His tears went from a dripping faucet to a running shower. "Come on move," he shouted, slamming the horn and drawing beside the speeding police car on the two-lane road. "I love you," Majac said. A hundred yards ahead, a car was approaching. Majac slowed, fell back behind the police car when the officer waved him off and whispered to himself, "We're having a baby."

Thirty yards ahead of him, a bicyclist wearing noise-cancelling headphones, hopped the curb and swerved into the intersection without looking. The cop slammed on his brakes, swerved to the left and skidded to a stop mere inches from the cyclist who had only seen the police car a second before it almost hit him. Less than a small girl's foot separated the cyclist from being a hood ornament on squad car 219.

Majac caught the police cars' brake lights in the corner of his eye, turned his gaze away from Tessa and slammed on his brakes. His Range Rover skidded on the wet street. In the brief interval between cussing at the cop for driving too slowly and looking happily at the woman who told him she was carrying his child, his nightmare shifted from bad to worse. Like the bullet stuck in his shoulder, his predicament stabbed him hard. Rain was falling; he was concentrating on Tessa; they were exceeding the campus speed limit; and, the cyclist wasn't paying attention, Majac could do nothing but watch as his car skidded on the cobblestone road and slammed into back of the police car.

The sound of crushing metal filled the air. Tessa's airbag deployed and punched her in the face. Majac's airbag deployed; slamming him back into the driver's chair. His ears rang. His eyes shut. The silence returned.

When he woke, Majac left his keys in the ignition and pushed open the driver side door. Solomon and Leona were unconscious in the back seat. Majac staggered past the police car as the officer inside radioed in the report of an accident involving a police car in front of the Bernheimer building. He walked around the front of the police car and then back to his Range Rover. His shirt was covered with blood. His eyes were filled with tears. His face was drenched with sweat. But none of that mattered. All that mattered was that he got Tessa to the hospital. As he stumbled past the spot where his front bumper was welded to the police car's back bumper, his right leg failed him and he stumbled onto the trunk of the police car. He regarded Tessa. Her eyes were still closed. He gathered himself, pushed up off the police car, and started to walk, determined to get to his fiancé.

A crowd of bystanders who had witnessed the accident started to gather on the campus street, pulling out their phones to take pics and video.

After checking that the cyclist was unharmed, the policemen rushed to the rear of his patrol car where he stopped to look at the damage created where the two vehicles collided.

Majac strained to look over the Range Rover hood and into the car. He willed Tessa to wake up and look at him. He roared with determination as he journeyed those last five steps to the passenger door. "Don't worry, Baby, I'm coming. You're going to be all right." He coughed, reached the door and yanked on the handle. The door didn't open. He yanked again. Still it didn't open. He looked at the door unlock button on the dashboard and yelled for Tessa to wake up and press it. Half crying, half laughing and completely exhausted, Majac yanked on the door handle a dozen times as he tilted his head to the sky and shouted, "Nooooooo!!!'

The sound of a man in agony shifted the police officer's attention away from the crash site.

Majac stopped shouting. Angry, exhausted, and bleeding from a gunshot wound to the shoulder, he whispered, "I love you," in a barely audible voice. He dropped his head against the windowpane, put his hand on the window and closed his eyes on the way down. Everything went dark, as Majac blacked out before the officer could reach his side.

While Majac drove, police and emergency rescue personnel crowded the frenzied crime scene in the coffee shop back at the student union building. The Army vet sat on a stool next to the body of a slain campus police officer. He stared at the dry rivulets of blood that ran along the man's face. He was lost in his own separate reality. His eyes glazed over. His mind drifted toward the darkness of his past. He thought that if he looked hard enough, the answers would all curl out through the officer's bloodstained cheeks. That his ghosts would whisper an explanation in his ear and tell him why he too hadn't died.

After answering a barrage of questions from Seattle police, EMTs sat him on a gurney and took him to an ambulance. He was conscious, responsive, and he asked several times about the woman in the green dress. The EMT evaluated him for almost fifteen minutes then placed a cold compress on the back of his head and told him to sit back and rest. He'd be all right.

The Army Veteran was tough. He thought about how if Vietnam couldn't kill him, what made two street punks think they could? "What happened to the woman in the green dress?" the vet insisted.

"I don't know, sir. I didn't see her." The EMT answered a call on the radio. "I need to go help my partner," he told the vet before leaving him alone in the ambulance.

When he was certain that nobody was paying him any attention, the Army vet stuck the compress in his pocket, rifled through the ambulance for some painkillers, since the EMT hadn't given him any, quietly opened the back door of the ambulance. Accustomed to the disapproving stares— stares that no longer bothered him as long as no one hit or harassed him— he kept to himself. He ignored the students who had probably never noticed him on campus before and, as was usual in his daily routine, walked away from campus unnoticed.

33

Stop the World

AMBULANCES ARRIVED TWENTY MINUTES LATER. They took Majac, Tessa, Solomon and Leona to an off-campus hospital. Flight plans would have to be cancelled. Wedding plans would have to be put on hold. But first, phone calls would have to be made.

The police officer who had been escorting them, retrieved Majac's wallet and found his military ID. Through a series of phone calls, he eventually got Majac's Executive Officer on the line. From his familiarity with his commanding officer and their meeting at Majac's bachelor party, the XO instructed the police to call Jaz Stevenson.

When his phone rang, Jaz had just entered his family home where Crystal and the girls were busily gathering books and digital tablets to occupy themselves during the trip to Pennsylvania. "Yes, this is Jared Stevenson," Jaz said, answering the call from the unknown caller ID. His jaw dropped when the voice on the other end of the line explained that Commander Charles had been shot. For a minute he stood silent, mouth agape, then finally recovered when he heard Crystal call his name. It was the third time she'd called him.

"Jared," she said again, "What's wrong?"

Jaz dropped his cell phone into his blazer pocket. "Majac's been..." He paused, unable to say the word. "He's...This can't be happening."

"He's what?" Crystal asked, zipping shut her daughter's backpack. "Please don't tell me he's gotten cold feet? I will kill that boy!"

"No, he's been...shot?" Jaz was stunned. "He's at the hospital."

"He's what?" Crystal asked. She stopped packing and shifted her complete focus to her husband.

"We gotta go," Jaz said.

"Where?" Now scared for her husband, Crystal dropped the backpack on the floor and stood directly in front of Jaz. "Jared Stevenson, you need to talk to me. What is going on?"

Jaz blinked a hundred times. "That was the police. He said there was a shooting at the University and Majac was shot. He's alive but unconscious and they took him to Northwest Medical Center."

"Oh my God," Crystal exasperated. "We gotta call Tessa."

"Tessa was with him. She's been shot too."

Crystal's eyes flooded with tears. They hugged each other, exchanging phrases of *Oh my God, what happened* and *let's get out of here* before Crystal snapped into action and ordered the girls to grab their backpacks and get into her car. Her mind was in panic mode, not Mommy mode, making her words to her girls sound harsher than she intended.

"Jared, lock the front door," she ordered as she grabbed her purse from the hall table. "Oh my God," she said pulling her phone from her purse, "Oh my God. I need to call Leona."

"Leona...Pearson?" Jaz asked in a stunned tone.

"Yeah," she said. "She's the only family Tessa has out here."

"Fine," he said calmly. "You call her. I'll drive."

~~~

While Jaz drove, Crystal called the hospital to find out what she could. After being informed that there were four of them brought in together, Crystal submerged into a trauma induced stupor. As Jaz sped north, shaking Crystal back into reality as he weaved through traffic on the I-5. Once she regained her bearings, she called and informed Jennifer Fleming.

When Jennifer hung up, her first call was to Luke. She told him that she needed a favor. Then she called home. She told her housekeeper she was going to the hospital and to make sure Ayrikah ate dinner and studied for her Spanish exam. She called Micah into her office and told him that she was going to the hospital so he'd need to cancel his plans for the evening because she needed him to close up.

As midnight approached, Jaz, Crystal and Jennifer Fleming sat huddled together in a private room at the Northwest Hospital and Medical Center waiting to hear about Tessa's status. Based on the wall clock, she'd been in surgery for almost nine hours.

Crystal, unsure of what to do next and hating hospitals, commented about the uncomfortable temperature in the room. "Why do hospital rooms have to always be so cold?" she said to no one in particular.

Jennifer suggested she find a nurse and see if they could turn up the temperature. Before she could respond, a man wearing a white lab coat entered the room and said, "Anyone here for Tessa Ajai?"

"I'm her sister." Jennifer shifted close to Crystal and grabbed her hand.

"I'm Doctor Cassellas," the man said, "Your sister's sleeping right now and on her way up to the ICU. She lost a lot of blood before we could remove both bullets. She is out of surgery, but she's not quite out of the woods yet. She's probably going to be in intensive care for quite a while."

"And her recovery?" Jennifer asked.

"Like I said, she's not yet out of the woods."

Tears of frustration, grief and relief streaked the women's faces.

Doctor Cassellas paused for a moment to let the women digest his words. He knew they needed a couple of minutes to decompress from the shock of the tragedy before he gave them any bad news. "Her vitals are good and she seems to be extremely healthy. She should have no problem making a full recovery."

That note of concern struck a chord with Crystal. Doctors never overemphasize the good news about a situation unless bad news follows.

"So what's the bad news?" Crystal asked forcefully.

Jennifer winced as Crystal squeezed her hand tighter..

"Nothing we can confirm while she's still asleep," he said.

"Right now, we're more concerned about infection. We'll be able to better evaluate her when she wakes up."

"And when do you expect that to be?"

"Like I said," Doctor Cassellas reaffirmed, "right now she needs to rest and let her body heal. We'll let time run its course and go from there. Once she's settled in the ICU, I'll go back and check on her."

"When can we see her?" Jennifer asked anxiously.

"She's going to be asleep for a couple more hours while the anesthesia wears off. After that, it will just be a matter of time until she wakes up on her own. There's really no reason for you to sit around here and wait."

"Well we can't just go home and do nothing with her in ICU," Jennifer barked. She had always been protective of her Leona. Although Tessa wasn't her blood-sister, that maternal instinct transferred with a vengeance. "Her mother is the only other family she has, and she is in Pennsylvania, so we're not going anywhere until she wakes up or her mother gets here."

Doctor Cassellas knew how emotional times like this could be. He said, "If you would like to see your sister, I can let you see her for a few minutes, but keep it short. She needs her rest. She is sedated and very weak, so she most likely won't know you're there."

"Thank you Doctor," Jennifer said.

"A nurse will come get you and take you to her room after I've had a chance to check on her."

After exchanging a moment of silent stares with the doctor, Jennifer asked, "What can you tell me about my other sister, Leona Pearson?"

The doctor checked three other patient folders before he came to hers. "Looks like she's going to be just fine. Says here she had a concussion, a lacerated ear which we sewed up and a couple of bruised ribs. Oh."

"Oh what?"

"What we've learned since she woke up is that her kidney is not functioning properly. Her chart shows she only has her left. How long ago did she lose her other kidney?"

"About ten years ago," Jennifer answered.

"That's promising," the doctor said. "That means it is strong."

"But?" Jennifer said sharply.

"We have her on antibiotics and we'll see how things go over the next twenty-four hours; but unless things change drastically, she will most likely need a kidney replacement."

"Most likely?" Jennifer asked.

"Yes ma'am. Tests and time will determine what happens next. But for now, we wait."

"Then for now, we can go see her."

"Not tonight I'm afraid. Visiting hours are over for the evening."

"Well, our parents are dead and I'm her big sister, so you better send a nurse in here to take me to her room, or my husband, Senator Luke Fleming will be having this hospital president's head for breakfast." Jennifer never pulled the Luke card, but for the first time in a hundred years, she felt it necessary.

Upon Jennifer's insistence, Luke Fleming made a series of phone calls. At 7am Friday morning, a man knocked on Momma Charles' front door shortly after dawn. He had a long face and a French-vanilla complexion. His nose was broad and flat, and his eyes were round like the orbs on an animated forest creature. Standing tall in a black suit and cap, the driver introduced himself to Angel who welcomed him inside where Momma Charles anxiously awaited his arrival.

Crystal had called Majac's sister just before midnight east coast time and told Angel what happened. At the same time, Jennifer called Tessa's mother. The driver put their luggage in the trunk then helped Momma Charles in the car while Angel locked up. Twelve minutes later that same process repeated at the house where Tessa lived as a child with her mom, Mabel Ajai. Having gathered his charges, the oddly handsome chauffeur drove to the Tuskegee Executive airport where a private jet awaited.

A magnificent sun crested over Mount Rainier late that Friday morning as the Seattle Knight's private jet landed at King County International Airport carrying Tessa's Mama Mabel, Angel, and Momma Charles. Jaz and Crystal sat on the tarmac in a limousine chauffeured by Luke's personal driver, waiting to escort them to the hospital. Luke's secretary reserved luxury suites at the Chambered Nautilus Bed and Breakfast Inn. At the hospital, the driver handed Angel his business card and told her to call when she was ready to go. He departed the hospital, and took their luggage to the hotel situated ten minutes away.

It was past noon when Jaz and Crystal escorted the trio of women up to the seventh floor. The family waiting room was a comfortable suite furnished with three love seats and two recliners, a mini-fridge, microwave, a 55-inch television and a brown bookshelf stacked with three shelves full of books, magazines and board games.

When they entered, everyone appeared to be praying. Mabel took a broad sweep of the room and noticed a handsome, silver-haired man in a business suit sitting alone in the corner. Although she'd never been to Seattle before, he looked familiar. His head was down; a cell phone was in his hand. His lips barely moved. His eyes looked closed. She couldn't tell if he was praying or talking on the phone.

Jaz cleared his throat to gain everyone's attention. Crystal introduced Angel and the mothers to Leona's sister Jennifer and Jennifer's husband Luke. After the introductions, Jennifer hugged the women from Tuskegee, holding onto Mama Ajai like she'd die if she let go.

That's it, Mabel thought staring over Jennifer's shoulder. *Senator Luke Fleming.* Mabel was an avid watcher of the political news channels and she knew she recognized the man in the corner's face because she'd seen him several times either talking to reporters at the Capital building or on the Senate floor. When Jennifer released her, she snapped out of her celebrity realization moment and asked, "Where's my baby?"

$$\rightarrowtail$$

Majac awakened to sunshine beaming through his room window. Tired and groggy, he looked around trying to figure out where he was. His skin was flushed red with the trauma of surgery, waves of color moving over his face and neck. All sorts of medical equipment surrounded his bed. There was an IV tube in his right arm and from the looks of the almost empty bag hanging from the metal pole, the nurse would be in soon to change it. The other bed in the two-person room was empty. Luke had made a phone call to the hospital president and arranged the private, two-bed room for Majac and Tessa. As soon as she was released from the ICU, she would join her fiancée.

A throaty snore from the other side of the bed disturbed the silence. He drew his focus away from the window and turned toward the right where he caught sight of two large feet in black socks resting on the end of his bed. After retrieving the family from the airport, Jaz came to Majac's room and was now sound asleep, snoring loudly, in the bedside chair.

Majac's throat was dry and scratchy. He strained to form the words, "Hey Man, get them big dogs off my bed." When Jaz didn't move, Majac slowly moved his left leg and pushed Jaz's feet off the bed.

The sudden movement of his feet crashing to the floor startled Jaz into consciousness and his eyes popped open when his feet hit the floor. "Good morning Partna," Jaz grumbled. He shifted into a sitting instead of laying position. "About time your lazy butt woke up."

"Hey," Majac said weakly. His eyes, clear and bright with thought, slowly scanned the serenely calm, white-walled, sterile-looking room. Then, as the memory of the coffee shop set in, panic encouraged him to try to sit up. "Uggh!" he gasped, falling back on the mattress.

Jaz stood and placed a hand on his chest. He looked in his eyes and told him, "Calm down Partna. You ain't ready to run just yet."

Majac loved Jaz like a brother, perhaps mostly because there had never been any type of rivalry between them, just pure unadulterated friendship. Meeting in grade school and practically growing up together, they rarely competed when it came to sports, girls or anything else. Despite being king of Hammond High, Jaz's status as the school superstar never interfered with their friendship. When it came to Majac, Jaz never played the *I'm a superstar so I'm better than you* card. No matter the situation, they'd always been able to talk about any- and every-thing. Despite his territorial issues or rivalries with others who may have had issue with his celebrity, Jaz had always been down to earth when it came to Majac.

"Where's Tessa?" Majac demanded.

"Tessa is up in the ICU. She came out of surgery last night, but she hasn't woken up yet."

"I need to go...Uggh,'" Majac winced as he attempted to sit up again.

"You need to lay right there and relax. The doctor said he'd come get us as soon as she wakes up. Right now, we're all just waiting. I know you love her, but for now all any of us can do is wait."

"I need to see her," Majac demanded.

"All right," Jaz said. "I'll go let the nurse know you're awake."

"Thanks, Bruh." Majac nodded his head, felt the pain in his movement, and swallowed painfully; realizing that sitting up on his own was too much to bear. He closed his eyes and a tear streamed down his swollen cheek.

Jaz wiped away Majac's tear, clasped his friend's hand and then left the room. When it was only the two of them, friends since they were snot-nosed kids, Majac and Jaz truly were brothers to the core. There in that hospital room, with Majac laid up, unable to move, nothing had changed.

By dinnertime Friday, his medications had subdued the pain enough to help Majac move from the bed to a wheelchair. Accompanied by his Momma and his about-to-be Mama-in-law, Mabel Ajai, Majac sat as Jaz wheeled him up to the ICU where Tessa lay sleeping. He parked Majac at her bedside then waited outside the door with the mothers.

Alone in the room, the door closed behind him and the rest of her visitors either out in the hallway or downstairs, the desperation to hold Tessa in his arms enveloped him like a heavy wool blanket. He wanted to hold her and pull her to his chest. At that instant, everything he knew to be real was gone. He held her hand, closed his eyes and wanted his dreams of her to be real. He wanted things to be normal again.

"Look at us," Majac said, his head on her bed. "Three thousand miles away and almost twenty years from that skating rink and I'm still here trying to pick you up."

In the summer of high sophomore year, Majac copied Tessa's address on a piece of paper, put it in his pocket and smiled at her broadly. "Have a good night ladies," he said as the two girls walked away. On his day off a week later, Majac knocked on Tessa's door.

"Hello, my name is Anton Charles," he began, figuring that the woman who opened the door must be Tessa's mother. Her suspicious uncharitable gaze so penetrating, Majac feared that she knew about the sex dreams her daughter had inspired. He was a cocky, six-foot teenage basketball player and this squat, brown-skinned little woman who opened the door had him squirming. "I'm a friend of Tessa's," he spat quickly. The lie relaxed him.

"Tessa," Mabel Ajai called stepping back. To Majac's surprise and relief, she moved away from the door, allowing him entrance into the small, narrow house. She did not invite him to sit down on the plastic covered furniture in the living room. The house smelled of cigarette smoke, incense and brownies. He wondered who smoked as the short woman glaring at him called for Tessa a second time.

Majac heard footsteps on the stairs, and then, there she was in tight cutoff jeans and a halter top. Her hair was in rollers, but Majac thought she looked beautiful. For a moment, a brief flicker of excitement bloomed in her eyes, then she quickly blinked it away as her mother inquisitively looked back and forth from her to the boy, trying to figure out what was going on and who was this strange boy. Tessa knew right then, standing in her mother's foyer, that he would be the man she would eventually marry.

"Hi," he said softly.

"Hi." Tessa turned to her mother and raised her eyebrows, dismissing the elder Ajai with a glance.

Mrs. Ajai folded her arms and rolled her eyes with a 'This is my house' look. Raised eyebrows accompanied a verbal "What?" that said she wasn't going anywhere.

"Sorry to barge in like this Mrs. Ajai," Majac interjected, trying to break the tension, "But...well..."

"Let's go outside," Tessa interjected, taking Majac by the arm.

"Outside?" Her mother's eyes shifted to her daughter's hair rollers.

"Yeah, outside," Tessa cooed, sweeping past her mother into the kitchen and opening the back door. The back porch was small, but big enough to hold a wrought iron table set with two chairs. Majac sat down beside Tessa. Flowered cushions shielded them from the hot iron, heated by the eighty-five-degree day.

"I wanted to make sure that you got home all right."

"And yet you waited a week to find out." It was a statement more than a question.

He had never met a girl younger than him who seemed so comfortable in her own skin. Her calm demeanor left him nervous, anxious and at the same time excited about how mysterious she was.

"Are you all right?" she asked.

"I don't know about you, but knocking on your door was the hardest thing I think I've ever done." Majac blew what seemed like frigid air into the summer afternoon heat.

Tessa tucked her bare feet under her legs on the cushion. Her olive-toned skin was burnished by a slight tan. He noticed a mole just below her left ear. She said nothing about how he had just shown up at her door unannounced. She just sat beside Majac as if they already knew everything of importance about each other. "And now you're here."

"I'll leave if..."

"So, you might as well stay and keep me company," she continued without regard to whatever he planned to say next.

"I don't remember ever seeing you there before," fumbled out of his mouth a beat later when he realized that she wasn't kicking him out.

"I'd never been," she said. "My girlfriend heard it was a fun place to be on Saturday night. It was her idea to go."

"And did you have a good time skating?"

"It was all right," she shrugged. "Never as good as you hope it'll be."

"Then you should go every week until it is." he beamed. "Once you become a regular, you'll love it."

"Every week...?" She laughed as though the idea was ridiculous. "I don't know that my feet could handle all that skating." Her eyes went wide with a slow, sly assessment of him that silenced them both. Then she asked, "How long have you worked at Skate World?"

"Two years."

"Do you like it?"

"Yeah. Yeah, I like it. Especially on Saturday nights when pretty new girls decide to show up," he joked, surprising himself with the subtlety of the humor. It was new to him, but he liked the way he felt afterward.

"Do you always do stuff like this? I mean, track girls down." Tessa placed a foot on the edge of her chair, hugged her knee and stared at Majac the way she looked at him a week ago when he helped her up off the floor after she'd fallen for the fifth time.

"Believe me, this is the first time I've ever done anything like this." Now he was sweating profusely—partly from the heat, partly from anxiety. "Sitting here with you is blowing my mind."

Tessa stared at Majac, trying to decide if he was a deranged serial killer who put on the skater uniform on a Saturday night trolling for unsuspecting victims, or actually, just a boy with a serious jones for her.

"You know my name, but I don't know yours," she said.

"Anton. Anton Charles. And, I owe you an apology." He hoped this new strategy would get him off the hook and speed things up.

Shading her eyes from the glare of the sun with her long, red fingernails, Tessa gave Majac one last look that took in everything about him she could see and everything she expected. "I'm hungry," she said. "Do you want to take me to get something to eat?"

"Sure," he said anxiously. He knew that she knew his response was way too fast to be considered cool. But even though he knew that she knew, she didn't show it. "Um, but not like that right?"

"What?" she grinned. "You can't eat with a barefoot girl?"

Majac was speechless. The girl with the rollers in her hair was mad cool. And he liked it.

"No, silly," she laughed. "Let me change then we'll go."

Twenty minutes later, Tessa came out of the house wearing big, dark sunglasses and a petite, yellow, sleeveless sundress with navy blue flowers that flowed innocently over every curve of her body. The rollers were long gone and her auburn hair was pulled back in a bun. Her mother watched out the window as Majac and Tessa walked away. "What would you have done if I wasn't home?" Tessa asked after buckling her seatbelt.

"Kept coming back until you were."

Tessa laughed. The sound was light and uninhibited. She removed her sunglasses and stared at Majac again. Her hazel eyes now gazing at him, were a crystal ball that revealed the real meaning of why she hated the other boys who had previously courted her; how she had just been marking time, stalling, waiting, for this. Waiting for him. It was as though it finally hit her what she had done and she was holding this thought in her mind, measuring it to gauge the full weight of why she was sitting in his car beside him. Tessa put her sunglasses on and stared straight ahead. Majac reached over and touched her hand. Without looking at him, she entwined her fingers in his.

When Majac opened his eyes, all of those memories were snuffed out by the truth of tubes and machines controlling her breathing and monitoring her heartbeat. He kissed her hand. Pressed it against his face. Hard sobs racked his body as he cried for the love of his life to wake up.

"Your mom's here. She can't wait to see your pretty eyes." When that didn't gain a response, he planted a kiss on her forehead and spent the next twenty minutes explaining to his sleeping fiancée everything he wanted them to do on their honeymoon. "Please wake up for me real soon because I miss your smile." He finished with, "You are loved, Baby Doll. Our friends, our moms and our sisters are all here waiting for you to wake up."

Smiling, he looked at Tessa's sleeping face and said, "You're my girl. You've always been my girl. And I'm your man. You're still here. I'm still here. This is us. After all we've been through since high school, we're still going strong. I love you and I'll be waiting right here when you wake up. I need you to let go of whatever is keeping you asleep and come on back to me so we can go get married and spend the rest of our lives together. We've come too far, Baby, to let some stupid bullets keep us from our happily ever after. Okay? All right? Just come back to me, Baby." When his pain returned to the point of being unbearable, he gave her another kiss and motioned to Jaz, who, wheeled him out of her room, out into the hallway and down to the family waiting room.

As visiting hours ended Friday night, the Stevensons, Charles', Jennifer Fleming, and Mabel Ajai approached the end of the first 24 hours spent in the Northwest hospital waiting room. Tessa's surgery had taken nine hours; Majac's only four. He had awakened almost 12 hours earlier. Her breathing machine removed; Tessa was breathing on her own but was still unconscious.

Saturday morning came. Majac and Tessa's wedding day had arrived. Their wedding party should have been primping to watch their friends walk down the aisle and jump the broom. But instead, they'd all spend the day taking turns visiting their still unconscious friend, sister and daughter. Until she woke up, the wedding was the last thing on their minds.

All except Luke, that is. He'd left the hospital at the end of visiting hours Friday night with Jennifer's explicit orders to go home with Ayrikah and make certain she got up and off to volunteer at the nursing home Saturday morning. As soon as he dropped their daughter off, he'd be on his way to his office and the business of catching up on whatever state politics he missed while sequestered under his wife's guard at the hospital Friday.

$$\rightleftharpoons$$

After breakfast Saturday morning, Jennifer had Luke's chauffeur drive her to the bed and breakfast to retrieve Momma Charles, Mama Ajai and Angel. Crys Stevenson was sitting with Vivienne and Solomon Alexandré when they arrived. Jaz had gone to visit with Majac. Once settled in the family suite, Mama Ajai blurted out, "Somebody please turn on the news."

Crystal picked up the remote from the table next to her and instinctively turned the channel to the station where she worked, KABC.

"No Sweetie," Mabel insisted, "I wanted to watch the national news."

Before Crystal could change the channel, Jennifer wheeled Leona into the room and stopped her wheelchair at the sofa next to them. "Miss Mabel, Missus Charles, I'd like to you meet my sister Leona." Tessa and Majac's mothers took turns hugging Leona, whose eyes were glued on Solomon, as the women peppered her with questions about how she felt..

In the three years following his wife Mareschelle's death, Solomon had sparingly dated. His haphazard time with Jordyn, along with the dozen or so meaningless dates with other women, helped him realize that he was definitely a one-woman man. Things with Leona seemed right. Time spent with her felt genuine. For the longest time following Schelle's death, he felt guilty spending time with other women. The months he'd spent with Leona did not make him feel that way.

Lawrence used his clergy privilege and visited Friday morning before normal visiting hours began. Solomon bared his soul to his long-time friend and pastor, and after their hours-long conversation he knew his heart was in the right place.

Before Lawrence left Solomon's room, Kenny called to say he was going to pick up Vivienne and bring her when he came. While he awaited their arrival, Solomon called Désirée. He informed her of Thursday's tragedy and she replied that she was closing the office and heading to the hospital. In turn, he asked her to run a special errand on her way.

Once he'd heard more than he cared to remember about that terrible morning, Solomon stood and said in a commanding voice, "Excuse me everybody." He walked toward Leona. All eyes turned in his direction and the chatter dulled to a murmur. They all seemed to release a collective gasp when Solomon dropped to one knee in front of Leona's wheelchair and removed a velvet box from his pocket. "Leona Pearson, you are a treasure and I absolutely love you." His Cheshire cat grin immediately brought her to tears. "I can't bear the thought that I almost lost you. This is not the way or place I wanted to ask, but I can't let another day go by. Will you...?"

Before he could continue, Leona shoved her hand at him. "Yes...Yes!"

The rest of Solomon's speech was short, sweet and elicited the intended effect. When he finished, every woman in the room was crying.

Lost in the excitement of Leona joining the fray was Crystal never changing the channel. "Hey, everybody be quiet." Amidst the commotion of celebrating Solomon's proposal, Jennifer noticed a familiar image on the TV. "Turn it up Crystal, they're talking about the shooting."

As video from the coffee shop played, they all listened intently to the news anchor report that police were looking for the unknown hero who, after fighting off the shooters at the University café, disappeared before police could interview him.

Leona smile at the memory of seeing her father face-to-face.

"The police have this sketch of the man," the reporter said, "but do not know his name." In the upper corner of the TV screen was an exploded video still of the man wearing an army jacket. "Anyone who might know his name or whereabouts," the reporter continued, "please call the police at the number on the bottom of your screen."

"Oh my God," Jennifer said, breaking the silence in the room.

"What's wrong, Baby?" Vivienne, who had been engrossed by her cell phone, looked up at the TV for the first time. Her gaze landed on the familiar image of the nameless man on the television screen.

"That can't be him," Jennifer said.

Vivienne gasped. In that split second, she mentally shaved the scruffy beard from the man's face. Beneath the dreadlocks and scraggily exterior, he was as dashing as she had remembered. She stared at the television wide-eyed, and remembered the nameless man—their past, a distant, long-forgotten memory. "That looks like..." Vivienne said, turning to Jennifer.

"Like Leona's daddy," Jennifer said, finishing Vivienne's sentence.

"Really?" Vivienne asked, her head tilted back away from Jennifer.

Leona stared at the TV like it was the first time she'd ever seen a television. In a little girl's dreamy voice, she said, "My Daddy's a Hero."

34

Awakenings

"CAN YOU WALK WITH ME, Missus Senator Lady?" Vivienne stood and took Jennifer's hand. "I need a cup of coffee." Downstairs in the hospital cafeteria they each bought coffee. Vivienne added a banana and a bowl of oatmeal. Jennifer a sausage, egg and cheese croissant.

"Ummph," Viv looked at Jennifer's breakfast. "A sandwich like that would have my blood sugar screaming."

"Mine too," Jennifer replied. "But my nerves are about shot and as much as I know I shouldn't have it; I need it right now."

"Hell girl," Viv said putting back the oatmeal and picking up the same sandwich as Jennifer. "I need it too."

"And hell," Jennifer said. "if it sends us into shock, we're already at the hospital." The women shared a laugh, paid for their food and sat down.

"This ain't fair," Jennifer said. "We are supposed to be enjoying a wedding today, not stuck up in some hospital as Tessa fights for her life."

"I know," Viv Alexandré said, placing her hand on top of Jennifer's. "All we can do is pray and put it in God's hands."

"I need God to put his hands on the men who shot my…well…sister."

"They said grace and Jennifer started eating.

"Jennifer," Viv said. "Back when your mother and I were young, you had to get a blood test before you got married. Do you remember that?"

"Yes, Lord," Jennifer said. "I did too. And I hate needles."

"Well they don't require that anymore. I wonder why they stopped?"

"Just like everything else, Honey…budget cuts. Girl you know how tight things are these days. Luke talks about budget cuts all the time."

"Well, I think we should talk to the kids about having a blood test."

"Who exactly do you mean by kids?" Jennifer frowned at the insinuation in Viv's suggestion. She chewed her food slowly as she sorted her words. "I am sorry ma'am. I know we haven't known each other long," Jennifer started. Her voice now icy and stern. "And this whole shooting thing has a lot on all of our minds. I don't know what you're thinking about my sister, but I'm going to go real slow right now and ask you to explain yourself before I get upset and get real nasty in here."

Viv Alexandré took a deep swig of her coffee. She took a bite of her sandwich, just to taste it; in case she didn't get to finish eating it once their talk was through. She cleared her throat and took another swig of the coffee before she started talking. "How much do you know about the guy on the TV?"

"Are you talking about my stepfather, Mister Courtney?" Jennifer said.

"Yes, Baby." Although Viv was certain she had a good twenty years on Jennifer, she called her baby as a way of emphasizing her seniority and thereby demanding her respect. "What can you tell me about him."

"Do you know him?" Jennifer asked.

"I might," Viv replied. "He looked familiar. But I haven't seen the person I'm thinking of in a long time."

"It's been a long time since Leona and I have seen him too.

"What can you tell me about him or his family?"

"We didn't spend much time with his family. I remember going to a cookout where my mother got into a fight with his sister. We left early and after that we almost never went to any of his family functions."

"Did he only have the one sister?"

"If memory serves me, he had two sisters and a brother."

"What was his brother's name?"

"Everyone called him Mayfield. But I don't know his real name."

"Do you remember where his family lived?"

"Missus Alexandré, where are you going with all of this?"

"May I call you Jennifer?" Viv asked.

"Yes Ma'am."

"I've sat back and watched a whole lot happen this morning, Jennifer. I watched that pretty sister of yours come out and greet us after going through that hell at the school. I've watched my only child propose to a woman I barely know. I don't think he's brought her by the house a handful of times to sit with me. And he's never brought her to church. And to top it off, I think I just saw my brother-in-law on tv wanted by the police for questioning?"

"Your brother-in-law, who?." Now Jennifer was completely lost. She thought people Vivienne's age always took their husband's last name, unlike some more progressive women of today. "I never knew. I never heard different, so I just assumed." And like Leona, she assumed Alexandré was her married name, and if so, Courtney Franklin being her brother-in-law made no sense.

"My brother-in-law, Courtney Franklin. It's been years, but I know whose face I just saw." Her statement was matter of fact, not meant to be presumptive or callus. Viv Alexandré explained how things fell apart when Curtis said he was shipping out and couldn't tell her when he'd be back. How he left and never called nor wrote. How when she hadn't heard from him in two years, and the Army said he wasn't dead, she marched right down to City Hall the next Monday and filed for divorce.

"I changed back to my maiden name when I divorced his twin brother, Curtis 'Mayfield' Franklin. I couldn't stand that wastrel and I wasn't going to go through life carrying the name of a despicable, low-life, coward of a man like Mayfield. And, I changed my son's name because I didn't want him to carry that burden either." She picked up her coffee and mumbled, "Best thing I ever did was divorce that wastrel."

"Ohhhh wow." Jennifer leaned back in her chair as if the breath had been sucked out of her. Jennifer held up a hand as she continued. "If you don't mind me asking, when was the last time you saw Courtney?"

Viv took a bite of her sandwich and closed her eyes. "Shaking her head, she said, "It has to be twenty-five years since I've seen Courtney. Let me ask you girl, do you remember his momma's name?"

Jennifer thought for a moment before her eyes lit up with recognition. "Yes ma'am. I remember it because it was really unusual to me. Her name was ..."

"Toni Iris," Viv blurted out before Jennifer could finish.

Jennifer's eyes almost jumped out of the socket when she called her name. "That's right. Toni Iris," Jennifer confirmed. "I used to think that was the most beautiful name I'd ever heard."

Viv looked down at her plate and shook her head. "Well, Miss Senator Lady. Now that my fool of a son done went and proposed to his first cousin, I think we have a little bit of a problem to solve."

Jennifer uncharacteristically plopped her hands atop her head and exhaled deeply. She had seen the pure joy on Leona's face when Solomon dropped to one knee and proposed. Now, less than a half hour later, she couldn't imagine how could she go destroy her sister's happiness.

Vivienne and Jennifer finished their coffee and sandwiches in silence. When their food was finished, they sat holding hands, both knowing how unpredictable life could be. They both knew how easy it was to fall for a good-looking man who was capable of saying everything a young girl wanted to hear. Finally, Viv said, "Well, if we're going to tell these kids what we think we know, I'll need something a lot stronger than coffee!"

They laughed, despite them both knowing there would be no humor involved in revealing their newly shared knowledge.

Just then, Angel rushed into the cafeteria "Ms. Vivienne, Mrs. Fleming; Tessa's awake."

～

Doctor Cassellas beamed like a schoolgirl when he recognized Jaz in the waiting room. Jaz signed an autograph to help him refocus. Then the doctor asked, "Which of you is Mrs. Ajai?" He took from the smile on Mabel's face that she'd already heard the good news.

"When can I see her?" was Mabel's response.

"Soon," the doctor said. "Very soon. She just arrived in her room, and when they are finished settling her in, the nurse will come get you."

Tears flowing, Mabel walked to the doctor and hugged him tight.

He forced a smile and politely patted her on the back. "Mrs. Ajai," the doctor started. "Tessa is awake and stable for now, but there are a couple of things we need to talk about. Do you mind if we talk in private?"

"Everybody here is family, Doctor." Mama Mabel barked. "Say what you gotta say." Despite her tears, Mabel was surprised to hear herself speak in such a firm voice.

"All right then," he said. "That's the worst of that news for now."

"What does *that news* mean?" Leona asked forcefully.

"Umm, like I said she's very weak," Doctor Cassellas stammered. "Her body's been through a significant amount of trauma, but we expect her to make a full recovery."

"But *that news* is not the bad news, is it?" Jennifer asked impatiently.

"Spit it out, Doctor?" Mama Mabel said again in that firm voice. "We're all adults here."

"Yes, well, where the second bullet entered, it caused some severe hemorrhaging to her lower intestine and uterus. She lost a lot of blood during the operation, but we were able to stop the bleeding, and like I said, Ms. Ajai should recover fully. Unfortunately," Doctor Cassellas inhaled deeply, "we weren't able to save the baby."

"Excuse me," Leona shouted.

"Lord, have mercy, Jesus," Mama Mabel sobbed loudly. Her knees buckled and Jaz caught her before she hit the floor.

"Take the wheel, Jesus," Momma Charles said. "Take the wheel."

"I'm sorry, but the baby didn't make it. We couldn't stop the bleeding in time to save her. She was only ten weeks, and in her weakened state, the trauma was too big a battle for her."

Crystal and Jennifer wrapped their arms around Mama Mabel and guided her to the sofa. Her tears flowed and her sobs came loud and hard.

Majac shook the doctor's hand. "We know you did all you could doctor." His eyes were watery with unshed tears. "Thank you."

Majac's tears didn't fall until he saw his mother's. He wanted to say something, but sitting in that wheelchair listening to what was pouring out of the hearts of the two grandmothers—who now wouldn't be— was breaking his. He knew he needed to talk to Tessa, but he didn't know how to conjure the words to comfort her when he was hurting so deeply.

He got up from the wheelchair, kissed both of the beautiful mothers on top of their heads and sat between them. He wrapped his good arm around Mama Mabel, hoping he could squeeze into her all of the love he had for his fiancée and their now deceased child.

Majac winced when Momma Charles rested her head on his shoulder.

Mama Mabel turned to him, tears in her eyes, a smile on her face. "And just think," she paused, refocused and said, "I almost didn't let you in my house that first time you came chasing after my baby."

Majac kissed her on the forehead. Then they laughed, and sat, and cried together.

Momma Charles and Majac waited outside after escorting Mabel down to Majac and Tessa's room. When her daughter's head shifted toward her, Mabel's eyes immediately filled with tears. Her chest tingled with a silvery tightness. And just like that, her daughter was five years old again, aching to be held and comforted. Mabel took a deep breath and wiped her eyes. "Hi Baby."

Tessa lifted her head. A baby bird desperately lifting its beak for food. "Hi Mom." Her voice barely above a whisper.

Mabel sighed with relief when she heard her daughter's voice. In that moment, her stubbornness fell away. She stopped reminding herself that she had mocked her daughter's decision to move to Seattle. But now, her daughter's voice was like warm milk. And hearing it, made all of her defenses and justifications fall away. All of the rawness she'd harbored for Majac when Crystal called her with the news, faded into oblivion. Mabel hugged, kissed and talked to Tessa for almost twenty minutes before telling her, "That Boy is waiting outside to see you."

Despite her continued reluctance, Tessa's meek smile encouraged Mabel to return one of her own. She leaned down, hugged her daughter, kissed her face several times, then told her she'd be back soon before exiting the room.

Momma Mabel waited outside with Momma Charles as Majac entered.

"Hi, Baby," Majac said softly.

"Hi, Handsome," Tessa whispered.

"I've been waiting for you to wake up so I could tell you how much I love you." He said, tears falling without abandon.

"I love you too."

He lifted her arm from her side, careful not to disturb the long tube leading to her I.V. Tessa shifted painfully to make room for him to join her. He kissed her cheek, then laid his body next to hers on the narrow hospital bed. With some effort, and pain caused by his own injuries, he managed to pull her arm around his shoulder as if wrapping himself in a blanket. He buried his chin on her chest just beneath her collarbone. The hospital sheets and gown carried an antiseptic smell, but as he settled in against the curve of her body, her familiar scent of lavender came to him. Lying in Tessa's hospital bed, Majac pressed lingering kisses against his fiancée's cheek.

"Do you have any idea how much you've changed my life since you've come to Seattle?" he said. "Lying up in that hospital bed without you had me thinking back to how selfish I used to be. How you've dealt with me being so self-centered and stuck on making my career. I just want to thank you for being so wonderful and selfless.

"When I couldn't get you out of that car and everything went dark, I thought I would never see your face again. At that moment, I was convinced that no matter how hard I tried to do right, the worst was always meant to happen to me. All I could think about when the car crashed and your eyes went closed, was that if you died without waking up, I'd never get to tell you how much you touched my life. How you changed me in so many ways and that if I never got to look into your beautiful eyes again, I hoped that you could hear my voice, remember me and love me forever.

"But now that I have you back, I want you to know that I am going to give you every bit of the man I am and that I will never let anything come between us."

"Yeah," Tessa said. "I guess it has been a pretty rough road getting here."

"But now, all that's changed," he said. "The love of my life has come back to me. I know today was supposed to be our wedding day, but as soon as we're both cleared to get out of here, I will do whatever it takes to get us married as soon as possible."

Tessa smiled, craned her neck and kissed his forehead.

"Hell, everybody that matters is already here at the hospital, all we need is a preacher. I can have Jaz go down to the hospital chapel and bring the hospital preacher up here to marry us right now."

"I love you Anton Charles. I love you for life." In the tiny space that was Tessa's recovery room hospital bed, the two lovers laid wrapped in each other's arms sincerely pouring out their hearts.

A half hour later, Doctor Cassellas accompanied in the two mothers. "I'll give you all another ten minutes, then I need Ms. Ajai to try to get some rest."

When he stepped out, the mothers joined their children bedside. Momma Charles kissed Tessa and told her she was sorry about her grandbaby, but God had a plan and even though she might not know what it is, she was happy that Tessa was alive.

Majac told the mothers that he was staying until Tessa went to sleep. Then he was going to find the hospital chaplain, because it was their wedding day and they were having a wedding.

The four of them smiled, cried and laughed through a shower of tears. When they couldn't think of what else to ask, Tessa reached for her mother amidst a flood of tears. Majac stood from the bed, held his mother and wiped away the tears that started to fall the moment she started talking. Mama Mabel took his place at Tessa's bedside and comforted her child. Serenaded by their own crying, the quartet hugged, kissed and caressed each other until the nurse entered the room and asked them to step out so she could check on her patient.

35

Solo Once Again

BLOOD TESTS CONFIRMED THEIR KINSHIP. Solomon and Leona, the children of twin brothers Curtis and Courtney Franklin, sat solemnly as Jennifer Fleming and Vivienne revealed what they'd recently discovered about the coincidence of their shared mutual understanding of the twins. Their mother-figures spoke softly and showered them with consoling words, but nothing they said could soften the blow of those devastating test results. The foundation of their relationship had crumbled, broken, and fallen into an abyssal unknown. Solomon felt like the ground beneath him had broken and swallowed him whole. Numerous times throughout their relationship, they'd both thought that looking into each other's eyes was like looking into a mirror. They thought it was love. Now they knew different. Jennifer stood by Vivienne's side as she answered any and all family tree, blood test, paternity and fidelity questions asked by the newly revealed first cousins.

It was two weeks after the shooting before the doctor deemed Leona strong enough to undergo her kidney transplant. Jennifer couldn't donate hers because of her diabetes. Tessa offered to donate hers, but her blood type was incompatible. After a blood test confirmed their type match and a subsequent DNA test confirmed what her almost-mother-in-law had told them, Leona received a new kidney from her first cousin, and man she loved, Solomon Alexandré. Despite the success of the surgery, the kidney donation seemed like a consolation prize to being his wife, but in addition to his heart, she would now forever have another part of him inside her.

Jennifer, her daughter Ayrikah, and Solomon visited Leona every day until she was released. Instead of going home, she was pleased to find that Jennifer had retrieved linens from Leona's house, and redecorated the second guest suite at the Fleming's mansion for her use. Jennifer teleworked from home until Leona was cleared to return to work full-time.

That summer was probably the most miserable in Seattle history. Or at least in Solomon's memory. At first he visited Leona every day. As June turned into July, more visits became phone calls. By the end of July, he was down to calling twice a week. He vowed to Leona that he'd find her father. Despite the best efforts of everyone he knew in Seattle, nobody was able to locate his father's twin; his long-lost uncle; the man now known to him as Courtney Franklin.

⌁

Why is it that every time I see you, you are in a suit?" Leona asked Solomon as he greeted her and Jennifer with hugs on the sidewalk outside Woody's Bar and Grill. "I know you don't see patients on Friday, so can't you relax the dress code like the rest of the world. Geesh, if I didn't know you better, I might think you didn't know how to relax?"

"What? I like suits," Solo replied, striking a pose to impress her. "I like the way they make me look and I feel comfortable when I wear them."

"You LIKE the attention you get from all the ladies when you wear them," Leona chimed.

"I LIKE the attention I get from you when I wear them." It was a Friday night in late September and they were getting together with friends to celebrate Majac being reinstated to full duty as the Captain of his ship. "If you want to see my draws hanging out and my jeans sagging like those guys in the music videos, I could dress down, but that's not me. It's not my personality. It's not how I like to look."

"Since you put it that way, I like it too." The text message that vibrated her phone read that Majac and Tessa were already inside. "And that particular suit hangs very well on you," she said before she slid her arm inside his so that he could usher her inside.

Solomon accompanied Majac to the bar for drinks. Jennifer, Tessa and Leona stood near the hostess table chatting with Desmond, his arms flailing, as he pantomimed a memory in his normal kinetic storytelling fashion. Jennifer was pressed against Leona's right side, her arm on one of her shoulders. Tessa was on Leona's other side, her arm around Leona's waist. When Des finished, the women erupted in laughter.

Solomon's hovering waned since her release from the hospital, but he still watched Leona intently. He'd never heard her laugh so exuberantly. Jennifer and Tessa had reclaimed her and didn't have to promise her anything. Didn't offer her anything more than sisterly love, and she asked for nothing more in return. His delusion, prior to the shooting, was that Leona was to be his savior. In their new reality, he was hers.

Afterwards, Solomon and Leona, driving separately, followed Majac and Tessa back to the Hang Suite. Leona was going back to Solomon's to pack the couple of personal items and clothes he'd convinced her to leave there for when she stayed the night. It was her first time back there since leaving the hospital. Being inside his place knowing that she could now be there as his fiancée intimidated her. It was difficult leaving a place you've grown to love. The memories, sights and sounds contained in those rooms, within those walls, suddenly became haunting. She was just about overcome with tears.

"Hey Viv," he said into his phone as he headed into the kitchen.

"Tell Aunt Viv I said Hi," Leona called to his back.

She picked up a picture album from the coffee table in front of the fireplace. She'd given it to him for his birthday. She held it to her chest and a whiff of the smoky wood reminded her of one of the last nights they had sat there, flames flickering. Solomon on the floor at her feet. She in the oversized chair behind him. They had traded stories about travel. Him about a college trip with his boys to Cancun. Her about marching in a revolt in Malaysia. She heard echoes of her distant laughter as she collected things. She recalled the memory of the soft plop on her back during the pillow fight as they watched a boxing match. In the end, Leona socking it to Solo, causing him to lose his breath, his balance and the pillow fight.

"I didn't know you were that strong?" Solo said from the floor.

Leona knew. She saw the man she loved put himself under tremendous pressure trying to solve other people's problems. She felt like she had grown so much in their relationship. Although they were both professionals, adults with individual personalities, when it came down to bare facts, they were still nothing more than a man and a woman—in love.

"Why are you so hard on yourself?" she asked him one day while taking a walk down by the Sound.

"I don't think of it as being hard on myself. More like, I don't know... Driven."

"If you could wish for anything, and I mean anything, right now; what would it be?"

"Come on Leona, that's kid stuff."

"Are you too grown to wish?" she challenged. "Well, I'm not. And I truly hope that I never get that grown. Not when it comes to wishes." She stared at him until he blinked. "So, what would you wish for?"

He spoke without thinking. "I'd wish to be drafted by the Seattle Knights and play my entire NBA career in my hometown."

Leona stopped walking.

"What?" Solomon raised his eyebrows to her reaction.

"You'd waste a wish on that? Wow. I understand focus is one thing, Baby. But I figured you to be more creative than that."

"What would you wish for, Ms. Pearson?...Money?...Fame?"

"I'd wish for love."

"All women do."

"And every man should. Solomon, I'd wish that God would send me somebody to love me right. I'd wish for a love that made me melt from the inside out. That fairy tale, Princess and The Frog, forever kind of love"

Then Solomon reached down and grabbed a handful of violets. "Would you settle for some flowers from an admirer?"

"That's a start" she huffed and started to walk again. As he quick stepped to catch up with her, she continued. "When people realize what is important to them long after it is gone, their hearts shout out "WHY" after the loss. It's so weird sometimes to see someone special leaving your life. They never ever disappear in a poof. An evil trick being played out in life's spotlight. You see them leaving almost in slow-motion, inch-by-inch vanishing from your world. Or you see them behind shadows everywhere you go throughout your day. If you make eye contact, your heart shatters into a thousand imperfect pieces, with no curves or matching edges that allow you the opportunity to put it back together. They leave you thinking; What went wrong? Could I have stopped it? Why does it hurt so badly?"

Leona answered Solomon's doorbell to find Majac and Tessa standing on the porch. As Majac took her bag to the car, Leona walked to the kitchen, her heavy heart weighing on her shoulders like Atlas simultaneously carrying Mars, Jupiter and Saturn. Solomon was still on the phone with Aunt Viv, listening more than talking—as it always was.

"I'll call you back Ma," he said, hanging up without waiting for a reply and lowering the phone from his ear.

Leona saluted him from the doorway and laughed. "Well My Dark Knight, time for me to hit the trail."

"Call me when you get home."

"We'll talk."

"And don't be out there kissing no frogs."

Leona laughed out loud. Her smile lit up his entire world.

Solo laughed with her. He wasn't in a laughing mood, but if she could laugh, so would he.

She came to him, kissed him on the cheek, thumbed away the red smudge, then wrapped her arms around his neck in what could have almost been considered a choke hold for her squeezing so tightly. After a beat of silence and a long sigh, she whispered, "Nothing will ever stop me from loving your heart. You will always be my Superman. My Dark Knight." That time, she didn't wipe away the red lipstick.

It's odd or maybe funny how the older a person gets and they come to deal with loss or have to suffer the loss of a loved one, how reluctant they become to say goodbye to those that are still with them. They find themselves saying things like so long, see you later, good night, but rarely ever goodbye. Leona hadn't said goodbye.

Solomon stood framed by the front door, with the phone by his side, tears washing down his face as his two new first cousins, Leona Pearson and Tessa Charles drove away.

Silence filled the Hang Suite. It was almost eleven that night when Solomon closed the door and stepped back into his space. The space that had been changed by another's scent, another's laughter, another's hopes and dreams living within the walls. And now, with the elements of another gone, the makeup of the space changed once again. But not back to the original state—oh no, not hardly. The original state for Solomon could never be restored. Never be regained. And without her, he thought, there was no desire for it to return. In that solitary moment he suffered the realization of what was now missing; her image, her scent, and especially her voice. Her soft laugh falling away. So real, yet so elusive. After the anticipation of almost a year of courtship, he now realized that he once again no longer had someone to share his life with. Someone to share... the ups and the downs, the whatever days. It was the body of a woman lying next to him at night. A body with skin that was soft to the touch; that yielded to his fancy. It was an open ear waiting to be filled, never tiring of hearing about his intense thrill of his best days, the lonesome depths of his worse days and the boring mediocrity of his normal. With one pull of a trigger, all of that was taken away from him.

At times, we are all insecure in one way or another. All vulnerable. Vulnerability is nothing but a gap in the spirit. Someone else can fill that gap, but only if you let them. And only for as long as you let them. For a fleeting moment, Leona filled that gap for Solomon. And that moment changed his life. Same way the cheerleader and sorority girl, Mareschelle Betancourt, had changed his life years ago back in college.

He had twice fallen head over heels for a woman. Twice experienced what he thought was true love. Once fulfilling that love all the way to the altar and six years beyond. This time, only forging forward as far as a proposal. Now that Solo was once again hopelessly single, he had to rethink things. His future. His career. His inept ability to keep and protect the woman he loved.

36

Sea No More

MAJAC WAS RELEGATED TO THE Physically Unable to Perform list through the Fourth of July. While his arm was in a sling, he rode a desk at a Squadron building at the base. Returning to his ship, even though it wasn't going out to sea, would wait. His XO called daily to update him about the ship and stopped by twice a week to have talks about the crew. After three months of daily therapy, he was finally cleared for full duty in September.

That third Sunday night in October, Majac stood in the shower as hot water soothed the muscles jittering nervously in his neck and back. He was returning to the ship the following morning and later in the week getting underway for the first time since the shooting. He jumped when the glass shower door opened.

"Relax, Baby." Tessa stepped in and pressed her front against his back. "Nobody but little old me. And you know I won't hurt you." One of her favorite songs filled her head and she started to hum, her melody vibrating against his back. "I wish we could've done this in on our honeymoon."

"Yeah, me too," he said. "But next year will be here in no time."

After the nurse kicked them out of Tessa's hospital room, Majac got everyone together in the guest waiting suite. Jaz found the hospital chaplain and with his help, planned the wedding in the hospital chapel. Jennifer took care of the flowers, picked up Leona and Tessa's dresses and hired a violinist. Jaz picked up Majac's tux and Solo got Desmond to cater.

Tessa and Majac were both in wheelchairs for the ceremony, but despite the circumstances, it was the happiest day in both of their lives. Back in the guest waiting suite, they stood for their first dance. It only lasted two minutes before she was tired, but those two minutes of *Heaven Brought Me an Angel* made Tessa smile like there was no tomorrow.

Three hours passed as their party ate, laughed and joked away the realization that the wedding had taken place in a Seattle hospital vice a church in Pennsylvania.

After the shower, he built Tessa a fire. She grabbed a romance novel titled *Chemistry Matters* and sat atop a floor pillow. He looked down at her from the sofa as she read. The curve of her smile brought back the memory of the Saturday he introduced her to Jaz and Crystal's daughters. He recalled figuratively having to drag Tessa to the playground date at Mercer Island Park that day. She insisted she had too much work to do to be wasting time at a park. He knew better; she just feared meeting his nieces. When they pulled up to Crystal's house, she and the girls were waiting for them at the head of the driveway. He parked, opened the car door and the girls rushed to meet him. After hugs, they climbed into the back seat while Majac informed Crystal where they were going and what time he'd have them back.

"Take your time," was the extent of Crystal's response.

"Miss Tessa Ajai, this is Laila and Monica Stevenson," Majac said as he pulled out of the driveway. "Ladies, this is Miss Tessa."

"Are you his girlfriend?" Laila, the younger of the girls, asked.

"Yes, Sweetie. I am his girlfriend."

The girls giggled loudly as Majac exited the gated neighborhood.

"Nice to meet you, Miss Tessa," Monica, the older daughter, said once her laughter died down. "I'm Monica and that's my little sister Laila."

"Well, I've heard nothing but wonderful things about the two of you."

"Yeah," Laila chimed, "And Uncle Majac has told us all about you."

"You don't say," Tessa purred, cutting her eyes at Majac. "I sure hope his description of me has done me justice?"

He saw quickly that Tessa was beginning to put on airs.

"I don't know what that means," Monica said, "but he did tell us you were very smart and he showed us pictures of you and him."

"And you're even prettier than your pictures," Laila giggled.

"Thank you Honey."

"They must be talking about when I told them how pretty and sophisticated you were."

Laila put her hand over her mouth to stifle a laugh.

"What?" Tessa turned to face Laila.

"He said you were beau-ti-ful!" Her words exaggerated for emphasis.

"Tell me again how beau-ti-ful you think I am Commander Charles," Tessa laughed "but louder so the world will know."

"I'm sure," Majac said with a wink, as they arrived at the playground, "that wherever you go, all the world knows you're there."

"Uncle Majac," Laila called from the top of the slide. "Catch." She had struggled to get to the top of the slide and was waiting for someone to catch her down at the bottom.

"I got her," Tessa said as she avoided kids like landmines in the playground sand, making her way to the slide. The little girl smiled, and whirled down the slide, finding comfort in Tessa's arms.

"Together?" Tessa suggested.

Laila stuck her finger in her mouth and giggled a yes. The two ran around and made their way back up the slide. When Tessa looked down, she saw Majac standing there.

"Come on," he said. "I got you."

"You can't catch us both," Laila squealed.

"Where's your faith? You'll never touch the ground."

"No way," Tessa shouted playfully. "Move."

Majac looked surprised. "Feel that?" He made a muscle for Monica. Strong," he growled.

"Strong," she growled back.

"Strong, strong," he began chanting.

Monica grinned at him and began chanting with him. Soon the entire playground had joined in.

"Okay," Tessa laughed from the top of the slide. "Look out below, here we come." And they came whirling down the slide, the wind pushing them with abandon. Majac bent his knees and caught them, but their momentum knocked him onto his back.

"See?" Tessa said as she and Laila practically sat on Majac's chest.

"See what?" he chuckled, "I said you wouldn't hit the ground."

Everyone watching laughed along with him.

"Whoa," Tessa began to tilt over. "Don't let me fall Anton."

"Don't worry, Baby. I won't ever let you go."

I won't ever let you go, Majac thought as he sat in front of the roaring fireplace. That was his promise then and it was still his promise now. They'd survived the worst day of their lives, complete with gunshot wounds, a car crash and ultimately the loss of their baby girl. But they hadn't let each other go and as long as there was breath in his body, he planned to keep his promise to never again let her go.

Wednesday night, he'd have to drive to the submarine base in Bangor to get his ship underway Thursday afternoon. But this Sunday night he was going to spend every waking moment loving the love of his life. His Soulmate. The woman he almost lost. The woman he hoped would one day give him a child. The woman he now called his wife…Tessa Charles.

⌒⌒

Twelve weeks into the underway, Majac received an email from Leona. Tessa was back in the hospital. After reading it, he typed a response: *Leona, thank you for informing me about Tessa. Please give her this letter along with a kiss and a hug from me.* The letter read:

> *'Okay, so what I've learned from your sister's email is that you are possibly, at worst, back in the hospital or at home but not doing well at all.*
>
> *I'm hoping, praying, wishing, ready to beg, borrow or steal to do whatever is necessary to make you better. But in the absence of my own healing powers, I want you to know that you are on my mind.*
>
> *I'm thinking of you. I'm praying for your recovery and hope that when you get this, it brings a smile to your face. You know thoughts of you always bring a smile to my face.*
>
> *I miss my friend. My Lover. My Wife! I can't wait to talk to her again. And I want her to know that I Love her like nobody else in this world. Talk to you later. Hopefully soon.'*
>
> *Your Anton*

After that, he couldn't get Tessa off his mind. He received no additional emails from either Tessa or Leona through the next week. Whenever he wasn't completely engrossed in some ship function—training, observing

394

an evolution, leading a qualification board or running drills—he was wondering what she was doing. Half of his days were consumed contemplating if he should email her just to say hi. He wanted to be back at the base so that he could just call to hear her voice and have her hear his. He'd spend his nights thinking about missing the holidays with her. He wanted to cook for her on Thanksgiving, buy her the most special gift for Christmas and shower her with roses and unique jewelry on Valentine's Day. Tessa was his heart. She was his once in a lifetime special woman and he wanted her to know that, more than anything right now.

A week before Majac's boat was to return to base, the ship was tasked with the role of the enemy submarine during a Destroyer Strike Group exercise. The scenario required Majac's sub to go to its most heightened security posture called battle stations. For more than four hours that afternoon, it moved silently below the northern Pacific Ocean hunting and tracking three surface combatants while simultaneously trying to avoid being detected by them in return.

The training team simulated several minor equipment failures throughout the ship to test the crew's ability to react to casualties. All of these were directed from the Central Control room under the guidance of Majac, his XO and the ship control party. During the first three hours, THURGOOD MARSHALL had managed to simulate firing two torpedoes and sinking two of the three ships tracking them. Ten minutes into the fourth hour, they secured from the final casualty fire drill. They received firing orders that directed them to execute a missile launch against the final simulated enemy ship.

Majac was at the Conn, the officer who controls driving and fighting the ship, as was required of the Captain during battle stations. Whenever he wasn't directly receiving reports from his crew, his mind wandered. Despite the buzz of war all around him, thoughts of Tessa and their unborn baby consumed him. Despite his years of training, years of riding submarines and executing hundreds of war scenarios throughout his career, Majac could not focus on the mission at hand.

"Captain," the XO said, "target is acquired. Missile two, ready to fire."

Maybe it sounded crazy but sometimes a woman can come into your life and like a force of nature, turn your world upside down. Not always for the worse, but change your daily routine, your way of thinking, your outlook for the future. With her, you finally see why people say relationships can lift your spirit when she brings out all of the good you have to offer. You want to offer all of it back to her in a way that you have never wanted to do anything for any woman in your past. With her, you realize how dramatically different and rewarding life could be in ways that you never realized before. The part that men don't always seem to understand is that she makes you feel this way without doing anything abnormal or extra in her mind.

"Captain," XO repeated, "target is acquired. Missile two ready to fire."

"Standby XO."

The time he'd shared with Tessa was the best he'd ever had with a woman. She made him feel more alive than a dozen energy drinks washing down a bottle of no-doze. They talked about everything; sports, music, travel, politics, family, and even sex, with an ease he'd been unable to find with any other woman. She wasn't intimidated by the beautiful out of towner that he'd brought home to his father's funeral and she was too much of a lady to settle for being the other woman.

"Captain," the XO shouted, "Missile two is ready to launch. I need the order, Sir."

No matter how loud the XO shouted. No matter what alarms, buzzes, beeps or bells went off around him, Majac couldn't focus on the missile launch decision. His every thought was about Tessa, about losing his unborn child, about being shot and almost losing the both of them.

Unable to give the order to launch, he picked up the Control Station microphone in the middle of the problem and announced, "This is the Captain, now secure from battle stations."

Groans immediately surged across the Central Control room. Without addressing the elephant in the room, Majac stared blankly at his XO. After a beat of complete silence, he exhaled, "XO has the Conn." Then he walked out of Central Control and returned to his stateroom. Behind him, inquiring voices chattered quietly before one singular voice boomed, "This is the XO, I have the Conn."

When all reports were received that the ship had been returned to normal steaming, the XO turned the watch over to the watchsection Officer of the Deck, then made his way to Majac's stateroom. He rapped three times on Majac's door, then after a beat, slowly pushed it open.

"Come in XO."

"Ship's secured from battle stations, Sir," the XO said timidly. "Nav has the…"

"I got it XO. Have a seat."

"Can I get you a cup of coffee, Skipper?"

"No Joe. Just sit down."

"This summer's been a rough one on me Joe. Getting shot. Losing my baby. She was a girl, Joe. Did you know that?"

"No Skipper, I didn't." XO Joe knew, but placated Majac anyway.

"Ever since that day, one week has run into the next, the summer months ran into each other, and I have no bearing on where I'm headed Joe. I'm struggling to accept that no matter what I do, my unborn child, the one thing in the world I wanted more than anything else, is not coming back."

"I'm sorry for your loss, Sir."

"I'm lost Joe. There's a storm cloud stuck in my head. A dense fog. Work. This underway. I go through the routine of my day, but I can't seem to concentrate on the details. I got you and Ship's Sec killing yourselves trying to keep me on task and that's not fair to you. You have your own jobs to do."

"My job is to ensure the ship runs safe, Skipper; I serve at your pleasure."

"I appreciate that Joe, but you need a Captain you can rely on, not one you have to babysit. If I keep walking around this ship playing the brave Captain, pretending that I didn't just lose my child, somebody is going to get hurt—or worse. And I can't have that on my conscience."

"Maybe you just need a little more time to get your mind right, Skipper. What you went through was a hard thing. Any lesser man wouldn't have made it this far without breaking."

"I just…" Majac held out his hands as if reaching for something. A curtain of guilt fell over him. Tears fell from his eyes. "I just wanted to see her face, Joe. I just wanted to hold my baby. Just once."

"I'm sorry for your loss, Skipper. I can't say I know what you're going through, but I will…"

The XO continued talking, but Majac wasn't listening. His thoughts were consumed with images of how he pictured his unborn child's face. With thoughts of her first steps. Her first words. Her first day of school. With taking her to the park to play like he and Tessa had done with Jaz's girls. When the images of his daughter faded and the XO's voice came back into focus, Majac blinked hard. Tears streamed down his face.

"Tell Suppo that I'll take my dinner in my cabin tonight."

"Aye, Skipper."

"And get squadron on the line and let them know that we need to return to port. I need to talk to the Commodore about my relief."

"I'm sorry, Skipper. What?"

"I'm done, XO." Majac said.

"Excuse me, Captain?"

"Riding boats Joe," Majac replied. "I don't love it no more. That Lady of the Sea is no longer calling my name."

37

Goodbye Tears

IT WAS ALMOST HIGH NOON on that cool Sunday morning when Solomon parked next to Leona at Lakenhurst Park. They shared a hug then walked quietly along the cobblestone pavement amidst a maze of sycamores and elms. During their time together, that park had become their getaway place. The park was empty save the presence of a couple of die-hard joggers. As they walked, their hands unconsciously gravitated towards each other, but pulled away nervously when they touched. Leona's smile looked pasted on. She had called and asked him to meet her there after breakfast. He agreed with a counterproposal for them to meet after the early morning church service. She acquiesced.

Solomon figured that his presence was a strain. When they emerged in the clearing facing the river, they sat side-by-side on a composite bench made of recycled plastic water bottles.

"I think they remember us." They were quietly watching a flock of birds—both ducks and swans—circle near the water's edge. Solomon flipped a silver dollar in the air. "Are we ever going to find love?" Leona took such a long time to respond that he wasn't sure she'd heard him.

"Don't worry. We will," she said. "We found each other. Right?"

Solomon put his arm around her. When he regarded her, she felt like nobody had looked at her since the shooting. In his eyes, she was still his Red Velvet. She was a story. One with a past and a future unwritten. He held Leona in one arm and flipped the coin in the air again with the other. "You know what these are good for?" Solomon said, catching the silver dollar in his hand.

"What?"

"Wishes." He threw the dollar across the lake and it skipped like a flat stone. The birds fluttered into activity. Three of them dove beneath the surface thinking it was food.

"What did you wish for?" Leona asked.

"I can't tell you."

"Since when? I thought we could tell each other everything?"

"I can't tell you what I wished for," Solomon said. "But I can tell you that I've learned a lot about myself over the past year and sitting here now, I like little of what I see."

"Well I like everything I see," Leona said reassuringly. "And everything about you."

"Thank you for that." Although he appreciated her words, he did not want to be reassured right then. He wanted to live with the brutal truth about what he had done to her. "But what I want," Solomon added, "is to repair what I can of the damage I have caused."

"What damage?" she asked. "You didn't fire that gun. Someone else did. That wasn't your fault."

"Not that Leona. I'm talking about proposing to you and getting your hopes up about marriage. About buying a house and having kids together. I'm sorry for the pain I've caused to you."

"Like wanting to be my husband?"

"Your ex-fiancée."

She contorted her face. Wriggled her lips.

"Not ex just yet," he said.

"Yes, Solomon, my ex; and now my first cousin. We've been through this; you are single again. Get used to it."

"I don't want to get used to it. Do you know how long it took to find you?"

"I'm sure you won't have to for long." Leona giggled and punched his shoulder gently. Her laughter sounded tinny, determined. A faint echo of the way he loved to hear her effervesce. "Sisters will be coming out of the woodwork once they learn that Doctor Alexandré is Solo again. Just wait and see."

"Not holding my breath."

"Are you kidding me? A tall, healthy, straight, black man. Really into kids. Doesn't do drugs. Doesn't drink—a lot." She giggled, then continued. "Sweet. Goes to church. Doesn't have a temper. Hell boy, you'll be fighting them off with a stick." She paused, then giggled as she said, "How did Biggie put it, *You're not only a client, you're the Player President.*"

He shook his head, genuinely less uninterested in those possibilities than in the possibilities that he was going to miss now that he and Leona were no longer a couple. But he played along because he knew her intentions were good. "You forgot good-looking," he said.

"Yes, how could I ever forget good-looking! Oh my God, Doctor Alexandré, how handsome you are." Leona laughed, held his hand and kissed his cheek. "I didn't forget. I just didn't want to inflate your already big head." Another soft punch. Another kiss on the cheek.

"When I listened to pastor's sermon this morning, I thought about how the message was for you. Probably more for you than for anyone else."

"What do you mean?"

"I think, no, I know it in my heart, that God wants you to go out there and find the absolutely right man for you." A lone tear rolled down his cheek. "To find your true husband."

"Solomon, you don't know how much it hurts me to tell you this, but I have pondered, no, obsessed over our DNA results. I've had Tessa using her work resources. When I'm not at work, I've torn this city apart trying to find Courtney Franklin. To find my father."

"I know what you mean," he said. "I'm surprised we didn't run into each other as much time as I spent looking for him."

"Funny thing is now that I think back, I can remember seeing someone resembling him during my walk to work each morning, but I never thought enough about it to really pay attention to the man."

"Seriously?"

"Yes. And it was probably him who left those great smelling incense on my windshield."

"Wow, that's crazy. If it was him, I wonder why he never approached you?"

"I don't know," she continued, "but my biggest fear is that he wandered off to some homeless shanty town after the shooting and died all alone. For all we know, he could be some John Doe laying in a morgue.

Silence enveloped them. She leaned on his shoulder again.

He wanted to say something about the homeless man. The man they would forever know as her father and his uncle, but he couldn't let go of the fact that he never really knew his own father. "You are a very special woman, Leona Pearson."

She snapped her fingers twice from left to right and said, "I know."
He laughed and she joined him.

"Leona, I want you to know that I still care deeply for you." He felt a little teary eyed. He sniffed it away and tried to play it off.

"You better," she smirked. "You almost married me. And on top of that, you're my first cousin. And all of my other first cousins are like my brothers and sisters, so like me or not, you're stuck with me, Mister."

"You are one of the only two women with whom I've shared my heart and I don't want anybody else. I'm so sorry. I wanted. No, I want You!"

She shrugged and wiped her eyes. "Not a lot we can do about it now. Time to move on." She paused, became teary eyed, dropped her naturally feisty veneer. She smoothed her hand across his back, trying not to cry.

"I'm sorry, Babe" he said a second time. Tears rolled down his cheeks.

"I'm going to be ...". She sat up straight and wiped away her own tears this time, then pasted on a happy-time smile before she spoke again. "We, Mister, are going to be just fine." She took his hand in hers. "With God's help, we'll get through this. We're going to find love again. Maybe not together, and I hope not right away." That brought a smile to both their faces. "And together, we're going to find both of our fathers." Her eyes widened, and so did her smile. "But think about it; now that I'm your cousin, you can tell me all of the crazy secrets you wouldn't tell me when I was your girlfriend."

"Huh," he guffawed. "Not a chance in hell."

Again, they laughed out loud.

"We'll see," she said bumping shoulders with him. "I'm persistent. And I ain't going nowhere."

"Me neither." He pulled her into an embrace. "You're going to make some lucky man a wonderful wife one day."

Leona dropped her head onto Solomon's shoulder. Then she laughed.

"You care to share?" Solomon lifted his shoulder to nudge her head.

"I was just thinking," she said. "We got one thing going for us."

"And that would be...?"

"Well...we didn't make the mistake of getting matching tattoos!"

The uproar of their joint laughter stirred the birds.

Then they held hands and shared tears—both happy and sad—as the birds played in the water. A recently engaged couple—now first cousins born to twin brothers—they sat silently and said goodbye to their individual images of Mister and Missus Solomon and Leona Alexandré.

38

Pomp and Circumstance

GOOD AFTERNOON LADIES AND GENTLEMEN. I am Captain Troy Chambers, Chief Staff Officer of Submarine Squadron TEN and Master of Ceremonies for today's retirement ceremony honoring Commander MacArthur James Antonio Charles. Please rise for our National Anthem"

After the national anthem played and all guests were seated, Captain Chambers returned to the podium. "Twenty years ago, an eighteen-year-old boy from the small town of Tuskegee, Pennsylvania joined the Navy and started a life like none he had ever imagined. During the years that followed, his travels would span the globe as he sailed to foreign lands, visited exotic ports of call, participated in historical military moments and to hear him tell it, sailorized a boatload of beautiful women."

The audience laughed at the Captain's attempt at humor.

"But I'm not here to steal all of Anton's thunder," Captain Chambers continued, "I'll let him tell his own sea stories. What I would like to say is that this young man from humble beginnings grew up to become a fine naval officer and a great human being. His dynamic leadership was pivotal to force readiness and in training sailors and junior officers. His vision and direction were critical in assuring the United States maintained undersea dominance. The Navy is a better service for having Anton. His leadership and professionalism will live on in those he leaves behind to serve our great nation." Captain Chambers read aloud the citation that accompanied the Legion of Merit medal—Majac's end of service award—then called for Majac's XO to join him onstage.

Majac's XO picked up the shadow box and stepped to the podium. "On behalf of the wardroom of the USS THURGOOD MARSHALL, I present you this shadow box in recognition of twenty years of superior and faithful service to the submarine force, the Navy and our country."

They held the shadow box while the photographer took their picture.

After the XO returned the shadow box to the awards table, Captain Chambers called out, "Flag detail post." Five Sailors, including a Seaman carrying a folded American flag, a Petty Officer Third Class, and three officers ranking from Ensign to Lieutenant marched onto the stage. As the senior man, the XO fell in line in front of them before they stopped directly in front of Majac. These men represented all of the previous ranks Majac had held while in the Navy. Five of them executed an about face movement so that they, like Majac, were facing the junior Seaman.

A recording of Ray Charles singing *America the Beautiful* played softly in the background as Captain Chambers read the story of the struggle of our nation's flag, *Old Glory*. Each time Captain Chambers announced one of Majac's promotion dates, a Sailor saluted, received the flag from his junior, performed two distinct right face movements and faced his senior, ready to pass on the flag. Finally, Majac's XO received the flag, performed two final facing movements, saluted his Skipper and stood in front of Majac while Captain Chambers read:

"Anton, at your request, this flag was flown on June 25th, the date that you first joined the Navy, onboard the fifth SEAWOLF Class submarine, USS TUSKEGEE (SSN 25). It comes with a note from your Commanding Officer on TUSKEGEE, Retired Admiral Carl "Flip" Skipworth:

> Dear Anton:
> Of the thousands of Sailors who served under me during my Navy career, few were similarly as charismatic. Through tireless contributions in the thankless and merciless world of submarines, you somehow made the best of the toughest of situations. Your vision and decisive actions allowed you to prevail in a difficult profession. You are truly a Man of Honor.
> I am honored to have served with you and wish you the best as you leave the Navy to start your next big adventure.
>
> Sincerely, A shipmate first and a friend forever,
> Flip Skipworth

The XO extended his arms and presented the flag. Majac saluted him, then took the flag and held it close to his chest, briefly thinking of his father, knowing how proud he would be if he were there to bear witness.

Again, the XO saluted then performed an about face movement. In a hushed voice he spoke, "About face...forward March!" The flag passers exited the stage and posted themselves at the bottom of the steps, switching their roles to later become Majac's side boys.

Majac placed the flag on the table with his other awards.

Captain Chambers read Majac's retirement orders then said, "Ladies and Gentlemen, I present you Commander Anton Charles."

As he stepped to the podium, he paused and looked over the crowd trying to recognize all of the smiling faces. Despite all of the anxiety from within and good vibes streaming his way from the faces in the crowd, he was saddened because his deceased father was not there to share in this day. He panned the crowd for a comforting face to help him through his speech without too many tears. There were faces that belonged to family, faces that were immediately familiar, faces that looked like they should be familiar and a couple that he probably should've, but just didn't remember. All in all, the turnout was a lot larger than he expected. After ten seconds or so, he found the face he needed...Jaz Stevenson. He smiled a familiar smile and Jaz returned a smile that only the two of them knew its meaning. Now in his comfort zone, Majac was ready to talk.

"WOW, Twenty Years!" Majac said proudly. "There are so many stories to tell and good times to share that I can't imagine where to begin. My Father was a big fan of the phrase the best things in life are worth waiting for. Well let me tell you, that it doesn't get much better when the wait is over and you finally take command of your own submarine. This truly is the greatest job in the world!"

Majac smiled gratefully and wiped a tear from the corner of his eye. Over the next ten minutes, he recounted his brief time as an enlisted man, thanking the officer who encouraged him to apply for and mentored him through his transition into the Naval Academy. He talked about life as a midshipman; about life as an Ensign aboard his first submarine, USS HARRISBURG, and the wisdom of a certain Chief Litchfield that has stuck with him to this day. He reminisced about his time in San Diego as a submarine Engineer, his staff jobs in Japan, Texas and at the Pentagon. "I want to thank all who have helped make each tour of duty special. The petty officers and seamen who bore the labor of my success. The Chiefs who trained me, and my fellow officers who made me feel welcome in every wardroom that I served. Tears welled up in the corners of his eyes when he began praising his crew. "To my Executive Officer and the great men who sail THURGOOD MARSHALL, thank you for making my tour successful, and moreover, making it enjoyable! You made every single day I came to work on OUR boat, the best day ever."

He paused to read his notes. A huge clap of thunder rang out in distant sky. "I'm almost done," he said as the audience looked towards the ominous black clouds. "I promise that I'll get you all out of here before the rain comes." Twenty seconds later a flash of lightning lit up the horizon. "Okay, God, I get it. I'm hurrying." The audience laughed in appreciation of his humor. "Before I get off this microphone, I should at least read the part of the speech that I wrote down last night while I was reflecting on my career and nursing a glass of Courvoisier with my best friend.

"To my fellow heroes of the Silent Service; you brave Americans who never rest in defending the ideals, principles, and values of our nation. For that noble duty, I thank you. Just as your spirit is tireless, my gratitude is timeless. I will worry about you when you are called into danger and I will salute you when you return victorious! I will marvel at your achievements and I will gain strength from your example. But after all is said and done, I will miss you, as I take my leave. Leadership is a trait that is learned, not taught; My friends, you have taught me well. God Bless you, your families and God Bless America."

The crowd came to their feet and applauded for a while as Majac returned to his seat. They remained standing while the Subase Chaplain, Commander Jones, delivered the benediction. Captain Chambers returned to the podium and prepared to conclude the ceremony. "Anton would like to invite all of you to enjoy pupus and share sea stories with him immediately following the ceremony at the Oceanside Officer's Club." He paused and took on a stern face. His order of, "Side boys, Atten Hut!" accompanied Majac's walk to the podium.

Captain Chambers read a Navy poem called The Watch, which details a sailor's life at sea coming to an end and those he trained taking charge of what he leaves behind. After the words, *Shipmate you stand relieved... We have the watch,* Majac rendered one final salute and said, "Request permission to go ashore."

Captain Chambers returned the salute, "Permission Granted,."

Majac did a sharp about face and stood at attention.

"Boatswain's Mate prepare to pipe a shipmate ashore."

The Boatswain sparked his whistle to pipe him ashore. Majac departed the stage, through his gauntlet of saluting side boys, as Captain Chambers announced, "Commander, United States Navy; Retired; departing!"

39

Knock Knock

By four o'clock that afternoon, more than a hundred guests had gathered in the yard behind the Hang Suite. Blue and white canopies were tented over a dozen picnic tables. Six to eight people sat at each table eating, laughing, playing cards or just sharing loud conversation. Cornhole boards, beach blankets and lawn chairs covered the grass everywhere there was not a tent. Those who had remembered to bring their bathing suits were splashing in the pool.

Inside, Majac had changed out of his uniform, showered and was now dressed to party. He gazed into a large mirror to take one last accounting of himself before he made his entrance.

Music thumped in the backyard. The DJ, who was encouraging more men to join the women on the dance floor, started playing his favorite line dance song. Bushes and a high fence surrounding the backyard provided shade and privacy. Strings of red and yellow pepper lights with circuitry processed through the amps to make them pulse to the beat of the music were strung throughout the trees.

Majac exited his back door, grabbed a beer and made his way to the tent covering the grill and food tables where Solomon's mother and the ladies from the church auxiliary were busy directing Tessa and Crystal's traffic. Vivienne cooked a pan full of fried chicken—because her chicken was her son's favorite. At Solomon's request, and with Majac's sizeable love gift to compensate for their efforts, she'd had the church auxiliary prepare enough food to feed a mega-church congregation—twice over. Although they all spoke English, the church lady chatter was far too fast to decipher.

The food tent bustled with activity. Women, all close to his mother's age and none of which he recognized, scurried to and fro carrying various platters of meat, pans of baked macaroni, veggies, pasta and potato salads, tomato and onion salad, green beans and collards, and tons of biscuits.

Vivienne stood guard at the entrance to the food line. Majac snuck up behind and wrapped his arms around her. He said thank you, and gave her a big kiss on the cheek. She smiled when she recognized his voice. Being the guest of honor, he reached out and lifted the lid from a pan to steal a pinch of anything he could get his hands on that smelled so good, but Vivienne slapped his hand away. "You wait, just like everybody else."

"You better stop tripping Anton," Tessa giggled. "Before you draw back a nub."

Majac rubbed the back of his hand. A five-second Mexican standoff ensued but he quickly caved. It vexed him that Vivienne wasn't going to step aside so he could steal some food, but he was not going to spoil his day by going to war with her. Despite their rough start, they'd grown closer through his time living in her son's rental. He strapped on a smile and asked, "So where's your son?"

"Let me take you to him," Viv said, grabbing his arm and ushering him out of the food tent. Solomon was nowhere to be found. After a couple of minutes of looking, Magic convinced Viv that he could negotiate his way around without her guidance. She released his arm and hmphed her disgust as she walked away.

Leona and Jennifer sat poolside watching as their cousin, Micah, climbed out of the pool followed by his boyfriend, Troy. Solomon, seeing Troy struggling to pull himself up the ladder, put a hand on Troy's swimming trunks and pushed him out of the pool.

Troy took a good look at Solomon once he followed them out of the water and smiled the grin of To Wong Foo. "Unh," he sucked his teeth. "Strong hands and all the rest of that too," Troy followed, snapping his fingers three times in a 'zee' motion. When Solomon was standing directly in front of him, Troy said, "Thank you handsome."

"Excuse me?" Micah bared his fangs at Troy.

"I was just thanking him for being so helpful," Troy said.

"And that's all you were doing?"

"Well I mean, a body like that deserves to be thanked properly."

"Not by you," Micah snapped. "Don't make me cut a bitch out here."

"Whatever bitch," Troy blew Micah off and turned his attention to Leona. "Anyway girl, that man right there is gonna make some pretty babies one day."

Leona sucked her teeth at the comment, but didn't reply. She handed Solomon a towel. "Would you do me a favor, Handsome and get your mom and Miss Phyllis some water?"

Solomon wrapped the towel around his waist and vanished to get the drinks.

Vivienne watched on the sideline as her chivalrous son bopped off to retrieve her water. "See that. That's how a real man treats a woman," she said bragging to her friend Phyllis.

"Girl, your nephew is right. He's going to make you some pretty grandbabies," Phyllis said. "I just hope we're still around to see them."

"I don't know about you," Vivienne said, cutting her eyes at Phyllis, "but I ain't going nowhere no time soon."

"You two need to mind your own business," Leona flamed on Micah and Troy when Solomon was out of earshot.

"Shoot girl," Troy said licking his lips and gazing in Solomon's direction. "If you can't give him some, somebody else damn sure will."

"Don't get slapped, Ho," Micah growled. He threw his cup of water on Troy. "You need to cool your hot ass off."

"Whatever," Troy catted. "I was just stating the obvious. That man is hot."

"Don't nobody need you telling what we already know," Micah said.

"Meee-oowww!" Troy said, snapping his fingers at Micah this time.

"You know what Bitch," Micah said angrily. "Your hot ass really needs to cool off." Micah rushed Troy and pushed him back into the pool. Troy, being an agile man, reached out and grabbed Micah before he lost his balance, dragging his boyfriend back into the pool with him. When the two men splashed in the water, the crowd who'd heard the cat fight laughed out loud at the divas' expense.

"I don't know about you, Girl," Jennifer said to Leona, "But I love a little drama."

"Yeah, you can't get through a black cookout without it."

"Now you know all these people weren't going to get together without someone showing their ass."

"Well, long as nobody messes with you or me, I'll be okay."

As soon as the words left her mouth, it hit her and burst wide open. It felt like Leona's head had burst wide open. She'd been attacked while she was vulnerable, distracted. She screamed, bent over and grabbed her head. Her fingers were drenched. Warm liquid dripped from her hair. "What the Hell?" She cried out like she was going to kill somebody.

"Oh, I'm sorry," a voice said from behind. He found her sudden anger funny as hell.

She turned towards the house and saw Solomon only a few feet away. He was laughing hard now. Colorful water balloons were in each big hand. Balloons that she had helped him fill with water and left in the kitchen. On his way to get bottled water, he had commandeered the water balloons and attacked her.

"You hit me in the head with a water balloon?" she yelled at him. "You know I didn't get in the pool because I didn't want to get my hair wet." She stood waiting for an apology. Instead of apologizing, he threw a purple balloon. She turned and it hit her on the back, exploded, sprayed against Jennifer and the two people standing next to them.

"What are you twelve? Put that down," she yelled. "I'm not playing. Put that..." She raised both hands, covered her face and turned sideways. The next balloon burst on her hips. When she uncovered her face, her look of determination was downright scary. "Oh, it's on now! On and popping." She caught the next water balloon he threw. Threw it hard back at him. Made it explode against his chest. "Let me get my hands on some balloons" she said. "This here is about to get serious."

Before the guests had arrived, Kenny and Lawrence had helped them fill almost a hundred balloons. Filled them all with warm water just in case people brought their children to the cookout. Now, like two children themselves, they ran around the yard, declaring their own personal war.

Kenny, Desmond, Lamont and Lawrence rounded the pool from behind opposing ends of the fence carrying two metal tubs filled with balloons. People started grabbing balloons as the guys passed. Grabbing balloons, running, screaming, shouting and playing as if they were children. A yard full of adults having fun in a backyard oasis where their daytime responsibilities didn't exist. For the moment they were children. Little boys hitting little girls. Little girls hitting little boys. Balloons exploding. Water splashing against tables, chairs, some bouncing off the fence. Hundreds of colorful water balloons redecorating the yard.

Loud screams accompanied unbridled laughs. Leona was once again a rambunctious little girl with wild hair. The child of a woman with fine hair like the manes of Guyanese or the West Indians. A child with the same beautiful flavor skin as her mother. Fine, soft hair like her mother's mother, but less powerful and more delicate. In a flash, she thought of playing in the backyard with her mother and sister as a child. Tears welled up in her eyes. She dropped her arms and started to slow down as the din of laughter from everyone playing around her began to fade. Began to fade off into oblivion as thoughts of missing her dead mother invaded her mind.

The water balloon fight had dozens of people running out of control, acting like heathens—in her mother words—chasing each other and having a ball. It only took a couple more minutes, but soon all of the water balloons were gone. Then, two blinks later, she watched as if watching a movie as Solomon stood ten feet in front of her and tossed a water balloon directly at her. The sneaky bastard had hidden one. When the balloon exploded in her face, the thoughts of her mother were all gone. She focused on the man who treated her as if she were the most beautiful girl in the world. A man who always wore suits and rarely behaved like a little boy.

Laughter reverberated loudly throughout the yard. The guffawing and snickering was contagious. Everyone from eight to eighty was acting juvenile, laughing so hard they could barely stand. They'd had a water balloon fight. Fought a great war that lasted no more than ten minutes. Battled with a playful fierceness in which—although sides were never declared— both sides unanimously declared victory in the end.

They were soaked when they finally went to each other. They held each other and laughed; clothes and skin sticking. Amidst the combination of clatter around her and her flustered state, Leona struggled to understand him when he asked, "So now do you accept my apology?"

She stared at him for a minute. Looked deep into his eyes for the meaning behind his words. The question was familiar, but the pretense was a blur.

Before she answered and without speaking another word, he lifted her, carried her in his arms and walked quickly across the pool surround.

When Leona realized where he was taking her, she shouted with all her might, "Yes, Solomon, I forgive y…!" But it was too late.

Before she could finish her sentence, Solomon leapt into the air. Leapt as high as he could with Leona in his arms, held her and splashed in the pool.

"I'll be going to law school at night." Majac was talking about starting his new life. He and the guys were sitting at a table playing dominoes. "During the day, my official title at Puget Sound Shipyard yard will be Deputy for Warfare Systems Integration."

"Sounds like some Xbox video war game stuff to me," Jaz said.

"Not every brother can be King of the Hill like you." Majac stared at his dominoes. He was holding double fours and double sixes.

"Like me?" Jaz said.

"Yeah," Majac said. "All brothers can't be the big stick mandingo who easily rules the basketball court with brute force and swag since charming words and charisma won't work."

"So says the Navy Commander who goes to war with missiles and battleships," Jaz said.

"You guys all right," Solomon asked.

"Yeah," Jaz answered. "No worries Doc, we just chopping it up."

In the distance, the sound of a siren blaring became increasingly louder.

"No different than leading your team to the NBA Finals." Majac said.

"Big difference Bruh." Jaz slammed down a double five domino. "Gimme twenny fools." He smiled at his tablemates while Desmond recorded his score. "And besides," Jaz continued, "worst thing that happens if we lose in the playoffs is we go home earlier than we want to." Next Desmond played the two three domino for twenty-five points. "Going to war gets people killed. So, tell me again who exerts all the brute force?"

Majac's slumped his shoulders. Cut his eyes at his Partna. Jaz was right. But fortunately for him, he was retired from the Navy. His life as the Warrior Sailor was behind him. War and the Sea were a thing of the past.

When the police arrived at the Hang Suite, they had trouble finding a place to park due to the volume of cars on the street. Like Moses parting the Red Sea, cookout guests moved as the two police officers entered the yard from Solomon's side of the house.

The DJ stopped the music when a buzz stirred from the crowd. Solomon stood up from the table where he, Majac, Jaz and Desmond were playing dominoes. He was startled to see two uniformed police officers coming onto his property. Being the property owner, he immediately moved to greet them. "May I help you officers?"

"The taller of the two officers said, "Are you Solomon Alexandré?"

"Yes," Solomon said skeptically. "If this is about the music, we can turn it down."

"Please turn around and put your hands behind your head."

"Excuse me?" Solo said. "C'mon now. All this over some music?"

"No Sir." The officer's tone was firm. "This is not about the music."

When Solomon didn't immediately comply, the shorter officer unclipped his gun.

"What then?" Solomon asked.

"Oh Lord," a woman cried.

"What's going on?" Vivienne demanded, joining her son's side.

"Please step back, Ma'am."

"Step back hell. We're just having a cookout. Now he said he'd turn the music down, so why don't you two just get the hell out of here. Who called the cops? I bet it was that nasty little cat lady across the street. I never did like her ass."

' Kenny and Lawrence stepped up next to their friend. "I'm Reverend Lawrence Didier. What seems to be the problem officers?"

"We need Mister Alexandré to come with us. We're not here to shut down the party. Nobody complained about the music," the taller cop said. "Mister Alexandré comes with us and you all can get back to your party."

"It's his house," Leona said. "Without him there is no party."

"I don't know anything about that Ma'am. I'm just trying to do my job. Now, Mister Alexandré will you please turn around?"

When the taller officer attempted to handcuff Solomon, Vivienne lunged in front of the officer. "NO!" she shouted, "You ain't taking my baby nowhere. Where's my gun. They got their guns; I'm goin' get mine. I'll be damned if they're taking my baby anywhere. You know cops kill black men. He's innocent. I'm his momma, I know he didn't do nothing."

The shorter officer secured Viv's arms and moved her to the side. "If you don't stop Ma'am, I'm going to have to arrest you too."

The din grew loud until Solomon yelled. "Ma stop!" The crowd was stunned to silence. A beat passed. Then he yelled, "Everybody Just Stop."

When he could hear himself think, Solomon turned his back to the officers, crossed his hands behind his back and said, "Kenny, call my lawyer." He allowed the taller officer to handcuff his wrists. The shorter officer cleared a path as the taller one led Solomon toward the front yard.

"In the name of God," Lawrence demanded, thrusting himself in front of the side yard gate. "What's this about officer?"

"Far as I know, Reverend," the officer's tone was devoid of feeling, "God wouldn't claim nothing to do with murdering a beauty queen."

Acknowledgments

First and foremost, I give glory to God for gifting me the health and strength to live life, and the sanity and mental acuity to pursue the passion of writing stories. I think people are at their best when doing what makes their heart happy. If nothing else, taking the time to craft stories helps me destress and reach my place of inner peace. I hope this project allowed you the chance to relax and enjoy the time away from the stress of the real world while you ventured into my land of make-believe.

I want to wish love and happiness to my children; Andrea, Brianna, India (Chrystina Jaye), and Chrystiaan (Chrys) Sexton. You are my legacy. Your smiles, and the twinkle in your eyes when you look at me, are the greatest joys of my life. I couldn't be prouder of the individuals that you have all become as young adults.

To my Beta-Readers; Kelynda 'Kellye' Sexton, Jennifer Lane, Stephanie Pough and Commander (Ret) Timothy P. Wadley. I thank you for gifting me your time. There may not be a Pulitzer Prize at the end of this rainbow, but I appreciate your support for my project. May not mean much in the big scheme of things, but your candor helps me be the best writer I can be. Get ready for the next Draft, it's coming soon to a Manuscript near you. Love You Guys!

And finally; to Mrs. Sabrina Lee Sexton. I Love You. Thank you for loving me and supporting me in whatever I do. My life truly began the day that God gifted me with YOU. And since that moment, I have only gotten better.

Enjoy the Read,
H. Adrian Sexton

CPSIA information can be obtained
at www.ICGtesting.com
Printed in the USA
LVHW111953100822
725535LV00001BA/14